D1043024

'A dark and unnerving psychological thriller that draws you deep into the lives of the characters and refuses to let go. This is a brilliantly written book; I could not put it down' Caroline Mitchell

'A chilling tale of the unexpected that journeys right into the dark heart of domesticity' Marnie Riches

'An unsettling and upsetting story that kept me enthralled, horrified and quite often, in tears. Dark, disturbing and peppered with his trademark humour, *A Suitable Lie* is a fantastic read, and, as a writer, Malone just gets better and better' S.J.I. Holliday

'Michael J. Malone is one of my favourite writers and his new novel does not disappoint. While on the surface this is a departure in genre for Malone, his incredible skill with language and prose remains, and his talent for characterisation really comes to the fore, creating a story that will I won't forget in a hurry. Malone is a massive talent … get on board now so you can brag you were reading his books long before the rest of the world' Luca Veste

'A tightly wound page-turner with real emotional punch' Rod Reynolds

'A disturbing and realistic portrayal of domestic noir with a twist. The humour and emotion laced within the darkness was just the right mix for a shocking yet compelling read' Mel Sherratt

'This searing depiction of an abusive marriage with the conventional roles reversed nonetheless manages to radiate warmth and integrity – and humour – in even the darkest situations. Malone's effortless writing style confirms him as a sharp new voice in crime fiction' Anya Lipska

'Really powerful. Seriously, I loved this book. A terrific read, I read it in one sitting. Disturbing reading at times but compulsive. It made the hairs on my neck stand on end. Loved it!' Martina Cole

'The slow-drip undermining of Andy's authority and sense of self feels very real and the psychological manipulation is painful to read about, so well has the author put the reader inside the mind of his main character. And Malone shows himself to be an expert plotter as well. A straightforward delineation of domestic abuse would have been engaging enough, but Malone throws in some twists and turns. Crucially these feel properly embedded in the story, rather than thrown together to obfuscate or confuse. It's a tough high-wire act, balancing believability with surprise, but the author pulls it off with aplomb. Excellent stuff' Doug Johnstone, *The Big Issue*

'Malone tackles the taboo subject of female violence against men with insight and compassion (for Anna is no one-dimensional witch), while creating all the hallmarks of a fine, page-turning psychological thriller' *Daily Mail*

'Wow! What an emotionally powerful read. It's by far the best fictional account of domestic abuse I've read and because of that, very difficult, even painful, to read at times. I found myself longing for Andy, the main character, to be happy again after the tragic death of his first wife. The way the relationship begins with Anna is so "normal", so believable, that, even though I knew it wouldn't end well (the blurb suggests as much – and it IS a psychological thriller after all), I was lulled into a false sense of security. I felt his happiness, and that made it even harder to read when things started going wrong. Dark, disturbing, tragic and frightening, there are nevertheless bright moments, as there would be in real life.' K.E. Cole

'A painful depiction of a man in turmoil' *Publishers Weekly*

'Highly recommended: *A Suitable Lie* is an intense, nerve-wrecking read' Thomas Enger

'Hits you like an express train' Mason Cross

'A slick thriller with a killer punch' Douglas Skelton

'A brilliant and disturbing novel. Be prepared to have your emotions not only stirred, but turned upside down and inside out. This book insidiously curls around you like a boa-constrictor – and it won't release you until you have read the final page. Thought-provoking, educational and if you don't feel anything when you lay down this book, then you must have a heart of stone. Malone will become stellar with this' Crimesquad

'Unsettling, thought-provoking, and absolutely riveting. Michael J. Malone steps into an uncomfortable and distressing subject and makes it relatable, accessible, real. I felt I could reach out and touch the characters, as though they could be someone I knew, someone I cared about … *A Suitable Lie* is a challenging and clever read' Lovereading

'Malone's writing is effortless, expressive and taut' Crime Review

'Malone handles his topic with sensitivity, coupled to a consummate understanding of narrative pace and atmosphere. An important book' Shots Mag

'Layered and intriguing. My attention never once wandered' Liz Loves Books

'Malone's writing style is first rate and his ability to transport the reader into the world he has created is beyond compare. Michael J. Malone is a key contributor to the Scottish crime fiction scene. I am impatient to see what he gives us next!' Eurocrime

'Funny and brutal, heartfelt and compelling. Highly recommended' Craig Robertson

'Talk about being put through the emotional wringer. Dark, compelling and recommended!' Mark Edwards

HOUSE OF SPINES

House of Spines

MICHAEL J. MALONE

ORENDA BOOKS

Orenda Books
16 Carson Road
West Dulwich
London SE21 8HU
www.orendabooks.co.uk

First published in the UK in 2017 by Orenda Books

A catalogue record for this book is available from the British Library.

ISBN 978-1-910633-86-1
eISBN 978-1-910633-87-8

Typeset in Garamond by MacGuru Ltd
Printed and bound by CPI Group (UK) Ltd, Croydon CRO 4YY

SALES & DISTRIBUTION

In the UK and elsewhere in Europe:
Turnaround Publisher Services
Unit 3, Olympia Trading Estate
Coburg Road
Wood Green
London
N22 6TZ
www.turnaround-uk.com

In the USA and Canada:
Trafalgar Square Publishing
Independent Publishers Group
814 North Franklin Street
Chicago, IL 60610
USA
www.ipgbook.com

In Australia and New Zealand:
Affirm Press
28 Thistlethwaite Street
South Melbourne VIC 3205
Australia
www.affirmpress.com.au

For details of other territories, please contact *info@orendabooks.co.uk*

Prologue

Someone was singing his name.

A pebble skittered off his bedroom window and his name was repeated in a harsh whisper.

Pulled from sleep, he opened his eyes on a thick darkness leavened only by the weak light from his *Bart Simpson* lamp.

He heard his name being whispered again. It was coming from the back garden, and he recognised the voice.

'Mummy?' What was she doing out in the garden in the middle of the night? He jumped out of bed, pushed his feet into his *Ninja Turtle* slippers and raced over to the window. Pulling open the curtain, he pressed his forehead against the cool glass and searched for her below.

There she was, in the middle of their back lawn, stepping from side to side with a graceful hop, her right arm trailing a sweeping arch to each side, her nightdress a slump of cotton in front of her feet.

Looking up, she spotted him and waved. 'Come, sweetheart,' she mouthed. 'Come and dance with Mummy.'

He waved back, but kept silent. He may only have been six and three quarters but he knew this was one of those occasions he should not wake Daddy. The thought of his father stilled him for a moment. If he did join his mother outside, might Daddy be disappointed in him? If there was one thing he hated most in the world it was the look his father gave him when he did something silly.

But Mummy looked like she was having such amazing fun. So, without further thought, he raced down the stairs, across the kitchen and out the back door.

'Aha,' she beamed as he skipped across the cropped grass towards her. 'The little faerie child is here.' She held her hands out to grasp at his. 'Have you travelled far? I hear the moon is a wonderful place at this time of the year.' With that she looked up towards the hook of moon tucked into a far corner of the glittering night sky.

Then her attention returned to him. 'You look cold, little faerie boy. We should dance to warm you up. Do you want to dance?'

He nodded. The part of him that desperately wanted to be a grown-up was not so sure, but this was one of those occasions when she was giving him her full attention. And that was something he craved. Often – too often – she was distant and sad, and acted like he wasn't really there. He'd stand in front of her and say, 'But Mummy, it's me', and she'd look at him, head cocked to the side. 'I have a son?' she'd ask, and he would feel tiny and invisible, and all the way back to his room he'd pinch at his arm, intoning, 'But I'm real, aren't I?'

So now, when he felt the warmth of her grip on his hands, he revelled in it.

'We do this…' She stepped to the side, and he followed. '…And then this…' She held his right hand up in the air and sent him into a spin. Then she showed him a couple of other movements, which he duly copied. As he did so he couldn't help but giggle; this was silly and fun. He loved it when he met this version of her.

And so, with the pattern of movement established, they danced and whirled across the lawn as light as moonbeams, to the music of a waltz that sounded deep in his mother's head.

They spun and stepped and danced until his breath grew ragged, until he looked up at his mother, begging her to stop; until his father's voice boomed out into the night.

Then all heat was taken out of the summer air and he felt a chill breeze stippling the skin across his back into goose bumps.

'Go to bed, please, son,' his father said.

'But, Dad,' he said trying to read his father's expression. 'Please don't be angry. Mummy only wanted to have fun.'

'Bed.'

He trudged back to the house. When he reached the door he heard a cry from his mother and turned. She was on the ground, and his father was on his knees behind her, gathering her to him, holding her nightdress against her breasts. Her head was thrown back, long hair trailing in the grass, the pale of her neck exposed to the sky and the beasts that lived there.

The boy's heart tightened with pain and sorrow. He wanted nothing more than to run to her and bring back her smiles, but his father looked over at him with an expression that stopped him.

'Bed ... please ... son,' his father said.

Even though his father's eyes were hidden under the shadow of his forehead, the boy could read his look. He'd seen it so many times. His father's greatest fear was lurking there. Would the boy become as mad as the mother?

1

Ranald McGhie wanted to slap the lawyer sitting across the table from him. Acutely aware of his threadbare cuffs; he pulled at the sleeves of his charity-shop tweed jacket in a vain attempt to disguise them.

The lawyer, who looked like he'd just stepped out of a shop window – Harrods or some other temple to consumerism – had hardly glanced at Ranald since he'd sat down. In fact, the man's whole demeanour was of someone keen to scrape a lump of shit from the sole of his shoe and hurry onto his next task.

'…the library was Mr Fitzpatrick's chief concern. And given the paucity of his living relatives, he was most anxious that you understand the enormity of the task it represents.'

'Mr…' Ranald began, pretending that he'd forgotten the man's name.

'Quinn.'

'Mr Quinn, how about you get to the point and save us both a lot of time?' Ranald took pleasure in pricking the man's pomposity. He was probably from Pollock and had managed to get himself a law degree and a cushy number working with the elderly relics at one of Glasgow's oldest law firms, thinking this meant he was more important than everyone who didn't work at the Bar.

'I'm explaining' – he huffed – 'Mr Fitzpatrick's last wishes, Mr McGhie.'

'Aye. But who exactly is Mr Fitzpatrick and why exactly have you dragged me in here?'

The lawyer sat back in his chair, a note of surprise on his face. 'Mr Alexander Fitzpatrick of the Fitzpatricks. One of the oldest merchant families in the city. Your mother, Helena McGhie née Fitzpatrick, was his niece.'

'She was what?' Ranald sat forwards in his chair. 'I think some-one's been selling you a load of shite, mate. My mother's name was Helen.' Ranald was a young man of considerable education and intellect, but, when faced with snobbery, he always found himself reverting to his working-class, Anglo-Saxon roots, reacting in an in-your-face, take-me-or-leave-me, kind of way.

Quinn opened a file and leafed through some papers until he found what he was looking for. He pushed the file across the desk towards Ranald.

'She dropped the "a" from her name. She thought "Helen" was better suited to her more…' he struggled for the right word '… prosaic circumstances.'

Ranald resisted the impulse to tell the man to shut up with his 'prosaic circumstances'; in fact he was more struck by the suggestion that his mother was from money. He opened his mouth, but the lawyer was handing him another document.

'This is her birth certificate. She was born on the 8th of November 1952. At the age of nineteen she met and fell in love with your father, an unemployed artist, Gordon McGhie. She became pregnant and, against the wishes of her family, went to live with McGhie.'

My dad was an artist? thought Ranald. Where the hell did Quinn get that notion? His father was a bricklayer, displayed no artistic tendencies whatsoever and decried – with a good deal of swearing – the notion Ranald had, as a teen, that he wanted to be a writer. But he and Mum went and died when Ranald was eighteen, so couldn't exactly stop him.

Ranald took a moment to think through the timeline of events. Mum met Dad when she was nineteen and fell pregnant. But he wasn't born until 1988. What happened to that first pregnancy? As if Ranald had asked the question out loud, Quinn answered:

'That first child was stillborn, Mr McGhie. And your mother dis-tanced herself so thoroughly from the family that we have no idea why she waited so long to have you.

'Mr Fitzpatrick kept a keen eye on you as you grew up. He often talked about you as the one that got away.' The lawyer grew thoughtful. 'He envied you your simple life, Mr McGhie.'

'Got away? My simple life?' Ranald was roused from his confusion. 'Living for months at a time with no income? Eating nothing but tins of beans and plain bread because my parents left me with nothing?' He was angry now: all that time he'd had a relative who was loaded – knew the difficulties he was in and did nothing to help.

'Still. You were safe. Dry. Not on the street.' Quinn raised an eyebrow.

'How the hell do you know that? How do you know *any* of this?'

'From time to time, Mr Fitzpatrick would … ah … check in.'

'Check in? What the hell does that mean?'

'He was delighted that you resisted the allure of a steady income and instead, followed your compulsion to work in the arts.'

'I write educational textbooks. That's hardly the arts.'

'You write for a living, do you not? And you had that poetry collection published: *The Unkindness of Crows*. 2012 wasn't it?'

'It was a pamphlet. And, again, how do you know all this?'

'Mr Fitzpatrick would ask us…'

'…to check on me.' Ranald ran his right hand through his hair. *What the hell?* Had he just dropped into the pages of a Dickens novel? Was there a camera crew hidden behind those oak panels? He needed to make some sense of all of this.

'He was saddened that you went off the rails slightly when your parents died, and he was concerned about your subsequent mental-health issues.' Quinn paused. It was clear that this wasn't because he worried he was being indelicate; he was simply checking his memory for the facts. 'Have you continued with the medication?'

'None of your business.' Ranald bristled. 'You mentioned a library?'

'Yes.' Quinn sat back in his chair as if relieved the conversation was back on a track he had rehearsed. 'He has … sorry, had, an extensive collection of books. One of the finest in the city, and he wanted you to look after it.' He placed his hands on the oak desk in front of him. 'It's a real treasure trove. Worth a fortune, I believe.'

Ranald thought about his one-bedroom flat above a chip shop in Shawlands. The aromas that would soon coat this 'treasure trove' of books, reducing their value considerably. As if reading his thoughts, Quinn continued.

'The library is not to be moved from the house. Mr Fitzpatrick was explicit in his instructions. Therefore, he has also left the house to you. He set up a trust fund to ensure that the utility bills would be paid. And the council tax. And there is an old couple who have been tending to the house and the gardens. Money has been set aside to pay their wages. But I'm afraid there's no extra for you personally, Mr McGhie. You will have a house, entirely free of cost, but you will have to continue in your endeavours as a writer.'

'I have a house?'

'You have a *very large* house.'

Ranald exhaled, his mind a whirl. He tried to picture his mother. To his shame, all he could see was her long dark hair and the point of her chin. She was from money?

'I have a house.'

'The fact may bear repeating, Mr McGhie,' Quinn said with a half-smile.

By Christ it does, thought Ranald. He could sell it. Buy that *gîte* he'd always fancied living in, over in Brittany. Write that novel he'd always promised himself he would write and say goodbye to all that educational crap.

'You won't be able to sell the house, Mr McGhie,' Quinn said, interrupting his thoughts – once more appearing to read them. 'It's owned by the family trust, of which I am one of the trustees. We're bound by law to ensure Mr Fitzpatrick's wishes are carried out to the letter.'

'But I can live there?'

'That is one of the conditions of access to the library.' Quinn's slow nod added importance to his words. 'It will be yours until you die, and then Mr Fitzpatrick hoped one of your issue would take over.'

One of my issue, Ranald repeated to himself. At this stage having 'issue' was highly unlikely. He'd never managed to keep a woman longer than two years. His ex-wife, Martie, regularly told him he was an easy man to fall in love with but a difficult man to stay with. Apparently he'd always had a remoteness, making him unable to commit fully to a relationship. Women sensed that, Martie would say, and it made them feel insecure.

Yeah, well, he would respond, when your wife has you sectioned, it kinda puts the spokes in the whole trust thing.

To which she would reply: If you're at the end of your tether and your husband is at the far end of an A-line roof over a twenty-foot drop, you need to do something.

It was an argument they had replayed several times. He'd known he was in the wrong, that he needed help; but still, being *sectioned* … by his own wife?

And because of this, Ranald was never able to completely trust Martie properly again, despite the fact that he was still in love with her.

His mind placed him back there, in that moment when he was balanced on the roof. He was invincible, he could affect the weather, he could have taken on God. Just a few months of pull-ups and push-ups and he would have had the strength to fly, he was sure of it. Truth be told, he envied that guy, now. Wished he would turn up more often, instead of this whiny, worthless version most people ended up meeting.

'Mr Fitzpatrick regretted that you never managed to stay married.' Quinn interrupted his thoughts. 'But he hoped that the medicine, and maturity might—'

'What? He even knew about the state of my relationships?' *And about the drugs*, he added silently.

'As I said…'

'He checked in.'

'Quite.'

Ranald studied Quinn's expression. This was real. This was all actually real. He had a house. He had a huge library. It must be huge, right? If this old fella was making such a fuss about it.

Quinn opened a drawer on the right side of his desk and pulled out a small brown envelope. He put it on the desk and pushed it across to Ranald.

'The key,' Quinn said, quite simply. 'There is a small piece of card inside with the address of your new home written on it.'

Ranald paused before picking up the envelope. Were the camera crew about to burst in now? The room remained still. The only noises from outside the room were the low hum of conversation and the clicks of a computer keyboard.

He opened the envelope, expecting a fanfare of trumpets. But the key was a small, insignificant thing. Cold to the touch. He read the address: Bearsden. A posh part of town.

'Everything you could want is in your new home, Mr McGhie. But if you want to move any of your…' Quinn actually sniffed. '… Your belongings from your flat in Shawlands, we can arrange for a removal van for you.'

'That's very kind of you, Mr Quinn,' Ranald said, emphasising the word 'kind' but meaning the opposite.

'The house is ready for you, Mr McGhie,' Quinn said with a note of relief. 'You can move in today. You'll find the housekeeper and the gardener – Mr and Mrs Hackett – have everything prepared. They're a pleasant couple. Worked for the family for years.'

Ranald sank into his chair, now weirdly reluctant to move. He even wanted the pompous old fool in front of him to keep on talking.

'You mentioned a … "paucity" of relatives? I'm it, then?' he asked.

'Mr Fitzpatrick kept an eye on all of you. You were deemed to be the most suitable for the task.'

All of you.

'Will any of the others challenge the will?' Ranald asked. He had a whole other family he knew nothing about. Should the fact that

Fitzpatrick rated him his best option mean he should also discount them?

'They have been adequately provided for by the trust, Mr McGhie. None of the others actually wanted the house. They are all well taken care of in the housing department. In fact, most of them see Newton Hall as a white elephant.'

Newton Hall. The house had a name?

'Can I meet them?' Ranald asked.

A buzzer sounded on Quinn's desk and a look of relief passed over his face. 'That's my next appointment, Mr McGhie. I'm afraid I'm going to have to…'

He stood up, and Ranald, with reluctance, followed suit. Quinn walked to his door and opened it. He held out a hand as Ranald reached him. His grip was tight, his hand cold. His voice low.

'My advice: Enjoy the house. Forget your new relatives. Mr Fitzpatrick didn't have a good word to say about any of them.'

2

On autopilot, Ranald found himself standing in front of the shiny aluminium door of the lift. He stared at his blurred reflection and then at the buttons on the panel as if unsure where they might take him.

A tiny, elderly lady – powdered face, hair piled high on her head, large pearl earrings – stretched out her hand and pressed a button.

'Going down, son?' she asked, looking up at him with an expression of concern.

'Aye,' he answered, most of his attention still in Quinn's office.

A musical note sounded and the doors opened. Ranald paused to allow the woman to enter before him. He followed. She pressed another button and the lift began its ponderous descent to the lobby.

Bugger me. A house. No, not a house. Newton Hall in Bearsden.

The doors pinged open. Before the old lady walked out, she reached out a hand and gripped Ranald's forearm. With a mournful expression, she said, 'Just remember, son, however bad you're feeling right now, all this will pass.' She offered him a smile. 'Look after yourself, eh?' And with her pronouncement made, she turned and walked smartly to the front door.

Ranald followed her with his eyes.

All this will pass? What the hell was she going on about?

Then he thought about where he had come from. The dazed expression he was undoubtedly wearing. The old dear must have thought he was dealing with some bereavement. The lift doors sounded a warning they were about to close. He jumped out before they did and made his way out of the building and onto the street.

He was greeted by a burst of noise. Buses and taxis motored past. Crowds of people bustling through that present minute of their lives.

The sun was shining. He turned his face up to it and felt the heat; had that mournful, Scottish thought that this moment was the only summer they might enjoy. He shouldered off his tweed jacket. What had he been thinking? That some stuffy lawyer would be impressed by it, rather than by his usual Superdry waterproof?

Ranald looked to his right at Central Station, then turned to his left and faced the shopping mecca that was Buchanan Street. While he had been inside talking with Quinn, finding out that his life was about to change, the rest of the world had been sailing on, taking absolutely no notice.

He palmed his trouser pocket to locate his phone. He pulled it out and pressed a number. It was answered quickly.

'What's up, Ran?' The familiar voice filled his ear.

'You're never going to believe this…' he began and only then noted the sense of excitement he was feeling.

Once he'd arranged a meeting and hung up, the thought occurred to him: the first person he'd decided to call – out of everyone he knew – was Martie.

He turned around and began to walk towards the train station. But he couldn't remember the last time he'd been to Bearsden. How did he even get there?

By now he had come to the junction where Gordon Street met Renfield Street, and there, in front of the green Victorian portico at the station entrance, was a line of taxis. He was going to be saving five hundred a month on rent; surely he could afford to take a taxi on this occasion?

There was a small queue of onward travellers waiting patiently for their rides. He stood behind a family: mum, dad and two-point-four children. The point-four child was an infant in a papoose-type arrangement fastened to its father's chest; looked like it was only weeks old. Tiny head covered in a dark fluff. Eyes screwed shut. Mouth pursed in a dream-filled pout.

It wasn't like him to notice such things. His default position was to look at kids and adopt the warding-off stance of a vampire hunter.

He felt his connection to the ground. Noticed his head was higher than normal. So this was what a good mood felt like? He had been in such a rush for his 9:00 am appointment that morning he'd forgotten to take his happy pill. Should he ask the taxi driver to take a detour to his flat in Shawlands so he could collect it?

Nah, one day off the meds shouldn't cause him any problems, surely?

A memory of the first couple of weeks he'd been on these current pills flashed into his mind. He'd been in a supermarket on day two. Mentally numb. Walking at a shuffle. Wondering how to form a smile of thanks when the cashier offered him his change. His doctor had reassured him that these side-effects would pass. He couldn't say how long they would take to fade, but surely they were better than the suicidal thoughts Ranald had experienced on the previous drugs?

Now, momentarily, he worried that a day or two off his pills might reintroduce that numb state of mind. Then he dismissed the thought. Things were looking up. His life was changing for the better. A little more cash. A new home.

And Martie had agreed to come over and have a look.

He felt a stir of excitement.

Yes. Things were definitely on the up.

⊣�muⱶ

The taxi driver was sharp-eyed and as lean as a marathon runner. Every now and then he'd take his eye off the road and study Ranald in the mirror. Normally, Ranald would resist making conversations with taxi drivers. But today the driver had him at 'Where to, mate?' and even before they'd reached St Vincent Street he'd told him everything.

'Lucky bastard,' the driver said. 'It's like something out of a book.'

'Aye. Good things happen to other people,' said Ranald. 'No me.'

'Mind you...' The driver threw him a sad expression via the

mirror. 'Like my old mammy used to say after a sunny day – we'll pay for it tomorrow.'

'What do you mean?' asked Ranald, reluctant to have *anyone* inject a note of negativity.

'Just sayin',' replied the driver, 'there's always a price.'

Piss off, thought Ranald, and stared out of the window to indicate that the conversation was over. If he was going to 'just say' rubbish like that, he could keep it to himself.

After a few minutes silence the driver piped up again: 'So this guy was like an old uncle?'

'My mum was his niece, apparently,' Ranald answered. He had trouble holding onto his resentment towards the driver, such was the power of his new state of mind. 'She had the audacity to want to marry a working-class guy, and her family disowned her.'

'That's tough, man.' Pause. 'Families, eh?'

Ranald nodded his agreement. Rubbed his hands together. They'd be drawing up at the house soon, and his excitement was mounting.

'Might mean you'll be able to get yourself a woman then, eh?' asked the driver. 'I mean to say … if you were married and inherited this house, your wife would be with you. So I'm guessing you're single. But women will be flocking round you now. Another bonus.'

'Keep your eyes on the road, Sherlock,' answered Ranald. He wasn't going to let the driver puncture his good mood again. 'The ex is coming over for a nosey later.'

'Oh, aye?' said the driver. 'Watch out for that, mate. Your marriage ended for a reason. A posh new hoose willnae paper over the cracks.'

'Fuckssake, mate. You don't half know how to put a dampener on stuff,' Ranald replied, knowing, though, that the man was making sense. He shook his head. That was Glasgow for you. Intrusive and interested. At times not a good combination.

'Here we are, mate,' said the driver as the car slowed and his brakes whistled their protest. 'I'll just go in the drive.'

There was a drive? Ranald sat forwards in his seat and looked out of the window.

The first thing he saw was a low wall bordering the road. Beyond that, mature trees of varying heights, a sweep of lawn and, a curve of pebbled drive.

And there. As large as a monument to a lost love.

The house.

3

The driver gave a low whistle. 'You lucky, lucky bastard.'

'You sure this is the right place?' asked Ranald.

They both craned their necks to look at the expanse of the building. All Ranald could take in were two, no, three rows of large windows; a red sandstone façade topped at one corner by a tower or turret of some sort. And in front of him a giant, dark, wooden door, flanked by two massive carved lions.

Oh, and what would you call that? A porch? It couldn't be as basic as a porch, he thought. There were four twenty-foot-high pillars holding it up.

'This is the address on the wee piece of paper you gave me.'

'Fuck me,' said Ranald.

'I just might, if I can move in,' laughed the driver.

'I suppose I better go have a look then,' said Ranald as he sat further back in his seat.

The driver chuckled, stepped out and pulled open the passenger door. 'At your service, m'lord,' he beamed.

Ranald climbed out of his seat. Once he was standing – he couldn't help but note the satisfying crunch of the gravel under his shoes – he pulled out his wallet.

The driver held up a hand. 'Naw, mate. This one's on me. It's fair made my day, so it has. I'll be telling folk about this ride for years.'

Just then the front door opened and an old couple stepped out. They were about the same height, with matching expanded waistlines. He was wearing a pair of dark-green overalls. She had a white apron over a simple black dress.

'You'll be Mr McGhie,' said the woman as she took a step forwards, holding her hand out. 'I'm the housekeeper, Mrs Hackett. And this is my husband, the gardener, Danny.'

Thinking it was strange how she had given herself the title of Mrs, and her husband was reduced to the more informal Christian name, Ranald stepped forwards and took her hand.

'Hello,' Ranald said.

Her grip was strong, her skin florid – she looked like she'd been living and working on a farm most of her days. But there was a stern cast to her expression as she studied him. Ranald imagined the message she was trying to get across: *I have my ways and you better not make my life difficult.*

'Danny,' the gardener said, as if he'd suddenly remembered his manners. He held a hand out. Ranald took it and nearly had his knuckles ground into a dust. While they shook hands Ranald was aware that the older man was yet to meet his gaze.

'C'mon inside, Mr McGhie.' Mrs Hackett straightened her back and clasped her hands over her large belly. 'Time for you to see what your mother deprived you of all these years…'

Ranald bristled at Mrs Hackett's words, determined he should defend his mother. But as he opened his mouth to do so, he felt something being slipped into his back pocket. He turned to see the taxi driver walking away.

'Just my business card, *Mr McGhie,*' he shouted over his shoulder, giving Ranald his title with some glee. 'Give me a call when you need to go back into town, eh?'

'Sure,' said Ranald. 'And thanks. Really appreciate it.' Then, deciding that this time he would allow Mrs Hackett her jibe, eager to experience his new home, he turned and followed the Hacketts inside.

The hall was the size of a tennis court. And in the middle sat a large, oval, marble-topped table, bearing a vase of white lilies. The walls were timber panelled for three-quarters of their height and the same wood had been used to construct a large, ornate fireplace on the far wall, a pillar at the stairs and the bannister. The huge space seemed oddly dim and gloomy to Ranald, despite the light streaming through the massive windows.

The window opposite the fireplace, halfway up the wide staircase, was like something out of a cathedral: stained glass portrayed a scene straight from the classics – a Rosetti-style maiden, with long amber hair and wearing a white, off-the-shoulder dress, was riding on the back of a swan across a watery landscape.

'It's based on the legend of Leda and the Swan. Beautiful, isn't it?' said Mrs Hackett with a proprietary tone as she followed his gaze. 'Mr Fitzpatrick was incredibly proud of that.'

'Stunning,' said Ranald, nodding his head in appreciation. He looked around, wondering what he should do next, where he should go. How else he could absorb exactly what was going on.

Perhaps realising what he was thinking, Mrs Hackett laid a hand on his forearm. Then she removed it with a little cough, as if internally reprimanding herself for crossing a boundary. 'There's a lot to take in, Mr McGhie. That door…' she pointed to the right of the stairs '…is a reception room. Visitors to the house are taken there, but you can investigate that at your leisure, the main thing is you need to know where to eat, where to sleep and where to relax. Everywhere else, as I said, you can explore in your own time. But first…' she turned and beckoned him to follow '…the kitchen and a cup of tea.'

At the far end of the hall was a door. This led onto a wide corridor. Here, the walls were painted dark green to waist height and white above that, with an ornate dado rail separating the colours. Here and there, white plaster Doric half-columns were set into the walls. Under their feet was a racing-green carpet, its pile so thick their footsteps were soundless.

'There is the smoking room.' Mrs Hackett opened one door for Ranald to get a glimpse of a high ceiling and dark wood panelling. The room was dotted with chairs covered in blood-red leather. Either side of a window there were bookcases full of leather-bound volumes, and despite the size of the window there was little light getting into the room. The view from the window was of the front drive and Ranald suffered a stab of anxiety. This was all too much for him. He didn't deserve any of it. He should phone the taxi driver before he was too far away.

He picked his phone out of his pocket. No signal. And before he could say or do anything else Mrs Hackett had stepped across to the other side of the corridor and opened another door. 'This is the ballroom.'

He took a step inside and heard the sound of his heel on the parquet floor echo through the large space.

'The family had many a grand occasion in here,' said Mrs Hackett with an almost self-congratulatory tone. Three floor-to-ceiling double windows lined the far wall, looking out onto a wide stretch of lawn bordered by oak trees. The other walls contained large mirrors set into ornate plasterwork.

Ranald felt uncomfortable with the grandiosity of the room and he stepped back out into the corridor closing the door behind him, with the thought that this was one space he wouldn't be re-visiting.

Further down, Mrs Hackett indicated another door. 'Here is the library.' She stopped so suddenly that Ranald almost ran into her. 'But in truth, Mr McGhie, the entire house is a library. The man was a book-obsessive.' She pursed her lips, allowing a little bit of warmth to leak into her expression: her version of a smile, Ranald guessed. 'I can't tell you how pleased Mr Fitzpatrick was when he found out you were a writer.'

Further down, the corridor turned to the right, leading to a large white door. Mrs Hackett pushed it open and entered. 'And here,' she said, somewhat unnecessarily, 'is the kitchen.'

It was large enough to house Ranald's entire two-bedroom flat. In pride of place was an expansive dark-green Aga with – he counted the doors – four ovens. Who needed four ovens? Again, the room was bright, thanks to light flooding in from the large windows.

'It's seen better days,' said Mrs Hackett, marching to the far side of the room and the kettle. 'But it has everything you'll ever need.'

She held the kettle up to judge the amount of water it held, then put it back down and flicked on the switch. 'Coffee or tea?' she asked.

'Aye,' said Ranald. 'Please.' Then he took notice of the question. 'Coffee.'

She bustled to the fridge and pulled out a plastic bottle. 'Mr Quinn told us you would probably be coming over today, so I took the liberty of doing a small shop for you: milk, butter, et cetera. Just some essentials.'

'That's very kind of you,' said Ranald, while thinking, *Well, that was grudged.*

'It's on your account,' she said, her tone suggesting it would be unlikely to happen again. 'Have a seat,' she indicated the large pine table, with enough seating for ten adults. 'Just so you know, after this cuppa you're on your own. I clean. I don't cook. Okay?'

'Yeah, sure.'

'Danny and I are not your servants, Mr McGhie. It's important you appreciate that from the off, and then there'll be no awkwardness, yes?' She pulled a mug from a cupboard and located the jar of coffee. The kitchen was filled with the sound of the kettle reaching the boil. Then, the chime of teaspoon on china as she stirred.

As Ranald sat down he realised that Danny hadn't joined them. He looked back at the door as if he expected to see Danny standing there like a sentinel. Mrs Hackett placed a steaming mug on the table and stood behind a neighbouring seat.

'Questions?'

'Aye, loads,' said Ranald, reaching for the mug. The act of bringing it to his mouth, testing it for heat and sipping, was enough to centre him in the room. 'This has all been a bit of a mind fu—' He stopped himself from swearing, not sure how Mrs Hackett might take it.

She gave him a small nod, acknowledging his effort at restraint.

'Mr Fitzpatrick took care of us handsomely,' she said. 'At the far side of the grounds is a converted stable. A lovely two-bedroom house where Danny and I live. We were gifted it in his will. We *own* it now,' she said with degree of steel.

Message received, thought Ranald. *Don't mess with Mrs Hackett.* Still, he could understand her setting out the situation from the start. After so many years working with one person, her and her husband must be concerned that their lives might change.

'The Fitzpatrick Trust pays our wages. I tend the house, Monday to Friday, nine till noon. Danny looks after the outside: house and grounds. In the summer, he works all hours. In the winter, just as much as the place needs.'

'Everything is immaculate,' Ranald said, taking another sip. 'From what I've seen.'

Mrs Hackett gave a small nod. But it seemed she took no pleasure in the compliment – was simply acknowledging it as an obvious truth.

'What can you tell me about my great-uncle?' asked Ranald, settling into his seat.

'He was ninety-nine when he died. Can you believe it? Just a few weeks off the century.' She shook her head. 'We've been with him for over forty years.' As if by magic, a hanky appeared in her hand. She dabbed at the corners of her reddening eyes. 'I miss him every day. Such a gentle man.'

Ranald took this to be her expectation of how he should behave as much as a character description.

She shook herself, pocketed the hanky and stood up. 'Ready to see more?'

'Please,' Ranald said with a quick look at his half-full mug.

'This way, Mr McGhie.'

'Please, call me Ranald. I'm not one for formality.'

Mrs Hackett pursed her lips then sounded his name as if it was on trial: 'Ranald.' With a tilt of her head she signalled she was satisfied and led the way out of the room.

In the corridor, as Mrs Hackett moved back down to the left, Ranald glanced to the right and saw a bronze door with a small, head-height window. He shivered, as he felt a chill work up the length of his spine.

'What's that?' he asked, taking a step back from the door. At that moment, the light in the corridor seemed to dim. A cloud obscuring the sun, perhaps. Ran's breathing deepened. Shortened. Sparks of energy fired in his thighs and fingertips. He clenched his fists, and bent his knees, not knowing whether to run or fight. A sane part of his mind questioned, *What are you doing, McGhie? This isn't a time for a panic attack.*

Mrs Hackett paused mid-step and looked back. Ranald pulled himself upright.

'That's the lift to what were your grandmother's and great-grand-mother's rooms – and to the tower room,' she said. 'It's broken. And locked. Mr Fitzpatrick never got round to getting it fixed.'

She quickly moved on, but something in her tone had registered with Ranald. A warning?

'Keep walking down the corridor past it and you'll come to the fitness room,' she added, seeming to make her voice intentionally lighter.

'There's a fitness room?' Ranald asked, mentally giving himself a shake to try and rid himself of the feeling of fear he'd just felt. He didn't want to come across to the help as totally crazy on his first day.

'Well, more of a suite, actually. Mr Fitzpatrick had a conservatory built about fifteen years ago. Installed a twenty-metre swimming pool and a sauna. There's also some exercise equipment. He must have had a rush to the head, because he never used it. But he did swim forty lengths every day. Almost right up to the end. Danny's sure that's why he lived so long. That and the coffee.' She smiled and turned to march on, actually saying, 'Come.'

Feeling like he was already being trained, Ranald followed. They were going back the way they came and about twenty paces on, Mrs Hackett paused at a door and pushed it open. 'If you're anything like your uncle this is the room you'll want to spend most of your time in. The library.'

Ranald stepped inside.

'Fuck me,' he said.

4

The room was a feast of browns and reds. Ranald judged that the walls were at least twenty feet high, that each wall was covered with a dark wooden bookcase and that each bookcase was full. There were several wheeled ladders, spaced at regular intervals, to allow the resident bibliophile access to the books on the highest shelves.

This was another floor space that could have doubled as a tennis court, but should anyone have been tempted to use the room for that purpose they'd have to have shifted the pine desk with a surface large enough to land a small helicopter, two red-leather Chesterfield three-seater settees and both leather wing-backed chairs. Then there were the numerous standard lamps dotted round the room, to ensure that wherever a reader might find him or herself, there was soft lighting available.

The only spaces empty of books were the floor-to-ceiling three-panelled window behind the desk and inglenook fireplace opposite it – which also had seating inserted, should a reader need to get closer to the heat on a winter's afternoon.

Ranald sent Mrs Hackett an expression of apology after his expletive. 'Wow.' He moved over to the desk, leaned against it and surveyed the room. 'I think I've died and gone to heaven.' So far, as he walked through the house he felt as if the weight of the place was pressing down on him, as if the centuries of formal human habitation were pushing him into a huge responsibility. But this room had a different feel. This was a room he could live in.

Mrs Hackett all but preened. 'Mr Fitzpatrick would be utterly delighted to hear you say that.' She looked around as if Ranald's presence allowed her to see it all afresh. 'It is quite something.' She paused. 'But just so you know, this is not a museum exhibit. Mr

Fitzpatrick would want you to read as many of the books as you could. He never bothered if anyone turned down the corners or bent back the spine,' she paused and shuddered. 'But what did drive him crazy was hearing that people took their books into the toilet. The idea of any ... matter ... finding its way onto the pages...'

Ranald laughed. 'I've read many books that were full of such matter.'

Her answering look was the reprimand of a stern school headmistress. 'Read as you wish, but don't take books into the loo and don't give them out to people. He hated it when people didn't return his books. He was a real hoarder.'

'I get that,' said Ranald.

'Just one more thing I need to tell you,' Mrs Hackett said. She looked at her wristwatch. 'Almost noon,' she murmured, then looked back at Ranald, her lips twitching in an almost-smile. 'The master bedroom is the first door on the right as you walk up the main stairs. The bedding is all brand new, as are the pillows and the mattress. Mr Fitzpatrick was bedridden for the last few weeks of his life and he was worried you might not want to sleep in a dead man's bed, so he left instructions that everything should be replaced.'

'Really?'

She walked to the doorway and out of the room. Ran followed to hear what she was about to say.

'Mr Fitzpatrick has been preparing for this day for some time, Mr Mc ... Ranald. He respected your mother's decision to remove herself from the family, so he was sure never to intervene in your life, no matter how much he wanted to. But he felt that anything that happened when he was dead was beyond that ... sensitivity.'

Ranald shook his head slowly. 'I really don't know what to say, Mrs Hackett.' He felt a surge of affection for the deceased man. His throat tightened and he felt his eyes smart. 'I wish I could have met him.'

Mrs Hackett studied him. 'You two would have got on, I'm sure. He was a lovely man, although he could be an irascible old so-and-so from time to time.' She rubbed her hands together. 'Right, I best be off, I have a husband who'll be looking for his lunch. As I said earlier, I took the liberty to put some food in the fridge, but if you need to go out to the shops, they're not that far down the hill.' She stretched to her full height, as if she was standing on tip-toe, then looked him up and down. 'You're a Fitzgerald, Ranald. Don't ever forget that.'

With that pronouncement, delivered as forcefully as any judge might pass sentence, she turned away and walked away down the corridor. Ran followed her with his eyes. Her large figure seemed to diminish in the poor light at the far end until she all but disappeared into shadow. What was that about? he wondered: *Don't ever forget you're a Fitzgerald?*

Ranald walked back into the room and sat down in the large, and of course, leather desk chair. He felt the give of the suspension and the chair rolling back a little. Then he put both hands on the polished wooden surface and examined the desk.

Apart from a bronze lamp on one corner, an old-fashioned phone with an answerphone on the other and a large leather blotter in the centre, the desk was clear of clutter. He stretched. Picked up the phone and listened. Yes. A dialling tone. A way to reach the world if required.

He took yet another look around the room.

This couldn't all be his. This was wrong. What had he done to deserve it all? His mind was drawn back to the taxi driver and his mother's fatalistic attitude: 'We'll pay for it tomorrow.'

Fate, destiny, providence – whatever the hell you liked to call it – had provided Ranald with this house. It was too much. Too much for the likes of him. And there was bound to be a cost.

He gave himself a mental shake. *Chrissakes, McGhie*, he thought. *Get a grip. It's just a house.*

Enjoy yourself.

Take a breath.

Savour.

But, before he knew it, he was on his feet, out the door, along the corridor and into the main hall. Then he was pulling open the heavy front door and darting out onto the drive, panting like he'd just run a marathon.

He leaned over, hands on his thighs, took a deep breath and tried to ignore the rapid beat of his heart. It was all just too much.

Fresh air, that's what he needed, he thought, closing his eyes and then opening them again. It was a lovely sunny day. He should go for a walk. He remembered Mrs Hackett talking about the village shops. That's where he could go. The shops.

As he walked towards the road, crunching over the gravel, he noticed Danny hacking at a bush of some sort with a large pair of shears.

'Awright?' Ranald asked him as he approached. 'Just need … just need a breather. This…' He turned back to the house. 'It's all a bit much to take in, you know?'

Danny nodded, but said nothing, his sombre eyes set deep in the tan of his face.

Something snagged Ranald's attention. Movement at a window on the first floor. Or was it? He stared. Nothing.

'Thought I saw…'

'A bit of a cloud. A breeze … and you think you've seen or heard something. Old houses will do that to you, Mr McGhie.' Danny nodded as if this would add import to his words. 'You'll soon get used to it.'

'The village?' Ranald asked, taking another step towards the road.

'It's a bit of a trek. There's a bike you could use, in the garage. But if you want to stretch your legs go out the drive and take a left. First right and just walk straight along that road. Half an hour at a good stride and you'll come to the Cross. There's a few shops there.'

Ranald's mobile phone pinged – a text alert. It was from Martie. She couldn't make it over after all. A crisis at work. Could she come tomorrow? it asked.

Disappointed, Ranald pocketed the phone without sending a reply.

'Another thing about old houses – at least hereabouts; apparently you get a terrible signal on your mobile,' said Danny. 'Or so I'm told.' His tone suggested he'd rather lose both his thumbs than have one of his own.

᛭

Five minutes into the walk and Ranald regretted his impulse to escape. What had Danny said? Half an hour? Already his calves were beginning to feel tight, it was too warm, the road was too narrow and with too many bends, the hedges were too high and he was sure a car was going to rip round the corner and toss him high into the air.

Get a hold of yourself, man, he thought. *Remember what your therapist said*: 'Centre yourself in the real world every day, and every day push yourself out of your comfort zone.'

Mindful that a car might be on top of him at any second he stepped off the road, his right leg almost in among the brambles, nettles and wildflowers that flourished in the lee of the hedge, and, as he focused on his breath – slow and through the nose – he turned round to look for his new home.

At first he couldn't see anything of it. The variety of trees before him was an arborist's dream, and there, like a giant's shoulder edging the hill, was a stretch of grazing land; but no house. In only five minutes' walking it had all but disappeared from view. Driving along this road you might not even know it existed. All of *that* was concealed by a dip in the land and an assembly of tall vegetation.

He shielded his eyes from the sun with his right hand. There. Above the trees was a tower, like a floating pavilion of brick and window. Cloud draped the sun and he was able to move his hand away from his forehead to study it better. And that's when he once again saw something. Was there someone behind the glass? He squinted. It was too far away to see properly, but he was sure this time he had seen some movement. Someone looking out towards him? He shook his head. Maybe Mrs Hackett was up there doing some overtime.

He wiped some sweat from his forehead with his sleeve and thought about his new cleaner and gardener. Pushing aside the thought that *he* had staff, he wondered what they made of him. After such a long time of looking after old Alexander they were in the middle of a period of uncertainty. Did they resent him? Danny had barely spoken a word and Mrs Hackett was as remote as the house now appeared to be. He frowned, thinking of his taxi drive from the city. Was the house really that far beyond Bearsden? It hadn't seemed like it. But now…

He began walking again, and, grateful for a breeze that greeted him as he rounded a bend, Ran's thoughts moved to more practical matters. When he got to the village, he'd look for a coffee shop, and then find a taxi to bring him back up here. No way was he walking all that way.

⳨

Eventually the road came to a junction. He looked to his left and saw nothing but farmland, turned to his right and was able to make out a cluster of red roofs. Civilisation. With the sight he felt a lift of energy. He lengthened his stride and increased his pace, and before long a row of large houses came into view. A car passed him. Then another, and Ranald realised this was the first traffic he'd seen since he left Newton Hall.

He came to a busy crossroads, with a set of traffic lights, and as he turned, deciding where to go, he almost collided with someone. An old man in a light-blue raincoat and a brown tweed flat cap was standing right beside him, staring at Ranald as if he'd seen a ghost. Appearing to gather his wits, the man mumbled, 'People should watch where they're going,' before turning to cross the road.

· *The natives are friendly then*, thought Ranald as he walked in the same direction as the old fellow in the cap. He was soon at the Cross and his eyes were immediately drawn to the War Memorial – a massive plinth on which stood a tall winged angel holding what Ran assumed was a fallen soldier.

He crossed another busy junction and spotted a wee coffee shop and mentally greeted it like it was an old friend. A pair of tables, each with two seats, had been arranged just outside the window. Ranald sped up, anxious that he should nab one before someone else got there first. The pavement was narrow, so the seat was a bit close to the traffic coursing past, but it felt like it would be a crime to sit inside on such a warm day.

He pulled the door open, stepped inside, caught the attention of the server, and ordered a black coffee. Then he went back outside and claimed his place.

With his back against the window, he turned his face to the sun and allowed his anxiety to dissipate a little. This was remarkable. What a library. And what a beautiful house. He couldn't wait to investigate the rest of it.

I should be doing that now, he thought. Why was he so intimidated by it all?

But then he gave himself a break, as his therapist had so often told him to do. It was a lot to take in for anyone. Least of all a man with his history.

He heard footsteps; a young woman was approaching the café. Loose, yellow, flowery dress. Long, straight black hair. She caught Ranald's eye and smiled. Then pulled out her in-ear headphones and said, 'You've got the right idea.'

Ranald nodded.

She's gorgeous, he thought. Then: *Better not sit down here; I've got so much nervous energy, I'll talk at you till closing time.*

She went inside. But came back out moments later and sat on one of the pair of chairs on the other side of the door. She rested a large leather bag on her lap and pulled out a book. Ranald craned his neck to see what the title was. *War and Peace*. He wanted to say that he'd probably got the original back at his house, then thought better of it.

'Good for you,' he ventured instead. 'I've tried that several times. Never got further than a third of the way in.'

She smiled, displaying a row of perfect teeth. 'This was my New Year's resolution. It's now, what, May? – and I've only got this far…'

She held the book up and Ranald guessed she was about a hundred pages in.

'That's actually good going,' he said. 'I'm giving myself an easier reading time these days. I'm reading one of those "Girls on the Train and the Bus with the Red Coat and the Cat Tattoo" books.' He was aware that he was speaking too fast, and thought he should force himself to slow down the next time he spoke.

She laughed. 'Sure you are. Show me a literary bandwagon and I'll go elsewhere.' She held up Tolstoy's offering. 'Hence this…'

'Anyway,' said Ranald, 'don't want to intrude on your reading time.' He pointed at her book. 'You want to be more than halfway through when it comes to next year's resolution.'

'Very true.' She offered him a smile and moved her chair so that she would be sitting with her face straight to the sunshine.

'We should take advantage of the weather while we can, eh?' he said needlessly. And then clamped his jaw shut. Had he misread the situation? Why was he always so clumsy?

He was saved from further embarrassment by the arrival of the waitress, who placed a large cup of black coffee in front of him and a tall latte on the girl's table.

He pulled out his phone in order to disguise his awkwardness and read the text from Martie again. He thumbed out a reply: 'No worries. Let me know when you can come over tomorrow.'

He sipped at his drink, leaned back in his chair, tilted back his head and stretched his legs out in front of him, just as a woman with her three kids and two dogs walked past.

'Some people,' the woman said, as she took evasive action.

One of her kids wasn't quite so quick. He tripped and stumbled into one of the dogs, who gave out a yelp.

'Really sorry,' said Ranald. 'I didn't see you there.'

'Clearly,' the woman said, before she gathered her brood and set off again at a clip.

The young woman beside him giggled. 'Couldn't have done that if you'd tried.'

'Just call me Captain Chaos,' he replied.

'Okay, Captain, my name's Suzy.'

Ranald nodded. 'Nice to meet you, Suzy. I'm only a captain on weekends. My real name's Ranald.'

'Think I prefer Captain.' She squinted her eyes against the light.

'Come back on Saturday, then.'

She laughed again and then picked up her drink for a sip.

'So how come you're not doing the wage-slave thing then? Student?' Ranald asked, feeling emboldened.

'I'm on holiday. You?'

'Just moved into the area,' he replied. 'Taking time out to meet the natives.'

'I know the feeling,' she grimaced. 'A house full of boxes?'

'Not exactly,' he replied. 'But it is a tad overwhelming.'

With a nod of understanding, she opened her book and began reading again. Ranald took another sip at his coffee. The feeling of foreboding he had experienced earlier seemed to have been dispelled by the heat of the sun, the coffee and the pretty young woman sitting only an arm's length from him. But the question remained: Why didn't he want to investigate the house? Most people who came into something like this wouldn't stop until they'd seen everything.

He took a breath, and recognised this reluctance for what it was. He struggled when something good happened to him, always certain that he didn't deserve it.

He looked up and down the street, trying to get out of his own head, and at the same time wondering how he could engage the young woman in conversation again. But before he'd come up with some suitable comment, the woman was packing her book away, sipping the last of her drink and sending a non-committal smile in his direction. Unable to help but feel he had a hand to play in her swift departure, he sat back in his chair, crossed his arms and gave a small grunt of disappointment.

Her seat was almost instantly taken, this time by a middle-aged woman, slim with long blonde hair, who eyed him with barely disguised curiosity.

He gave her a nod as she sat down. 'Lovely day,' he said.

She smiled in response, placed her large handbag on the table and rummaged around inside.

A second glance up at him, accompanied by another small smile prompted Ranald to say something more. 'I wonder how anyone can find anything in those.'

The woman blew her fringe out of her eyes, smiled more broadly and said, 'Don't I know it. I put my phone in the little pocket on the side and it always finds its way down into the bottom of my bag.'

The waitress appeared with her drink and Ranald heard the music of the teaspoon on china, as the cup and saucer came to rest on the table top. He cursed her timing. Unusually for him he was feeling chatty and he couldn't help but feel her sudden presence had put a halt to their conversation.

'Do you have the time?' Ranald asked once the waitress had gone back inside. The words were out before he could stop them.

The woman raised her eyebrows as if he'd just come out with the worst chat-up line ever. 'It's one-thirty.'

'Really?' he said. 'Where's the day gone?' Feeling encouraged by her open expression, he decided to try and push it. 'Come here often?' he asked.

'That's what you're going with?' The woman chuckled. She lifted her cup, examining him over the rim.

'Sorry, I'm just recently divorced. I've forgotten how I should speak to attractive women,' he said.

'Good comeback,' she laughed. Perfect teeth, light tan, hair that looked as if it had been straightened to within an inch of its life reaching her shoulders. Just a touch of cleavage. 'Just moved into the area?' she said.

'Yeah,' he replied. 'Just finding my feet.' He paused. Held his cup up in a kind of cheers motion. 'Is this it, then? The height of excitement in Bearsden?'

'Just wait till you have one of their fruit scones. That's when you know you've really lived,' she chuckled. 'So the ex got the marital home? Where are you living?'

Ranald smiled. 'I've just moved into Newton Hall.'

She sat forward, a note of *what do we have here?* clear in her face. 'I didn't realise it had gone on the market,' she said.

'It didn't,' replied Ranald. 'I inherited it.'

'You did?' She narrowed her eyes. 'You a Fitzpatrick then?'

'On my mother's side.'

'Right,' she said with a hint of excitement, as if pleased to touch on some old gossip. 'She was the one that got away. Helena, wasn't it?'

Ranald blinked, taken aback by the direction the conversation had moved in. But then again, he should have known. While Bearsden was part of the urban sprawl of Greater Glasgow, it did have a distinctly village feel about it.

'You knew my mum?' he asked.

'Knew *of* her.' The woman smiled. 'Is it true that the house is haunted?'

'News to me if it is,' answered Ranald. 'Don't all old houses have that reputation?'

'I used to work with one of the Fitzpatricks,' she replied. 'She said none of the extended family wanted to inherit the place. It gave them the creeps.'

Thinking he understood that after only spending a short time inside, Ranald disguised his uncertainty behind the action of taking a sip of his hot drink.

The woman's focus returned to her coffee, and silence fell on them, the only sounds the chime of cup on saucer and the passing traffic. While Ranald wondered what to say next he tried to study the woman without being too obvious. She was beautiful; he was flattered she was even giving him the time of day.

Before long, she took what appeared to be the last sip of her drink and got to her feet. 'Was nice talking to you…?' She left a space for him to reply with his name.

'Ranald. And likewise,' he replied. 'Hopefully I'll see you again soon.'

She smiled and walked away, and was at the end of the street before Ranald realised she hadn't given him her name.

⊩

Once the woman had left, Ranald felt the fun had gone out of his visit to the village, so he drank what remained of his coffee quickly and made his way to the small supermarket where he filled a basket with some essentials, and something for his evening meal.

He'd paid and was walking out of the shop door, when he heard his name being called. It was the blonde woman from the café again.

'I never told you my name,' she said and held out her hand. 'It's Liz.'

'Nice to meet you,' he said taking her hand in his. Her skin was warm and soft.

'How about you show me this haunted house, then?'

5

It had been a day full of surprises. And the latest was that they'd been back at Newton Hall only minutes before they were having sex. Ranald wasn't exactly sure how it had even started. All he knew was that Liz was the one in charge, seeming to find the main bedroom in the blink of an eye, and hauling him over to the massive four-poster they found there.

Afterwards, she rolled onto her back, propped her head up on the pillow and looked over at him. She seemed pleased with herself.

'I've always wanted to do that,' she said.

'What?' Ranald asked, trying to get his breathing under control.

'You know, do it with a stranger; and a younger man at that…'

Ranald turned away from her, locating his boxer shorts on the edge of the vast bed and slipping them on.

'What's that about?' she asked. 'I don't mind you being naked.'

He made a face. 'I've never been that comfortable with nudity.' A flash of memory and his father's angry red face was in his head. Where had that come from? he wondered. He forced his thoughts back into the moment and as if it might help, he reached over and down with his right hand to trace a lazy circle round Liz's belly button. He spotted a small tattoo on the inside of her upper thigh. It was a small, pink heart. He leaned over and touched it.

'I've got another one,' Liz said and held up her leg. 'On my ankle.' It was a blue butterfly. Small, about the size of penny.

'Another thing you always wanted to do – get tattoos?' he asked.

'Kinda,' she chuckled.

Ran lay down next to her, placed his head on her shoulder and closed his eyes. All this talking, all this moving, all of *this* was momentarily too much. He craved the balm of sleep with an intensity that was, most likely, unhealthy.

'You're not going to do that thing where you fall asleep, are you?' she asked.

'Nah,' said Ranald. 'Just resting my eyes.'

'Sure you are,' she said, reaching up and patting him on the head. 'I might just join you,' she added.

⊣⊢

Ranald woke to a panicked yelp. He felt the rush of movement as someone leaped away from him. Opening his eyes in fright he saw Liz pressed up against the headboard, the quilt held up to her breasts and her eyes as large as plates.

'Did you hear that?' she whispered.

'Hear what?'

'Oh my God. I've got to get out of here.' She jumped off the bed and rushed to put her clothes on.

Ranald climbed over to her side and stood up. Mystified, he asked, 'What happened?' As he spoke he noticed the room was decidedly colder. His skin prickled.

'Walk me out, please. Walk me out.' She didn't bother with her underwear, simply slipped her dress over her head and held her underwear and shoes to her bosom and marched swiftly out of the room.

Ranald jumped into his shorts and followed her down to the front door.

She only slowed down once she was outside. Grimacing from the pain of the pebbles on her bare feet, she hopped into her shoes.

'Liz, what's going on? What did I do?' Ranald asked, checking to see that Danny wasn't somewhere near.

It was still bright and warm. And now she was outside, Liz appeared to have relaxed a little. She gave a little laugh. 'Oh my God, that was weird.' She placed a hand on Ranald's arm. 'I'm so sorry. It must have been a dream.' She exhaled. 'But Christ, it was so real, you know?'

'What did you see? Or what did you dream?'

Liz pressed a hand against her lips as if holding back the answer. 'Och, you'll think I'm just a daft woman.'

'What was it, Liz?' Ranald reached out and took her arm.

'There was this face. A woman's face. Oh my God, it was horrible. One half of it was kind of in shadow, you know? She shouted at me; I could even feel the heat of her breath on my face as she did it.'

Ranald released his hold on her and crossed his arms. He felt cold despite the hot day.

'What did she say?'

Liz laughed. 'I'm being silly. It was just a weird dream,' she replied. She brushed her hair away from her face with her fingertips. Then she leaned forwards and kissed him on the lips. 'Thanks for a lovely afternoon.' She made a face. 'Not sure I want to repeat it after that horrible dream, mind.' She turned and started walking towards the road where she'd left her car.

Ranald followed her. 'Liz, what did this woman say?' He had no idea why it might be important, but for some reason – the look of genuine fright he'd seen in Liz's eyes; the chill of the bedroom – he had to know.

Liz stopped walking and turned to stare at him. 'You're taking this seriously, aren't you?'

'I'm a writer,' he shrugged. 'I pay attention to what people dream.'

'It *was* a dream. I'm sure of it now.'

'And?'

'The voice I heard – in my dream, or whatever – it shouted at me. Really loudly. I can still hear it.' She paused. 'She said: "Get out, he's mine."'

6

On his own again, confused at the speed at which everything was happening Ranald headed straight for the library, seeking the solace of its books. He needed to be surrounded by the muffle and hush of the bound word. There, his body cushioned by soft leather, he breathed in the smell of hundreds of years of literary works and allowed his heartbeat to settle. It felt as if the rows of spines around him formed a sanctuary, protecting him from the burden of the unknown, unexplored rooms that surrounded him.

His breathing almost back to normal, he pushed all thoughts of Liz and what she thought she'd heard from his head and sat at the desk.

What a load of crap, he told himself. She heard something. *Yeah right*. She'd just wanted to get away from him and that was the best thing she could think of; *that's* what had happened.

He felt the heat from the sun through the window at his back, rose from his chair and opened it.

Sitting again, he tried to enjoy the warm breeze that curled its way inside, and turn away from the harsh, self-deprecating thoughts his condition never failed to produce. Thoughts that at times he felt powerless to stop.

Distract yourself, he heard his therapist saying in his head. So he pushed back the chair and pulled open the middle drawer under the desktop. Inside, to his surprise he spotted the shine of a chrome-coloured laptop. Old Uncle Alex was more modern than this house first suggested, then. He pulled the laptop out of the drawer, set it on the desk, opened it and pressed the on button.

A box appeared asking for a password.

Just guess, he thought, and typed in his mother's name. Nothing.

He tried the name of the house. Same result.

He closed the lid and replaced the laptop in the drawer.

Next he pulled open the top drawer on the left side of the desk. Inside were a black fountain pen and four black moleskin notebooks.

His interest was roused. Might he meet his great-uncle somewhere in the pages of these books?

He picked out the top one and placed it on the desk with some reverence. But as he did so, part of his mind acknowledged that this was an act of avoidance. Any other young man in this situation wouldn't rest until he'd examined every room in the house. At this thought, a knot of anxiety tightened in his chest. It was too much. Much too much. *A little at a time, Ranald. That's what your doctors would say*, he told himself.

He opened the notebook and began reading. The handwriting was difficult to decipher at first. Vowels were often placed too close together and the '–ing' at the end of words was reduced to a shape that resembled an upside-down L. But within a couple of pages he got the hang of it and realised it hadn't really been worth the effort.

At the top of the very first page, underlined, were the words 'A Commonplace Book'. He'd never come across that before. What on earth was a 'commonplace book'? And leafing through the pages he came across aphorisms: 'Do the right thing, it will gratify some and astonish the rest'; random facts: 'Polar bears can eat as many as eighty-six penguins in a single sitting'; and even the odd recipe.

If there was a message contained in these pages, it was passing him by. Nor was he gaining any insight into what his great-uncle was like. He brought out the other notebooks and, leafing through them, found they contained more of the same.

He put them all back in the drawer and closed it.

That was a waste of time.

He now noticed a hollow ache in his stomach. Was it the return of his earlier anxiety? But then he realised he hadn't eaten for hours. Making his way along to the kitchen he spotted the plastic bag full of provisions he'd bought at the supermarket just inside the door. At least he'd had the presence of mind to carry them in here before Liz and he got intimate.

What a surprise that was. He was hardly a catch and yet on his first day at the house he'd met an amazing – but flighty – woman. Was that the kind of time he was in for?

His head spun at the thought; he felt both thrilled and terrified at the prospect. After years of therapy, he had become aware that he was prone to wide leaps in mood and energy, and that he often didn't realise what was happening until it was all over and he found himself lying in an exhausted slump, too tired to even sleep.

He closed his eyes and performed the breathing exercise he'd been taught – feeling his feet on the floor and bringing his awareness to his diaphragm.

Calm, he thought. And then food. Eggs and bacon. You couldn't go wrong with an omelette.

Once it was prepared and on a plate, he found himself eating it at the corner of the table nearest the window, his back to the expanse of kitchen. There was just too much space to be comfortable in this house. And it was too quiet. He needed to find a radio or a TV – a noise generator of some sort.

And then he heard the echo of Mrs Hackett's voice telling him about the fitness suite. A swimming pool. He could give that a try. He tidied his dishes away, not wanting Mrs Hackett to think he was a slob and went in search of the pool.

Turning right out of the kitchen, he walked past the lift. Remembering his strange reaction when he was first here, almost involuntarily, his hand reached out and touched the metal door. *Ouch.* He pulled his hand away as if he'd just received a jolt. It had been cold, like touching the fur of frost on the wall of a freezer.

He touched it again, bracing himself for another chill, but second time around the door felt like it should: solid and merely cool. Where had the shock come from, then?

Very strange.

He reached out for the handle. Mrs Hackett had said the door was locked – so what was the point of trying it? He felt like the kid who'd been told a knife was too sharp but then tested it for himself and was cut.

But before he had a chance to turn the handle, a cool breeze on his neck reminded him of his original destination: the pool. He was off, half walking, half running. Swimming had always held a special place in his heart. It was a real treat as a kid to be taken to the local swimming baths by his dad – away from the family home and all its uncomfortable oddness. The smell of chlorine and the high echo of children's voices never failed to give his gut an excited lurch: normality; like being a part of other people's more regular lives.

He felt that excitement now as he approached a pine door ahead of him and pushed it open.

'You beauty,' he said as he entered the wide space.

The surface of the water wore a lazy ripple and sparkled in the late-afternoon sunlight coming in through the wall of glass that looked out onto the garden. The other walls were stone clad. He slowly turned to the right and left, taking it all in. He noticed what looked like a small sauna tucked away in the corner.

His attention went back to the pool and for a moment he was tempted to jump in fully dressed.

A white plastic lounger sat to his right. Beside it a rack of towels. Placed on the top towel was a pair of swimming goggles. Did he have Mrs Hackett to thank for this? All he needed was a pair of trunks.

Who needs trunks? This was his pool. He could just skinny-dip. Then he thought of Liz's reaction to him putting his boxers back on. She found that strange. Was it really? And that memory of his father. Why had he been so angry with him, and why had the recollection of it popped into his head at that moment?

If Danny was out in the garden, though, he'd be able to see into the pool area. Ranald walked down and round the pool to the window. He looked out into the garden and saw a vast lawn so neat it might have been cut with nail scissors. Around the lawn were large trees and bushes. Borders full of all colours of flowers. And there, in the far corner, a summerhouse.

There was no sign of Danny, or Mrs Hackett for that matter, so he decided he could risk his naked swim. Feeling incredibly self-conscious, he turned back to the pool, kicked off his shoes, pulled off his clothes and jumped into the pool before anyone could see him.

⊥⊦

He counted out twenty laps, enjoying the ache in his arms and the kiss of the water on his skin. He hadn't done this for a while. He used to get a mile in on a regular basis, but was long out of the habit. He did a quick calculation. In this pool a mile would be about eighty lengths. Was he up to that?

Maybe not today, but he'd give it a try in the morning.

He swam a length on his back, then swam to the far side of the pool and leaned on the edge, arms on the tiles, the water supporting his legs as he lazily splashed them.

This was the life. Like the library, the pool felt like a place separate from the rest of the house, which gave Ranald an inexplicably uncomfortable feeling. Here he felt he wasn't being judged. Watched. Felt like a more relaxed version of himself.

Then a low note of loneliness. Wouldn't it be nicer to share it with someone?

He looked out into the garden and read its invitation. It must be early evening by now, but the sun would still have some heat in it. He should be out there getting some more fresh air. He climbed out of the pool and, wrapping one of the white cotton towels round his waist, he opened the middle glass door.

A couple of sun loungers sat on the patio, in the shade. He pulled one out into the early-evening sunlight, lay down and closed his eyes.

Wow, what a day. Summoned to a lawyer, given a new house, met a woman, go for a swim – no wonder he was knackered.

Breathe, he told himself.

But he knew this was easier said than done. He decided to try a relaxation exercise one of his counsellors had taught him: going through each muscle in his body, tightening then relaxing it. Gradually his breathing slowed. He could feel the heat of the day receding. And with it the sound of birdsong. His head felt heavy and he was aware of how slow his breathing had become.

Sleep claimed him…

… and he was at the door of the lift. The memory of the icy touch sparked in his fingertips. He reached out and gripped the metal handle. It was cool this time. He pulled. It opened.

A wooden-framed mirror was on the floor, leaning against the wall. He sat before it and crossed his legs. But the face he saw was not his. It was that of a much older man, with a full head of white hair and a wealth of worry worn into his expression.

Then, like a lover's exhalation, he felt a murmur of heat on the back of his neck, before something silken was pressed there. Lips. He groaned, feeling his desire build and receiving the kiss like a benediction.

'Hello, my love.' It was a woman's voice he heard. It sounded as if it floated from a shell plucked from a deserted beach. 'Welcome.'

The glimpsing kiss on his skin was both tease and torment, bringing with it the ache for more. He never wanted it to end. He stretched his head to the side to allow easier contact. A hand stroked his chest. He looked into the mirror, expecting to see himself and a woman beside him. But he saw nothing, and strangely, thought it didn't much matter. Drunk in the moment, he closed his eyes and savoured the touch.

His thighs weakened, his breath quickened. He was becoming aroused. He arched his back and heard himself beg: 'Please.'

Moist breath filled the curve of his ear. The words 'Not yet,' sang like a lament.

Then…

'Ranald? Is that you, Ran?'

Someone shook him.

He recognised the voice. He opened his eyes and he was back on his sun lounger in the garden, immediately awake and conscious of his lingering arousal.

'Martie?'

7

'What are you doing here? I thought you couldn't make it until tomorrow.' Ranald struggled to escape the clutches of his dream. And the desire it had inspired. With a deal of self-consciousness, he sat forward protectively on the lounger.

Martie looked around as if to direct her gaze anywhere but towards him. 'Is this for real?'

Ranald smiled. 'Yup.'

'I knocked on the door for ages. Got no answer.' She crossed her arms and turned to the side, clearly embarrassed that she'd caught him like this. 'So I walked round the side, thinking I must be in the wrong place. I expected someone to shout "Stop, police!" any second.'

'Surreal, isn't it?'

'Bloody hell,' said Martie. She took a step back and looked up at the length of the building. 'It's beautiful.' She looked back at him, arms out. 'You off your meds? To get yourself like…'

'Just forgot to take them this morning.' Ranald read the accusation in her question and resisted the impulse to bicker.

'They take weeks to get out of your system,' Martie began. Then stopped herself from going any further, too. 'Why don't you go and put some clothes on and tell me what the hell is going on.'

🜊

Ten minutes later they were in the kitchen with a mug of coffee in front of each of them.

'I thought you couldn't get away from work,' Ranald said.

'I texted you back about an hour after you replied to me to say everything had been sorted and I'd be over later.'

Ranald pulled his phone from his pocket. 'Nothing.'

'Hmm, you might need to change your mobile supplier if you're getting shit reception here.'

Ranald made a motion to suggest he'd get round to it. 'Fancy a tour?'

Martie was on her feet instantly. 'Lead on, Jeeves.'

He showed her the library, the ballroom and the main hall, receiving a series of gasps and wows.

'I haven't fully investigated the upstairs yet,' said Ranald, neglecting to mention his earlier visit there with Liz. 'Fancy a wee look?'

'Aye,' was the tentative answer. Then, 'Don't be trying anything on, though.'

Ranald gave her a half-smile and began climbing the stairs. As he went he noted the depth of the carpet's pile, the shallowness of the treads and that the staircase was wide enough for half a dozen broad-shouldered men to make their way up, side by side.

At the top of the stairs, he pushed open the first door. 'The master bedroom.'

'With a giant four-poster bed,' said Martie, '…which looks like it recently saw some action…' Her eyebrows were raised.

'Ah,' Ranald said and felt his face heat. He sped over to hurriedly fix the sheets. 'Isn't it great?' he said when he was done.

When he'd come in here earlier with Liz he had been too distracted to take in the space; now he looked at it as if for the first time. The massive bed was made of dark oak, but was still dwarfed by the room. White linen drapes hung at each of its posts. The large windows were dressed with similarly luxuriant curtains and placed with care between them was a large oak bookcase filled with what looked like memoirs and biographies. His great-uncle must have enjoyed reading about the rich, the famous and those with celebrated minds before he went off to sleep. Ranald looked at the low three-seater sofa at the foot of the bed. Beside it was a small table and lamp. It seemed like Uncle Alex had established good reading positions all over this house.

'What do you think's through those?' asked Martie, pointing.

He turned to see that the far wall had two sets of white double doors. 'I haven't had a chance to fully investigate.' He scratched at his head. 'I'm guessing one of them leads to the en suite. No idea what the other one is.'

Martie pulled open one set of doors. 'You've got an actual dressing room.' She walked inside and ran her fingertips over shirts, trousers and suits hung in neat rows. Then she pointed at the shelves of t-shirts and jumpers. 'Wonder if any of these will fit you,' she said and looked at the clothes he was wearing. 'Those are about ready for the bin.'

Ranald studied the clothes on the shelves. 'These all look pretty new.'

Martie was examining the label on a brown cashmere jumper. 'This is a medium – your size. And it looks like it's barely out of the packet.' She paused, and grew sombre. 'What the hell's going on here, Ranald?'

He shrugged. 'Mrs Hackett – the housekeeper – said that my great-uncle had been preparing for my arrival for years. Maybe this…' he indicated the clothes '…was part of all that.'

'Try something on,' Martie urged, seeming to drop whatever thought was bothering her. 'One of the suits. Go on.'

She looked along a row of suits in grey, navy blue and black. Chose a grey one and handed it to him. 'I'll turn my back while you get dressed.' She gave him a tired smile.

Ranald felt a slight twinge of sadness, then shucked himself out of his clothes. He pulled on the trousers first, then took a white shirt off a hanger, put that on and finished off by shrugging on the jacket.

Martie turned back to face him and smiled her approval. 'It's like it was made for you.' She walked over to him and stroked the lapel of the jacket. 'Beautiful material.'

Ranald walked over and stood, feet wide, in front of the mirror on the back of the door. 'Aye, no bad,' he said, seeing himself smile.

'Lovely,' said Martie, gently placing a hand on his shoulder. 'Shoes?'

Ranald chose a pair of black ones from the row under the shirts, slipped them on and moving back to the mirror preened a little. 'Don't I look like the swell?'

Martie said nothing. She walked past him over to the windows and looked out onto the garden. Ranald joined her. She had crossed her arms as if warding off a sudden chill.

He nudged her with a shoulder. 'Sorry you dumped me now?'

'Shut up,' she gave a small smile that betrayed her growing unease. 'Doesn't this worry you?'

'What do you mean?'

'It all feels just too good to be true.'

'Jesus, you're like the taxi driver that brought me here. Can't you just be happy for me?'

'Course I can, Ran.' She turned to face him. 'I am. Happy for you.' But her eyes were full of concern.

At this, his stomach gave a little twist. She still cared.

'Just don't get carried away, eh?' she said. 'Enjoy it now, but get back into your routine. Keep the work going. Stay on the meds.'

'I am on my meds.'

'Really? Then what was that when I first saw you in the garden?'

Ran snorted. The way she said it sounded almost jeering, which was rich, considering one of her complaints when the doctors put him on the pills, was the libido-suppressing side-effects.

Ranald took a step back, feeling his expression sour. He fought down his irritation. 'I haven't stopped taking the pills. I'm not going to do anything stupid, Martie. And you're not my fucking mother.'

'That's not fair, Ran. Just because I'm not married to you anymore doesn't mean that I stopped caring...' She shook her head, as if trying to rid her mind of old offences.

Ranald turned away and faced the window. *Here we go again*, he thought.

'I'm sorry, Ran,' Martie said. 'It's just...'

'Just what, Martie?'

'Lots of people are bipolar, Ran. It's nothing to be ashamed of, but you need to keep on the meds, keep on the regimen that the doctors gave you.' She moved closer to him, prompting him to face her. When he did she placed a hand on his shoulder, just for a moment. 'I'm worried that all of this…' she drew a big arch in the air '…will throw you off from your…' She shook her head and crossed her arms. 'Sorry. I'm overstepping.'

Ranald stuffed his hands in his pockets, his mouth shut tight in case he said something he might regret.

'You witnessed a terrible thing, Ran. Your mum and dad…'

Ranald's eyes drifted to the bed. And for a moment it wasn't the huge four-poster he saw. It was his parents' ordinary double at home, the day he'd found them…

He shook his head. 'I thought you were going to leave it, Martie?'

'You never talked about their suicide properly, did you…?' she said and faced up to him, her eyes bright, seemingly desperate to help. 'To anyone, really.'

'SHUT UP.' His hands were down by his sides, and he was gripping his trouser legs as if that might stop him from forming fists. No, he'd never spoken to a doctor, or his therapist about it, no matter how hard they'd tried. No matter how many hours of talking about anything and everything else; no matter the number of tricks and leading questions they'd used, the space and time they'd given him. He'd never really even talked to Martie about it, apart from telling her about the initial discovery. And that's the way it would stay. That subject was permanently closed.

'If you don't stop talking now…'

'Sorry,' Martie said and took a step back. 'Sorry. I … again. Overstepping.' She crossed her arms and held one hand under her throat, her eyes soft with apology.

Ranald heard the creak of a door in the back of his mind. What lurked behind there was dark and dangerous and had to remain out of sight and hearing. He imagined the door slamming shut, and saw a large key being turned.

'Anyway…' He fought to loosen the tension in his shoulders and arms. 'Bygones, eh?' He forced a smile.

'C'mon downstairs,' said Martie forcing a light tone into her words. She looked at him, checking that he was back in a calm place. He nodded to signal that he was. 'You need to show me the rest of the house, and I want to have a look at the books in that amazing library.'

'I should get out of this suit first,' he answered, still feeling a tremble from the force of his emotion.

'Why?' asked Martie. 'There's loads if you get this one dirty. And besides,' she smiled, 'you look good in it.'

⊣⊢

Sometime later, having looked at the other three bedrooms in the same wing as the master, as well as the TV room, and the big reception room with its massive, ornate, white marble fireplace, low, red damask sofas and its assortment of oil portraits of what looked like members of the Fitzpatrick family, they found themselves in another wing of the house, one that stretched beyond the kitchen.

It was Martie who spotted the small passageway that ran along the side of the lift and followed it along to a narrow set of stairs. 'I wonder where these go?' she said.

The dark, cramped space felt unpleasant to Ranald, but she was already up the first flight, and he had no choice but to follow.

The first-floor passageway in this wing was even dimmer than the rest of the house. Despite several large windows, there seemed to be less light, and the walls were painted in a darker colour, the curtains of a heavier material, and there were a lot more wooden fixtures and fittings.

The effect was of a grand hotel whose time had come and gone. It all needed a lick of paint, the windows opening, new curtains. Something. The space looked unaltered since Victorian times.

'These must be my grandmother's rooms,' he said. 'The house-keeper told me they were up here. My grandmother took them over after *her* mother died.'

He imagined his great-grandmother pacing along these halls, a queen in her domain, primped and primed servants trailing behind her, anxious to do her bidding. His grandmother, just a little girl, watching and learning. Perhaps her mother left such an impression on her that she couldn't bring herself to make any changes to this wing when she inherited it?

Martie crossed her arms and shivered. 'It's colder up here, somehow.'

As they continued along the corridor Ranald could almost smell the memories in the air, carried there with a trace of lavender and camphor.

That was strange. Camphor? He remembered his mother was a fan. She'd used it as a disinfectant. Applied it when he had an ear infection and again to a cold sore. He'd never forgotten the smell, but until now he'd forgotten about her using it on him.

'You smell that?' he asked Martie. 'Camphor?'

Why would Mrs Hackett use camphor in this part of the house and nowhere else? Tradition? Perhaps that was what his grandmother insisted on while she was alive, to protect her thick skirts and coats from moths. And, judging by the look of this wing, tradition was important to her.

Martie was looking around, mouth slack with something approaching awe. 'This is amazing.' She paused and looked at him. 'What was that you were saying about camphor?' She breathed in deeply through her nose. 'I can't smell much to be honest, which is surprising in such an old house. Your cleaning woman must do an amazing job.'

There were four doors off the main corridor. He opened the first. Large windows, framed in dark, heavy curtains, faced him. In front of them sat a chaise longue. Cream material framed in dark wood. Against the main wall was a massive, ornate bed. A wooden head-board reached halfway up the wall and two posts stretched beyond that, supporting a canopy. A bed fit for a queen.

A dead queen, a voice sounded in his head.

He dug his hands in his pockets. This part of the building was off. He tried to work out what was giving him that impression.

'I don't like it up here,' he said to Martie. 'Being empty of people for so long must have weighed down the air or something.'

'It *is* cold,' she said, 'but it's amazing. Like a step back in time.'

He walked over and touched the smooth, cool, dark wood of one of the bedposts. He looked over the mattress and thought of someone who had been important in life, lying there in state. No one who still breathed would want to sleep there, surely. The remainder of the room was similar. A dressing table, chest of drawers, a chair and a wardrobe. He walked over to the wardrobe and opened it. Empty. He closed the door, thinking it was that sturdy you could upend it, take off the doors, install some seating and sail the Atlantic. The Victorians clearly didn't plan obsolescence into their objects.

He looked around the room. Where had Martie gone? His back prickled, as if he didn't like being left alone. Stupid, he thought. She was just exploring. And he was going to have to live here by himself.

And then he was distracted. The chair by the bed snagged something in his mind, like a hook caught in flesh. It pulled. He approached the chair and sat down in it. Allowed his buttocks and thighs to sink into the cushion. He stretched his legs out. Good back support. A good seat to read in for a few hours.

An image entered his mind: his uncle sitting in this chair, after his sister died, trying to commune with her ghost. They had two different sections of the house, but surely he would have missed her presence after her death. Ranald imagined Alexander sitting here, and he was saying the word sorry, over and over again.

Where did that come from? And to whom might he be apologising?

He stood up. Shook his head. This house was doing things to him. *Apologising*. He snorted at his own imaginings.

At the far end of the room was another door. He walked over and opened it onto a large bathroom, which was also accessed, it turned out, by one of the other entrances in the corridor. Again, it looked like time had paused at the door to this room. There was an ornate sink and a mirror against the wall, a large fireplace and a claw-footed bath in the middle of the floor. The pipes and fittings were all brass. And they were all gleaming. Mrs Hackett was certainly earning her money in here.

He left the bathroom, walked across the corridor and opened the next door. This was an oak-panelled sitting room, dominated by a large fireplace with two low, cream sofas lined up on either side.

This was much more comfortable. He could imagine a woman at leisure here. In fact, dotted everywhere were clues as to how she might have passed her time. Embroidered cushions, in various shapes and sizes and colours and displaying any number of images from flowers to kittens, graced every seat.

'Now, this is lovely.'

He jumped, twisting round to see Martie in the doorway, her face shining.

'The other rooms are a bit, you know, formal,' she said, not seeming to notice his fright. 'But I could see myself totally relaxing in here.'

There was something missing though. He looked around and spotted a small table with a tray set with all the things you would need to make yourself a cup of tea. As if the owner had just stepped out to go shopping.

Photographs. That was it. There were no photographs. And now that he thought of it, this was the same throughout the house. Other than the family portraits in oil hanging in the downstairs reception room, and Leda and her swan, there were no images of anyone in this house.

Surely that wasn't normal. Even in his wee flat in Shawlands he had a couple of framed photographs: one of his mum and dad, taken while they were courting, on a visit to Rothesay, he remembered them telling him. The other was of him and Martie.

Despite the absence of photographs, this space felt so personal and feminine, he felt like an intruder. He stepped outside, signalling to Martie that they should leave, and pulled the door shut, sending an apology to his grandmother.

ᛏᚻ

Back in the peace of the library with its view of the back garden, Ranald felt himself relax. Under the soft light of the lamps that had been spread around the room with obvious care, they began to browse the spines of the many books.

'Every room we've been in has a bookcase full of books,' Martie said, head to the side as if it had just occurred to her. 'Apart from your grandmother's rooms. This house is like a library.'

'Dream come true,' Ranald agreed. And the mention of dreams made him wonder if he should drag some bedding down here and sleep on one of the sofas. The master bedroom was great. Really luxurious. But it was so big. Apart from the pool, this was the only space he had felt comfortable in so far.

While they browsed, Ranald kept as much of an eye on Martie as he did on the books. She looked good with her new, short hairstyle. It showed off her large eyes and slender neck.

While pretending to be engrossed himself, the better to study her, he watched her pluck a book from a shelf and run her fingertips over the leather cover as if afraid her skin would erase the gilt writing. It pleased him to see her so enthused about books. They had met during their first year of an English literature degree course. A period of study, Martie asserted, that ruined her love of a good read.

Eventually Ranald's neck grew too uncomfortable, looking up at the shelves for so long, so he took a seat on one of the leather sofas.

Martie looked over at him and smiled.

'By the way,' she said in a stage whisper, 'do we have to speak quietly in here?'

He gave her a bored look. 'Very funny.'

She placed the book she had been looking at back on the shelf and plucked out another, opened it in the middle and stroked the paper with reverence.

'Seen anything you fancy?' he asked.

'Oh man, loads. Your great-uncle had an amazingly eclectic taste.'

'Apparently the trust that owns this place was instructed that I could treat the books as I liked. But they can't leave the premises, and I can't … take them into the toilet.'

'That's specific.'

'So, you're welcome to come back anytime you want a browse.'

Martie glanced up from the book. Gave him a look. 'Don't, Ran.'

'Don't what?' he asked with a sinking feeling.

She replaced the book on the shelf, walked over and sat beside him. 'Don't read anything into this other than the fact that I'm a friend who's delighted for you.' She put her hand on his. 'We're friends, Ran. We work better that way. If you can't see it, maybe I should stay away from you.'

With an expression he hoped hid the strength of his feelings and mirrored her tone and mood he said, 'Don't worry, Martie. I know that. And anyway…' he crossed his arms '…there's a nice young lady I just met.' He pictured the girl in the café and hoped Martie had forgotten about the messed-up sheets on his bed. 'I'm taking her out for dinner at the weekend,' he lied.

'Good,' said Martie. 'Brilliant, in fact.' She patted his leg. 'And, hey, the weekend is tomorrow.'

Ranald thought for a moment. 'Shit, I'd totally lost track. Of course. This is Friday.'

'And think of all those cool clothes you can wear. She won't know what's hit her.'

'Let's have a drink,' Ranald said, and stood up in an effort to hide his awkwardness and the internal voice that was intoning *shitshitshit-shitshit*. He'd hoped the fact she'd come over so quickly was a sign she still had real feelings for him.

'Wine,' he said. 'I'll have a rake through the kitchen cupboards and see if I can rustle up a bottle.' As he spoke he turned away from her in case any of his thoughts were leaking onto his face.

8

Martie left soon after the wine bottle was opened. She only had half a glass. Any more, she said, and she'd get a taste for it and would soon be over the drink-driving limit. But Ranald guessed, with a slight drop of his shoulders, that she was afraid sharing some wine with him might send him the wrong signal.

At the front door, she pecked him on the cheek, as if he was a brother of whom she was hugely fond. 'I'm so happy for you, Ran, really.' She stepped back from her hug and looked into his eyes. 'Keep in touch, eh?'

'Aye,' he replied, faking a smile.

She took a few steps towards her car.

'Still got that old mini I see?'

'I love my wee car,' she said. Before she stepped inside, she faced Ranald again. 'Good luck on the date. Let me know how it goes?'

Ranald smiled and thought, *Sure I will*.

He watched as she drove off and stayed at the front door until she was long gone, the vast hulk of the house behind him suddenly feeling like a mausoleum. He looked up at the night sky but the lights from the house made it difficult to see what was happening in the atmosphere above his head. There was a full moon, its silvery light diffusing across part of the night sky.

He shivered despite the fact that the heat of the day hadn't dissipated, and walked back into the house. It was great that Martie wanted to come and see him, but did she have to always go on about his illness? He was better, *much* better – he hadn't had an episode for a couple of years now.

He hated hearing those words, even in his own head – bipolar – the three syllables of his personal shame. Why did she have to remind him? That faux concern of hers really irritated him. He took a step forwards and kicked out at the stones under his feet, listening to them as they bounced and clicked off into the darkness.

Moving back onto the step he took a seat and listened to the sound of Martie's car as she wound her way back into her own life. She could stay there for all he cared, if all she was going to do was badger him about his medicine.

Anyway, what did she know? What did she matter? He had a house that he had to pay nothing for – he had security for the first time since his parents died. He was a man of property – even if that property did chill something inside him. And he was on his own and that was just fine by him.

⊤⊢

Upstairs in his bedroom he hung up his suit and put the shirt back on its hanger. Wearing only his boxer shorts he climbed onto his bed and centred himself on the massive mattress and threw out his arms and legs, making a star shape. This is what you called a bed, he told himself, trying to search for the undeniable positives in his new situation. His old one, back in his flat, sagged in the middle and gave him a sore lower back. This one was the height of comfort.

He reached over to turn off the bedside lamp. But the bed was so wide he had to do a graceless, crab-like scrabble to the edge.

Light off, he clambered back across to the middle of the bed, pulled the covers back and edged under them. He made a clear attempt to savour the cushion of the pillow and again, the comfort of the mattress. He closed his eyes and felt the heat build up. He kicked off the covers.

Opened his eyes again.

Had he locked all of the doors?

The front door locked automatically when you closed it, but was the door of the conservatory locked? He tried to recall what he'd done when he'd come back inside after Martie left. He couldn't remember if he'd turned the key or not.

Shit. Better check. It was a good area, but a house like this – far from any other – would surely be a target for thieves. Was there an alarm system? He'd have to check with Mrs Hackett in the morning. But first he had to check the pool door.

He ran down the stairs and when he neared the door that opened to the corridor that led down to the conservatory, he became acutely aware once more of the huge space he was inhabiting – the darkness that surrounded it. Apart from the Hacketts in their house at the far end of the garden, there wasn't a living soul for miles.

A mad axeman could be waiting for him behind any of the doors in this house and no one would hear his screams.

For God's sake, man.

But still.

He pushed open the door, and before he stepped into the corridor he reached for the light switch. Only when the way in front of him was fully lit did he step beyond the doorway. Arms crossed, walking as fast as he could, but pausing at each doorway to listen for noises he made his way to the fitness suite.

With a start he realised that the pool door was indeed unlocked. He turned the key, then raced his way to the other side of the house and back up the stairs to his bedroom as if he was being chased by a demon.

Heart racing from his sudden exercise, he lay in the middle of his bed and closed his eyes once more.

Right, Ranald, don't be stupid. You're safe, he thought. No one was going to touch him. And how nice was this bed? he reminded himself as if that might push the fearful notions from his mind.

He turned onto his side, pulled his knees up and let his head sink into the deep cushion of his pillows.

Despite himself, he opened his eyes yet again.

There was just so much space around him. And it was so hot. He wiped sweat from his forehead with the back of his hand, thinking he should really open the window.

He looked up at the ceiling; it was sliced in two by a long, narrow blade of moonlight entering through a gap in the curtains.

Moonlight.

Dancing in the moonlight with his mother: the memory was so sharp it was like he was back there once again.

He recalled a sobering moment: looking into his mother's eyes and seeing a cold stranger there. He tried to pull his hands out of her grip, but she held him fast.

What was this house doing to him – dredging up these memories from a past so deeply buried that ten years of therapy had been unable to reach them? Ten years of experimenting with a combination of legal drugs. Eight of them before his official diagnosis.

He needed air. It was so warm his pulse was pounding in his neck, thumping in his ear against the pillow.

He edged off the bed, walked over to the window and opened it. The breeze was a welcome relief against his bare chest. He took a deep breath, left a space open between the curtains to allow the fresh air to circulate in the room and went back to the bed. Without thinking about what he was doing, he pulled the white gauze curtains of the four-poster closed. It was only as he lay down that he understood the impulse he'd had to do it: he'd automatically been aiming for that feeling he had as a wee boy when he would create a den in the dining room. He'd place the biggest bed sheet he could find on the table, so that it reached down to the floor on every side and no one would be able to find him. Then he'd pull every cushion off the sofa, stuff them under the table and set up his little reading station.

When he was there, nothing could intrude and he would be lost in the worlds of Enid Blyton, C.S. Lewis and Robert Louis Stevenson. And so his love of books had been fostered.

With the thought of this old sanctuary soothing his mind, Ranald drifted into a state somewhere between sleep and a haunting memory.

ᛏᚺ

He woke with a start. His arm was numb. He was cold. Where had his quilt gone? Where the hell was he?

Bright light pushed at the thin skin of his eyelids. Then he realised he was not lying on the soft cushion of his mattress, but on a harsh, thin carpet. He rubbed his eyes as he tried to work out where he was. He sat up. He must have sleepwalked.

That hadn't happened for a long time.

He looked around.

At his back was the door of the lift.

He scratched his head. How weird was that? And he realised with a start that he was naked. How had that happened? Hadn't he gone to bed in his boxers as usual? He cupped a hand over his groin and listened, trying to hear if anyone was in the house. It wouldn't do for Mrs Hackett to come in for work and find him sitting naked in the corridor.

He got to his feet, putting a hand on the lift door for support. The door felt warm. Where was the cold buzz he got from it the previous day?

His mind felt foggy – a sense that his dreams were still with him. There was danger and comfort there. A woman. A smile. A kiss. But also something feral. Disturbed. A voice echoed in his memory: *You're mine now.*

Wasn't that what Liz thought she'd heard? A voice saying that very thing?

He rubbed at his forehead. *Shut up, McGhie.*

He took a breath and dismissed his thinking as idiotic.

He looked along to the door into the conservatory. He should go for a swim, that would clear away these bizarre thoughts.

╫

One of the benefits of swimming he'd somehow forgotten was the meditative state he would go into, as he felt the stretch and pull of his muscles, and the rhythm of lifting his head and to the side, breathing in, then dropping it again and exhaling into the water.

Forty laps later, with a satisfying ache in his arms, chest and shoulders, he climbed out of the pool, located a towel and wrapped it round his waist and looked out of the expanse of window at the ordered greenery, saw nature curbed by blade and brawn. Judging by the clear sky he was in for another day of sunshine, and he vaguely wondered why that thought didn't fill him with cheer.

╫

Fortified by a plate of bacon and eggs and carrying a mug of coffee, he walked into the library and took a seat behind the desk. The heat of the day fell on his back through the window. He would take time to enjoy the sunshine later, he thought; first he'd like to get a handle on Alexander Fitzpatrick.

The notebooks. He'd discounted them the day before, but if they were full of stuff that the old fella found important then that would surely be a good indicator of how the man's mind worked.

He pulled the four notebooks out of the drawer and arranged them before him on the desk. Only four? There must be more somewhere. He took a sip of his coffee and opened one of them in the middle. At the top of the page was a quote from a movie:

'Film: *In a Lonely Place.* "I was born when she kissed me. I died when she left me. I lived a few weeks while she loved me."'

Ranald wasn't sure how to take that.

He read it over again – 'when she kissed me' – and he was back in his dream of the previous night. A pair of ruby lips poised over him mid-pout, and then a sudden and sharp arousal.

He tried to distract himself by dipping back into the notebook. A few pages on was a quote from the man who was thought by many to be the Godfather of modern Scottish crime fiction, William McIlvanney: 'Praise is lovely, but it's like a hotel: you can't live there for any length of time.'

Choosing another notebook, he opened it near the back and read a few lines that weren't attributed to anyone. They read like scraps of poems. Was his great-uncle a writer like he was? This set off a surge of excitement. How sweet would that be if they had that in common?

He read on. The words seemed pressed onto the page with no discernible pattern – random thoughts that had blown through his great-uncle's mind. Nothing linking them other than the fact they'd come from him.

'…the day the sky fell in … her smile has a shadow … like a wordless tongue … her name was Jennie … Jennie full of grace … regret is a weight, a sodden cloak.'

Were these memories or random impressions?

Then on another page, Ranald read a short poem:

I should learn to listen.
Allow the words to settle
in that padded room between denial and acceptance.
But it would be easier to place one foot
on the low wall of a high bridge,
spread my arms crucifix-wide, lean forward
and will flight into the span of my arms.

What was that about? Something in it spoke to him. The words carried a sense of needing … and foreboding? Who should Fitz have listened to? What had he denied?

Closing the notebook he was studying, Ranald pushed his chair back from the desk, his fingers clasped as if in prayer, pressing on the underside of his nose. From what he had read he was sure he would have liked Fitz. But did he and Great-Uncle Alexander have more in common than blood?

A phrase echoed in his brain and found a point of resonance. He winced at the recognition.

'…in that padded room between denial and acceptance…'

9

The next day Ranald woke early, and the wrong way round. That was, his feet were at the head of the bed and his head at the foot. How had he got like this? He didn't remember any nightmares or thrashing about in his sleep. In fact, feeling more alert than he had in a long time, he realised he had just enjoyed the best night's sleep he'd had in ages. Might it have been the return of his sex drive?

And wasn't that a miracle of sorts? That he could actually do it.

He recalled what Liz had said about sex with a stranger. He hadn't confessed that his only similar experience was a solitary and disastrous one-night stand before he met Martie. Married life with her, and his session with Liz yesterday, were the sum total of his sexual adventures.

He thought about Liz's dream – or vision; whatever it had been, it had terrified her. Had it really been an act – a way of getting out of the house? If it was the case, she was a brilliant actress.

Had he had any dreams the previous night? Could that explain the way he'd woken up? He scanned his memory as he stood at the sink and washed his hands, but failed to remember anything.

It was Sunday, he thought. What would today bring?

A swim? It was best to keep that good habit going. Then breakfast and another root through Fitz's notebooks. Also, there was more of the house to see. He should go exploring, and with that thought, a question: why hadn't he explored the entire house already? Was he somehow afraid of what he might find? He frowned. What was making him think like that?

What he should really do was get across to his flat in Shawlands and pick up a few things. Speak to his landlord and hand in his notice. Most of his stuff could go to one of the charity shops on the street down the road from the flat. Surely they'd be able to make good use of his things.

With a sense of purpose, Ranald made his way, naked, down to the pool. Why bother putting clothes on? He was going to take them off shortly anyway, and there was nobody to see him. And he was beginning to like this naturist thing. It felt liberating. He'd been Mr Serious most of his life. He saw his father's angry face and mentally gave it the finger.

Time to let go of the mental shackles, Ran.

⊦⊦

After his swim, as he dressed and dried himself, Ranald wondered at his sense of unease. In his previous home Ranald had a routine, a pattern that informed his day, but here he felt rudderless and uncertain. He heard Martie's voice in his head; her warning that if he didn't follow his therapist's regimen he might end up back in hospital. But he dismissed it.

After all these years he knew what he was doing.

People. He needed to be near people. He recognised that was why he'd gone to the café on the first day. Although he was on his own it gave him the illusion that he was in company.

However necessary he knew it was though, being around other people could be exhausting; having to pretend that you were fine, having to make sure your mask was in place for every moment of every conversation. Being terrified that if it slipped, even for a second, people would get a glimpse into the sham of a human being he really was.

Shawlands. He had decided that he should go to his flat. Get his stuff sorted. That would help him feel more grounded.

He dressed in his old jeans and a clean t-shirt. Found a dark-brown, linen jacket hanging in among the suits. Checked himself in the mirror, and preened a little. Much better than his usual scruffy self. That would give his old neighbours something to talk about.

He returned to the library to use the house phone where he called for a cab.

†⊢

Stepping inside his flat it felt like he'd been away for two years, not two days.

Was this really how he used to live? This lack of space; the untidy, barely clean, sorry mess of it?

In the bedroom, he pulled a suitcase out from under the bed, then began going through his wardrobe. The clothes he wanted to bin, he threw on the floor. The others went in the suitcase.

When he'd finished, he realised choosing a suitcase had been a mistake. Two pairs of jeans, a couple of t-shirts and a pair of running shoes hardly made an impression on the space. So he shoved them in the hold-all he used for the gym instead. He spotted his phone charger on his bedside cabinet and threw that in as well.

There was nothing he wanted in the kitchen. The bathroom told a similar story. Shaving gear, deodorant and bottle of aftershave – Hugo Boss – that Martie had given him for his twenty-first birthday. He loved the smell of it, just kept forgetting to put it on.

There, beside the aftershave, was a blister pack of anti-depressants; and the other drugs too. He could never remember their names. He reached for them. Paused. Did he need them? He'd never felt better. Besides, they were already leaving his system, as was evidenced by the return of his libido. It was kind of nice having that back. Reassuring almost: be a human being, have a sex drive.

Also, if he started up again, would it be back to the side-effects he'd experienced when he'd first taken them: staring into space all day, trying to locate a spare thought? He wasn't going back there.

In the living room, other than his books, DVDs and laptop, there was nothing he wanted. He looked at the TV. It was a thirty-two-inch flat screen. The height of his ambition only a year ago.

Back at Newton Hall there was a whole TV *room*. And for a moment it felt as if a cold hand clutched his belly.

He shook off the negative thought. His wireless connector thing.

That would have to come too. He prayed that would work there. Living without a mobile was acceptable; existing without a broadband connection was not.

Once he was finished, all he had to show for his time at this flat was a small holdall of clothes and a box of books and DVDs.

Pathetic.

As he was about to dial for his taxi, there was a knock at the door. He opened it to be greeted by the neighbour across the landing, Donna Morris.

'Everything, okay, honey?' she asked as she breezed inside. 'Where you been?' She stepped into his hallway, turned and faced him. She smiled broadly. 'You no ring. You no call?'

As usual, Donna had her long, grey, shoulder-length hair loose and was wearing neck-to-toe cheesecloth and sandals. She was as lean as a walking cane. Her face was unlined, but her eyelids had a slight droop. Ranald guessed she was in her late sixties, but she always fended off his questions about age with a wave of her hand and a comment along the lines of it being a construct of commercialism and her having no truck with any of that.

He recalled that one night, after a walk around Chinatown and sharing a bottle of wine with him over a Chinese meal, she had described herself as an 'egalitarian, socialist, Bolshevik, humanist, feminist who hates labels. An anti-labellist, if you want...' Then she had added, in a dramatic tone, '...with a touch of the psychic about her.'

'Really?' Ran had asked. 'That bit's much more interesting than the multiple, political personality thing you've got going on.'

Donna had changed the subject, but Ran had pressed her. 'Do you see dead people and shit?'

'That's not how it works, honey,' she replied. 'Wasn't Jack Nicholson amazing in that film?'

'It was Bruce Willis.'

'I'm talking about *The Shining*.'

Then Ranald had dared to ask, 'Could you speak to my mum and dad?' He would never have asked the question if he hadn't been half-pissed. And instantly, judging from her expression, Donna realised she'd made a mistake telling him about her abilities.

'Listen, Ranald,' she said, 'we don't go messing with that stuff. Besides, the information comes in at random.'

'But…' He'd had an urgent need to know more.

'But nothing, son,' Donna had said. 'We've both had too much wine.'

'But…'

'Tell you what – my … whatchamacallit … my gift, is a bit random. But if I get anything, I promise I'll tell you. Okay?'

Ranald had realised that was the best he was going to get and he'd allowed Donna to change the subject back to the movie.

Now, as he wondered what had prompted that memory, Donna stepped forwards, pulled him against her chest and pecked his cheek.

'You've lost weight. Have you not been eating?' Pause. 'Nice jacket.' She ran her hands down the sleeves. 'Nice material. You look so handsome. Where did you get it?'

It was part of their shtick that she was the mother he'd never really had, so if ever they didn't see each other for a few days, she'd ham it up for him. Underneath the fun and bluster, though, was the kindest person he'd ever met.

'Is that the kettle I heard going on?' she asked. 'Hang on. If you're going to offer me a coffee, do you need me to fetch some milk from mine?'

'You're a nutter,' Ranald said. 'Let me put the kettle on and while I'm in the kitchen I'll check the fridge.' He hugged her again, surprised by how much he'd missed her.

'What's this all about?' she asked, hugging him back. 'You miss your Auntie Donna, our Ranald?'

Ranald could hear the pleasure in her voice.

'Go on into the living room and I'll sort the drinks. I've got…' Before he could finish what he was about to say, she had left his side and stepped into the living room, saying something as she went. But she halted abruptly. As he walked into the kitchen she was behind him.

'Hang on,' she said. 'That bag and that box on the living-room floor? You coming or going?'

'I was just about to tell you…'

She stepped closer. 'What is it?'

'Something … well I guess you'd call it something amazing … has happened.'

'Aye?' Donna moved closer.

'Okay – the highlights: I've got a new house worth a fortune, a family I never knew I had, *and* I got my leg over on the first night.' Ranald tried to inject some enthusiasm into his voice, at the same time acknowledging to himself that it was an effort.

'Son, I'm fair chuffed for you. Who was she?'

Ranald smiled. Donna cared little for material things, but she was a sucker for romance.

'The woman was lovely. She made me laugh, but it's not going to go anywhere. Are you not curious about the house?'

'Go on then, if you must,' she said, eyes rolling up to the ceiling, faking a lack of interest.

As he talked, however, her eyes grew larger and larger. Her mouth opened. And then her eyes began to moisten.

'What's wrong?' he asked.

'Absolutely nothing, Ranald. That's just bloody amazing.' She dabbed at her eyes with the pad of her right thumb. 'It's about time something good happened to you, son. You really deserve it.'

Ranald picked up the mugs of coffee. 'C'mon through to the sofa and I'll tell you the rest.'

In the living room, Ranald told her all about the house – the library, the pool, the ballroom … studiously avoiding any mention of the quiver of anxiety he had in most parts of the building.

'You had no inkling about any of this?' Donna interrupted.

'None. My parents never talked about things.' *Any* things, Ranald realised. Perhaps that's why he was so poor at communication. 'At family events, it was only ever people from my dad's side. My mum always claimed she was an only child and her family were all dead.'

'All because your dad was working class,' said Donna. 'Fucking industrialists.'

Donna rarely swore, but when she did, it was usually to do with the sins of capitalism. She looked away from him, out of the window at the roofs across the street.

'Aww, son' – she turned back – 'you've been the best wee neighbour I've ever had here. I'm really going to miss you.' She dabbed at her eyes again.

'We'll keep in touch,' Ranald said. 'You can invite me over for movie nights. And you can come over to mine to use the fitness suite.'

'Cheeky sod,' Donna managed a smile. 'Besides. These big posh houses in Bearsden and such are not for the likes of me.'

'What?' demanded Ranald. 'What happened to Bolshevik Donna who goes wherever the fuck she pleases?'

'She got old and disaffected.'

'You have to come and visit me, Donna,' Ranald insisted. 'You'll love the library. You can read as much as you like. The books can't leave the house, so that means you'll have to come regularly.'

'Aww, Ran,' she reached over and patted his hand. 'We both know you don't mean that.'

He did, but didn't want to show any disappointment that this was her impression of the situation.

'Besides,' she went on, 'you need to get yourself some pals. Mates. Hang out with some blokes and watch footie, drink beer, or whatever it is you men do when you get together.'

This was an often-discussed topic when Donna came to visit. After she'd queried the state of his love life, or lack thereof, she'd lecture him on the benefits of same-sex company.

'A young man shouldn't be on his own as much as you are.'

It was Ranald's turn to roll his eyes.

'Have you invited any of your buddies over for a read-around?' she smiled to let him know that she was only half joking.

'You know I don't have any buddies,' he replied. 'And that's one sure way to kill off any burgeoning friendship.'

Ranald gave a mental shrug. Most of the people he knew were female. That was just the way it had turned out. He had one male friend through primary and secondary school: Patrick Connolly. They'd shared an obsession for Marvel comics and Nintendo Gameboy. Neither of them was into football, meaning, at best, that the other boys treated them as if they weren't there; at worst, they bullied the pair remorselessly.

Ranald went on to university to study English, met Martie on the first day and she became his constant companion. And in that heightened bubble of discovering love together for the first time, he saw no need for anyone else in his life.

The conversation with Donna ran its course as the coffee dried up in their mugs.

'Right.' She stood up. 'This has been lovely. But my carrot and coriander soup isn't going to stir itself.'

Ranald followed as she walked out of the room, into the hall and pulled open the door. Before she stepped outside onto the landing, she offered another look of support.

'I'm so happy for you, Ran. Now keep in touch, eh? Make sure you feed yourself properly? You've got my number on your phone if you need to get in touch? And yeah, we have to do that movie night soon.'

She gave him a hug that had a note of finality about it, as if she didn't believe the movie night would ever happen. 'When did we Scots become such a hugging nation?' She shook her head. 'My parents will be girning in their graves.'

Her eyes then grew distant. She shivered, refocused and looked up at his face as if debating whether or not to say something.

'The dark-haired woman? Keep away from her. She means you harm.'

10

A dark-blue Land Rover was in the drive at Newton Hall when Ranald's taxi pulled in. There were two or three people inside but Ranald was unable to see exactly who they were.

'Got you back just in time,' said the taxi driver.

Ranald fished out his wallet and paid the fare. Then he picked up his bag and the box, climbed out of the car and went to greet his visitors.

A man got out of the driver's seat. It was Quinn, the lawyer. He smiled broadly when his eyes lighted upon Ranald – but his expression lacked any warmth. Then he walked forwards, arm outstretched, inviting Ranald to shake his hand. Ranald shifted the box in his arms and with an awkward movement, took the lawyer's hand. It was too warm and way too moist. Ranald made a mental note to wash his hand as soon as he could.

'Mr McGhie, how are you? We just thought we'd pop in to see how you're settling in.'

We, wondered Ranald.

'So lawyers now do Sunday house calls do they, Mr Quinn?' said Ran, turning to appraise the man who'd climbed out of the passenger seat.

'You're part of the family now, Ranald.' Quinn sounded Ran's first name as if he was trying it out for the first time. 'So we thought it was time you met your cousins, Marcus and Rebecca Fitzpatrick.' He put out his arm as the other man strode towards them. 'Marcus, this is Ranald.'

Marcus was tall, flat-bellied and broad-shouldered, with a full head of grey hair. Clearly middle-aged, he brimmed with health, looking like he'd just left the changing rooms at the rugby club after a hard session on the practice field. His demeanour oozed privilege; Ranald felt as if he were being weighed up for a shoplifting charge.

Marcus took Ranald's hand and gave it a vigorous and too-lengthy shake, as if he was trying to demonstrate he was the alpha male. Ranald immediately pictured him at the imagined rugby club, surrounded by ageing ex-public schoolboys, all of them at the height of society and crowing at the fact.

'Going to invite us in?' asked Marcus.

'Ah…' Quinn looked back at the Land Rover and then at Marcus. 'Rebecca? Is she not…'

'Migraine,' Marcus offered. 'You know how she is.'

Ranald looked over at the vehicle. In the back seat he could just make out the shape of a woman with dark hair.

'Please,' said Ranald turning away and holding his hand out towards the doorway.

Once inside, Ranald led the way to the right and the corridor down to the kitchen. Then he turned; Marcus and Quinn weren't behind him – they were making their way straight for the big reception room to the left of the main hall. Ranald took a deep breath then dropped his stuff in the hall and tailed after them.

Without waiting for an invitation, Marcus took a seat on one of the room's vast red sofas and, hitching up his cream-coloured chinos at the right knee, he crossed his legs. He leaned back, his arms stretched out. 'Perhaps a wee snifter would be in order?' he said looking pointedly at a low cabinet leaning against the far wall. 'It's five o'clock somewhere, surely?'

'Yes,' said Quinn looking at his wristwatch. 'Here, actually.'

Taking the hint, Ranald walked over to the cabinet and opened a couple of doors. Inside he found bottles of brandy and whisky, water, ginger ale and lemonade, as well as crystal glasses.

'What would you like?'

'A cheeky wee malt for me,' replied Marcus. 'On its own, thanks.'

'Just a bottle of water for me,' said Quinn. 'Wouldn't do to risk the breathalyser these days.'

Ranald poured a generous measure for Marcus and himself, then he picked out a bottle of water for Quinn and carried the drinks across the room to the seats.

'How are you settling in, then, Ranald?' asked Quinn.

Ran nodded, trying to disguise a small choking feeling as the strong drink hit the back of his throat. 'It's quite a place. Still trying to get my head round it all, to be honest.'

As he spoke into the hushed gentility of the room, with his forebears looking down on him from their portraits on the walls, Ranald was acutely aware of the difference in their accents. Glasgow had never been allowed into the speech of either of these men, but it was there in his vowels and consonants, like a wee black dog growling from the corner of the room.

'If I may,' Marcus took a sip of his drink, 'I'll give you the full picture. The man you inherited this house from was my father, William's, uncle. Alexander died without issue. My father had two children. Myself and my sister, Rebecca.' He paused. 'Next time we visit, we'll try to get her out of the car.' He guffawed as if that was the funniest thing he'd heard all year. He took another sip. 'Your mother was my father's younger sister.' He looked off into the distance. 'I have few memories of Aunt Helena. Rebecca reminds me of her. Changeable, like the Scottish weather.'

Ranald considered what Marcus just said and about the timing of events. He judged his cousin to be in his early forties, so he would have only been an infant, if that, when his mother left Newton Hall. She would have miscarried her first pregnancy around the same time as Marcus's birth. So how would Marcus possibly remember her in any detail?

Marcus read what must have been an expression of puzzlement on Ranald's face. 'Ah, yes, the family legend,' he nodded. 'Daughter leaves, never to speak to any of us ever again.' He raised his eyebrows. 'She used to sneak in when Grandmother was out of the country. Borrowed a few bob from my father I believe, over the years.'

'What?' asked Ranald, looking from Marcus to Quinn. 'I thought you said she kept her distance?'

'So I was led to believe,' Quinn responded keeping his face rigid.

'If I remember correctly...' Marcus scratched at the left side of his face, the kink of a strange light in his eyes. '...Aunt Helena and Father had a strange relationship. One minute they'd be squabbling, as only brother and sister can. The next...' He tailed off as if unsure whether or not to go there.

'The next, what?' demanded Ranald, feeling emboldened by the strong liquor.

'Well...' Marcus held his arms wide as if to indicate an openness. 'I was only a teenager the last time I saw her, and, well, you know how clueless teenage boys are.' He threw his head back and issued one of his hearty laughs. It sounded like a pronouncement of his convivial nature; if Ranald heard it one more time he was going to grind a good centimetre off his back teeth. 'But there was this one afternoon, I was supposed to be playing rugby, but I got sent home – tummy bug or something. Anyway, when I came in, I heard some noise coming from Father's study. I walked in and Father and Helena jumped apart as if they had just been scalded.' He brought his eyebrows together, his forehead deeply furrowed. 'No idea what they were up to. Nothing dubious I expect.'

As Ranald tried to work through whatever Marcus had just said, his cousin knocked back the remainder of his drink and stood up. 'Right,' he said loudly. 'Best be off. The wife will be carving into the Sunday roast as we speak.'

Ranald stood up with some relief.

'You must join us one Sunday,' said Marcus.

That was an invite that was never going to arrive, mused Ranald. But he kept his thoughts to himself. 'That would be ... splendid,' he answered instead.

'Excellent,' said Quinn rubbing his hands briskly together. 'I'm sure you two will become the firmest of friends.'

Ranald forced a smile and they all shook hands.

Ranald closed the door on them before they'd even reached their car.

Going back into the reception room, he picked up his unfinished whisky and walked over to the window to watch as the car drove off. Neither Quinn nor Marcus gave the house so much as a glance. Probably too busy gossiping about him, thought Ranald. Finding plenty of fault.

At his first meeting with Quinn, the lawyer had stated that the other members of the Fitzpatrick family were adequately compensated in the old man's will. Ranald wondered if that was how they saw the situation. Had they been aware he existed? Or had they been assessing the size of the old man's estate in the months before he died? If the latter was the case, his appearance must have come as a massive shock; a challenge to their dreams of further wealth.

And what was all of that about his mother and her brother? What was Marcus trying to suggest? That their affection for each other was something other than the usual family bond? He might have only been in his teens when his mother died but he knew her well enough to question that. Sure, she had her problems, but...?

If Marcus's memory was to be believed, however, what were she and William up to?

Ranald drained the last of the drink and noted the warmth in his gut as the whisky reached it. This whisky-drinking was going to take some getting used to. What he didn't think he'd ever get used to, though, was his cousin Marcus. And his other cousin, Rebecca, hadn't even bothered getting out of the car to say hello. Ranald couldn't help presuming she was every bit as condescending as her brother. He was willing to bet that the 'migraine' was a convenient excuse to postpone meeting him.

Forcing his cousins' unpleasantness to the back of his mind, he went upstairs and changed into shorts and a t-shirt, then went down to the kitchen and made himself a meal.

While his food was cooking he set his phone to charge. Knowing Martie as he did, she'd have left him a couple of messages after her visit the other day, worried that her rejection had set off a black mood.

Once he'd eaten, he judged that the phone would have enough

charge, so he turned it on and waved it slowly at the window to see if it might pick up a signal. Nothing. Maybe the garden beyond the pool might be a good place. Moments later, he was standing there, in the warm evening sun, holding his phone at various heights and angles. Finally, walking further away from the house he had success. A beep. Then another.

He dialled his messaging service.

The first one was from his agent. That was a surprise – he hadn't spoken to the guy in months. He said he had a commission to talk over with Ran; could he phone the office first thing on Monday?

The next one was from Liz. An apology that she'd run off the other night. 'I'd never had such a vivid dream before.' Then a small laugh. 'Maybe it was the product of a guilty conscience?' Cough. 'Anyways. This is a small town, really, so I don't want there to be any awkwardness between us. Be sure to say hi next time you see me.' Then a half-whispered, half-sung, 'B-ye.'

He hadn't expected that. She'd obviously had a nice time. Might she be up for a repeat performance? But there was just one thing that troubled him: he couldn't remember giving her his number.

He felt warm. Too warm. On the brink of suffocation. The air was leaden in his lungs and his skin was clammy from head to foot.

He was aware of something – a hand on his chest. Hot breath in his ear. Teeth nibbling on his lobe. Then the mouth was pressed against his neck and kisses trailed to his collarbone.

A groan sounded out in the room; he realised it was coming from him.

'Please, don't stop,' he said.

He felt a hand on his inner thigh. It stroked his stomach and then moved back down to his thigh.

He exhaled. The feeling was exquisite. Nothing else mattered beyond his skin and beating heart.

Then he woke with the suddenness of a gunshot.

Disorientated, his heartbeat heavy against his ribs. His pulse was hard in his throat, and he was lying on something hard. Where the hell was he?

His eyes adjusting to the dim light, he could see that he was in a confined space. Three walls were covered in a red-and-gold patterned wallpaper. The remaining wall held a mesh door and to the side of it a column of buttons with numbers on them – 1, 2, 3 and 4.

He was in the lift. And he was naked. There was a seat in the corner. He drew himself up onto it then immediately thought, why wasn't he pulling open the door and getting the hell out of there?

And how did he even get *in* here? This door was locked the other day. How had he managed to get inside? He searched his memory. He'd gone to bed in his room shortly after dinner – still lightheaded from the whisky he'd drunk. He'd read a little, and then…

He heard a cough. As if someone was trying to get his attention.

'Hello?' he said, looking up at the small window in the lift door.

Then he heard a peal of laughter. A note of pure pleasure.

'Who's there?' he asked. His system was charged with adrenalin. He was trembling. He needed to get out of here. Now. He crossed his arms as if to hold in his mounting panic. Should he shout for help?

And then he realised the truth of his isolation. He could scream for days without anyone hearing him. Not even the Hacketts.

Another cough.

He looked up, this time at the wall opposite the door. There was a mirror at head height – matching the height of the window in the door. He saw movement. Something passing out of shadow, partly into light.

It was a woman. Long, dark hair hid one side of her face. She wore a robe that was open to the navel, showing a glimpse of her breasts and a lean stomach.

'Welcome,' she said.

11

'Mr McGhie, Mr McGhie.'

Ranald sat up in his bed, his body charged with fright at the loud voice coming from outside his bedroom.

'Just checking you're at home, Mr McGhie.' It was Mrs Hackett.

'Yes,' he said, coughing to clear his throat.

'I'm just about to leave for the day. Thought I'd better make sure you were okay before I left. Sorry to disturb you.'

She was about to leave for the day? Really? It was almost noon? He edged over to the side of the bed, realising as he did so that the quilt was down at his feet. He stood up, feeling dizzy.

In the shower, under the hot stream of water, he gathered his thoughts. There was a vague, unsettling build-up of energy at the back of his mind. He tried to push it away. It had been set off by Marcus's comments about his mother, and he wasn't going there. For the good of his health he couldn't afford to. Besides, the man was full of nonsense.

Splinters of his previous night's dream then slid into his mind. He'd been in a lift – the lift, surely. There was a woman. A vivid image came to him: her eyes. Knowing. Demanding. Welcoming. Captivating. He could have stared into them for hours.

His heart beat a little faster as he recalled her voice, her touch, the arousal he'd felt. What was happening to him? It was certainly better than the numbness of the last few years. *You don't appreciate what you've got till it's gone … and then you get it back*, he thought. He was human, vital, male, after all.

He turned on the cold water, with the thought that if he didn't he might be in this shower all day. He gasped as the cold water streamed down his back and chest.

Exiting the shower, he dried himself, dressed and went down-stairs, meeting Mrs Hackett in the corridor to the kitchen.

'Good morning, Mr McGhie.' She tilted her head to the side as if in judgement. 'Sleeping till all hours? Up working late last night were we?' Her tone made it clear that she would be surprised if it had actually been work that kept him up.

Were you so familiar with my great-uncle, Mrs Hackett? was what he wanted to say. Instead he made a non-committal noise.

'Do me a favour…' he said in a feeble attempt to show who was really in control. 'Please call me Ranald. That whole Mr McGhie thing feels weird.' He shot her a smile and, before she could respond, walked past her and down to the kitchen. Before he got there he turned. 'One thing? Is there a working broadband connection in the house?'

'Yes there is, Mr … Ranald,' she answered, bustling towards him. 'I'll find the password. The wifi signal has trouble getting through some of these walls, so Mr Fitzpatrick had boxes put in the kitchen, the library and up in the master bedroom. Oh, and in the TV room.'

'Right. The TV room. I did *some* exploring. Mostly in the library to be fair.' He made an apologetic face. 'Me and books: I'm obsessed.' He didn't want to tell her that the sheer scale of the place was still giving him the creeps.

'Mr Fitzpatrick would be so happy to know that, dear.' She gave a little bow, and Ranald thought that he had momentarily been trans-ported onto the set of a period drama.

᚛ᚆᚁ

Having put the coffee pot on, he retrieved the bag he'd left in the hall the previous afternoon and pulled out his laptop. Back at the kitchen table, he plugged it in, powered it up and sorted out the internet connection.

He was in.

Connected. And the world was back on its axis.

He had forty new emails. Most of them he could delete without action; all bar one. It was from his agent, Douglas McIntosh, and had been sent that morning at 9:01 am:

'You haven't answered my calls. On the piss, you lucky boy? All that whisky and sheep-shagging, eh?'

Douglas was from London, and, like several southerners Ran knew who'd never been to Scotland, he had a strange view of what life might be like up here.

'We have an exciting project to talk over with you', the email went on. 'Big bucks!! Call me ASAP.'

This time last week Ran would have been on the phone to Douglas as soon as his fingers could flash over the numbers. This week? Life was just too interesting – and not a little disturbing – to be bothered with anything as basic as work.

Still, as Quinn pointed out, there was nothing in his inheritance that would keep him fed, so a job was still a necessity.

The coffee pot signalled with some spurting noises that the drink was ready so he poured himself a mug, stuck his laptop under his arm and walked through to the library.

On the way, he paused to have a look through the mesh of the small window on the door of the lift. His head blocked out any light, so he saw nothing. He shrugged. What had he expected to see? It was simply a vivid dream he'd had, that's all. Already it was fading, leaving him with nothing but a lingering mix of emotions: hopefulness, a suspicion of joy. And there, elbowing its way past the others: a low-level sense of anxiety. Odd, he thought, and walked on. How could he have all that in his mind at the same time?

In the library, he picked up the desk phone and phoned his agent.

'Ranald. Bloody hell, are you a difficult guy to get a hold of these days.'

'Sorry, Douglas,' he answered. 'Life's been a bit hectic.' And very confusing.

'It's unlike you, Ran. You had me worried.' This was a lie. They both knew that Ranald was likely to go AWOL from time to time.

But when he did get on it, he was a good worker. Focused, on point and always on time.

Douglas was already talking about the mooted project: '...a new imprint ... Pearson ... they want you ... liaise with Scottish Qualification Authority. Edinburgh meeting...' Then. 'You getting any of this, Ranald?'

'Sure. I'm hearing you loud and clear, Douglas.'

It was all very workaday. Boring, and as functional as a Wellington boot. He wanted to soar. Use words that would move people. Tell stories that would shift minds, change worlds. Not this shit, time after time after time.

'...initial advance ... three months' work ... seven grand.' Pause. 'Ranald, should I call back when you are less distracted?' Douglas sounded a little ratty. 'These guys need an answer yesterday.'

'Yes,' Ranald replied. 'Yes, of course I'll do it, Douglas.' Then, with a note of resignation: 'It was always going to be a yes.'

'Right. Excellent. I'll fire off the contract. Usual thing. Print off the last page, sign and stick in the post, yeah?'

Ranald hung up and sat back in his chair, more than a little surprised at his reaction to this offer of work. Until now he'd been devoid of ambition – more than happy to take these scraps of work that would help pay his bills. Where was this desire to write creatively coming from?

He swung round on the chair and looked out of the window. The sun was high and strong. He could almost see heat rising from the grass.

A walk. He stood up. A walk round his garden. He should get out of the house and survey the property properly instead of spending all this time surrounded by these stuffy books. He looked at the nearest shelf and sent a silent apology.

⊣⊢

Even a former flat-dweller like him could appreciate the time, effort and organisation that had gone into this garden over the years. The place was gorgeous, he thought as he stood under the shade of a towering rhododendron and its profusion of pink blooms. Birds sang overhead, the warm air was like a balm on the skin of his arms and face; a butterfly even flitted past on the breeze.

It was like he'd been transported into a Disney movie.

He heard footsteps and turned to see Danny walking towards him. He was wearing green overalls; his single nod to the warm weather was rolled-up sleeves.

'Afternoon,' said Ranald, as he watched the older man move towards him. For someone so slight he moved as if he possessed a larger, more muscular body.

'Aye,' Danny agreed when he got closer. He looked up at the rhododendron. 'Must be a hundred year old, that. At least.'

Ranald almost said, *Is that how long you've been here?*

'Been out in the cars yet?' Danny asked as he wiped sweat from his forehead with the inside of his wrist.

'Cars? There's cars?' Ranald asked.

Cars? What other surprises did this house have in store for him?

Danny must have deduced from Ran's look of bewilderment that he had not seen the cars, because he gave him a frown that said, what kind of man are you? And beckoned him on.

Ranald followed Danny along a well-rutted path, one car wide, with only a fraction of the pebbles that graced the drive at the front of the house. It moved beyond the giant rhododendron and between a pair of giant fir trees, with reddish, wide trunks.

'Mr Alexander got the cars – one in the eighties and one in the nineties,' said Danny over his shoulder. 'Must have been a mid- or late-life crisis. Barely used them. Told me it was because he couldn't read while he was driving.' Danny shook his head at the total nonsense of it. 'But he did get them serviced regular like. And he asked me to be sure to turn the engines over every other day.' Danny stopped as if he'd had a thought. 'Here. You can drive, can't you?'

Ranald laughed as he nearly collided with the man. 'Never needed to learn, to be honest.'

'Dearie me,' said Danny. 'What a waste.'

They reached a wide outbuilding with tall, green double wooden doors. Above them stretched a crow's foot gable end in the same stone as the main house. Danny pulled a key from his pocket and unlocked the door.

'Gimme a hand here, son,' he said to Ranald, and began to pull at one door, indicating he should pull on the other.

When he saw what was being unveiled, Ranald gave a low whistle. He peered left and right, looking into each windscreen.

'They're nice.'

He thought Danny's expression of pleasure at the unveiling deserved more enthusiasm, so he nodded several times and added, 'Beauties.'

'You don't know anything about cars, eh?' said Danny, clearly reading the truth of his indifference in his tone. 'The dark-blue one with the low roof, two doors and long bonnet. That one is a Ford Capri. 1980 model, three-litre engine, just under twenty-five thousand miles on the clock...' As he talked, he walked into the garage and round the car, trailing his fingertips over the body, with a touch that would please a lover. 'A car similar to this went for just under fifteen grand recently.'

'And who owns it?' asked Ranald, thinking how that cash would come in nicely at this point.

'You do,' said Danny. 'The will did say the house, the grounds and everything in it – apart from the stables – should go to you.'

Ranald stood in front of the Capri, hand resting on his forehead. Bloody hell. He looked at the other car. 'And this is a Mercedes. Even I recognise the symbol.' He admired the gleam on the chrome. 'You've obviously looked after them over the years.'

'Just doing my job, Ranald.'

It was more than just doing his job, Ranald thought. There was a good deal of love gone into the care of these vehicles.

Then he had a thought: 'Where are the keys?'

Danny nodded to a small, black metal box fitted into the wall. 'Should be unlocked,' he said.

Ranald walked over, opened it and pulled out two sets of keys. He juggled them from one hand to the other, feeling the weight of them.

'Which car do you prefer?' he asked Danny.

'Oh, that's difficult,' Danny replied. He scratched his neck. 'If I was to be forced to say, I'd go for the Capri. That was a real moment in time, so it was.'

Ranald looked down at the keys resting on each palm. Read the Ford symbol and threw those keys over to Danny.

'It's yours.' He shrugged. '*One* car's too much for me. After all these years of looking after them, you might as well get some pleasure.'

'Mr McGhie, I really don't know what to say.' Danny's face had grown a beautiful shade of pink, and his eyes had moistened a little. 'I really can't accept this—'

'Sure you can,' Ranald interrupted. 'I'll get on to Quinn and ask him to draw up the paperwork. Frankly, I'm disappointed that old Fitzpatrick didn't think of this himself.'

'Now, Ranald … I won't hear a word said about your uncle. He was a great man.' Then Danny went back to studying the car keys resting in his palm. 'I don't know what to say.'

'Say thanks,' said Ranald, and feeling rather pleased with himself, he walked out of the garage and towards the house. But halfway across the lawn, looking up at the ranks of windows, knowing there was no one behind them, he realised he couldn't quite face going back inside. So he changed his direction and headed for the road to the Cross and the café.

ᛏᛰ

His street-side table was taken, so with a slight huff in his step, he pushed open the café door and took a seat at the back of the room. When he sat down, he felt something in the thigh pocket of his shorts, knocking against his knee. He undid the flap and pulled out one of the moleskin notebooks he'd found in Alexander's desk along with a pen. He didn't remember putting those in there.

The waitress approached him. He ordered a coffee and while he waited for it tried to recall when he could have picked up a notebook and put it in his pocket without realising it.

Then, sitting by the window, he spotted the *War and Peace* girl from his first visit. Her head was down, her eyes focused on the page of her book. Ranald tried to guess if she was much further on from the last time he saw her and wondered if he should go over and speak to her. But she looked so engrossed in the passage she was reading, he felt it would be rude to interrupt her.

He opened the notebook in front of him at a clean page, and, glancing over at the girl again, he felt words starting to form in his head. He picked up the pen, and soon they were making their way onto the pristine paper. They were without form or rhythm, but he savoured their pull and allowed them to take him, like a feather borne on a rising breeze.

His drink arrived. The musical chink of teaspoon on china enough to pull him from his imaginings.

He looked down at the page and read what he'd just written:

I watch from here, you are there,
unseeing behind a curtain of quiet.
Your silence disturbs me.
Makes me want to intrude.
Extend a finger and prod that space under your arm,
where nerve meets laughter.

He assessed his words. Some nice ideas. Needed work though. He sipped his coffee. Looked over at the reading girl then back down at the page.

The café door opened and an old man walked in: light-blue raincoat and tweed flat cap. It was the old fella he'd almost tripped over at the crossroads on the first day he arrived. The man stared at him a moment, so he offered him a small smile. But he made a sour face and negotiated his way round the tables to an empty seat at the far end of the room.

Suit yourself, thought Ranald, and returned to his poem.

Minutes later he heard footsteps and someone came to a stop in front of him.

'Hi, Ranald. Come here often?'

He looked up to see Liz smiling down at him.

'Sorry about the other day,' she said. 'Don't know what got into me.'

She was looking good. He felt himself smiling. 'Been sunbathing?' he asked.

'How can you tell?'

He pointed to the bridge of his own nose. 'Some new freckles coming in through the tan.'

'My, aren't you the observant one.' She crossed one leg behind the other, as if rubbing her thighs together, and leaned over him. 'I can't stop thinking about you,' she said quietly.

Ranald wasn't quite sure how to respond to that, but his body felt a jolt of pleasure.

'I saw you in the window as I walked past,' she murmured. 'Thought I'd come in and say hello.' She glanced around to see who was looking. Decided no one was. 'And use their loo. There isn't one on this street.' She laughed, and leaned further forwards. 'Just give me a minute. One knock and I'll let you in.' She winked, stepped away and turned down the corridor that led to the toilet.

Was that a genuine invitation, wondered Ranald, or was she just having a laugh? He looked around the café. Someone had to have noticed their exchange. But no, everyone else was locked into their own world.

He counted to sixty. Then another twenty, because the sixty was a bit too fast. That would amount to a minute, right? As he counted, anticipation of the pleasure to come almost made him dizzy. Was he really going to do this? It wasn't something he'd ever pictured himself indulging in. Not him. Not difficult, quiet, anxious Ranald. When he stood up his thighs were weak and his pulse hammered in his throat. He wasn't sure how he would make it down the corridor, let alone…

He found himself knocking on the door of the toilet. It opened and Liz reached a hand out and pulled him inside.

ᛁᛕ

Once they'd finished she kissed him on the cheek and, with a delighted grin, said, 'I'll go out first. Count to twenty, then follow me out, okay?' She gave him another peck and left the tiny room.

Ranald pulled up his pants and shorts, then stumbled over to the large mirror on the far wall and, leaning over the sink, stared into his own eyes. Did that really just happen?

He left the toilet and returned to his table, expecting Liz to be sitting there. But she was nowhere to be seen. The waitress walked past just as he sat back down. He tugged at her arm. 'Did you see the woman I was talking to earlier? Did she leave a message for me?'

'No, son,' the waitress said, with what Ranald thought might be a knowing smile. He felt a blush rise on his cheeks and turned his face down to his notebook, mumbling, 'Thanks.'

He reached for his still-warm coffee and, with his mouth at the lip of the cup, he looked round the room. No one was staring. No one was looking at him and laughing.

Bloody hell. He sat back in his chair.

Finishing his drink, he picked up his notebook and pen and walked to the counter, paid the waitress, leaving a generous tip, and left the café, feeling uncommonly relaxed.

Enjoying the press and heat of the sun overhead, he walked past the Cross and onto the winding road that would take him back to Newton Hall, a little swagger in his step. For the first time in days, his mood was carefree. He couldn't help but feel that Liz's attentions were bolstering him. How could he have been so wary of his good fortune? He should be revelling in it.

As he rounded a bend and caught sight of the tower of his house – his house – rising above the trees, he thought it was time he properly investigated the whole house – all of its nooks and crannies. And as he picked up his pace, he couldn't think for a moment why he had been holding back. What was the worst that could happen?

12

By the time he arrived back at Newton Hall his thighs were burning, his calves were tight and his breathing was laboured. He hadn't realised how unfit he'd become recently.

Pausing before he entered the front door, he became aware that the sun's power had weakened, and on the far horizon, across the fields, he saw a battalion of clouds. It seemed like he'd got home in good time. Once inside, to allow his breathing to slow, he walked slowly across the hall and down the long corridor past the ballroom and library towards the lift. His usual path was to ignore the small passage to his left here in favour of turning right, and on to the kitchen and fitness suite.

Trying to ignore a sudden sense of unease and to hold on tight to the decision he'd made on his walk back from the Cross, he forced himself to turn left. As he did he traced the wall on his right with his fingertips. Behind this wall the lift waited. He shivered at what he'd experienced just that morning. Don't go there, he told himself.

Ignoring things had worked so far, right?

He could feel his reluctance build. A low level of discomfort grew into something bigger as he pressed on towards the bottom of the narrow staircase. He felt his shoulders rise as he tensed … in preparation for what? He'd felt like this when he was here with Martie, and they'd found nothing untoward. So why was he now so skittish?

He put a foot on the first stair, like a child might test a parent on a dare, fearing a word of warning.

A shadow flitted across the landing above him. His heart thumped.

'Hello?' he shouted. 'Anyone there?'

He waited.

'Mrs Hackett?'

You're imagining things, Ranald, he told himself. That was just a cloud passing the sun, and Mrs Hackett was finished for the day. Steeling himself, repeating that he was being stupid, that this was his home, he began to move up the steps.

The staircase was cramped and dark, the walls seeming to crowd in on him as he slowly climbed higher.

As a small boy, he was terrified of going upstairs at his parents' house whenever there was no one else up there and it was all in darkness. He even started going out to the back garden to pee, such was his concern that scary things were waiting for him in the dark of the first floor; that was until a neighbour spotted him outside and reported him to his father.

You're not ten, Ranald, you're nearly thirty. And there are no demons, and paranormal events are limited to the TV and film world.

Then another voice in his head said, *Tell that to the woman in the lift.*

When he reached the landing, he looked around and paused for breath, waiting for his heartbeat to slow. He willed his anxiety to settle, seeking comfort from the luxurious feel of the place, but it appeared to him now as a luxury born of darkness and oppression. Even the air felt heavier here. But see, he told himself looking around, there was no one about. He saw the lift door for this level and made himself approach it, holding out a hand. It was simply cool and smooth, as it should be. There was no life in there. It was just an empty space.

This was his house, he thought. He would not be cowed by it.

The one room he had been almost comfortable in when he was up here with Martie had been his grandmother's sitting room. Perhaps if he went in there for a moment or two it would reset his anxiety and allow him to relax into the rest of his investigation.

He pushed open the door and stepped inside. Making his way over to the window, he looked down into the garden and saw Danny on his knees by a flower border, his attention focused on what Ranald guessed must be weeding.

This moment of normality helped his pulse regulate, and he looked around the room, determined to take in more than he did when he was last here with Martie. Tucked away in a far corner he spotted a small desk with a high-backed chair. He made his way across and sat down. Hands on the smooth wood he imagined his grandmother at work here. Did she have a habit of writing a journal, like her older brother? He pulled open the central drawer just under the desk top, but found it empty. He heard something shift inside, ducked his head to look and spotted a small key in the back. He closed the drawer and checked the others. They were mostly empty, with just a pen in one and a small trinket box in another. The bottom drawer on the right was however locked.

He pulled on the handle again. It refused to give. Why would one drawer on a desk that contained almost nothing be locked?

Guessing it might fit, Ranald retrieved the key from the centre drawer and inserted it into the tiny lock. He gave it a twist and pulled the drawer opened. With a pang of disappointment, he saw that it was empty. But then his eyes adjusted and he realised he was looking at a cardboard folder that filled the bottom so neatly it was like lining paper.

Using the nail of his index finger he reached under and prised it out. It was thick – something plumped it out in the middle. Why had someone locked this away up here?

Feeling a little trepidation, he walked to the nearest sofa and sat down. What was he worried about? Surely there was nothing. He opened the folder.

Inside there was a small pile of what looked like letters, handwritten on small rectangles of cheap notepaper, yellowed with age. The writing was in black ink, tight cursive letters that looked like they'd been written by someone young. Why that was his impression, he had no idea; yet without even reading the words, he could tell a young person wrote these. Had his grandmother received them? Had she written them? Why would she save them all these years?

He focused on the first one and began to read.

Dear Ma and Da,

This is my very first New Year away from home, so I thought I would write to you and send you a little present. It's not much, really, but I saw it in a shop when I was out with the young miss, and I thought you would like it.

They do things different up at the big house. We like New Year better than Christmas, but here, they celebrate both. You should have seen the clothes I had to dress the young mistress and the young miss in! And the Christmas tree they had in the ballroom – it was bigger than our whole house. And the food on the table was a feast. It would have fed everyone on our street for a week! I kept my little brother a sausage roll. I folded it up in a napkin, hid it in the pocket of my pinafore and took it up to my room. Then I realised it would be mouldy before he got near it, so I ate it myself. It was delicious. Tell him sorry.

I miss you all very, very much and I'll write again soon.

Your loving daughter,

He struggled to read the signature. Where everything else was neat and tidy, it was like a rushed scrawl.

Well, that was all very nice. A young girl off to work in service for the first time, writing home. But why would his grandmother save it? And then it occurred to him that it hadn't actually been sent, had it, if it was still here?

He scanned some others. They were all similarly written. A young woman excited to be working and able to contribute to her family income. It seemed every penny was crucial; from what he could gather, her father had been suffering from an old injury he got in 'the Great War' and couldn't work more than three days a week.

This was hardly earth-shattering stuff. But something in the tone caught him; in the voice of this young girl. There was an honesty in her prose and an engaging unaffected manner. He couldn't help but feel sure this girl would have grown into a fine woman. But what was the link to his grandmother?

He skipped a couple and chose another at random.

Dear Ma and Da,
I hope this letter finds you all well.

How is my little brother? Getting bigger? Are you still giving him
bother for climbing that tree in the park? I used to love that tree. I'd
hide in among the leaves and pretend I was a bird.

The trees in the garden around this house are just like those in
the park. The garden itself almost feels like a park, it's that big. They
have two men and a boy working on it all day, every day. I climbed
one tree up the back, where I hoped I was out of sight of everyone in
the house. I found a branch that could be my perch, where I would
be safe. But I forgot to put my coat on and it was so cold I had to go
back inside.

Cook saw me and I thought she would give me a skelp, but she
laughed and gave me a warm scone just out of the oven, and now
every time she sees me she calls me little birdie. It's nice to have a
friend.

I miss you all very, very much and I'll write again soon.

Your loving daughter

Ranald found himself smiling as he read this letter. He was getting
more of a sense of the girl. But a word or two stuck in his mind. She
needed a break away from someone – or everyone perhaps. She was
glad to have a friend. And that word 'safe'. Why would it take hiding
up a tree to make her feel safe? Somehow he felt like that was the
point of the letter. In her quiet, straightforward way, she was trying
to communicate something – something beyond the regular. Was
this why the letters had not been sent?

He flicked through them. There were perhaps another half dozen
before he came to the last one. Starting to read, he hoped the girl,
whoever she was, had indeed found her safety.

Dear Ma and Da

There is so much I want to tell you all, so much I am unsure of, but I don't know where to start. The big news is about the war. It has got everyone up here all of a tizzy. Some of the younger ones are excited at the thought of adventure, but the older ones remember the last war and are afraid. I never thought I'd say it, but I'm glad Da was injured and won't be asked to fight again.

The young master is being sent to London. I heard his parents talk about it when I was in the garden with the young miss. They were relieved that he was getting an easy posting.

When I have a bit of free time – not that I get much – I love to explore the garden. There's a quiet corner I found up the back, where even Cook can't see me. I know I'm too big for such things, but when I'm there I go up a tree and pretend I'm a bird – a homing pigeon, and all I need is for someone to open up the coop and let me out. Then I'd come flying home to be with you.

I miss you all very, very much.

Your loving daughter,

Ranald stood up and went over to the desk. He studied the inside of the open drawer to satisfy himself that this was indeed the last letter. Whatever had happened to her? Again, she was talking about hiding. He read one line again – 'all I need is for someone to open up the coop and let me out'. Did the girl feel she was in a trap?

He tried to read the signature again, and got nothing. Poor girl. What had happened to her? Who did she need to get away from?

Something occurred to him, and he scrolled through all of the letters to confirm it was true. Every letter ended in the same way, except for the very last one. The words 'I'll write again soon' were missing.

⊦

Mind full of the young woman in the letters, Ranald left the sitting room and continued his exploration. Who was she, what happened to her, and why were the letters there? He shook his head, resigned to the fact that he'd never know. More to wonder about in this place of shadows and wide-open spaces. His anxiety quelled now somewhat by the thoughts of this young woman who'd inhabited these spaces he turned back to the staircase and climbed up to the next floor to see what it held. Here the furnishings were much more basic. Looking left and right he saw that this corridor was much narrower than the one below and ran the full length of the house. He could see bare floorboards either side of a narrow carpet runner. Less money had been spent up here. These must be the old staff quarters, then. He counted the doors lining either side. All this space. What a waste when there were families struggling to get decent homes. He tried the first door he came to, turning the handle. But the room was locked. He frowned and tried the handle again. Gave the door a push.

Then he heard it – a noise coming from beyond the door.

Had it been him, pressing against it? His heart in his mouth, he held his ear to the dark wood. He could definitely hear a knocking, scratching sound. He shivered and took a step back. But this was his home, he should really investigate. It was probably the branch of a tree touching the glass of a window.

But, what if it wasn't? His former anxiety rose suddenly, engulfing him like a wave, and he all but ran back to the stairs. But instead of descending into the darkness, he headed upwards and found himself on a small landing outside another door to the lift. To the left of that was yet another flight of stairs, these almost as narrow and steep as a ladder. Where did they lead? His pulse racing, as if he were mindlessly fleeing some wild creature, he leaped up them, using his hands as well as his feet to climb.

And with a feeling of immense relief he emerged in a space flooded with light.

This must be the tower room that Mrs Hackett had mentioned,

the windows of which he had seen from the road and from the drive below. He walked over to the nearest. The view was remarkable. All the terror he'd felt downstairs fell away, as he turned a full three hundred and sixty degrees. He could see for miles. One half of the sky was a clear sweep of brilliant blue, the other half covered in epic, monstrous clouds that thrust into the ozone. A storm was on its way.

Looking down and to the left he saw an expanse of green fields sliced through with stubbled lines of tree and hedge, and here and there, like widely scattered jewels, golden fields of rapeseed.

Over to the left was the massive grey, spiky, spread of human life and achievement: Glasgow. He'd never seen it from this angle before. He would have to come back regularly to study it. His stomach flipped: that would mean dealing with getting up here, climbing the gloomy, claustrophobic staircases. He shuddered at the thought of going back down. He frowned. Told himself not to be daft. The only thing he had to worry about was his vivid imagination.

He lowered his gaze from the view and assessed the room. Each of the four walls was taken up by matching floor-to-ceiling windows, and in the middle of the floor sat four, large cushioned armchairs. Each of them positioned to face a different window. He sat in one and appreciated the view again for a moment. And then sat in each of the others.

Is this what his great-uncle did when he came up here? Depending on the time of day, choose a chair that gave the best outlook?

He sat down on the first chair again and stretched his legs out in front of him. He wondered what Liz would make of this. He should bring her up the next time they met. That's if there was to be a next time. While he was walking home from the café, he'd half expected to bump into her on the road, or even see her standing at the top of the drive. But, no, she had completely vanished.

Was she happy only with this sort of contact, or would she want or expect more from him? Either was fine, he thought. She was fun, very good looking. Good for him.

He looked around the room again. Other than the chairs and

windows, and the narrow staircase that allowed entry, there was nothing else in here.

Then he noticed that the cushion he was sitting on felt a little bumpy, so he stood, turned, picked it up and gave it a shake. Before he set it back in place, something stopped him: a small black triangle poked above the springs of the chair's base: the corner of a notebook.

With a sense of excitement, he picked it up, replaced the cushion and sat back down. Why was it here? Did Alexander mean to hide it? But from what and who? Maybe it was simply one he'd left here for whenever he was up here reading and an idea occurred to him.

Holding the book closed on the palm of one hand, Ranald traced the cover with his other, as if a light touch from his fingers might access some of his benefactor's soul. He sent a mental note of thanks to the old man. It would have been nice if he'd got in touch sooner, perhaps when his parents died. Or at least when he was still alive, so he could explain all of this…

He opened the cover and read the first page. There was no note to say that this was a commonplace book like the others, but, like them, there were scraps of what Ranald assumed were his great-uncle's own poems, images and observations. As he read, Ranald grew sad. The overwhelming impression he was getting was that Alexander was a lonely man, someone who observed life from the edges but was rarely a part of it. At times he seemed to be relieved and almost taking comfort at that remove: unable or unwilling to join in. Other notes suggested this was a great source of loneliness.

At that realisation, Ranald felt a surge of affection for the old man. For all his wealth and connection, he didn't do well socially. He may have been able to deal well with money, but appeared to have failed in those small, daily transactions that human beings use to help form connections and mutual trust.

He read some more and came to a passage about a father and son playing football in the park. The father trying to remember long unused skills, while the boy continually looked from the ball to his dad, tongue sticking out of his mouth, not caring that his dad wasn't very good, happy only to have his undivided attention. There was a poignancy to the words. And envy, perhaps?

The words snagged in Ranald's mind, like cloth on barbed wire. Was Alexander's father too remote? As a boy had he craved that sort of attention? Ranald searched the mental scraps of his own childhood. His father was a taciturn man, but made up for that by being tactile. He often reached out to touch Ranald as he passed him, in the house or garden. A hand on his head. A pat on the back. Reaching out to hold his hand when they crossed the road. He never told him he loved him – those words would have been locked behind the cage of his version of masculinity – but it was there, in those moments, as clear as a spring morning.

And then he was gone.

An image slammed into his mind. Walking into his parents' bedroom that fateful evening. Their still forms on the bed. Too still.

He shook his head violently as if that might remove the memory. He was not going there. Not now. Not ever.

But a boy needs his father. Ranald felt his eyes sting with emotion. For those short years he had had his dad by his side, a safe anchorage, a quiet but solid point of reference; and, in early childhood, a figure of respect, almost of veneration.

Then Dad had blown all of that up with his act of ultimate betrayal. Choosing death with his wife, rather than life with his only child.

As had been his habit for years now, he acknowledged the old hurt while simultaneously pushing it to the side of his mind. There was no benefit in going back over all that.

He turned back to the notebook. It was clear from his great-uncle's words that he didn't have much of a bond with his father. Nothing like Ranald had with his.

Something shifted in his mind. Softened. He'd been so resentful for so long that his parents died while he was struggling to find his place in the world that he hadn't taken time to realise that when they were with him, they were *with* him.

But still, how could his dad…?

Enough.

Ran dipped back into the book. With a sense of relief, he found some lines that were less introspective: an excerpt from a poem:

There was a woman from the north,
who danced till the lights slept, and then
when the world emptied its heart into her eyes
she wept till the lights re-gained their colour.

Where did that come from?

Then:

'This morning I watch from here. You are there. Unseeing, behind a curtain of quiet while within your mind's ear dances a discreet miracle of words.

Your silence unnerves me. Makes me want to prod, extend a finger and pick at that space under your arm where nerve meets laughter.

I see you from the counter as I collect my coffee. I approach your table. Cough, apologise, smile. Cough again. You motion absent-minded assent with casual arm and flicker of smile. I sit in the empty chair opposite and sip.

And watch. And find myself needing to share in your content.'

Wait. What the hell is happening here? He knew these words. He wrote some of them just a little while earlier.

He pulled out the notebook that was still in his pocket, opened it and read:

I watch from here. You are there,
unseeing behind a screen of silence.
Your quiet disturbs me.
Makes me want to intrude.

Reach with a finger and prod in that space under your arm, where nerve meets laughter.

No.

It was like he'd written an early version of Alexander's words.

He closed the notebook. Crossed his arms against a sudden chill. This can't be real. Some odd dreams he could handle. After all, such a big change in circumstances was going to dislodge something in his subconscious. But this – finding words that he'd written earlier that same day, in a notebook of his great-uncle's?

They weren't just similar words. They were pretty much the same. Identical thoughts and observations. What the hell was happening here? He threw the notebook away from him as if it burned, sat back in the chair, and pulled his knees up to his chest.

He forced himself to breathe more slowly. There was an explanation. There had to be. But how could this happen? He got up and scuttled over to the notebook, picked it up and read the words again.

Almost identical.

He fell into a crouch and began rocking back and forwards, knocking his forehead with the fist of his right hand. What was happening here?

Then he caught himself and stopped. This was the very behaviour Martie had described him as showing the first time she came to see him at the hospital. With trembling legs he moved over to the nearest chair and sat on its edge, desperately trying to control his impulsive movements.

This wasn't his imagination. He wasn't dreaming. The words were there in black and white. Was the house somehow affecting him? Was he beginning to adopt his great-uncle's … what? Mind? Memories?

Oh, come on, Ran, you're being ridiculous.

And then, once more, came the worry that had haunted his mind since that first moonlight dance all those years ago: Was he as mad as his mother?

13

Randall remembered wanting to speak to his father about his late-night dance with his mother, but in the days that followed it he didn't get the chance to be alone with him. The expression of disappointment on his father's face stuck with him though, and eventually, unable to bear how much it troubled him, he sought his father out.

It was a Sunday afternoon and Dad was out in the garden pulling up weeds. Ranald watched what he was doing for a moment then fell to his knees and began to copy him.

'None of your pals about, son?' Dad asked, pausing in his task and looking over at Ranald.

'John's got the mumps and Stuart's mum and dad are taking him somewhere.'

Sitting in his present, Ranald could bring no further detail to mind concerning either of these boys. When he pushed at his memory for more there was nothing but a vacuum.

'Don't pull on that one,' his dad had chided next. 'That's a flower.'

'And flowers are good, right?'

'Right,' Dad smiled.

Ran looked down at his father's hands and forearms. Saw the strength coiled in their leanness; the soil clumped around his short dark hairs and embedded under his nails. He turned his attention to a piece of grass among the dark loam and pulled it out. There was just a tiny amount of resistance and then it lifted as easily as a bird's feather.

'Good man,' said Dad and nudged him with his arm.

Ranald felt warmth fill his chest and head. Everything was okay. His father still loved him. He ducked his head to hide the smile that was spreading across his face and reached for another errant blade of grass.

'Am I going to be mad like Mum?' he asked, the words escaping his mouth before the thought occurred that he should stop them.

His father sat back on his heels and sighed a deep, long sigh. 'Mum is just very, very sad, son.'

Which Ranald knew was true; she'd kept him awake much of the previous night, crying on the other side of the thin bedroom wall.

'But sometimes she's happy too, right?' He studied his father's face. 'Like the night we were dancing?'

Dad took some time to answer. Ranald knew that he was trying to protect him by finding the right words. But he was clever, wasn't he? He would be able to understand, whatever explanation Dad came up with.

'Her brain works differently, son. Sometimes she's just so happy she can barely hold it all in, but then, for no reason at all, her brain switches and goes the opposite way, and she feels … too much sadness for her to cope with.'

'Will I be like that, then?' He had to press the question now; now that Dad was prepared to talk about it. 'Sometimes I feel really, really happy.' An image of his mum came to him as she danced in the garden, her face turned to the moon, bathing in its light.

'Nah, you're a McGhie. We're a sensible lot.' Dad ruffled Ranald's hair and he felt some soft pieces of soil crumble from his father's big hand, through his hair and onto his scalp, as if Dad's words were being sanctified by the very earth itself.

You're saying that because you don't want me to worry, he wanted to say. Everybody knew that Ranald, with his mother's pale skin, dark hair and high cheekbones, was every inch his mother's son.

⊦

All these memories. He stood up once more and looked out across the darkening landscape, the blue-grey clouds were closer than ever.

Was the move to this big, perturbing house – the place his mother had grown up in – reawakening the fears he'd suppressed for so long? Was that what all his dreams were about? His apparent sleepwalking?

Something occurred to him. Perhaps he had come up to the tower room when he was sleepwalking the previous night? It would explain why he'd automatically headed up here when he'd run from the darkness of the corridor a few minutes before. Perhaps he'd found this notebook on his earlier visit, read it, absorbed the words and then regurgitated them a few hours later? That was a rational explanation, wasn't it…?

But even he couldn't believe the human mind was that convoluted.

So what, then?

He needed to speak to someone. Talk this over. Maybe if he heard the words said out loud that would chase his worries back into the shadows.

He tucked the notebook back in place, left the tower room and climbed back down the stairs, all the while acutely aware that in the massive space of this house he was the only living being.

ᛏᛰ

Back in his bedroom he changed into some exercise gear and charged down to the fitness suite, set on using physical exercise to escape the turmoil in his head.

He started with press-ups, burpees and sit-ups.

Then chest press, shoulder press, squats and bicep curls. And back to body-weight movements that would get his heart and lungs working, and turn his thoughts off.

He realised that there wasn't a decent pattern of movement to any of this and sat down, breathless. He couldn't remember the last time he'd worked out like that.

To finish off, he stepped under the shower to wash off his sweat, then, naked, jumped into the pool. He splashed about and then swam to the window end, and, leaning against the edge, gazed out.

He looked across the expanse of garden. All of this and no one to share it with. He thought about Martie. He'd had no word from her since she'd left the other day. Of course, there was the poor signal issue up here. Perhaps she was sending him messages and they just weren't getting through? Or maybe it was deliberate. She wasn't sending him any messages for fear of suggesting she was still interested in him.

Perhaps it was time to accept facts. It had been three years they'd been apart now. That ship had sailed.

Still, it would be nice to share all of this with someone – friends; or even with someone special.

He thought back to his time in the flat. He couldn't remember craving company while he was there. Had the drugs anesthetised him to life? While he was on them they provided a numbness that meant he wasn't concerned about, well anything really. He fed himself, worked and slept and didn't care that was all his life consisted of. Didn't even notice. Apart from the occasional visit from Donna, he was mostly alone, and he had been fine with it.

Was all of this empty space emphasising just how much he was on his own?

He could go down to the stables and visit the Hacketts, perhaps. Pretend he was just passing. Getting to know the place. Wondering if he could borrow some sugar?

What he should do was check his emails and see if his agent had sent him anything about the proposal he had been talking about. He rolled that thought across his mind a couple of times then decided be couldn't be bothered.

He hauled himself out of the pool, collected a towel and went outside so the sun could dry his skin. As his head hit the back of the lounger, he heard a voice.

'Helloooo. Helloooo.'

He sat up just as a woman came round the corner of the house. It was Liz. When she saw him she gave a broad smile.

'Hey, handsome. I was just passing.' Her eyes were sparkling. 'And

I wondered if you might like to repay the … compliment … I gave you earlier.'

† ⊦

They made it up to the bedroom. Eventually.

Afterwards, he rolled off Liz, chest heaving and slick with sweat.

'Woman, you are insatiable,' he said.

'Yeah,' she smiled. 'That's what comes after twenty-five years of marriage to a man who prefers the entertainment at the nineteenth hole of his local golf course.'

She laughed at her statement, imbuing it with a humour it clearly lacked; Ranald couldn't help but hear the pain behind it. He turned over onto his stomach and looked up at her as she propped herself up on the pillows.

'Twenty-five years?' he said. 'What, did you get married when you were fifteen?'

'You're a charmer, Mr Ranald … you're not a Fitzpatrick, so what is your surname?'

'McGhie. But you can call me … I dunno … babes? Darling?'

Liz snorted.

Ranald coughed. Made a face of apology. 'Too early for endearments?'

She cocked her head to the side and looked as if she was tasting the words. 'You think too much.' She smiled. 'Right. A shower. You stay here and snooze.'

Ranald grunted in response and, burrowing into the mattress, closed his eyes. 'Sounds like a plan.'

It felt like only moments later that he woke to Liz shaking his shoulder.

'Ran, Ran, Ran!'

The note of fear in her voice roused him instantly. He sat up. She was holding a towel to her breasts. Water was dripping off her onto the carpet, and her hair was slick with shampoo.

'I need to get the hell out of here.' Her whole body was shaking.

'What's wrong? What happened?' Ran jumped out of the bed and pulled her to him.

'In the bathroom.' She pointed, her fingernail almost a blur, so violently was she trembling. 'There was this noise. Children crying.'

'It must be a cat. Or a fox or something.'

She looked at him, pleading. Her eyes filling with tears. 'It was coming from *inside* the walls. It was a child. A child was crying.'

14

That night, nothing he could do or say would allay Liz's terror at the strange noises she claimed to have heard coming from the walls. Ranald was in turns supportive, cajoling and calm. It was a big house. Massive. These old places conjured up all kinds of strange noises, he told her. Floorboards creaked, walls groaned, air in the pipes squealed. It was an aural feast that could lend itself to all kinds of ghostly imaginings, and none of it should be given credence. But in his mind, he was uttering a string of curses. How could she be so suggestible? What he didn't want to do was agree with her – tell her that he had been experiencing his own sense of uneasiness almost every day since he moved in.

Liz refused any of his practical explanations and insisted that she needed to go home. He stood on the drive, reluctant to go back inside, helpless and alone as her car sped away through the twilit fields.

ᛡ

Two miserable, lonely weeks passed. After that last evening, Liz became a virtual stranger. They'd pass each other in the supermarket at the Cross, or going in or out of the café, and Ranald would try to speak to her, but she offered him nothing, barely giving him a nod.

Outside the supermarket one day, he stood in her path and insisted they have a conversation about what had happened. She flicked her hair back and simply said she had heard what she had heard. It was like a child was trapped behind the wall. She'd had repeated nightmares over the past couple of weeks about it, each more vivid than the last.

'Sorry, Ran,' she said. 'That house gives me the willies. There's something wrong up there.' And judging by her expression it seemed she was extending that sense of wrongness to him too.

After they parted and he headed home, he couldn't help thinking her description of the house was correct.

His great-uncle's gift had somehow become a trap.

And then, as he had done repeatedly over the past two weeks, he thought about the poem in the notebook. Didn't that simply reinforce everything Liz was saying? Perhaps he should speak to his old neighbour, Donna. He remembered her telling him all about 'connected-mind theory' – the belief that we all, often without realising it, tap into the same universal consciousness. Perhaps she would be able to explain away the fact he and his great-uncle had written virtually the same words, in the same kind of notebooks.

But what if she didn't? What if she held his arm in that way she did, stared into his eyes as if he were nuts and argued that he should be back on the medication.

He sighed; no way was he going there. The anti-depressants and anti-psychotics he'd been prescribed over the years were evil. He was no longer going to be a sucker for the lies of big pharma and government. They were only interested in huge profits and keeping the population docile. The responsibility for his health lay with him. Clean eating, exercise and work, that was the way forward. That was how he was going to maintain his equilibrium.

But what if the dreams, the sleepwalking – finding himself over and over again in odd places around the house – didn't stop?

He came to a halt in the middle of the lane. The green hedges formed a thick, soft barrier on either side, but through a gap, in the distance, he could just see the tower room, floating above the trees, like a siren to tempt the weary onto the rocks below.

He didn't want the dreams to stop. Yes, they were disturbing, if he thought about them logically. But he couldn't help but be honest with himself: he enjoyed the time he spent in them. Each evening he looked forward more and more to what might greet him in his sleep.

His dreamscape was becoming ever more reassuring. Seductive. And desperately satisfying.

Even when he was awake and going about his daily routine, the woman in the mirror was there, like an aftertaste from his dreams. Her perfume hung in the breeze that curled around the garden, her soft, low voice woven into the pattern of birdsong and chirruping insects.

No, he thought, *I don't want the dreams to stop.*

They lingered in his mind, holding his loneliness at bay. When they were with him it didn't matter that he had no meaningful contact with anyone else. Sure, he wandered to the Cross every couple of days, but the odd word with the café waitress didn't count. And, yes, he saw the Hacketts about the house and garden. But they didn't really engage with him. They were pleasant enough, but they held him at arm's length. A word here. A sentence there. God forbid that they should spend any more time in each other's company than was strictly necessary.

No, his dreams were a positive. They relieved the anxiety and stress the move had provoked in him. Just thinking about the one from the night before – the one that would surely come when he went to sleep – picked him up.

He gave the tower another look and started walking again, noting the elation triggered by simply thinking about the dreams – about her.

The weather since he'd move into Newton Hall had been consistently dry and unseasonably warm. He would take to the patio when he got back. Thirty minutes on his back, thirty minutes on his front. He knew that, under the weight of the sunshine, his mind would move to her presence – to the woman he sensed in his dreams. And the prospect of the bliss he knew he would feel made him pick up his pace another gear.

He had considered – a couple of times – that he should get back into the habit of charting his moods, as his therapists never tired of recommending that he should: 'managing himself' as they called it.

He even had an app on his laptop that he had used. When he saw the scores jump from one level to another he was supposed to take more care. Acknowledge that he was moving from stable to high; from stable to low.

Without pausing to consider the consequence he grasped the branch of a bramble that reached out from the hedge beside him and snapped it off. He didn't need an app. He was in a good place. Why bother?

Then the pain registered with a gasp, and he looked down at his hand. He'd gripped the frond too tightly. Dots of blood appeared on his palm. He flexed his fingers, noting a couple of sharp pangs that hadn't reduced after he let the plant go and used his teeth to pluck out the tiny thorns.

He shook off the pain, wiped his hand on his shorts, turning his mind instead to her. If only she was real, corporeal. They could share the good fortune of this house together. Sit out on the patio in this heat. Then, when it got too hot, jump side by side into the pool, splashing each other. And they would talk. Talk endlessly. Or else walk silently by each other's side, wandering these sunlit country lanes.

He caught onto himself and shook his head. 'Ranald you're going crazy,' he said, out loud. Then he thought: *No you're not.* He wasn't harming anyone. A rich internal life could be a source of content-ment, couldn't it?

What harm was there?

╬

The weather did, of course, break.

Rain fell for two days straight. The sky, as clear as a newborn's con-science for weeks, became laden with clouds so heavy they appeared to be sinking closer to the earth with every passing minute.

Water constantly dripped from the eaves, giant puddles formed on the drive and lawn as the parched and baked earth struggled to deal with the volume.

Ranald's mood took a dip too. On the third day he found himself standing at the pool door, eyes on water that fell like a thick, opaque string from the guttering above him. When he came to he questioned how long he had been there. The only clue was an ache in the soles of his feet.

Enough, he thought. The fact that he'd been all but hypnotised by water falling from the gutter was a sign: he'd dipped into a low mood now. The temptation was to curl up on his bed – retreat into sleep; try to meet her.

No, he had to do something. He should go for a walk. There must be an umbrella somewhere in the house.

His journey to the Cross was uneventful.

Inside the café, there was a different waitress, but she gave him a large smile. One that suggested a degree of familiarity.

Desperate not to look like an idiot, but keen to understand, Ranald asked hesitantly, 'Have we met?'

She leaned forwards and hushed her voice so that no one else could hear. 'Are you telling me you were high the other day?'

He reared back, uncertain. 'High?' he asked.

'You were the life and soul in here last time you were in.' She reached out to him and poked his shoulder. 'Demanding we bring in a karaoke. You even asked old Agnes Weir if you could marry her.'

'I did?'

'Eighty-two years old and never been kissed, she said when you left. You fair made her day.'

'I did?' he repeated. It felt as if his guts were shrinking. He hoped the woman couldn't read his cringe.

'You told her you knew everybody at the BBC and you'd get them to film the wedding,' the waitress said with a giggle.

'Man,' Ranald moaned.

'That must have been some batch of weed,' the waitress said under her breath as she moved close again. 'You have to get me the number for your supplier.'

Ranald tried to turn his confused frown into a smile, ordered his black coffee and took his usual inside seat, against the back wall.

When the waitress brought his coffee, he took a sip and sat back, fighting to ignore the tremor through his mind as he replayed the conversation he'd just had with her. He crossed his arms. How had he managed to forget he'd been down here the other day entertaining everyone? God. What an idiot.

He looked around the room. Apart from the waitress, not one other person had registered his presence. Or so it appeared. They'd probably been staring at him while the waitress was talking to him, and now they were back at their drinks, minds stewing with unanswered questions: Isn't that the one who was behaving like a raving loon the other day? Who was he? Why was he always on his own? Why can't he get a woman? Must have something wrong with him. Must be a deviant. How can he afford to be in here in the middle of the day? Doesn't he have a job?

He told himself to shut up with all the negativity.

But they *were* looking at him, he thought, as he tried to distract himself by stirring his coffee. Of course they were. They knew who he was and they were eaten up with jealousy. They'd probably heard about his bout of manic behaviour and put it down to the rich kid showing off. He had come from nowhere and he now owned all of that. Facebook and Twitter would be full of all kinds of nonsense. He was weird. He was dangerous. They would be posting any old nonsense.

There were two couples among the café's patrons. As he watched them, his loneliness built and he felt envy take residence in his gut, curling up there like a malicious black cat.

He brought out his notebook and pen, placed them on the table in front of him and began to write in an effort to shut off his train of thought.

Minutes later he read what he'd written:

He picks his seat with care on a Sunday.

Alone in the café. Square table.
Heavily thumbed novel, coffee and cake.
And space for three more people.
He kisses the rim of the cup. Sips, swallows and licks
at the foam teasing the corner of his mouth.
An intimacy of one.
He watches couples for clues. A smile. A look. The briefest of
touches.
Words without sounds. How to effect that comfortable
indifference
couples wear while reading weekend print?
He reads his book. Thinking he should drain his coffee
continue his read at home.
But where's the company in that?

He sighed and read the last line again: 'But where's the company in that?'

And there was the rub.

The door opened. He looked up, hoping it might be Liz and that she might be in a better mood. They didn't need to have sex or anything, just passing the time of day with him would be some sort of result.

But it wasn't her, it was the *War and Peace* girl. And she was carrying the book under her arm. She shook the rain from her hair, spotted him, gave him a little wave and walked over.

'How's you?' she asked. 'Have you been away? You look great.'

Been away? Again he wondered how long it had really been since he was here.

'Cheers. Just been in the garden. Who needs to travel abroad when we get that kind of weather?'

'Well, if the sun comes back, get right out there again. It suits you.'

That was all the encouragement he needed. 'Why don't you join me? I've got all these seats to spare.' He pointed at the other three chairs at the table.

She looked taken aback at the suggestion.

'Shit,' she replied wearing an apologetic expression. 'I'm just in for a takeaway coffee. Got to get back to the house. But thanks, that was kind of you.'

Ranald fought the heat that was working up his neck. Don't blush. Don't blush. Why was he blushing? Hadn't done that since he was in his early twenties.

'Ach, they're not very comfy anyway.'

She smiled and walked over to the counter as he chided himself, calling himself a loser.

He watched her at the counter and noted the book. She had just decided to take her book out for a walk, had she? Shit excuse. Then he felt ashamed that if she had come in here for a quiet coffee and a read, he'd scared her off with his awkward invitation. So, before the waitress started working on her drink, he stood up and walked out.

When he got back to the house, he realised he still needed a distraction. Loud noise and lots of movement – the illusion at least of company? So he went up to the TV room, set the volume high and watched mindless shows, his mind barely following what was happening.

Every now and then his thoughts would stray back to *War and Peace* girl and he still felt the heat of a blush, even thought she had said no so nicely. She could have laughed at him.

Finally he headed for bed. He stripped off and before he climbed under the covers, pulled the bed curtains closed. Tonight, he needed to forget there was all this space around him. He needed his wee den.

But he remained awake for what felt like an age. Although the rain had returned, it was still warm outside. His head was too hot against the pillow, so he turned it over to the other side, hoping it would be cooler against his skin; but soon that heated up, too.

He got out of bed, opened the window and left the curtains open in the hope that a breeze would enter and dispel the oppressive heat. It didn't work.

This was Scotland, he thought. This country didn't get weather like this. What was happening? Body hot in the sticky air, he stretched out on the bed. Then changed position, turning from one side to the other. From the bed he could see out of the open window. The oak trees fringing the garden were black against the sky, louring over the house like sentinels.

Eventually, blessedly, his brain shut down and let him sleep.

⌐⌐

Sliding into wakefulness, even before he was fully alert, he felt a sense of wrongness.

He opened his eyes to a weak light, enough to see that his breath was misting in the air. It was so cold he was shivering. He pulled himself up into a seated position, bringing his knees to his chest.

Was he dreaming? Last thing he remembered, he was too warm to sleep.

From the weak light coming in from the small window he could see that he was in the lift. He felt a tremor of fear. Trying to damp it down he stood up, located the seat in the corner, sat down with his feet on the chair and with his chest on his thighs. Steeling himself, he looked across at the mirror.

She was there. A back view. A shoulder clothed in a dark fabric. Black hair piled high on her head. The pale of her skin and the line of her neck and cheek shone as if holding some form of internal light. Her eyes were in shadow.

'My love,' he heard. 'I've missed you.'

Equal parts fear and relief washed over him. 'And I you.' He didn't speak but the words sounded in the space between them.

'Close your eyes and let me show you how much.'

Unable to refuse, he closed his eyes. Felt a hand on each knee and warm breath on his inner thigh like the promise of a thousand hours of delight. Then a hand gripped him. Moved slowly.

Disappeared.

All sense of her was gone. Then she returned, fingertips trailing the length of his body, reading his skin like braille, as if she knew the exact route his nerves took and the precise amount of pressure required.

Again, she stopped.

He groaned. 'No.'

A fist in his hair, pulling his head back and exposing his throat, and it felt like she might tear a handful of his hair out at the roots.

Her mouth was hot at his ear. 'Are you mine?'

He nodded, afraid to move too much, aware of the exquisite pain in his scalp. Fear bloomed in his mind, clogged the words in his throat. Fear that she was real. Fear that she might withdraw from him forever.

'Are you mine?'

'Yes,' he said in a croak.

Then a sudden shout: 'Are you mine?!'

'Forever,' he gasped.

15

He woke inside the little space created by the curtains of his four-poster bed. His eyes were burning with fatigue and his forehead was damp. He turned and borrowed deep under the quilt, willing his mind to find sleep again.

The lift.

He sat up with a start. He'd had a dream again, hadn't he?

There was a sense of it in his mind, but it was as if the detail was hidden behind a screen of smoke. He poked at this with his mind, and reeled back from the sorrowful feeling that was released, and the image that it prompted. Him lying in an open casket.

Jesus.

Enough.

He jumped out of bed. Grabbed a towel from his bathroom, wound it round his waist and made his way downstairs. As he passed the lift, he paused, lingered with his hand flat on the door as if trying to sense what was behind it.

He heard a voice from his right.

'Ranald, are you okay?'

He turned. It was Mrs Hackett. She was staring at him with a strange look on her face. And she was keeping well away from him. Presumably because he was standing there in nothing but a towel.

'I was just going for a swim…'

'The lift won't take you to the pool, Ranald,' she said pointedly.

'Where's the key?'

'It's broken, Ranald. So it doesn't matter where the key is, does it?'

'The key please, Mrs Hackett? Why don't you simply tell me where it is?' He felt strangely authoritative.

Something in his gaze must have made her blanch. 'Mr McGhie, you're making me feel quite uncomfortable. Please go and have your swim, and then I'll answer any questions you have about keys and lifts.'

'Right,' he said. 'Sorry.'

He wasn't, but he realised that, if he wanted the woman to talk to him about the lift he'd have to cover up. He decided to forego his swim for the moment. This was too important.

'Wait here, please,' he said. Then he ran upstairs and threw on his t-shirt and shorts.

When he came back down, Mrs Hackett was looking irritable at being kept waiting. But then she examined his face. 'Ranald, are you sure you're okay?'

'Never better.' He pointed at the lift. 'The key?'

'Why are you suddenly so interested in this?'

'Why are you not just answering my question?'

'Well, I never.' Mrs Hackett held a hand to her heart. 'Mr Fitzpatrick would never have used that tone to me.'

He took a breath. His anxiety to work this out was making him aggressive; he knew that wasn't fair.

'I'm sorry, Mrs H. I just really need to know. Could you please tell me where the key to this door is?'

Somewhat mollified by his placatory tone, Mrs Hackett gave a little huff and shifted her feet, signalling that she would answer his question, but he wasn't fully forgiven just yet.

'I never use the lift. It used to give me the creeps, actually.'

Ranald raised his eyebrows, thinking, *Just tell me*.

'Yes, yes…' She picked up on his irritation. 'Mr Fitzpatrick told me one day that the lift was broken, and he'd locked it in case anyone used it and got stuck. Which was a bit strange, I remember thinking, because there was rarely anyone in the house apart from me and him.'

'Did Rebecca and Marcus never visit? What about Quinn?'

Mrs Hackett made a dismissive noise. 'Rebecca and Marcus rarely came. In fact, I'd all but forgotten what they looked like. And Quinn never ventured beyond the front drawing room. Couldn't see past that drinks cabinet, if you ask me.'

'And my uncle never tried to get someone in to fix the lift?'

'He said there was no real point.'

'And the key?'

She shook her head slowly. 'Not sure.' She shrugged. 'Never using the thing, I didn't think to ask.'

'Where might he have kept a key like that?'

'There's cupboards and drawers all over this house. It could be anywhere.'

His mind crowded with disappointment and no longer entirely sure why he was so adamant that he should gain access to the lift – outside of his dreams, at least – Ranald slumped against the wall.

'Sorry, Mrs Hackett, I don't know what's got into me this morning.' He smiled full beam, hoping that would win her favour. 'A strong coffee will sort me out.'

'Not too strong, Ranald.' Now they were back on good terms, it seemed she was happier to call him by his Christian name. 'You don't want your sleep affected.' As she said this she gave him a pointed look.

He let it go. But what the hell did she mean by that? Was he looking that tired?

'If you have no more questions, Ranald, then…'

'Thanks, Mrs Hackett. Sorry to be so…' he tailed off and turned away towards the kitchen.

Once there he set up the coffee machine. Feeling tired once again, and guilty for the way he'd spoken to Mrs Hackett, he sat down and rubbed his eyes. For a moment he even thought about going back to bed.

He'd be fine once the caffeine hit.

Dark-brown, liquid heaven splashed and spluttered into the glass jug. He poured some into a mug and started to drink.

Why would his great-uncle lock the lift? Was it really something as basic as the fact that it was broken? The most obvious answer was usually the right one, his dad used to say. But in this instance, Ranald wasn't buying that. Why was it a regular feature in his dreams? Something was going on here.

If Alexander did lock the lift, where had he put the key?

As he thought back to Mrs Hackett's responses, her body language, he was sure she had been skirting the question, hiding something. But what?

If he couldn't find the key, he had to get a locksmith in. Whatever he needed to do to achieve it, he had to open that door.

After the coffee jug was drained, he moved through to the library and searched every drawer in the desk in case he'd missed it when he'd rifled through previously. Nothing. Next, he tried the reception room, working his way through all of the cupboards and drawers there, under the watchful eyes of his deceased forebears. Still nothing.

Next, he tried his bedroom and the TV room, with similar results.

He tried the other bedrooms in his wing of the house. Both of which had large oak beds and matching giant wardrobes, straight out of an antiques showroom. Dark walls and heavy curtains completed the feel of bedrooms that hadn't changed in decades. It was as if Alexander had run out of energy while doing the modernisations and thought, why bother, no one goes in here. And while these rooms were bright enough, all having large windows, they had an oppressive feel, lacking the energy that constant inhabitation brings.

They also lacked anything that might constitute a key.

He thought about the little key safe in the garage. When he opened it the other day the only keys he could remember seeing were the ones for the cars. But it was certainly worth another look.

He ran out to check but, once again, found nothing.

Trudging back into the house he sat back down again at the kitchen table. He considered trying the bedrooms on the way up to the tower room, but he discounted that idea. Something told him it would be a waste of time – he wasn't sure what, but as he rubbed his thoughts against it, like he might rub his thumb against the ridged edge of a coin, he decided his intuition was solid. Mrs Hackett had talked about Alexander's *mother's* rooms. And, after her, his *sister's*. Alexander was of a generation most likely forbidden access to family member's private spaces, and if they were known as *their* rooms that must have had the whiff of an official dictate for him. He might, perhaps, have entered that space after his sister died, for a wee nosey, but Ran doubted he would have ever felt comfortable lounging there.

Then, without articulating the need to, as if directed by some internal force, he stood up and walked to the kitchen cupboards nearest the door and opened the top drawer. For a second he paused, questioning what he was doing – what was prompting him. Then he ignored the question. Now that he was doing it, it made sense.

In the drawer he found pens, assorted sales leaflets, some packs of AA batteries, a couple of birthday cards still in their cellophane wrapping … and a key.

Instantly he knew it was what he was looking for.

He opened his fingers. Felt the weight of it and regarded it sitting there, in the middle of his palm: a threat wrapped in a promise. It looked like a key that might open a treasure chest, an attic room or a box labelled 'Pandora'.

At the thought of the Greek legend, he tilted his hand and allowed the key to drop into the drawer. But it rested there for no longer than a second before he picked it up again.

He told himself not to be daft. It was time to go and look. These dreams were haunting his every waking thought. He had to discover the truth of things. It would prove his worries were groundless and he could relax, get some work done and get on with his life.

But what if…

Mouth dry, heart thundering at his ribs, and the thought that he was going crazy rattling in his mind, he walked along the corridor to the lift.

As he thought it would, the key fitted the lock perfectly. He twisted the metal shaft and, with just a little effort, the mechanism moved and the lock clicked open.

Before he could stop himself, he had pulled open the outside door.

16

With the main door open he was faced with a metallic mesh concertina gate. He reached for the handle and pushed the gate along its runners until it was fully open.

He didn't step inside.

Couldn't step inside.

It's only a lift, Ran. Get a hold of yourself.

He had an idea. Walking back into the kitchen, he lifted one of the chairs, carried it back to the lift and used it to prop open the outside door. If that closed while he was inside, he didn't know how he would handle it.

Light flooded in from the corridor.

Then it dimmed.

He looked over his shoulder, down towards the main hall. But there was nothing. Probably the sun ducking behind a cloud.

Ignoring the slight tremble in his right knee, he stepped inside the lift. He looked at the red wallpaper with its gold fleur-de-lys motif. The red carpet. The low-legged, small chair in the corner. It was wooden, the centre of each arm cushioned with the same cloth as the seat cushion and the back insert. It was a parlour chair, he thought. Then he asked himself how that little nugget of information had dropped into his mind.

Wherever it had come from, the chair, the wallpaper, and yes, the mirror, were all familiar. Far too familiar. If he had only been in here in his dreams, why was everything in it instantly recognisable?

There was a draught. A breeze. On it floated a scent he recognised.

The kitchen chair shifted; its weight was insufficient to hold the outside door. With a brushing sound, it closed.

'No,' he shouted and reached out, but he wasn't quick enough.

'My love,' he heard. The sound was musical, reassuring. He stepped back further inside the lift, shaking his head, refusing to believe that this was happening.

'You should have a seat,' he heard. 'It's tiring, isn't it?'

Almost paralysed with fear and uncertainty, he managed to nod his agreement, and sat.

'Who are you?' he asked, hearing the panic in his voice. He sent the command to his legs to rise from the chair and leave, but his limbs remained unresponsive.

'I know who *you* are. You are my love.' He heard a smile threading through the answer.

'I don't understand,' he said, and heard a note of anxiety in his reply.

He looked up at the mirror. And there she was. The woman from his dream. Her shoulder. Dark cloth with a white lace trim. The back of her head. A quarter view of her face. Long, brown hair in waves and curls.

'What do you need to understand?' Her cheek moved as if her face was forming a smile.

'This isn't happening,' said Ranald, thoughts jumbling in his head, commands he sent to muscles going unheeded. He should leave.

Run.

This wasn't a dream. He was wide awake.

'And yet here we are, my love.'

Not happening, thought Ranald. *Not fucking happening.*

And yet.

'Who are you?' he asked in a whisper. 'Why are you in my dreams? My head?'

'Why not? Can't you feel it?'

'Feel what?'

'Our love.'

Ran exhaled. Glanced down at his hands. They were quivering. He needed to get out of here. But again his muscles refused to obey his brain. Then a moment. A memory. Walking in the garden. Catching a glimpse of a slender ankle. A long skirt, its edges damp with dew.

'We do enjoy our walks.'

'We do? What's happening here?' He knocked his forehead with his fist. He should get back on his drugs. That was the explanation. He needed to be taking his medication.

'Close your eyes.'

He did.

'Lean back.'

He did, questioning at the same time why he was being so acquiescent.

'Keep your eyes closed.' Her laugh was a chime. Silver on crystal. Somehow he didn't feel at risk.

Then he felt a hand slip into his loose grip. The weight of someone sitting on his lap. A head on his shoulder.

'Please hold me.'

He did, knowing he had finally slipped beyond the veil and into madness.

17

From that day, Ranald felt like his normal, everyday life was dimming. His physical presence fading into inconsequence. If he were to die, who would even notice?

He began to follow a simple and apparently straightforward routine. On waking he would shower, go for his morning swim, then it would be coffee and breakfast. Then he would go to the library, answer his emails and work on the project Douglas had sent him. Lunch. More coffee. Then work.

But all of this he performed as if on automatic, his body behaving at a level that would ensure functionality. Pushed to a dark corner of his brain, there was a version of him cowering in a corner, terrified for his sanity. Was he going mad? Really mad? Had a life of cruel disappointment, mental health issues and powerful medication pushed him over the edge?

Because, in the late afternoon, after all the mundane tasks were taken care of, he would select a book from the shelves of his library and carry it along the corridor to the lift, biddable as a puppy. Once inside, he would be welcomed, then he would sit and begin reading aloud to her.

He didn't need to be informed that she would enjoy being read to, he just *knew*.

The first book he chose, completely at random, was *Heart of Darkness*. He picked it out because it was a slim volume. Then, when he saw it was the Conrad classic, he thought, why not?

'Did you like that?' he asked, when he closed the last page. Not sure himself how he felt about it yet.

'I like to hear your voice.'

For their next read he picked another short book: *The Awakening* by Kate Chopin. When he finished it, his first thought was that, to his modern sensibilities, the actions of the main character were nothing that would cause concern. But to someone of that time, it must have been scandalous. Women were mere chattels then, surely? That this woman had the audacity to pay attention to her desires would have caused a bit of a fuss.

He waited for *her* reaction. Wondered if it might give him more of a clue as to who she was.

'So sad. Why are these people all so sad?'

He didn't know how to answer that.

His next read, again at random was *The Turn of the Screw*. Sure, he'd heard of the book. Who hadn't? But he knew next to nothing about it. There was a film, wasn't there? A governess, some strange children in a big lonely house. Her 'wanderings' in the garden. Wishing someone would appear to her. It all felt so familiar. Then a male figure appeared to her in the tower. Everything grew silent, the hour no longer friendly.

"'…and even as he turned away still markedly fixed me. He turned away; that was all I knew.'"

Ranald stopped reading. He felt a moment of clarity. A stab of insight into his fog of dreamlike acceptance. He was reading a ghost story to a…

'Why stop, my love?'

'I'm tired,' he said as he stood up.

'See you in your dreams.' Her voice followed him as he walked along the corridor. A feeling of unease both stippling the length of his spine and thrilling his mind.

And yet, a thought that felt like a betrayal: *Dear God I hope not.*

18

His body betrayed him time and time again. He gave in fully to her demands. She would beckon, and he was like a spark shot from the fire, only to fall back into the flames. His mind lived in two places. Regret and joy: shame that he was so easily seduced and elation at the seduction.

This was not real, he would tell himself.

But the feeling, he would reply, was like nothing else. The pleasure centre in his brain was sending up flares, firing messages to every atom in his body, telling it to relax and let it happen.

But. It. Is. Not. Real.

It certainly felt as if it was, he would think as his head fell back onto the cushion and he rested, allowing his breathing to adjust to normal.

Then, when the sweat had dried and his pulse slowed, the reality check. That's when his work would come in handy. Losing himself in the act of trying to inject sense into an educational text, he found most worries would recede.

From time to time he would walk into the Cross. Buy food in the supermarket. A coffee in the café. People were beginning to recognise him now. A few actually stopped to chat, despite his monosyllabic responses. Most would just give him a nod or a smile.

And the further he walked from the house, the stronger the feeling grew that he was not in charge, that he was a pawn in someone else's game. But still the pull was there, like a curser blinking in the corner of a computer screen. It was tiny, but he was incapable of ignoring it, and soon, with a heavy mind and light heart, he'd be winding his way back to Newton Hall, almost singing, 'I'm home, honey,' as he walked in the door.

One day, as he left the café, intent on the internal voice telling him to get back home, he brushed against someone going in. He mumbled an apology and took a step outside.

'Ran, are you okay?' It was Liz; her face was pulled into an expression of concern.

'I'm fine, thanks. Why do you ask?'

'Just…' She withdrew slightly. 'Sorry. Just wondering. Haven't seen you about for a few…'

Ranald mumbled something and walked off.

She was there again the next day.

This time she put her hand on his sleeve. 'Ran, are you sure you're okay?'

Pulling himself out of his thoughts felt like an exhausting climb to a high peak. He looked at her, puzzled why she should ask this, and why she would ask it two days in a row. 'Yeah. I'm fine. Tickety-boo.'

'Join me for a coffee?' Smile. 'I do hate sitting on my own.'

'I'm just…' Ranald looked off into the distance.

'Please? Five minutes?'

With barely disguised reluctance, he stepped back inside the café and took his usual seat.

Liz sat across from him. She seemed smaller, less confident than when they had been together. 'I can understand why you wouldn't want to talk to me,' she said. 'I was pretty rude.'

'S'okay,' Ranald replied. 'You were freaked out.'

The waitress came over to the table, and stood over them with pen poised over her small notepad.

Smiling up at her felt like a barely remembered reflex. But he found he almost enjoyed the sensation. It was like he was greeting an old friend. He tried to remember the last time it had happened, and then heard a vague nagging thought: he should try harder, before he completely lost touch with the real world.

'These older women,' he addressed the waitress while nodding over at Liz. 'Can't keep their hands off me.' And a sense of humour? Wherever that came from, it was welcome. Then he remembered that had been his habit. Whatever was going on in the battleground of his mind he could usually disguise it with the mask of a smile and a well-timed joke.

Was he so out of practice at being around other people?

Ranald, you need help.

He stiffened his spine and sat up. Nonsense. He was fine. Completely in control.

Liz laughed. 'You'd be so lucky.' She sat back in her chair, relief evident in her pose. They gave the waitress their order and she hurried away.

'So, what have you been up to?' Liz asked, reaching over to play with the sugar dish.

'Oh, you know. This and that,' Ran replied, watching Liz arrange the paper straws that held the sugar. 'You?'

'Trying to ignore the fact that I'm still married. That I had a good wee thing with you…' She pushed the sugar dish away. 'Why do I always have to tidy things up?' She put her hands under the table as if hiding them away and laughed.

Ranald joined in, catching some energy from her good humour.

Their drinks arrived. Ranald nodded his thanks at the waitress and picked up his cup. As he put it down, he noticed an old lady in the far corner looking over at them.

'Do you know that old dear over there? The one with the cropped white hair?'

Liz turned to look. The older woman waved. Liz turned away, shifting her chair slightly so that the woman was no longer in her view.

'No idea who that is,' Liz said under her breath. 'Crazy old bitch. Look at her waving.'

'Looks like she's certain she knows one of us.'

'You know what they say: old age brings along a few unwelcome friends.' She sneaked another glance at the woman and then ducked her head, holding her hand up as if hiding. 'Christ, she's coming over.'

The lady arrived; she wore an aquamarine scarf and tan raincoat. 'I knew it was you soon as I saw you,' she beamed at Liz. 'How are you, dear? I haven't seen you in an age. Don't often get a chance to come over to Bearsden. Not since my sister died.'

She turned her attention to Ranald and, as she did, she shook her head and held a hand to her throat. 'My, I must have just taken a wee turn. You look so like someone I used to know.' She held a hand out as if to touch Ran's face but then remembered herself and pulled it away. 'Oh, dear,' she said, confusion in her eyes. But then it was replaced by certainty: 'I never forget a face…' Her eyes flitted from Ran to Liz.

'I'm sorry,' said Liz. 'I'm pretty positive we've never met.'

'I never forget a face, dear. A name, maybe.' She smiled.

'Sorry,' Liz said, her face a little twisted; she was clearly torn between telling the old dear to piss off and feeling sorry for her. 'I've never met you.'

'You were at school with my daughter, Hannah Talbot, weren't you?' Then to Ranald: 'Thick as two peas they were.' Her smile was radiant at the memory, but faded suddenly, and she held a hand to her throat once more.

'How is … Hannah?' Liz asked, making a quick face at Ranald as if to say, might as well try and please the old dear.

'She died…'

'I'm so sorry…' Liz began. But the woman waved off her sympathy, her hand in the air.

'It was a few years ago now, dear. Time heals, or so they say.' She looked once more at Ranald. A moment of study. 'Still waiting on it, though, son.' Her smile was pained. Turning back to Liz, she said. 'Anyway. I could have sworn…' Her eyes glazed over.

Liz gave her a conciliatory smile but said nothing. Ranald could see the indifference in her expression.

Mrs Talbot accepted the unsaid message and, trying to disguise her discomfort, stepped away; but Ranald could see the hurt in her eyes.

When she was out of earshot, he said, 'That's a shame.'

'Crazy old bat,' said Liz in a whisper. 'Accosting random strangers in public.'

'She was certain she knew you. You have no idea who she is?'

'None whatsoever,' Liz replied. 'And she was giving you the once-over. Wonder who she thought *you* were.' She sipped at her drink. 'At least it kept us from another awkward silence.'

'We were having an awkward silence?'

Liz raised her eyebrows.

'Well, maybe a little,' Ranald said.

'Jesus, she's coming back. Quick. You pay the waitress for the coffees and I'll get you outside.'

Liz rushed out of the door and a bemused Ranald walked over to the café counter to pay. As he walked past Mrs Talbot, she held a hand up.

'Oh, dear, looks like I've upset your friend.' She looked away, and then back at Ranald, as if determined to assert her sanity.

'Don't worry about it. She often runs out on me, too.' He managed a smile.

The old woman peered into Ranald's face. And then her eyes widened in surprise and not a little shock. 'My. It's finally come to me…' She held a hand to her chest. 'You're the spitting image of Alexander Fitzpatrick – from the big house.' She searched his face. 'You'll be the great-nephew that just moved in? Had a wee fancy for him when I was a girl. Such a handsome man. But I was too young, and he wouldn't have been interested in the likes of me, anyway.'

'Right,' said Ranald, wondering how he could politely escape.

'I heard it wasn't too easy for him at the end.'

'Aye,' said Ranald, without commitment.

'They say the house got the better of him,' she said with a sage nod and a look full of portent.

A sudden panic seemed to grip Ranald, and with a quick, 'Got to go', he left the café.

Outside, Liz was waiting on him, tapping her foot.

'What did the old dear say to you?'

'Nothing really. Just apologised again.' Ranald didn't want to discuss the woman's comments about Alexander. What she said about the house had rattled him. If that's what she'd heard, was the rest of the town saying it, too? Whatever they thought happened to him, were they all waiting for him to go the same way?

He felt himself walking faster. He told himself to calm down and managed to rein in his anxiety. 'Where are we going?' he asked.

'Don't know where you're going, but I'm going home.' Liz looked up at the darkening sky. 'Hopefully I'll get to my car before the rain starts.'

'Where do you actually live?' Ranald frowned. 'You know, I know very little about you.'

'I prefer to preserve the mystery, Ranald. Don't you?'

They stared into each other's eyes.

She gave him a little shove. 'It was good to see you, Ran,' she said.

'Good to see you too, Liz.'

As he watched her walk away, his phone sounded an alert. He plucked it from his pocket. It was a text from Martie: 'Hey Ran. Soz not been in touch. How's life in the big hoose? Don't be a stranger, eh?'

She'd finished with a double x.

He read it and felt a surge of resentment. Then gave himself a telling-off. In any case, they weren't really kisses. They were exes. A double reminder he and Martie were no longer together.

ᛏᚻ

Back at the house, Ran made straight for the library.

He checked his email. There was nothing. Not even a phishing email for Viagra. He soon found himself perusing the shelves for a book to read; it was only after he had discounted a number of them that it occurred to him that he was choosing a book with *her* in mind.

Was that such a bad thing? He was experiencing a whole side of literature that he had previously ignored. But perhaps he should go with something that was home grown. Since briefly studying his fellow Scots at university, he had passed by much of their writing. Time to remedy that?

From his previous browsing he knew his great-uncle had reserved an entire bookcase worth for Scottish writers, so he walked over to it. Something modern, he thought as his fingertips lit on a number of spines.

His hand came to rest on Jackie Kay's *Trumpet*.

He loved her poetry but hadn't read her longer work. He looked at the cover, turned it over and read the blurb. It was about a jazz trumpeter called Joss Moody who pretended to be a man. Even had a wife and foster child. He wondered how someone could keep that pretence up, and at how the author might keep that narrative running.

He opened the book to the first page and began to read as he walked over to the leather sofa. Before he even sat down, he was there, in Joss's world.

⊣⊢

Only when the light was so weak that he could feel his eyes working too much over the words, did he surface. Must be past ten, he thought, so he took the book to bed and lay, propped against a mound of pillows, on top of the covers with the four-poster's curtains pulled shut.

His eyes soon grew heavy and he realised that his focus was wavering and the words were having less of an impact. He'd close his eyes just for a minute, then he'd finish the chapter.

The bed really was very comfortable. His breathing slowed. He should go and switch off the light. He tried to open his eyes, but they were too heavy.

In a minute.

Liz popped in to his mind. It was nice to spend some time with an actual human.

Then he thought about Martie. He really should reply to her text. His nonsense thought about the two kisses was just that: nonsense. She was his oldest friend. He missed her and he would benefit from having her in his life. He'd just have to accept the fact that friends were all they would ever be. His spirit wilted a little at the thought.

Still. He remembered all those days they spent walking, chatting, drinking coffee, going to the movies. Watching a film just wasn't the same since they'd split up. He needed her there beside him to read the shorthand of his responses. It made watching movies more of a shared experience. Nobody could read his movie-induced snorts like she could.

And she'd absolutely love the TV room. She'd revel in the big, soft chairs, the giant lump of a TV.

There was no point in asking Liz to come back and watch a film. She was completely freaked out about the house. That was just not happening.

He should really turn out the light.

In a minute.

He turned onto his side, pulled his legs up in a foetal position and let out a long, slow breath.

The next thing he knew, he was walking in the garden and *she* was by his side, her hand in his, warm and as light as a bird. He must have said something funny because she was laughing, musical and soft. A sound that brought a lightness of spirit. Then they were in the tower room. He was in a chair and she was sitting at his feet, on the floor, her head on his knee. He ran his fingers through the satin of her hair.

Then they were on his bed. Fully clothed. She was at his back, lining the curve of his body with hers, the weight of her arm on his side, their hands clasped and at rest over his heart.

'This is what you could have,' she said, her lips brushing over the fine hairs on the curve of his ear. 'For eternity.' Then she was on top of him. Pinning him down onto the bed. 'This is what you could have,' she repeated.

He tried to see her face in the shadows of her hair, but could only see a strange light coming from her eyes. And her teeth.

She gave a sharp intake of breath. 'But I can smell other women on you. Their perfume.'

He sensed her withdrawing from him.

'No,' he said. 'Please…'

They were on a lawn; he was standing in the sunlight. She was walking towards a row of tall trees at the far end. Before she reached them, she half turned, her right arm reaching out behind her and towards him, like an invitation. *Come, hold me*, it said. But his bare toes were curling into the lush grass, taking root in the light.

'I'll miss you, my love,' she said just before she became one with the darkness in the border of the trees. 'But … you've betrayed me. I can't stay if you want others…'

Don't go, he thought.

Then out loud. 'Please don't go.'

But she was gone, her leaving as final as the act of turning over the last page of a much-loved novel.

He fell to his knees. Her disappearance so brutal his legs couldn't hold his weight. *What is it?* he asked himself. He recognised the feeling, that was for sure. The mass of it there on his chest, as black and as unforgiving as a lump of coal. As familiar to him as the Scottish outline on a map. He'd just never given it a name. Since his parents died he'd gone with the flow of just existing, knowing this weight was as much a part of his life as the need to breathe, but looking at it head on, giving it a name, was beyond his capacity.

Only now, in this moment, with her moving out of his sight into a dark farewell, could he name it. Possess it. Take the necessary collection of consonants and form that one mournful syllable.

Loss.

19

The doorbell rang. Wondering who it might be at this time of day, Ranald pushed his chair away from the desk and walked into the hall on bare feet.

Opening the door he was met by big smiles, which quickly transformed into barely concealed expressions of shock on the faces of Martie and Donna.

'What are you both doing here?' He stood with one hand on the door, the other in the pocket of his shorts.

'Well ask us in, then, Ran,' said Martie.

'Nice to see you, too, son,' said Donna. She looked at the front of his t-shirt and made a face. 'I always change my t-shirts every two weeks, whether I need to or not.'

What was she talking about? 'You don't wear t-shirts. And since when did you two know each other?'

'How about asking us in?' asked Martie. 'We're getting a bit wet here.'

'It's raining?' Ranald looked beyond her out into the drive and saw puddles among the slick shine on the pebbles. He stepped back. 'Well, seeing as you're here…'

Martie huffed. Donna silenced her with a warning look. Ranald tried – and failed – to work out what that meant.

He stepped back to allow them in. Martie passed him and walked into the hall with a small smile. Donna paused at the threshold, looked around as if suddenly unsure then crossed her arms as if bracing herself before stepping inside.

'You okay?' Ranald asked her.

She gave a little smile and a nod, before reaching out to touch his arm. 'Great to see you, son.'

'Come on through to the kitchen,' he said wondering what had suddenly happened in Donna's mind. 'There's a kettle and every-thing. Not sure there's anything to go with it other than water.' He gave a laugh that sounded false, even to him. What *were* these two doing here?

'Your flat is still empty,' said Donna in a slightly arch tone as they entered the kitchen. 'Someone should sort that out. There was a lot of half-decent stuff in there, and some people might be able to make good use of most of it.'

Ranald nodded his agreement, and filed it to the back of his mind. He'd get to it eventually. He filled the kettle, switched it on and started rooting around for mugs, tea and coffee. Then he realised that all the mugs were in the dishwasher. He opened it to find that it was full of crockery – some of it clean and some of it dirty. He pulled out three mugs and rinsed them under cold water as he tried to work out how the clean and dirty thing had happened.

'Must have added dirty dishes to a clean load,' he said out loud.

'What?' Martie had a worried expression on her face.

Ranald felt the heat of a blush. 'Sorry. You do that, don't you, when you live on your own. Talk to yourself?'

Both women looked at each other, then at him, and at the same time said, 'No.'

The kettle came to the boil, and while trying to recover some sort of equilibrium he made the drinks.

'So, to what do I owe the pleasure of this visit?' Without waiting for a reply. 'And how long have you two known each other?'

Donna was the first to reply, and as she spoke she was obviously attempting to gauge his state of mind. 'Oh, not long after you moved in across the landing. I met Martie one evening when she was leaving. You know me.' She smiled. 'Mrs Busybody. There was a gorgeous woman leaving your flat. I had to know who she was.'

'Then we connected through a friend of a friend on Facebook.' Martie added.

'But I still don't understand what brought you two over here … together?'

'My last text to you was three weeks ago, Ran,' replied Martie. 'No reply.' She held her hands out, palms up, in a *what's-going-on?* gesture.

'We're worried, son,' added Donna softly.

Three weeks? That text from Martie had been three weeks ago? His mind presented an image of Liz leaving him outside the café; of him reading his phone. Three weeks had passed since then? He looked beyond through the window into the garden as if any changes in the trees would give him a clue about how much time had gone by. But there was no sign he could interpret. Three weeks would put them into August.

He looked from one woman to the other. Martie was wearing an expression that was four parts concern and six parts pissed-off. Donna, despite her ever-present smile was also showing signs of worry.

'Last I saw you, you were working on a bit of a tan,' said Donna. 'You look like you've turned into a vampire now.'

'You could also do with a plate full of doughnuts,' Martie said looking at his non-existent belly.

'You know how I get when I've got a job on. Everything else fades,' Ran replied.

The sudden appearance of these two women was giving him a strange sense of dislocation. Like two different worlds were being brought together. He took a deep breath in an attempt to adjust and felt like he was a diver returning to the surface from a long way down.

And then he thought of *her* and his longing. It was a coil in his jaw muscles. A hitch in his gut. It seasoned everything his mind touched. Since the night she accused him of betraying her, of thinking about other women, she had been absent. And not since his parents died had he felt an absence like that. He tried to fix his expression before it betrayed his thoughts, but he wasn't quick enough for Donna.

'I've seen that look before,' she nodded slowly. 'There's been a woman. She dumped your scruffy arse and now you're feeling sorry for yourself.'

'What? No,' Ran replied, leaning back in his chair and crossing his arms.

Martie tutted. 'Of course.' She looked at Donna. 'You're right.' She reached across the table and patted Ranald's arm. 'Whoever she is, she's not worth it.'

Ranald moved his arm out of her reach. 'That wasn't patronising in the least, Martie.'

But if anyone could read him it was these two. Feeling hot, he pushed his chair away from the table and crossed his legs.

'That's not it at all,' he said. 'Work's just taken its toll on me these last few weeks.'

Donna sniffed the air sharply as if taking in a noxious smell. 'What's that?' she said and looked at Martie. 'I smell pants that are on fire.'

'I smell bullshit,' said Martie. The two women grinned at each other. Now that they could see Ranald was alive and functioning they were relaxing.

'Christ, you two are like a double act.'

'Dumb and dumber,' said Martie.

'Hinge and Brackett,' said Donna.

Ranald enjoyed the good humour between them and felt a slight easing of his spirits. He stood up. 'How about a tour of the place? Martie's seen most of it, but you've not seen it at all, Donna.'

Donna got to her feet. 'Thought you'd never suggest it.' She walked over to him and studied his t-shirt. 'That stain there looks like Brazil.'

Martie joined her. 'And that one looks like a wee boat in profile.'

'Maybe it's some kind of sign? You're going on a trip, Ran.'

'Aye,' said Martie. 'Who needs tea leaves? This one – coffee? – looks like a shower head.'

'Yup,' agreed Donna. 'I think there's a wash in your immediate future.'

Ranald threw his hands up. 'Right. Okay,' he smiled, realising he hadn't used those muscles too much recently. 'A shower and a change. Then I'll give you guys the tour.'

†⊦

Sometime later, having walked through most of the house and gardens, they were back in the kitchen, nursing another coffee.

'Well,' said Donna as she sat back in her chair, 'isn't this something?'

'Did you ever find out more about your great-uncle?' Martie asked.

'Not really. I found some notebooks full of quotes and stuff that must have meant something to him. And I came across some poems he wrote. But not much about the man himself.'

Martie leaned forwards, rested her chin on both palms and lightly drummed on her lips with her fingers. 'This is great, eh? But he might have done more for you while he was still alive.'

'All those years you were struggling…' said Donna.

Ranald made a face. 'I get it, though. I'd been brought up in a working-class home. All of this coming to me after my parents died? It might have gone to my head. Sent me off the rails.'

'Aye, cos you're totally together now, eh?' Martie said with more than a hint of sarcasm.

Donna fired a warning look at her. 'Whatever his thinking was,' she said to Ran, 'he came good in the end.' She raised her coffee mug. 'Here's to you, Great-Uncle Alexander.'

Ranald smiled at Donna.

Donna winked back, and looked around the room as if judging where it was in relation to the rest of the space she'd been walking through. 'Is there more?' she asked, sitting upright in her chair. 'I could see a kind of tower thing when I was out in the garden. It would have been right above here.' She looked at the ceiling.

'Aye,' said Ranald. 'I keep forgetting about the other wing of the house.'

'Get you,' said Martie. '"Wing of the house."'

They all laughed, the women both savouring Ranald's good fortune, without the slightest suggestion of envy. For a moment Ranald felt blessed for having them in his life.

'Don't know why,' he said. 'But I've barely spent any time in that part of the house. The library, the kitchen and the pool are enough for me really.'

'What's above us, then?' asked Donna.

'The floor directly above us is where my grandmother had her rooms. The next floor up is old servants' quarters. Above that is the tower room.'

'Cool,' Donna said. 'Lead on Macduff.'

Both women stood, and Martie said to Donna, 'There's a lovely sitting room up there. Wait till you see it. The rest is a bit too grand for my tastes.'

'Tell you what,' said Ran. He rubbed at his eyes, suddenly feeling exhausted. Perhaps because he had mostly been on his own, the ladies were too much for him. He didn't want to be rude and tell them to leave, but perhaps a little break from them would help? 'I'm done with the whole tour-guide thing. Martie knows the way. Why don't you guys go for a look yourselves?'

They nodded at each other. 'Sure,' said Martie.

They left the room and Ranald walked to the kitchen window and stared out into the garden, probing his thoughts for a sense of *her*, like a tongue brushing against a chipped tooth.

Would she be jealous that these two women were here? There was no need. His relationship with both was platonic.

Might it drive her further away? For longer? He sent his thoughts to her: *Missing you,* he said. He felt the ache of it.

Nothing.

He groaned and leaned against the sink. Then he pushed himself away from it again. Enough, he told himself. Two of his favourite people were here, he should go and be with them. Feeling a surge of energy, he made his way through to the stairs that led to his grandmother's rooms. Halfway up the stairs he heard low voices and became aware they were talking on the landing just ahead of him. He heard his name.

He stopped and pressed himself against the wall.

'…I'm so worried about him, Donna.'

'This has been a big adjustment for him, honey,' Donna said. 'He'll come out of it fine.'

A pause, and he imagined Martie shaking her head. 'I had to have him committed the last time he was like this.' A sniff as if she was fighting back tears. 'I can't do that again. He hates me as it is.'

'He doesn't hate you, Martie. And it won't come to that. Once he deals with all of this, the old Ranald McGhie will be back. Better than ever. You just wait and see.'

'Did he ever tell you he was the one who found his parents?'

Silence. He hadn't. And he imagined the look of shock on Donna's face. Ranald crept up another couple of stairs so he could hear better.

'Thing is, Ran just retreated from everything. He couldn't handle it – and who could blame him? And there was no one else, so I had to help see to all the formalities. We'd only been going out for about six months and I was left with … this. I don't know how I coped with it all.'

Ranald sagged against the wall, pinned there by the immensity of his guilt. He really was a worthless excuse for a human being. How could he have left poor Martie to deal with all of that?

Another big black tick on the shame chart.

'Fortunately, this lawyer guy turned up…' Ranald perked up. 'Said he was from his mother's family and he would pay for the funerals and arrange to sort out all of their personal effects, so that was a huge help.'

What? Why didn't he know this? Was she talking about Quinn?

'He was a very old man,' Martie continued. 'Truth is I thought he was far too old to still be working as a lawyer.' She paused. 'And now that I think about it, with Ran looking so thin and with his hair like that … maybe the man I met wasn't a lawyer at all. Maybe it was…'

Alexander? thought Ranald.

There was a long pause. And then Donna spoke, and Ranald could hear the tenderness in her voice.

'Aww, honey, don't upset yourself.'

'It's this house. Being here. It's somehow bringing it all back.'

There were some shushing noises from Donna.

'Then it all got a bit … murky. That's the only word I can think of to describe it. And of course I couldn't say anything to Ran, he was in a mess…'

'What happened?'

'The old lawyer guy swore me to secrecy. Even tried to pay me off. I used the money he gave me to get a private therapist for Ranald…'

That's how that happened. He'd gone to the doctor, prompted by Martie, but the doctor told him there was a six-month waiting list, at least, for that kind of service. And then suddenly, he had an appointment. Then followed years of sessions, sitting with a very large woman who kept pressing him, without success, to talk about his parents.

Why hadn't Martie told him any of this?

'This old guy must have had a lot of money, and a lot of powerful friends.'

'Why do you say that?'

'Oh, Jesus, I've held this in for all these years…'

For crying out loud, Martie, he wanted to shout, *what was it?* It was all he could do not to run up the stairs and force the words out of her.

'The official version was that it was a double suicide, some sort of lovers' pact. They said that Ranald's mother's state had become so desperate that she'd killed herself, and his dad found her, and full of grief swallowed all of her remaining pills.'

'And that's not what happened?' asked Donna.

'I was there when the post-mortem verdict was delivered. Just me and the old guy … The doctor who did the post mortem was some kind of family friend. They were suspiciously pally – him and the old guy – and suddenly I was asked to leave the room and told to forget everything that I'd just heard.'

'And what did you hear?'

'No,' murmured Ranald. He clasped his hand over his mouth. No. He didn't want to hear this. But he was frozen solid. Unable to move.

'His dad was the first to die. And from the contents of his stomach they were able to tell that he'd been *fed* a fatal dose of drugs with his evening meal, and then…'

Oh, dear God, thought Ranald. He caught an image of his mother at the stove. Dad never cooked a meal in his life.

'Donna, I can never forgive myself. I've kept this back from Ranald all of these years.'

'But you did it with the best of intentions, Martie.'

'I did, and I hate myself for it, Donna.' Martie paused. 'But when's the right time to tell your damaged boyfriend that his mum killed his dad before she killed herself?'

20

Ranald was back in the kitchen when they walked back in, sitting on a chair, cross-legged, as if he'd hadn't moved since they left. He kept his hands in his pockets to hide the trembling.

They looked at him, but their eyes were back in the rooms upstairs.

'Absolutely fascinating,' said Donna.

'It's like stepping back in time,' agreed Martie.

Ranald gave her a taut smile, and she cocked her head to the side as if she couldn't read its purpose. He was saying, without speaking, *I heard you, I know everything, and I understand but I don't know if I'm capable of forgiving you. Or myself.*

That he'd given her this burden was surely the greater sin.

'So, that was your great-grandmother's space?' asked Donna. 'And your great-uncle Alexander had the wing at the front?'

'Did Alexander ever marry?' asked Martie.

'Not as far as I know,' replied Ranald.

'Your grandmother had your mum, Helen—'

'Turns out her real name was Helena,' Ranald interrupted, aware that his mouth was soured with a bitter taste. This was all becoming too much. He needed them to leave.

'Your gran have any other kids?' asked Donna.

'Yeah, William. He had two kids, Rebecca and Marcus,' Ranald replied, thinking, *Go, please go.*

'You met them?' asked Martie. 'What was it like to find out you had this other family?'

'Interesting,' said Ranald. It was the best he could come up with.

Please just go.

Martie tutted. 'You're one of them now, Ran.'

Donna's eyes narrowed. 'These cousins of yours, I wonder how happy they were when they found out about you. All this –' she looked around '– they must've thought it was going to them.'

'They must have been shocked,' said Martie.

'Aye.' Donna leaned forwards. 'Family intrigue. This house must be worth a couple of million at least. Bet when the old fella was on his deathbed they were counting the pennies.'

'If they were, too bad. They got stuff. I got the house. It's all about the library, apparently. Alexander wanted his books protected.'

'The whole house is like a library,' said Donna as she looked over at a couple of bookshelves in the kitchen that, unsurprisingly, contained cook books.

'Except the rooms above here,' said Martie. 'Now that I think about it, I don't think I saw a single book.'

Her tone prompted a rebuke from Donna.

'A lack of books doesn't make you a bad person,' she said.

'Yes, it does,' Martie and Ranald said at exactly the same time, and he was relieved that his mask was back in place.

'We need to have a movie night soon,' Donna said. 'I'd love the chance to get a good rake through his film collection.'

'There are so many classics up there you wouldn't believe it,' said Ranald.

They settled into a few moments of silence before Donna finished her coffee and placed the empty mug on the table.

Please leave.

'I think our work here is done, Martie,' she said. 'I detect a positive change in Mr McGhie since we arrived.'

Ranald breathed, felt the air flow as if down to his toes. He'd managed to fool them both. He exhaled and, dragging up some last ounces of vigour, he smiled. He worked hard to make it as genuine as possible.

'Yes,' said Martie. 'I believe the intervention has worked.'

They phoned a taxi from the library and then walked to the front of the house to wait.

When it arrived, after kisses and hugs and promises of more visits in the very near future, Martie ran to the car.

Donna paused however, reached a hand out and took a grip of his forearm. 'See all that stoic man stuff – it's total rubbish, Ran. I can see through your act. If you need someone to talk to, give us a shout, eh?' She gave him a little smile, her eyes deep wells of sympathy. 'There's folk here that care about you.'

Throat tight with emotion, he didn't trust his voice enough to speak; he could only nod his head in response.

Message delivered, Donna took a step back, turned and walked quickly to the taxi. The car then drove off and Ranald was left alone on his doorstep.

He stepped back into the house and closed the door. Then he turned and slid down the wood until his legs were spread out in front of him. They'd left just in time. He had no idea how he could have kept that performance going.

The maw of the house yawned in front of him. He unfocused his eyes and looked out into the cave-like gloom. Furniture, doors, stairs, windows, all of it blended into wraiths and shadows and whispers. None of it held meaning. All of it held threat. He was real once, and now he was falling, falling, falling into a deep shaft. His lips felt swollen, his throat constricted, his limbs encased in concrete.

He was upside down.

He was wearing his organs on the outside of his skin.

A black snake was sliding across the wooden floor towards him, risen from a swamp, and the house shivered in anticipation of its bite.

21

He didn't remember making it back up to his bedroom, but he did remember standing by the window, thinking he should open it and jump out. But it took less energy to move across the room to his bed, so that's where he went.

⊤⊢

He was unsure how long he was there. It was certainly days, but how many, he couldn't count. All he knew was that he was weak with hunger and that he had a good length of stubble on his chin. Dragging himself up, he managed to shower, shave, and eat something.

In the kitchen, having established some sort of normality, his mind finally began to filter through what he had overheard.

Dad.

His dad hadn't abandoned him after all.

He had always known his mother was unwell, and great though her loss was, there was an explanation for it. Difficult as they were to process, her actions could be understood. But that his father had also chosen to abandon him had been a way more difficult idea to bear.

Now, he didn't have that to worry about. But that relief was tainted with the knowledge that his mother had killed his father. The news left him reeling.

Why would she do something like that? He knew paranoia was a frighteningly real aspect of bipolar for sufferers, having been there himself. Had his mother become convinced that his father was somehow a danger to her?

Or perhaps, desperate need to end her own torment, and knowing how much he loved her, she decided to take him over to the other side with her to save him from living through that bereavement?

Jesus.

He should know better than to try and rationalise the irrational thoughts of someone in that manic phase.

But there was another thought he had to lock down. If that was what his mother was capable of, was the son …?

This house. He looked around at the thick walls. The Fitzpatricks. He was one of them, and whatever set his mother on that path was part of him.

As if in search of answers to questions he couldn't begin to articulate, Ranald made his way along the corridor and up the dark, narrow staircase to his grandmother's wing.

The previous time he'd been here he'd heard Martie tell Donna the truth about his parents. The memory of her admission was almost enough to make him sag to the floor. Just in time, he stuck a hand out and bolstered himself against the oak bannister. From there he lowered himself onto the top step and took a breath. Poor Martie, what had she done to deserve him?

Then he felt a moment of panic. When he'd been in the hospital, the nurses and doctors had taken his full history – spent a lot of time asking about his mother. The word 'suicide' had hung in the air above every conversation. But *now* – now he knew she was a murderer – not just a suicide victim. How might that knowledge have affected his treatment? Surely that would have been important. Had his team missed out on a vital piece of information that would have improved his chances of a full recovery? That would have meant he would now be more stable?

That Martie would never have left him…?

Enough. Stop, he told himself. *Breath.* There was nothing that could be done now to change any of that.

He heard a noise. His head whipped round. It came from the end of the corridor to his left. Everything told him to go back downstairs to the safety of the library, to hide himself behind the wall of spines.

But he found himself getting to his feet and walking carefully along towards the sound.

There was a small window at the end, bracketed by rich brocade curtains that tumbled to the floor. The light coming in through the glass was weakened by the branch of a giant tree that was in heavy leaf. He examined the window. There was nothing to suggest the noise had come from here.

He turned to his side. This door then?

He placed a hand on the wood as if that might transmit something of what was inside. Listened. Got nothing. With care, he reached for the handle, turned it and pushed the door open.

This was a much smaller room, and although the furniture was solid, it was much more basic. A single bed had been pushed against the far wall, dressed in a plain, navy-blue bedspread and pillows. A desk sat under a window. He stretched his neck and could see that, if someone was sitting at this desk, they would have a good view of the gardens. He moved closer and looked down to the left; from this vantage point he recognised the patio that was just outside the pool conservatory.

Looking around the room, the furniture set was completed by a chair and a wardrobe that looked like it was a smaller cousin to the one in his grandmother's bedroom.

A door was tucked into the far corner of the room, by the window. Something caught his eye on the glass. A small crack and a blot of blood. Had some poor bird just flown against it? That must have been what he just heard. He let out a sigh, suddenly realising he had been holding his breath in anticipation. There was always a reason, he reminded himself. No need to go scaring himself.

He opened the door to see a small bathroom with the same type of dated fittings as the other bathroom on this floor.

He turned from the door and surveyed the room. Was this a servant's quarters? Did his grandmother have her own maid? Or would that have been his great-grandmother. They lived in a grander style back in those days.

He moved over to the chair by the bed and realised with a start that it was the same chair as the one in the lift. Standing in front of it, he felt a mix of anxiety and anticipation. He sat down and closed his eyes.

After just a brief moment, he felt her ease herself onto his lap. Her head lay on his shoulder. Her hand sliding into his.

Her words in his ear.

'You came, my love.'

22

It felt like he'd been hidden away for so long in Newton Hall, and so altered by the things he'd learned and his time there, that when he did venture back into the city he was somehow convinced that everything there would have changed. And yet, here he was, in the real world, in Quinn's office just off Gordon Street, and it was exactly the same as the last time he'd been here. He found himself constantly touching things to check if they were solid, not imaginary.

How long ago had it been since he last visited? A couple of months? Was that all?

A gust of wind and rain hit the window as if aimed there by a powerful hose.

'This weather?' said Ranald to fill the silence, adding a smile after he mentally checked that his mask was in place. He felt a sudden urge to go up to the glass and press himself against it, as if the rain outside would somehow reach him and dampen the heat in his brain and heart. She was back and he wanted nothing more than to be in Newton Hall with her. Being here, he felt too far from her.

'Very autumnal, yes,' Quinn said as if impatient to begin. 'Thank you for coming in, Mr McGhie.' Quinn's tone was at odds with his words. 'I would have come out to the house … but I have to charge the trust for more time when I do it that way. I'm sure you understand.'

Ranald offered him a smile, hoping that it was convincing. 'S'fine, Mr Quinn. Time's money and all that.' He realised he was staring, and turned his face away.

'Quite.' Quinn pushed an open folder across the desk to Ranald and offered him a pen.

Ranald took the pen, felt the weight of it and looked down at the document in front of him. 'What am I signing?' An ant crawled across the page. He slammed a hand down on it, so hard that Quinn sat back.

'An ant,' Ran explained, but when he looked at the paper it was perfectly clean. No squashed bug.

Quinn coughed and focused on the papers. 'This transfers the car into Daniel Hackett's ownership, as per your request.'

The use of Danny's full name threw Ranald momentarily. 'Ah, right. The car.' He'd almost forgotten he'd done that. He scribbled his name in the place provided, aware of the slight shaking of his hand as he wrote.

'And there are some … ah … other papers for the trust. You are required to be a trustee and you need to accept your position by signing here.' Quinn flicked off the top page and with a long and surprisingly lined finger indicated where Ranald should sign.

He did so.

Feeling strangely reluctant to leave the man's company, despite how obvious it was that Quinn had little time for him, he anxiously sifted through his mind for a question. A moment ago he had been anxious to go home, and now he didn't want to leave.

'What can you tell me about my grandmother and my great-uncle?'

Quinn pulled the papers towards him and closed the file. 'I'm not sure I'm the one to ask. I am the family lawyer, not chief gossipmonger.' He flicked a smile at Ranald.

'Oh, come now,' said Ranald and wondered at his use of such an old-fashioned phrase. 'It's perfectly understandable that I might be curious about a family I never knew I had.'

'Why not give Marcus a call?'

'The impression I got from him was that he'd rather not spend any more time in my company.'

'That's not quite fair, Mr McGhie. I've always found Marcus Fitz-patrick to be a perfectly amenable chap.'

'To the family lawyer, perhaps. Not to the prodigal child. What does my cousin Marcus do, by the way?'

'He's a lawyer for a prestigious Edinburgh firm.'

Ranald leaned forwards in his chair, tucking his hands under his thighs, hoping that he didn't look too desperate. He needed to dig more into his family's past. There was so much that he needed to know. Why was he the way he was? Did the reason lie in the family tree? This man obviously knew something, why didn't he just answer the question? He decided that being direct was his best option.

'My grandmother took over her mother's rooms in the house. Isn't it unusual for siblings to share a house like that?'

'Not in families like yours – with such large houses. Your great-uncle never married. Your grandfather died while Helena and William were very young. The family investments hadn't yet recovered after the war so it was felt more prudent for everyone to remain living in the house. An elegant solution was worked out. Everyone was content.'

'Alexander never married?'

'There is one piece of the family story that I do feel permitted to share, Mr McGhie.' Quinn leaned forwards, a light now shining in his eyes. And Ranald had the distinct impression Quinn was a gossip, despite his protests.

'There was a scandal concerning your great-uncle. Just before he set off for the war…'

'He was in the war?'

'He had a posting in London, doing some admin type of thing … Initially. Then to everyone's apparent surprise, he actually sought out some front-line position. Not many did that when they had a cushy number.'

'And the scandal?'

'You have to remember this was a different age. Fine society in Glasgow in those days had barely moved on since the Victorian age. A young woman died. Anyway, the family kept it all hush hush because they were terrified of the possibility of scandal. It all calmed down when Alexander went off to war.' Quinn shook his head. Then, as if remembering who he was and who he was talking to, he sat up in his chair and brought his arms in to his sides, drawing himself back in.

'My next client will be here shortly, Mr McGhie…' He stood up.

Ranald got to his feet, his mind whirring with this new information.

Quinn escorted him to the door of his office and put a hand on his shoulder. 'Give Marcus an opportunity to prove you wrong, Mr McGhie. He is family, after all.'

'There's more to family than shared genetic material, Mr Quinn. That day you visited, Marcus made it quite clear how much interest he had in the new member of the family.' He nodded. 'Good day.'

7⊢

He'd taken the train into the city centre, and leaving the lawyer's office he walked back to Central Station, head hunched into his shoulders as if that might reduce the impact of the rain. He was just in time for the next train and took a seat in the first carriage with relief. Speaking to the lawyer, pretending to be human, had really taken it out of him.

Someone sat opposite him, by the window. He raised his eyes and saw that it was *War and Peace* girl – Suzy. As he looked for a book, she pulled one from her large handbag. It was *The Girl on the Train*.

She saw him and smiled. 'Nearly didn't recognise you with all that hair.' She gestured at his head. Then followed his gaze to her book and laughed. 'Girl on the train reads *The Girl on the Train*.' She shrugged. 'Does that make me a cliché?'

He nodded. 'How did you get on with *War and Peace*?'

'I finished it,' she said with a big grin.

'Congratulations.'

She gave a small bow.

The train moved off and a mother huffed into the space between them, along with her two young children. Whatever energy had been starting to build between Ranald and Suzy dissipated. She opened her book and began to read.

Ranald took his notebook from his pocket and, opening it at a new page, noted down the gossip from Quinn. Then he closed his eyes. Last time he'd written anything in here it had been like he was channelling Alexander. Should he have another attempt?

He began to write, allowed himself to scribble any old nonsense at first.

He looked over at Suzy, but her eyes were locked onto the page of her book.

He dropped his shoulders and closed his eyes again. The house appeared before his mind's eye. He opened his eyes again and began writing:

The rain hides the house behind a squall of rain.
The door slams and birds scatter like seeds shot
from a blunderbuss into the fertile air.
Disappointment contains itself to a grunt, a moan,
a blemish of brown.

He paused and read over his words. There was no sense in them whatsoever. So much for that idea. The train slowed to a stop and Suzy stood up, making ready to leave. He was so caught up in his thoughts he almost failed to realise it was his stop too.

He jumped up and got off the train just in time, and he and Suzy walked almost side by side along the platform and out of the station. With every step, Ranald debated whether or not he should ask if she wanted to join him for a coffee. And with every other step he told himself she would only say no.

She walked over to a small red Ford parked outside the station.

'Bye,' she said and ducked inside.

Fool, Ranald said to himself. *You're a fool.*

'Hi.'

He looked up.

She had stepped back out of her car, an uncertain smile on her face. 'I'm just heading to the café at the Cross for a wee coffee. If that's where you're going I can give you a lift.'

'Am I that predictable?' Ranald asked, walking towards her car.

'I'm Suzy, by the way,' she said as he got into the passenger's side and buckled up. 'In case you forgot.'

'I hadn't.' He had. 'I'm Ranald.'

'Nice to meet you, Ranald. Great name. Very Scottish. And a good combination with an Irish surname.' She put the car in gear and drove to the car park exit.

Ranald turned to look at her. Irish surname? 'My surname's McGhie, which is solidly Scottish.'

'Oh.' She looked surprised. 'I thought you were one of the Fitzpatricks.'

'Where did you hear that?' he said and instantly regretted the defensive tone in his voice.

She made an apologetic face. 'Sorry. In many ways Bearsden is really just a wee village. The waitress in the café…'

'I am a Fitzpatrick, kinda. The one that got away and then got pulled back in. But my surname's McGhie.'

'Sorry. I must sound like a total gossip.' She braked as she approached a T-junction and took a left.

As she did so, Ranald spotted a barber shop and made a mental note. It was high time he got the mop on his head sorted.

'I've a secret wee parking place,' Suzy said as they approached the Cross, aiming a wink at him.

'The benefit of being a real local instead of an incomer.'

'If you're an original Fitzpatrick, you're not really an incomer, are you?'

He chewed on that. 'Do you think people will give me the benefit of the doubt, then?' And after asking that he worried it might make him look pathetic.

'I think people are … curious.'

'Ah, right. So what are the gossips saying?'

'My mum knew your mum.' Suzy paused. 'Not that my mum's a gossip.' She made a face. 'Says she was a couple of years above her at the academy. Doesn't remember too much about her, to be honest. Said she was nice.'

Ranald nodded. That was what people did to show that they were listening, wasn't it?

'And everyone was impressed she ran away with the artist guy and gave up on all that money.'

That artist guy.

Dad.

Ranald felt his breath shorten. He saw his parents again in that bed, but this time with the knowledge of how they had ended up there. A noise sounded in his throat, like a throttled hiccup. Then he felt a flare of panic. He needed to get out of here. He put his hand out to the door and scrabbled at the handle.

'Sorry, Suzy. Could you just let me off? I've just remembered I need to…'

'Oh, right,' she said in a small voice, looking disappointed.

'It's not…' Ran began and shook his head unable to form a complete sentence. The thoughts of his parents began to wind round new thoughts about Alexander and the supposed scandal he'd been involved in. Brows would have been fevered as that situation was discussed and dissected. Reading between the lines, Alexander had not only signed up for a war, but had avoided any relationship with women for the rest of his life, because of the kind of small-town mentality Suzy was highlighting. Ranald felt claustrophobic at the idea of it. 'Could you just…' He looked ahead. 'Right here will do.' He tapped loudly on the dashboard. 'Please.'

She drew in to the side of the road. He opened the door.

'Thanks for the lift,' he said, without looking at her he jumped out.

⌐⌐

Such was his need to get away from Suzy, his movement along the road was half walk, half run. Almost out of breath he slowed up and found that he was outside the barber's he had seen from her car.

He'd said to himself he'd have a haircut, hadn't he? That's what normal, everyday people did. He needed to be normal and everyday.

He read the sign above the door – Dan and Stan's. Heart still thumping and breath still short, he pushed it open with a jangle. All the heads inside turned towards him and Ran felt himself shrink from their judgement, then they all went back to whatever they were doing – watching TV, reading newspapers, cutting hair. Both chairs were occupied, two barbers standing beside their customers. Another three men waited on the bench along the wall. Everything was calm. He was safe. The smell of the products and quiet buzz of the clippers was almost soothing.

'Have a seat, mate,' said the barber closest to the window. 'It's goin' like a fair the day.'

Two of the men on the bench bunched closer together to create space for Ranald to sit down. He nodded his thanks, sat and leaned back against the wall, crossing his arms as if that would diminish his presence. He was the son of a murderer. Did someone in this room know it? Did everyone? He shook himself and tried to focus on something other than his thoughts.

Both of the barbers had cropped grey hair. One had a full lumberjack beard and was skinny, while the other was clean-shaven and looked like he spent a lot of time in the gym.

Ranald worked out from the conversation that the muscular guy was Dan and guessed that his thin colleague must be Stan. The latter cut his customer's hair in silence while Dan kept up a monologue that was funny and camp and interspersed weirdly into the corrosive chatter in Ranald's head.

The word loser was still being chanted in his mind when he felt a nudge from the old man beside him. 'On you go, son. I've got all day. You've probably got a thousand more exciting things to do than me.'

'Hey,' said Ranald and took the seat in front of Dan.

'You're new,' said Dan, sizing him up.

'Just moved in.'

Dan stood behind him and looked down at his hair. 'Did they no' have barbers where you came from?' Wink. Then a smile. 'Just pulling your leg.' He began to run his fingers through Ranald's hair, pulling the strands high off his head, measuring where the cuts might be placed. 'What you for havin'? Want to keep it longish? Want to go soldier-boy crew cut?'

'Leave the man alone,' said Stan. His voice was deep, as if he grated his voice box every morning and smoked cigars of an evening. 'He's new. You need to break him in gently.'

'Oh, I'll break him in gently awright,' said Dan as he stood back, crossed his massive arms and studied Ranald's hair.

Ranald gave a shrug. He'd only ever gone into the barber's for a trim. And it usually ended up in the same formless cut. In the mirror he caught sight of a line of framed photographs on the far wall. Headshots of young men with a variety of styles, but he felt unable to suggest what Dan could do to his hair. It was suddenly beyond him to make this simple choice.

'Just whatever you think,' Ranald said.

'Short back and sides. Long layers on top,' said Dan as he fingered Ranald's hair. 'That will suit your face shape and that strong, masculine jaw.'

'Don't be fooled, mate,' Stan shouted over. 'When we leave here at night, he's as butch as a builder.'

'How very dare you,' said Dan. 'I've got a reputation to live down to, here.' He picked up the protective cape, placed it round Ran's shoulders and got to work.

Ran closed his eyes and focused all his attention on stopping himself jumping up and running out, still wearing the cape and his hair half cut.

A while later, the job was done and mirror was presented to the back of Ranald's head so he could nod and accept Dan's handiwork.

When Dan whipped off the cape, Ranald rubbed at the back of his neck. It had been a while since the skin there was bare to the air.

'Thanks,' said Ranald. 'What do I owe you?'

He paid at the till and included a generous tip.

Dan winked his thanks. 'You're the new boy in Newton Hall, aren't you?' he asked. And before Ranald could confirm the fact he continued: 'You settling in all right?'

'Aye, fine.' Ranald turned to fetch his jacket.

'Shame you don't have that long to enjoy the place, eh?'

Ranald swung back round in surprise. 'What do you mean?'

'Well, I thought…' Dan looked taken aback by Ranald's reaction. 'Or, I should say, I *heard* that when the old boy died the family were going to sell to a developer who was going to turn the place into luxury flats.'

So, everyone in the town *was* gossiping about him. 'You heard wrong,' said Ranald. 'I inherited it from the old boy and the family trust stipulates that the house and the library are to remain intact.'

'Shame,' said Stan. 'I heard one of the other big houses up your way went through something similar. The owners made millions.'

Ranald bit down on his irritation and left the shop without another word.

He was already a few steps along the road when he heard a voice behind him.

'Haud oan, son. I'm trying to have a word with you here.'

He stopped and turned. It was the old man who'd let him go for a haircut before him. And only then did he realise he was the old man he'd bumped into outside the house on his first day there. He hadn't recognised him without the flat cap.

'So you *are* one of the Fitzpatricks,' the man said, rubbing the back of his neck, as if annoyed the barber hadn't got rid of all of the hair clippings. 'Now that you've got that haircut…' He studied Ranald's face for a moment. 'Aye. I can see him in you. I used to see

Alexander tripping around the town like he owned it. Bit of a prick, to be honest.'

Ranald wanted to defend his uncle; instead he hunched his shoulders and pushed his hands deeper into his pockets.

'Once he got back from the army he was a different guy. But as a younger man he was up his own arse.'

'That's an accusation that could be aimed at any one of us, Mr…'

'Welsh. Ken Welsh.' He offered Ranald his hand.

'Ranald.'

They shook.

'Aye…' Ken began to walk along the pavement in the direction of the Cross, so Ranald kept pace with him. 'So they managed to rein you back in?'

'They did,' Ranald answered, wondering where he was going with that comment.

'I wonder how your mum would feel about that.'

Wanting to tell him to mind his own business, Ranald said, 'I knew nothing about her family growing up, so I had no reason not to accept the place when it was offered to me.'

A hearse drove past. An arrangement of flowers read "Son" on top of the coffin. The car that followed was a long, sleek limousine. Three people with black jackets and short white hair sat in the back, staring straight ahead. Ranald looked from the car to Ken Welsh and back again. He seemed to pay it no attention. Hadn't he seen it?

'True, son. True.' Ken slowly shook his head. 'Good job we don't know what's in front of us, eh?' He raised his eyebrows, signalling he *had* seen the car. So, it wasn't just in Ranald's mind.

'It's a small place this,' Ken went on. 'Folk have got long memories. Best not stir them up again.'

'What's that supposed to mean?' Ranald could barely contain his frustration now. He felt like shaking the old man, insisting that if he had something to say he should just say it.

'Your mum was in my niece's year at school. She was a nice lass. Not stuck-up like the rest of your family. I'm surprised she didn't leave you something to explain…' Ken slowed down as he reached a small Ford. He put his hand in his pocket and pulled out a set of keys.

'Why don't *you* explain, Mr Welsh?'

'Not my place, son.' He opened his car door. 'Not my place.'

⊥⊦

Back at the house, Ranald made straight for the pool. He didn't really have the energy, but it was a good habit and one he should try to maintain.

As he swam he fought to contain the mash of anxiety in his head and reviewed his meeting with Quinn, feeling a little pleasure at the way he'd handled the man. Aim for small victories, his psychiatrist once advised. His thoughts soon turned to Dan the barber and his take on the gossip about the house. If he sold it off as Dan suggested, and the trust made millions on the deal, how much might his slice be?

He swam a couple of lengths of the pool in a daydream, fanta-sising about what he could do with that amount of money. As he touched the wall of the pool and turned, though, he realised that, materially, he already had everything he had ever wanted. So, what would be the point of selling up? And wouldn't he be betraying Alex-ander if he did such a thing?

Considering poor old Alexander led Ranald quickly to the 'scandal' Quinn had mentioned. How could he find out what that was? And what about Ken Welsh? What the hell was that all about? Why hadn't he just come out and said what was on his mind?

He dived under the water, and as he resurfaced, the image of Suzy just before he got out of her car came to him; her crestfallen expres-sion. She was worried she had offended him. Everyone he'd spoken to that day had shared some sort of gossip about his family with him. He'd felt annoyed, panicked, even.

Perhaps the idea that Alexander had fled the country because of all the talk was something he could identify with; he'd certainly had his fill of gossips today. And how sad was it that Alexander had withdrawn from society and never met another woman?

He made another turn at the end of the pool. He should have asked Suzy for her number. Then he could have phoned her, told her he was an idiot and not to pay any attention to his strange moods. He should be fostering any friendships he could, not turning people away. No wonder he had no friends.

Tired from the swim, he climbed out and lay on one of the loungers. He began to feel drowsy and considered getting dressed and doing some work, but he couldn't be bothered. And yet the rest of the day and evening stretched ahead of him like a featureless landscape. Not for the first time he wondered at his own capacity for acting in his own worst interest. Work was surely the best antidote for loneliness, but here he was avoiding it, wallowing in his feelings of isolation.

His breathing slowed as he felt his body relaxing into sleep.

And what seemed like a moment later, *she* was there.

But this time she was snarling. Her teeth were large and sharp and stained with blood, ribbons of flesh stuck between them.

Ranald jumped up, out of his sleep, shouting a horrified 'No!' Adrenaline was sparking in his every cell.

'Again, you betray me,' he heard.

And then she receded. Her absence as final as a door being slammed.

And despite his revulsion at what looked like pieces of raw meat hanging from her mouth, he couldn't help but send out the message to her: *Please, no. I need you here.*

23

He heard the front doorbell ringing in the distance.

'I'm coming,' he shouted, although there was no way anyone at the door could hear him. Without bothering to make sure he was completely dry, he stepped into his boxers and jeans and pulled his t-shirt over his head. As he walked towards the door he tucked it into his waistband. But when he got to the door and saw who it was, he wished he hadn't bothered.

'Marcus,' he said, with false bonhomie. 'How nice to see you again.'

Marcus held his left arm out as if to highlight he had company. 'My sister Rebecca.'

She was a small, thin woman with short black hair and was wearing heavy-framed dark spectacles. Her eyes met Ranald's and as she hitched the gold link chain of her handbag over her shoulder she offered him a tight smile.

Marcus stepped inside and held his right hand out. He was wearing a dark suit, white shirt and blue tie, and was carrying a briefcase. He looked like he'd just stepped out of a boardroom. 'We were just passing and thought we would pop in,' he said, marching over to the reception room.

'How nice of you,' said Ranald, shaking Marcus's hand while wondering how quickly he could get rid of them. Rebecca was yet to utter a word. 'I'm kind of in the middle of something...' But he had no choice other than to trudge after Marcus into the reception room. He found him at the far end, already bent over, examining the drinks cabinet.

Marcus straightened up, holding out the bottle of malt whisky. 'A wee snifter, old boy?'

'Help yourself,' said Ranald, certain, however, that his sarcastic tone was lost on his cousin.

Marcus poured generous measures into a couple of glasses. 'Are you on the whisky or gin these days, sis?'

'I'll have what you're having,' she murmured and took a seat.

'Slainte,' Marcus said as he handed round the drinks.

The two men joined Rebecca over on the sofas.

'You were just passing…' Ranald began, leaving a pause for Marcus to fill.

But Marcus appeared not to notice. Instead he held the glass to his lip and took a generous mouthful. 'Old Alexander certainly knew his way round the whisky barrels.'

Ranald sipped his, feeling the drink harsh against the back of his throat. He coughed and felt himself flush a little with embarrassment. And then felt stupid. Why was he worried that this might seem less than manly? What did he care what Marcus thought of him?

He sat back in the sofa, aiming for a relaxed pose, lifting his right foot so it rested on his left knee, stretched his left arm along the low back of the sofa and took another sip. As he did so he tried to get more of a sense of his cousins and their experience of this house. Was it just bricks and mortar to them? Did they see nothing that he did?

'You're looking well,' said Marcus, looking at him as if for the first time. Then he added, 'Apart from the bags under your eyes, of course. Not getting any sleep?'

Ranald considered what his response might be, but before he could come up with a suitable answer, Marcus laughed and said, 'What are we Scots like? Can't give a compliment without minimising it with a wee insult.' He glanced at him again. 'What have you done?' He indicated his own head. 'For a moment it was like a younger version…' Then he shook himself. 'That's fanciful, Marcus,' he said, dismissing whatever thought had come to him. He looked to the side at Rebecca. 'What do you think?'

'Hmm,' she said as she sipped at her drink.

'I have a mountain of things to do today, Marcus, so if you could get to the point?'

While Ranald spoke he tried to read Rebecca. She looked poised and utterly familiar with her surroundings, as if she'd never been away from the place while Alexander was alive. No that wasn't it. He changed his mind as he watched her cross her legs and sit further back into her seat. She simply didn't care what he thought of her. And she really couldn't be bothered with his conversation.

What would she make of the woman in the mirror? Would she run screaming from the house if she saw her? Marcus seemed as if nothing could break through his strong sense of himself. Was Rebecca equally as robust? He felt an urge to test her, grab her by the arm and drag her down to the lift, push her inside and ask if she could sense anything. Anything at all? Someone else had to see what he did.

'I like a man who doesn't beat about the proverbial,' said Marcus, plucking Ranald from his thoughts. 'So I won't either. Dear old Uncle Alexander very helpfully put a business plan we were developing to the sword. I would like to enlist your help to breathe some life back into it.'

'Yes?'

'A firm called McIntyre Developments had offered him a substantial sum for the house and gardens. Their plans were ambitious: high-end apartments, minimum asking price, one million pounds.'

Ranald held Marcus's gaze and sent a silent thank-you to Dan and Stan for telling him about this. 'And how can I help?'

'I understand you are now a trustee of the family trust, yes? And, of course, you inherited the house, library and gardens. What if there could be a better split of Uncle Alexander's assets?'

'For example?'

'Here you are, Ranald, asset rich and cash poor. In your position of trustee you would be well within your rights, with the other trustees backing you, of course, to apply for a change in the will. Then we could sell off the house. You take a handsome share and set yourself up nicely for the rest of your natural.'

Ranald heard a noise. A bang from somewhere in the house

behind him. Was that *her* letting him know he shouldn't listen to these two? Letting him know to get rid of them.

He turned away from Marcus, then back to him, running over his last statement in his mind.

'I ...eh, I am set up rather nicely.'

'But asset rich, with nothing in your pockets?'

How the hell did Marcus know what his cash situation was?

'I do fine, thank you.'

Marcus snorted. 'Fine? Yes, you can go into the local supermarket and buy a tasty ready meal. Is that the limit to your ambition? Have you never thought of owning a nice wee cottage in the south of France, as *well* as a city centre flat in Glasgow? Wouldn't that be an attractive way of life? Say goodbye to all those boring writing commissions and write what you really want to.'

Rebecca interrupted. 'That's the kind of freedom that this money could buy you, cousin.' So she *was* paying attention.

'Can we rewind a little?' Ranald uncrossed his legs and clasped his hands together on his lap. He gripped tight as if that might lend him some strength to defy his cousins. 'You said that I'd take a handsome share. The house is mine. Why would I share *any* of the proceeds with anyone else?'

Marcus was nonplussed. 'We assumed you knew: if you were to sell up, under the conditions of the trust, the liquid asset that produces would then have to be shared among the other parties to the will.'

'The other parties being you...'

'...and me,' Rebecca said with a tone that was just on the right side of boredom.

Ranald chewed on this. Quinn had neglected to mention any of this during either of his visits. And it did seem rather too much of a coincidence that Marcus just happened to be passing the very afternoon Ranald had been to see the lawyer.

'I understand you and Rebecca have already benefitted...' He coughed to hide his discomfort at challenging him. '...from the will?'

'Yes. And?' Marcus bristled.

'If *my* assets were all to go back into the pot to be shared…' He fought for an even tone, a voice that wouldn't betray his nervousness. '…shouldn't yours, too?'

'That's simply not plausible,' Marcus answered. What little smile there had been on his face had now slipped. 'That money is accounted for.'

Ah. So, Marcus was in difficulty, despite all of his background, experience and undoubted assets.

'So's mine,' said Ranald, sitting back, telling himself he would not, should not give in to this man. 'It's very firmly in bricks and mortar, and books.'

'Bloody books,' said Marcus. 'The old bastard cared more for his bloody books than he did for his bloody family.'

'That's as maybe, Marcus. I'm happy with the current arrangement.' He braced himself for his cousin's response.

'C'mon, Ranald. This would be a much better way of doing things. We'll all make a hell of a lot of money.'

Ranald stood up. What would Alexander say? How would he respond? 'You have my answer, Marcus. And it's no. I have everything I need. I see no reason to entertain your proposal.'

Then, legs shaking, without waiting to see if his cousins were following him, he walked out of the room, across the hall to the front door. He pulled it open and stood, waiting.

Without meeting his eyes, Marcus appeared from the reception room, Rebecca just behind him, and traversed the hall, his shoes clicking on the stone tiles.

'I'll give you time to think this over properly, cousin.' Marcus made his tone softer, but in a studied way. In his hand he held a file, which Ran assumed he'd just take from his case. He brandished it in the air a little and dropped it on the table in the middle of the hall. 'Have a read of that. I think you'll be impressed.'

'My mind is fixed on this, Marcus.' He heard himself and thought of Alexander. The strategy of imagining he was the old man had helped him avoid being brow-beaten by his cousins. He saw shadows shift at the darkest end of the corridor, felt a breeze on his cheek and sent a silent thank-you.

Without another word, Marcus brushed past him and walked out of the door.

'Nice to finally meet you, Rebecca,' Ranald offered as she joined her brother out on the drive, but without acknowledging him, she walked over to the car and climbed inside.

꠸

Ranald was sitting cross-legged in a front corner of the garden, under a tree. Cupped in his hand was an amber leaf, surely one of the first to fall, and he was following the vein and thread of the lines that fed the burnt outer fringes before it had uncoupled from a branch and floated to the ground in a lazy spin.

How he got there he had no idea. And as he saw a taxi drive up, with Donna in it, he realised he was going to have difficulty explaining to her *why* he was there.

'Seem like a good idea at the time?' she asked with a smile, seeming to read his mind.

He struggled back through his thoughts. He'd been standing at the front door when Marcus and Rebecca left, and instead of going back inside he'd found himself aiming his body at the large green bulk of leaf off to his right.

'Mindfulness, you know?' It made some sort of sense. He looked at her. 'Not that it's not great to see you, what are you doing here?'

'Unfinished business,' Donna said as she huffed her large handbag into place in front of her, as if it might ward off the evil eye. 'Can we go inside?' She looked up into the sky, and then at him as if he was slightly nuts. 'It is raining.'

'So it is,' Ranald said coming into full awareness. He held his arms out to assess the amount of raindrops on his sleeves. They weren't so wet, but he was suddenly aware his hair, neck and shoulders were very damp.

Once inside Donna asked, 'Mind if we go up to your grandmother's suite?'

Surprised, Ranald said, 'Sure.' And wondering why, he began to walk in that direction. As they went, Donna kept up a stream of chatter. How lucky he was. What an amazing house. She and Martie had talked about nothing more all the way home after their last visit.

When they climbed up onto the landing, Donna said, 'We saw a sitting room up here. It was really cosy. Should we go in there?'

'Absolutely,' said Ranald mystified.

They went in, and they both sat on the same sofa, at either end, facing each other.

'I'm guessing there's a purpose to this visit?' Ranald asked. As he spoke he threw a look over at the desk in the corner and wondered again about the young woman who wrote those letters.

'You overheard me and Martie talking, didn't you?' Donna asked as she kicked off her shoes and pulled her feet under her.

He knew instantly what she was referring to. He nodded. She clasped her hands in front of her, closed her eyes and took a deep breath as if something else had just occurred to her. 'Camphor,' she said. 'You can smell it too, eh?'

He took a breath. Caught the camphor … and something else. 'Yeah…'

'Martie had no sense of it at all.'

'Right?'

'This is the only place in the whole house you can smell it.'

'And?'

'First of all. Martie: you realise why she held all that stuff back from you, don't you?' Her eyes roamed over his face. 'You don't resent her for it, do you?'

'I get it, Donna. Or part of me does. The sensible, mature part. The eighteen-year-old resents the hell out of it. I've spent the last … nearly dozen years hating my father for abandoning me. Except he didn't…' His throat and chest tightened. The room gave a lurch. He coughed. He would not cry. 'Anyway, what are we really doing up here?' He fought to regain his equilibrium and tried to change the subject. 'Why aren't we in the kitchen like normal people?'

'You sense it, don't you?' she asked.

'Sense what?' He played for time knowing exactly where she was going.

'I looked it up. Camphor.' She paused. 'There's none among your cleaning materials in the kitchen, by the way. I checked that time we were here – when you went to the loo.'

'Donna, why the cryptic…' He couldn't remember going to the loo while they were in the house.

'It's incredibly potent stuff. The Egyptians used to use it in their mummification process … There's good reason why moths hate it.' She laughed but threaded through her short burst of laughter Ranald heard her disquiet.

'I could have looked all of this up on Wikipedia if I was interested, Donna.' He softened his expression to show he was not irritated, just confused.

'They also used to use it, a long time ago, to treat mania.'

His mind delivered up an image of the woman in the mirror. This time her body was twisted at a tortured angle, but she was facing him and her eyes were shining a light that could only come from a place of madness.

'Right.' He blinked the image away.

'A long time ago.'

'Donna?' *Please stop. You need to stop.*

'I've never been more certain of something, son.' She clutched her hands in front of her and leaned towards him. 'This house has a troubled past, Ranald, and I would be so much more comfortable if you would sell the thing off and buy yourself that house in the south of France you've always dreamed about.'

'What? You're taking camphor, some mummies, adding a dash of mania and coming up with a haunted house?'

'Don't mock me, Ranald McGhie. I'm not saying the house is

haunted. I'm saying there's an energy here. A very old one, and it has caused your family a lot of pain over the years.'

'Donna, I hear you and I understand your concern…' He shivered, hearing the truth in her words. He understood more than he was prepared to admit and hoped his jocular tone would divert away from the truth.

'And now you're patronising me, Ran.' He could hear an edge of fear in her voice, and not a little panic. A chill ran through his heart, his lungs and down to his gut.

'I'm pretty certain that every generation of your family has had its victims, Ran. You need to break that cycle and get the hell out of here. Before it's too late.'

24

In the library, Ranald opened his laptop. The file he had been working on was on his taskbar, so he clicked on it intending to do some more work. But instead he found himself staring, unfocused, at the screen.

Trying to ignore what Donna had said was proving difficult. Was she right? Aside from the woman who visited his dreams, there *was* something strange about the house. Perhaps it was the amount of room here. It felt like every step came with an echo and every breath fell into space. Perhaps if weasel Marcus flogged it off he could buy himself something nice, with a pool and enough capacity to hold all of Alexander's books?

But then Marcus would win.

Ranald couldn't allow that to happen. Nor could he betray Alexander in that way.

He closed the laptop, stood up from his chair and wandered over to a bookshelf. He had no other aim in mind than to pick up a book he'd never read before. His fingers dallied over a Muriel Spark novel. He'd never read her. Time to remedy that. He hooked a finger over the top of the book and pulled it from its space. It was a hardback edition of four of her novels, led off by *The Prime of Miss Jean Brodie*.

He held it on one palm and held the other hand over it, palm down, as if the words might lift from the paper, transmit through into his skin and from there into his soul.

He took comfort from the notion, then carried the book out of the library, down the corridor and into the lift. He pulled the doors open, sat inside and began reading.

Next morning he woke up lying on the floor of the lift. He hadn't gone up to bed; instead, he'd read through much of the night and then slumped onto the floor, curling up there, waiting for *her* to enter his mind.

He didn't care that the last image of her was terrifying: a mask of fear, teeth and blood. There was more to her than that. Much more. There was love – enough for them both – and he would come here every day and night and show her how much he cared.

He stretched out on the floor, telling himself what he knew already: he was crazy. He stood up, placed his hands on his hips and bent backwards, trying to ease the ache in his back. He contemplated going upstairs and crawling into his bed, getting another few hours in.

Instead, he found himself plodding towards the pool where he took off his clothes and dived in. Sixty lengths later and he felt a little better.

A few minutes later, upstairs in his bathroom, he leaned over the sink and peered at his face in the mirror. His eyes looked as if they'd shrunk. The skin below them was puffy and shaded. He also needed a shave, but his hair was tidier than it had been for a long time. He turned to the side and counted the ribs he could see.

He shaved and had a shower to wash the chlorine off his skin. Then he went through to his walk-in wardrobe. All these clothes and he had barely touched them. He might look tired and in need of a good feed, but he could at least look like the young gentleman Uncle Alex hoped he might be.

He chose a pair of dark jeans, a cream shirt and a check jacket. He finished with a pair of tan brogues. Regarding himself in the mirror, he wondered if the clothes would be enough to distract people from his haunted face.

Downstairs, he made for the kitchen and surprised Mrs Hackett as she was on her way to the pool carrying a pile of freshly laundered towels. Hearing him coming, she turned to say hello. But her mouth dropped open and the towels fell to the floor. She almost gave a little scream but caught herself before the sound issued from her throat.

'My, Mr … Ranald … for a moment.' She held a hand to her mouth. 'For a moment I thought you were your Uncle Alexander.'

Ranald was disappointed. 'Really? Last time you saw him he was an old man.' He looked down at the clothes he was wearing. 'Maybe I should change into something younger-looking.'

'It's the hair. The clothes are very smart. I'm so glad you're wearing them after all the time it took to select them.' She gave him a small smile, tinged with memory. 'You look like a much younger version of the man I met when I first came to the family.' She stepped closer, studying his face. 'Don't know why I didn't see it before. The resemblance is…'

'Aye, aye,' interrupted Ran. 'You said already.' He felt uncomfortable and tried to disguise it by getting down on one knee and picking up the scattered towels. He looked like the man. He wrote like the man. He was even beginning to talk like him. It was helpful when he was working himself up to defy Marcus, but did he want to be affected by it permanently?

'I hope I haven't offended you. Your uncle was a fine-looking man in his day.'

Ranald put the towels on the table and began to fold them. He shook his head. That anyone should think he was bothered about his handsomeness quotient, if there was such a thing, was ludicrous. When it came to looks he was completely oblivious. It came from a lifelong desire to be invisible, he supposed.

'The clothes are okay?' he asked Mrs Hackett, smoothing down the lapels of his jacket.

'Very smart, young man.' She smiled her approval. 'So much better than those shorts and the t-shirt you were living in for the last few weeks.' She gathered up the freshly folded towels and walked away.

Moments later Mrs Hackett came bustling back into the kitchen and walked over to a cupboard where she pulled out some cleaning materials.

'Mind if I ask you something, Mrs Hackett?'

'Yes?'

'I've been hearing some gossip. That my great-uncle was involved in some kind of scandal way back.'

'Don't listen to gossip, Ranald.'

'I just want to know more about my uncle. What was he like? What kind of man was he?'

'Everything you need to know about Mr Fitzpatrick is in that library there.' She held a bucket of cleaning materials in front of her as if they helped form some sort of barrier against Ranald's questions.

'Where are all the photographs?' Ranald asked. 'I haven't seen any at all in the house. Isn't that a bit weird?'

'Not really,' Mrs Hackett said and gave a small shrug. 'Mr Fitzpatrick was more concerned with words than images. He was on his own for most of his adult life. Who takes photos of themselves?'

'Ever heard of selfies, Mrs H?' He surprised himself by managing a grin.

She gave a small huff of disapproval. 'Thankfully your great-uncle was never that vacuous. Anyway,' she managed to look at her wrist-watch without overturning the bucket of cleaning materials, 'I best be off. Work to do et cetera.' She began walking out of the room.

'What about my grandmother?' asked Ranald. If Mrs Hackett didn't want to talk about his uncle, maybe she would be more willing to talk about her.

She stopped and turned, her expression a request to clarify.

'What can you tell me about her?' Ran sat in one of the chairs round the kitchen table – a signal to Mrs Hackett that he wasn't going anywhere. 'I never met my gran; I don't know the first thing about her.'

Mrs Hackett moved closer, her features softened a little. What was that, sympathy?

'I was always blessed with good family ties. I can't imagine life without them.' Her eyes narrowed as she considered Ranald's situa-tion. 'All I can say is that Mr Fitzpatrick was the best of them. You're lucky you take after him.'

'When did gran die?'

Mrs Hackett thought for a moment before she answered. 'It would have been about 2006.'

'That was the year my parents died,' Ranald thought out loud.

'Cancer,' said Mrs Hackett, her mouth a cold line of judgement. It was the first time Ranald had seen any hint of a breach of her self-imposed stance of confidentiality. 'At her autopsy the doctors said her body was riddled with it. She must have been in enormous pain, but she never sought treatment, not until very near the end.'

'When in the year did she die?'

'As far as I remember it was the autumn,' Mrs Hackett said, her eyes clouded, looking into the past. 'I can remember the piles of leaves on the paths through the graveyard.'

'My parents died in September. Could have been only a matter of weeks before my grandmother died.'

'The minute, no, the second your mother walked out of that door, she was dead to your grandmother.' Mrs Hackett shook her head. 'I can't understand how a woman could be so uncaring about one of her children. She had a formidable mind, but I don't think her body could cope with the amount of poison it produced.' She gave a little cough. 'Sorry.' She immediately looked ashamed – disappointed in herself, as if she had broken her own rules. And without another word, she walked out of the room.

⸸

Minutes later, Ranald found himself upstairs, again, in his grandmother's wing. He sat in her lounge and was again struck by how different this room was to her bedroom and bathroom. They were austere, Victorian, and held little that softened the hard line of function.

Remembering what Donna had said, he sniffed the air for camphor, but failed to find it.

He was in an armchair by the inglenook fireplace and surveyed the room. It was like this space had been lifted from a generously proportioned country cottage and planted here inside the mansion. Was this her favourite chair? A standard lamp by his shoulder would have provided necessary light for her to embroider by, when daylight from the window was no longer sufficient.

There was not a book in sight. In that, clearly, she was nothing like her brother. But in the absence of photographs their tastes were apparently shared. He closed his eyes, trying to get a sense of her. Why was she so determined to close his mother out of her life? Surely marrying an artist wasn't all that bad? And if his father had been an artist he must have locked down his creative impulse to become a provider to his new wife, because he couldn't remember any evidence of it whatsoever.

There was an old chest by the window. A couple of embroidered cushions sat on top of it, which, upon first glance, had made him think it might be a small window seat. But from here, he could see that, in fact, the top was a lid.

He stood up, walked over to it, removed the cushions and lifted up the lid. Inside it held a small storm of paper. He rifled around. It was notepaper, of the kind he remembered using for letters. There were also packets of envelopes, brown and white, and two small packs of postage stamps. The image was not the queen. It was a robin peering out from the slot in a red letterbox and it cost nineteen pence. Only two stamps had been used.

He dropped the stamps and carried on searching. Next he picked up an instruction pamphlet for a television and a couple of unused birthday cards. They were of a generic feminine design: pink and flowery.

There, at the bottom, was a small, brown plastic wallet. He judged it to be about five inches by seven. His pulse rate raised. It was similar to a photograph wallet his mother had once owned. He pulled it out, carried it over to the armchair and sat down. He felt the rough edges with his fingertips. The seams were torn here and there, which suggested that it been regularly handled.

With a feeling of trepidation, he placed his thumb under the plastic ridge and lifted the folder open. The first photograph was black and white: a somewhat formal study of a woman and child. The woman was seated, wearing dark clothes. Her face was a blank, giving nothing away about her thoughts. The girl was wearing a white dress. Her blonde hair was in ringlets and one of her eyebrows was slightly raised, as if questioning the photographer. She looked – although he acknowledged he was a poor judge of a child's age – around ten. One thing he was sure of, however: it was his mother. It was there in her eyes. Unmistakeable. He felt his throat tighten. His longing for her was a dull weight on his chest, despite the terrible knowledge that she'd almost certainly killed his father. How could he still love her knowing what she'd done?

It had been the condition; it wasn't her, he told himself. And who could appreciate that more than him?

But still.

He closed his eyes and leaned his head back, feeling a dull, heavy spread of sadness throughout his body. *Somebody please take this all away from me,* he groaned. There was only so much of this he could take. A spine can only bend so much before it snaps.

He pushed out, away from his own head and returned his attention to the photograph, and his grandmother. She appeared formidable. Her lips did have a slight upward curve, but there was no real smile. And where his mother's eyes appeared to be questioning the photographer, his grandmother's eyes were sending a challenge. Who was behind the lens? Uncle Alex?

Then it occurred to him there was a physical distance between the two figures. No touching; enough space between them for a column of ice.

From what he was beginning to learn about his grandmother, he was surprised his mother had turned out the way she had. She could be stern, but she was also a lot of fun. She even joined in the kickabouts he and his dad had in the back garden, often forgetting to check the dinner in the process and serving up burnt potatoes with a grin and a challenge.

How much pain must she have been in to then do what she did?

And there, a memory of Dad at the dinner table, spooning some soup into his mouth, making pleased noises as the flavour hit his tongue.

Loving. Accepting.

Trusting.

The next photograph must have been from the same sitting: his grandmother and mother were both wearing the same clothes and in the same poses. If anything, they were slightly further apart.

Then came a picture of a couple at a church, taken from a distance. It was a bride and groom. He instantly knew who they were: his mum and dad. He even recognised the church door behind them. He'd seen plenty of similar photographs when he was a kid. They were standing facing someone. In the corner of the image, Ranald could make out an arm and leg, and the way they were positioned made him think these might belong to an official photographer. He frowned and held the photograph away from him. Did the scale and distance it was taken from suggest the person who took *this* picture was not part of the official party?

The next few photographs were also of the wedding, and also seemed to be taken from somewhere just beyond some official cordon.

He flicked through some more.

Here was a photograph of his mother. She was carrying a tiny bundle. To her right, on the wall, was a sign that read 'Maternity Ward'. Again, the image looked like it was a stolen rather than shared moment.

Something flashed across his memory.

Had he seen these images before?

He shook his head. How would that be possible?

The next to last photograph convinced him. It was taken from the rear. A couple walking, a small boy in the middle of them, holding both their hands. He was wearing a school blazer. Both of his feet were off the ground as if he was skipping in his excitement. Ranald couldn't remember the moment, but he could remember the blazer and the school in the distance. His first day at primary.

A sudden sense of sorrow weighed down on him. He imagined his grandmother looking through these photographs time and time again. For hours and hours. Tenderly touching his and his mother's faces.

What a waste. She obviously pined for them. Why hadn't she been in touch?

He looked at the last one.

Wait.

Who was this?

This was clearly from a much earlier time, judging by the formality of the pose and the clothes being worn. A man and a young woman sat on separate seats. Another woman stood just behind them, on the same side as the man. The seated couple wore dark clothes and both their faces bore sombre expressions. The woman was his grand-mother, looking like she might be in her teens. The man by her side must be his great-uncle. He had a short back and sides. Thick curls on top. Ranald studied him. So this was Alexander Fitzpatrick. Even he could see that their resemblance to each other was strong.

Then he looked at the woman behind his great-uncle. She was young, late teens perhaps. Her hair was long and black around her pale face, and she was wearing a dark dress with a white pinafore over it. She had a hand on his uncle's shoulder and, judging by the faint smile in his expression and the slight angle in his shoulders, the touch was welcome.

However, her expression suggested she was placing her hand there under silent protest, almost as if her skin might burn if it was held there for a second longer. Her eyes leaked pain, and it was clear her smile was costing her considerable effort.

Ranald drew in a deep, quick breath as recognition dawned. The hairs on the back of his neck stood on end. He looked closer. He knew this girl.

She was the woman in the mirror.

25

Ranald was back in the kitchen. He put the photograph wallet on the table and thrust his hands into his pockets, as if that would stop them trembling. What the hell was going on here? Was he losing it? What could possibly explain the fact that he knew that girl's face?

He sifted through memory and all of those dreams. She'd sat on his lap, head in the crook of his neck as if enjoying the deep rumble of his voice as he read. They'd walked hand in hand through shadow in the garden. At no point could he remember her face being clearly visible, so how did he know it was her?

Even though he was disturbed by all of this, he still felt a longing for her. He wanted to take that last photograph out, sit down and stare into her eyes.

But he dared not.

Despite this, he reached across the table. Allowed his hand to hover above the brown plastic. He retreated. He couldn't do this. Shouldn't be doing this.

Part of him recognised the displacement. He was lonely. His real-life relationships were all failures. He never failed to push women away, eventually. And that was why an affair with a dead woman – a half-face he'd imagined in a mirror – was preferable to flesh and blood, and certain disappointment.

But then…

It still didn't explain the dreams, the lift and the fact there *was* a woman in the mirror.

He stood back from the kitchen table and the wallet, creating distance. That was the thing. Distance. Get the hell out of here and maybe the fog in his mind would recede and he would be able to make some sense of all of this.

He marched along to the front door, and pulled it open to see Marcus standing with his finger poised to ring the bell.

'Ah, Ranald. Do you have a moment?'

Without waiting for him to respond, Marcus walked past and through into his usual space. Once there, he made straight for the drinks cabinet and poured himself a whisky.

'Aye,' said Ranald when he caught up with him. 'Do come in.'

Marcus threw his head back and drank the whisky down in one. Swallowed. 'Cousin,' he said. 'We need to talk.'

'If you are going to try and change my mind, Marcus you're wasting your time.'

'You can't do this,' Marcus said, and slammed the crystal glass on the top of the cabinet, so hard Ranald was surprised not to hear the sound of breaking glass.

'I'm sorry, Marcus, I can't not see to my great-uncle's wishes. I would feel awful.'

'Oh, give me a break,' Marcus said as he squared up to him. 'You didn't even know the old bastard. He ignored you for most of your life. Where does this ridiculous sense of loyalty come from?' There was a tightness in the man's face, the chords on his neck were standing out and his eyes were red.

'Marcus, what's wrong?' Ranald asked. Again, Ranald had the impression there was an importance here. A desperation even. Was his cousin in deep financial trouble?

Marcus turned away for a moment, as if he was using that time to gather his thoughts, but he turned back to Ranald, hard eyed and mouth a tight line of anger, as if he was a mere breath from losing control.

'You sanctimonious little prick ... don't pretend to care about me.'

'What the hell ...?' Ranald felt a surge of irritation in response, and his hands form into fists. Words crowded his brain. Smart answers. Cutting answers. *Alexander, where are you when I need you?* he sent out.

Nothing came back.

His shoulders slumped. He looked over at his cousin.

Marcus stared at him as if building up for another insult. And sure enough it came. 'You fucking inbred,' he said.

Wait. *Inbred*?

'What did you call me?'

'There could be two different lots of Fitzgerald blood in your veins, Ranald.'

Ranald looked at his cousin. Wanted to punch the smug out of his face. 'What the hell are you on about?'

'Do I need to spell it out? I gave you enough hints before.' His mouth stretched into a poisoned smile. 'My loving father. Your mother. Couldn't keep their hands off each other. It's why she left. And it's why she couldn't stay away.'

Ranald was in his face. His breath a harsh pounding. 'You're full of shit.'

'If only, Ranald old boy. Your mother's first child was fathered by her brother, William. The stillborn *thing* was another family lie, she had an abortion. Couldn't handle the guilt of fucking her own brother. I wouldn't be surprised if you and I were brothers.'

'Utter crap.' There was a ringing in Ranald's ears. The world had narrowed to the pounding of his heart and Marcus's mouth. 'Lies. All lies, you arsehole.'

'My father told me all about it on my twenty-first birthday. How's that for a loving parent, eh?' He stepped away from Ranald and sat in his usual spot, as if pleased to have told Ranald the story of his inception. His posture perfectly displayed his attitude. If he couldn't get Ranald to change his views, by God he would spoil his peace of mind. Marcus rested his right foot on his left knee, back in control now that he had spat out all of his bile. 'We could be brothers as well as cousins. How messed up is that?'

Ranald opened his mouth to speak. To shout. To deny. His mother and Marcus's father? He could see the taunt in Marcus's eyes. Even he didn't believe they were really brothers. It was just a provocation. Something to set him off balance.

He turned away, closing his eyes. Remembering his parents, how they'd interacted with each other. On her good days, there was no one who could match Gordon McGhie in his mother's eyes. Once she had left that house – *this* house – all she cared about was his father. More even than him, her own child, Ranald realised with a lurch and a grip of disappointment.

And his father shared that love. He would have made any bargain to keep her. Life without her would have been an inconsolable ruin. He would have opened a vein for her, of that Ranald was certain.

But, knowing all of that, she had beaten him to that final, irrevocable blow.

†

With a half-walk and a half-run Ranald made his way down to the Cross, wearing only his shirt, hunkered against the rain and the cold. He stood at the intersection under the watchful eye of the war memorial and watched the traffic flow as the lights changed. People. People in cars. This was life. Real life. People doing things in the here and now. Actions that were not debatable. This was visible. Verifiable.

How he envied each and every one of them. What he would give to be able to just do the simple things, engage in life, without this unceasing, accusing monologue going on in his head. Everyone else knew what they were doing, where they were going and why it mattered.

At the traffic lights, on automatic, he reached out to press the button that would make it switch to pedestrian mode. As he lifted his hand up he saw that his right wrist had a huge slash across it and his hand was coated in thick blood. Part of him shrank back in horror, another part wondered if it really should have the consistency of treacle. He held his left hand out to see a similar wound and a spouting of blood.

Had he managed to kill himself? Was he dead?

Would anyone care?

The lights changed. People walked past him to cross the road, but he stood there, unable to move, studying his hands.

He looked up and away, blinking, heart a furious bluster in his chest. No, this can't be happening. Then he looked back down to see his skin was an unblemished healthy pink.

Distracted, and without realising he had sent the command to his brain, he stepped out into the road.

The van swerved. The horn blared. A hand with finger extended and a loud voice shot out of the window: 'Wanker. Watch where you're going.'

Ranald staggered back onto the kerb, his hand to his heart, adrenaline sparking all over his body. He forced a breath.

'Ranald?' he heard. A female voice. 'My God. What are you doing?'

It was Liz, her face long and pale with shock. 'Did you just deliberately step—'

'Don't be daft,' he interrupted her. 'I was just in a wee dwam.'

'I've been in plenty of daydreams, Ranald, but I've never stepped in front of a van. Good job he managed to swerve out of your way or you'd be spread all over the road.'

Ranald looked down the street. The van was long gone and he felt a crush of disappointment that the van driver had been paying attention. Then all of this would have been over. No more of this constant distracting chatter in his head. And how could that not be a good thing? He would be doing everyone a favour. No more Ranald McGhie to worry about.

'You're soaking,' she said, touching his shoulder. 'You sure you're okay?'

Ranald tried to smile. 'Not got your man's tea to make tonight?'

He walked away, judging the traffic with more care this time, and crossed the road safely. He didn't bother to check whether Liz was following him, but thought that his rudeness must have scared her off. Which was just fine by him.

By the time he arrived at the café, however, he wanted to go back and apologise to Liz. There had been no need to have a go at her. She was just trying to be a friend. Before he pushed open the door he paused and looked back down the road. Liz was nowhere to be seen.

He walked inside and took a seat.

'Usual?' the waitress shouted over.

'Please,' he replied, then sat back in his chair and looked around the room. It was busy this morning and everyone was staring at him. Probably thinking, there's another of the Fitzpatricks losing their shit. To hell with them. He adjusted the wet material of his shirt, pulling it away from his shoulders.

There was a familiar face at one of the window seats. Suzy looked up as if aware of his attention. Without acknowledging him she went back to her book.

Somebody else he'd pissed off.

His coffee was delivered. He nodded his thanks and took a sip. An old man on the table across from him was reading a newspaper. One of the sections lay on the edge of the table, as if it was no longer needed.

'Mind if I…' Ranald pointed at the paper.

'Aye, nae worries,' the old man said.

Ranald picked up the paper, but found he couldn't focus on reading. He kept seeing the photograph. His mother. A woman who had a twisted relationship with her brother, if even a little of what Marcus had told him was true. The woman who ran away, only to bring her shadows with her and destroy everything she loved.

The girl with her hand on Alexander's shoulder. The aching smile on her face. Who was she? Her clothing suggested that she was a maid or servant of some sort. Who got a photo taken with the staff?

His grandmother looked decidedly unhappy, but that seemed to be her default position. In every single image he'd seen of her she looked like her teeth were coated in lemon juice.

Out of the corner of his eye, he spotted movement. Suzy was preparing to leave. He got to his feet and walked over, unsure of what was motivating him to do so. Just a second ago he was mentally cursing at everyone in the room.

'Listen,' he said. 'I just want to apologise for the other day.'

She looked at him. Expression blank.

'I was being a dick.'

'Yes, you were.'

'You were being kind and I was a total arse.'

'Yup. A dick and an arse.'

'Just wanted to say sorry.' He gave her a small smile, then turned and walked back to his seat.

As he sat, he realised she had followed him over. She stood, looking down at him, holding her books in front of her with both hands.

'And I'm sorry if I touched a nerve,' she said. 'You're new to the area. Must seem like everyone is staring at you, trying to work you out.'

'Och, I don't mind that, to be honest. People will be people.'

'You should put that on a t-shirt.' She grinned. 'Preferably one that's dry.' She nodded at his chest. 'Not bring an umbrella?'

'It's only rain.' He gestured at her books. 'What is it this time?'

She brandished the top one. It was large and looked like an educational text. 'Just something for uni.' She made an unhappy face. 'I've got some resits, but studying in the house all day makes me feel claustrophobic. So, I have a wee change of scenery every now and then.'

She made as if to move away. Ranald stood up.

'You said your mum knew my mum?'

'Yeah?'

'Do you think she'd be happy to talk to me about her?' He scratched his head and looked at the floor. 'I've … never met anyone who knew her during that part of her life.'

Suzy's face was a study in empathy. She reached out and lightly touched his forearm. 'Of course.' She thought for a moment. 'She's at home this afternoon. I'll text her and tell her I'm bringing the arsehole I met the other day for a blether.'

Ranald managed a smile. 'Deserved that.'

Suzy rested her bag and books on the table, took out her phone and thumbed out a text. When she'd finished she nodded towards the door. 'C'mon,' she said.

Ranald followed her out, feeling anxious what he might learn about his mother. Who was she before all of *that*? Before her innocence spoiled. Before her mind turned. He was back in the room with Marcus and listening to the accusations spew from his cousin's mouth.

What kind of people did he share his genes with?

🕇

Suzy and her parents lived in a modest bungalow just a few minutes' drive from the café. Ranald was afraid that when he sat in the car that there might be some awkwardness, but they managed to keep up a polite run of conversation until she pulled into the drive.

They were met at the door by a woman who was an older, shorter-haired version of Suzy. Tight, blue jeans and a pale-blue, short cardigan. Button nose. Plump lower lip. This was where Suzy got her good looks from, then.

'Hi there.' She held out her hand. 'You'll be Ranald. I'm Eve.' They shook hands. 'C'mon through to the kitchen.' She turned and, walking down a short corridor, said, '…that's where all the interesting stuff happens in our house.'

The corridor was filled with the light coming in through the glass front door and the walls were painted cream and displayed lots of family photographs, mainly of Suzy at various stages of her life.

Walking just behind Ranald, Suzy spoke as if she could read his glances.

'Man, they make me cringe every time I bring someone home.'

Ranald found himself wondering how many of these 'someones' were men and noted a stab of envy. He shut it down. He didn't deserve someone as nice as she was.

In the kitchen they sat around a small table on which sat a tray containing three mugs, a large teapot in a knitted cosy, a small jug of milk, a sugar bowl and a plate of sliced cake. It took Ranald straight back to his mother's kitchen and summer afternoons when neighbours would pop in for 'a wee blether'. Back then he hadn't been too bothered about the chat or the tea, but the slices of cake and the biscuits were a strong attraction.

'Haven't seen one of these in ages.' Ranald gave a weak smile, pointing at the piece of knitting enclosing the teapot. 'I thought people were too into their coffee to bother with tea these days.'

'Can't beat a nice cup of tea,' said Eve. She glanced at Suzy, pride evident in her smile. 'It's how we put the world back to rights. Shall I be mother?'

'You're the one with the credentials,' Suzy smiled back.

Ranald felt himself relaxing into the warm, accepting atmosphere generated by the two women, and registered a note of sadness drift into his mind, like a scent in the breeze; it had been so long since he had been included in such a mood. To disguise his emotion he reached for a slice of Madeira, and bit into the soft cake.

'Haven't tasted this for years,' he said mid-chew. 'Mum used to buy it every New Year.'

'It's like Brussels sprouts,' said Suzy. 'Why do most people only bring them out at Christmas?'

'Cos we can't stomach them any other time of year?' said Ranald.

'Sprouts are good for you, young man,' said Eve. 'Make your hair and nails shiny.'

'Mum, I don't think Ranald is all that bothered about shiny nails.'

'Oh, I don't know,' said Ranald, and held his right hand out as if for an inspection. And wondered at his capacity for hiding his true state of mind with a little dredged up humour.

They each picked up their drinks and sipped in a companionable silence.

'So, Helena Fitzpatrick was your mum?' asked Eve, just as Ranald bit into another slice of cake.

He heard *Helena* and for a moment forgot that was his mother. 'Yeah.' He collected himself and swallowed. 'You're about the only person I've ever met, outside of family, who knew her from that time in her life.'

'Can't say that I knew her all that well, to be honest. We had a friend in common. A girl who lived next door to me when I was a teenager was in her class.'

'What do you remember of her?' Ranald asked, trying not to look too interested in the answer. But of course, he was fascinated. When his mother was alive, she was just a normal person. She was *Mum*. And now he was realising that there was, of course, more to her. Much more, if Marcus was to be believed. Helen McGhie hadn't just appeared fully formed in that position. She'd had a life before him.

Eve paused, a flicker of memory lighting her eyes. 'I was a little bit in love with Helena FitzGerald. What style she had. What grace. All of us girls were incredibly jealous. Her brother, though – William – he was another story altogether. He liked to be seen as a bit of an eccentric, you know? Seemed to revel in the family's … strange … history.' Eve sipped her tea carefully. 'He was long finished with the academy when I arrived, but his legend seemed to follow Helena about.'

Ranald's heart gave a lurch when he heard William's name. 'I know next to nothing about my family, Eve,' he said, trying to control his tone. 'I've met my cousin Marcus, and his sister, Rebecca.'

'They'll be William's kids.' Eve stared into space. 'He died when Marcus and Rebecca were in their early twenties. From what I heard, they got too much money too soon and kind of went off the rails.'

'Really? Marcus is a bit arrogant, but other than that he seems to be fairly level-headed.'

'Well, bear in mind all this is based on small-town gossip. And to be fair, it was a few years back. I dare say Marcus has had plenty of time to have done some maturing.'

'Must be nice to find you have this other family,' said Suzy. 'After being on your own.'

'I only just met Rebecca, and I couldn't make head nor tail of her. But Marcus?' Ranald made a face. 'Bit of a dick.' He toyed with the idea of telling them about Marcus's demand that he sell the house, but decided to keep that to himself for the moment. 'You said something about the family's "strange" history…' He tailed off, hoping Eve would pick up the thread.

'You don't want to listen to that, son – it's just rumours and talk.'

But there was something in the way she spoke – a strange light in her eyes, a twist in the corner of her mouth – that made Ranald think she believed there was much more to it than that.

'I won't pay it much attention,' said Ranald. 'But it would be kind of helpful to know what I'm dealing with.'

'Well, there were the usual high jinks when Marcus and Rebecca were younger.' She turned to Suzy and smiled. 'Close your ears, young woman.' Back to Ranald. 'Drugs and sex parties, that kind of thing.' Then she added in a lower tone, as if afraid she might be overheard. 'Rebecca was a bit of a wild child. Far worse than Marcus apparently.'

'What about William? Did you mean he tried to live up to the family's … eccentricities? Do you know about those?'

'Not really. I heard my mother talking to one of her pals about Alexander Fitzpatrick making someone pregnant when he wasn't married. I'm not sure who the woman was, or what happened. She clammed up as soon as I walked in the room.'

'That was nothing to do with my mum, though?'

'No. But perhaps the pregnancy situation with Alexander was why her mother gave her such a hard time?' She shrugged. 'Who knows what goes on behind closed doors?' She smiled. 'All of us girls admired Helena. She turned her back on all that wealth for love. It was like something out of a novel … but it was just down the road.' She laughed. 'Listen to me. I'm talking rubbish. Don't pay me any attention, son.'

Turned her back on all that wealth for love? Did she really love him, or was Dad just some convenient patsy? Was he her chance to get away from a perverse relationship? He was doubting his own memories now.

They talked for another ten or fifteen minutes on more general topics, which was a relief to Ranald. Having come here to find out about his mother he realised that the more he discovered, the less he wanted to know. He'd hoped that Eve would say something that would cancel out Marcus's accusations; instead, subtle as her words were, they served only to add confirmation.

Ranald looked out of the window, to see that the rain had stopped.

'Best be off,' he said, standing up. 'Thanks for the chat and the tea.'

'You're welcome, son,' said Eve. 'I enjoyed talking about those times.'

'Want a lift back up to the Cross?' asked Suzy.

'Thanks,' said Ranald. 'I need the walk.' As he spoke he wondered if there was more to the offer, but Suzy's open, guileless face suggested she was just being kind. 'You've got studying to be getting on with, anyway.'

'Don't remind me.' She made a face.

'Yeah,' said Eve with a mock expression of reproach. 'My Suzy having a resit. Who'd have thought that would happen?'

'Don't start, Mum.'

'What?' she asked, assuming an innocent expression.

'My cue to leave,' said Ranald and he felt a pang of envy at their closeness. 'Never get between a parent and child talking about exams.' He thanked the women for their time and walked with Suzy to the front door.

As he stepped outside, he felt worried that he might have offended her by refusing her offer of a lift.

'You like movies?' he asked on the doorstep.

'Yeah.'

'There's a great TV room in the house. Why don't you come up some time and have a look through the selection. See what you fancy…' His voice tailed off as he worried that now he'd overstepped the mark. He ducked his head as if getting ready to take the blow of her rejection.

'That would be cool,' she said with a big smile. 'Would be great to have a break from all this studying.'

'Excellent,' Ran said, his grin as big as hers, and for a moment, remembered that this was what normal people did. 'It's a...' Just in time he stopped himself from saying the word 'date'. '...Just whenever, eh? I'm rarely out in the evening.'

⸸

As he walked along the road, he felt a couple of spits of rain on his shoulders. Looking up he saw, just ahead, a cloud towering like something out of a biblical epic – a jumble of greys formed a column from dark to light and every shade in between.

Picking up his pace, he reached the Cross and took a right. As he did he heard a car slowing down and a voice calling out.

'Still here?'

He turned. It was Liz. 'Get in,' she said. 'It's about to bucket down.'

He opened the door and climbed in. 'Sorry, I was a bit of an arse earlier.' It seemed to be his day for apologies.

Liz pulled away without a word.

'Who was the girl you were talking to in the café?' she said, after a minute or two.

'You spying on me?' Ranald asked, trying to inject a light tone into his voice.

'Aye,' said Liz. 'Cos I've nothing better to do.' She threw him a glance. 'I drove past just as you and she were walking out the front door.'

'Where are we going?' Ranald asked, although he knew exactly where. He felt a weight descend on him. He wasn't quite ready yet to face the woman in the mirror and find out the answers to the questions the photograph posed.

'I'm just taking you home. Then I'm off to make my man's tea.'

'Right,' Ranald said, with a slight feeling of disappointment. He didn't want to be on his own again. 'Want to come in for a wee while?'

'Please don't ask me to do that, Ranald. You know how I feel about that house.'

'You could just come round to the pool. It's a much newer part of the building. There'll be no weird shit going on there.'

Liz checked her mirrors. Indicated. Turned into his drive and drove slowly to the front door. She parked and pulled on the handbrake then twisted to face him.

'You really want me to come in?' There was doubt in her eyes. 'What does a young man like you want with a woman my age?'

Ranald decided to plump for honesty. 'Yes, I want you to come in. It's such a big house, I'm still not comfortable in all that space on my own. And as for your last question: you're good company.' *And you shed enough light to keep the shadows away*. He paused. 'And you're not that much older than me, anyway.'

'And I like some fun?' she grinned.

'I wasn't going to go there.'

She gave his shoulder a wee punch. 'See you.' Then: 'You sure the pool area is a newer part of the building?'

'Course it is. I don't think swimming pools were big in the Victorian era, do you?'

'Probably not,' she answered in a small voice. 'Fuck it.' She released her seatbelt. 'Anything spooky happens here, any weans greeting in the walls, and I'm going to have you, understand?'

'You'll be perfectly safe.' But as he said it, he thought about *her* the last time he'd entertained thoughts of another woman, and considered recanting the invitation.

Liz would be safe, he thought. But he wasn't sure about himself.

Ranald went in the front door and told Liz to walk round the side of the house to the pool conservatory, where he would unlock the door for her.

'This is lovely,' she said as she they met at the back of the house and she stepped inside. 'Do you use all of this?' She pointed to the exercise equipment.

'I'm full of good intentions,' he said. 'But I do swim a lot.'

'Looks really inviting,' Liz said looking at the cool, blue water.

Feeling a surge of energy Ranald stripped off and dived in. Surfacing, he pushed his hair away from his eyes. Treading water, he said, 'Come on in, the water's lovely.'

'I don't want to get my hair wet.'

'Why so coy?' asked Ranald. 'There's nothing like a skinny-dip.'

She sat on the edge of a lounger, her feet crossed at the ankles, her hands on her knees. She looked uncertain. Demure. Nothing like the sexually hungry woman with whom he'd previously spent time.

'You okay?' he asked, swimming over to the side of the pool. 'Can I get you something?'

'I'm driving, but a small glass of red would go down nicely.'

He climbed out of the pool, and picked up a towel. Wrapping it around his waist he walked along to the kitchen and moments later he was back with a bottle and two glasses.

'Just a wee one, mind,' Liz said. 'Does the sauna work?'

'I assume so,' Ranald replied. He walked over to it and flicked a switch. 'It'll probably take a while to heat up.'

Liz looked up at him and reached for the towel. 'I wonder what we could do until then?'

ᛏᛧ

After, they were in the sauna – Ranald on the upper bench, Liz below him, grinning at each other like a pair of teenagers.

Ranald's pulse was still recovering. He let his head fall back against the pine cladding and exhaled slowly. He could feel the push of his own personal darkness. It had been dimmed by Liz's presence but now it was starting to reassert itself. That piece of charred meat that wore his clothes, spoke with his voice, limped through life, was working its way back into the forefront of his mind.

'You're definitely getting the hang of this, Mr McGhie,' said Liz.

'Why, thank you …' Ranald replied as he tried to shake his head free from the path it was surely heading down. 'Sorry, I've just realised I don't know your surname.'

'Don't be daft,' Liz replied. She leaned forwards and touched his knee. 'I've never told you.' She cocked her head to the side. 'I like to maintain an air of mystery.' She was holding a towel in front of her and used a corner to dab her forehead. 'Warm, eh?'

'That's the general idea,' Ranald said, with some effort. He wanted to sleep. That was of course, his other comfort. Sleep and sex, if he could spend all of his time doing that he might have a healthy mind.

Liz stood up. 'I need a shower.' She walked to the smoked-glass door, pushed it open and turned to Ranald who was enjoying the view.

'Don't stare, it's rude. And don't fall asleep in here. That wouldn't be too healthy.'

With a groan, Ranald sat up, jumped off the bench and followed her out of the sauna. Lying down on a lounger, he closed his eyes. He heard the shower come on and a tuneful hum from Liz as she sang under the hot water. He sang along, grateful to have the energy of another human being nearby, an energy that would hopefully keep him from diving into the hell of his own thoughts.

'See that girl/ watch that scene/ digging the dancing queen.'

'Don't give up your day job, Ran,' Liz shouted.

He smiled. Thought about a retort, but couldn't think of anything funny. He breathed deep and slow. Deep and slow.

Deep and…

He was in the garden. The grass was cool and wet on his bare feet. Mist swirled round his legs. Shapes shifted in the fog ahead. Formed. Faded. Reshaped themselves. A breeze on his neck, like a kiss. Perfume. *Her* perfume. A sweet, light and heady mix of citrus, cinnamon and wood oil.

Her hand in his. Her skin warm and dry. Her bones, in his light grip as insubstantial as the mist that flowered and shifted around them.

Where have you been, he sent her. *I've missed you.*

Her hand was gone. The mist faded and coalesced at his side, like a long skirt might flare in a quick gust of wind.

Her face was in his. He could feel her breath on his nose. He leaned forwards, his mouth formed as if for a kiss.

'Liar.' Loud. Like a bark.

Teeth bared. Dripping blood. Gore wedged into the space between them.

'LIAR. You will pay.'

Fear squeezed his heart. Stole air from his lungs.

He saw her in a small room. Her hair hanging from her head in damp rags. Her shift was white and open, exposing her breasts and a pool of blood at her groin. She was holding something in her arms. Something pink and fleshy. Part of it was hanging from her mouth. Her eyes wide with the grief of a hundred bereaved mothers.

'Ranald. What have you done, Ranald?'

He tried to wake up, but he was snared in the fog of his dream as if it was netting.

'Ranald.'

A cold hand on his shoulder.

'RANALD.'

Reality thrust its way through the sludge of his mind. Something was wrong. He opened his eyes. Saw the face of Danny Hackett. His open mouth. Uneven teeth. The pale pink of his tongue flecked with saliva.

'Ranald, what the hell have you done?' Danny shouted at him, shaking his shoulder hard enough to bruise.

'What…'

Danny stood back and looked towards the water.

Ranald stood up and looked in the same direction as Danny. He couldn't make sense of what he saw at first. It was too strange. As if it came from his dream.

A fully clothed Marcus was standing in the water. He was holding Liz's slack body and wading to the side of the pool.

Ranald looked at Liz, trying to comprehend what he was seeing.

'She doesn't want to get her hair wet,' he said, and his voice sounded like it was coming from someone else.

Then finally the truth hit him. His knees buckled. He was desperate to look away, but he couldn't. He stared. Fixed his eyes on Liz. Taking in everything – the angle of her legs and arms as they hung from her body. Her head tilted back. Her soaked hair, one side of it plastered over the lower half of her face.

Above that, her eyes staring into an endless nothing.

Terrified and lifeless.

26

Ran woke up in his bed. He sat up so abruptly his head swam, his mind searching for some sense of where he was and when…

'Hey,' Mrs Hackett said. 'Take it slow, Ranald. You're in your bed.'

'What?'

His mind was sending him pictures. Grass. Shadows. A swimming pool. A small hand in his. Liz bent over, looking over her shoulder at him, her eyes large with lust as she urged him on.

Liz smiling at him in the sauna.

Liz lying in Marcus's arms. Dead.

'No, no, no, no…'

Fuck. No.

What the hell happened?

'What am I … how did I get here?' Ranald asked Mrs Hackett, desperately hoping she would tell him that he'd slept in. That everything going on in his mind was the after-effect of some vivid dream. Or that someone had slipped a powerful hallucinogen into his coffee.

He searched Mrs Hackett's eyes for answers. She gave a small, accepting nod, as if she was saying it was time to face up to what he had done.

'You were hysterical … after … so Danny and I brought you up here, put you to bed, while Marcus…'

'What did Marcus…?'

'First, you need to tell me what happened, Ranald,' she said as if withholding judgement. Then she breathed in deeply through her nose. 'Did you kill that woman?'

'Kill? What? No.' Ranald jumped out of the bed, taking a tangle of sheets with him.

'It was just you and her in the pool room when Marcus and Danny went in there. You were unconscious on the lounger.' She looked at his head as if searching for evidence of some kind of wound. 'And the woman was in the water.' She held a trembling hand to her mouth. 'Please tell me you didn't kill that poor woman.'

'No, absolutely not.' Ranald searched his mind for some kind of solution. 'We were in the sauna…' He paused. 'She's dead? Really dead?'

Mrs Hackett just stared at him.

Ranald's knees buckled. Mrs Hackett held out an arm, trying to catch him on the way down. His chest heaved. Every part of him trembled. His guts churned. His mind delivered an image of Liz's lifeless eyes.

Mrs Hackett joined him on her knees on the bedroom carpet.

'We were in the sauna,' he began again. 'After we … you know… Then Liz went for a shower and I fell asleep on the lounger.' He exhaled, a long juddering breath. 'Then, next thing I know Danny is shaking me awake … and Marcus is in the water with…' He couldn't finish.

Mrs Hackett stared into his eyes for a long moment. Then at some internal signal she looked away, and back again. 'For what it's worth, I believe you.' She shook her head. 'Must've been a terrible, terrible accident.'

Ranald struggled back onto his feet. He realised he was still naked from his swim.

'Shit,' he said, looking down at himself.

'Go get dressed,' said Mrs Hackett. 'We're all in the kitchen. Come down when you're ready.'

'Where's the…'

'Danny is seeing to it.'

'What, no police? We need to phone the police.'

'Get some clothes on. Come down and talk to us in the kitchen,' she said, quietly, but with a firmness that invited no dissent.

Ranald walked into the kitchen, his heart thick in his chest. He felt as if his blood had all but solidified. His fresh t-shirt was already wet with sweat.

Marcus was sitting in one chair, Mrs Hackett in another.

'Where's Danny?' he asked. His voice cracked.

'Clearing up your fucking mess,' replied Marcus. He was still in his sopping-wet clothes. His sodden hair was pushed back off his face, highlighting the strain there.

'Wait a minute.' Ranald felt a surge of energy, feeding on Marcus's open hostility. 'I don't know what you think happened here…'

'You were lying pissed on a sun lounger and there was a dead woman in the pool, Ranald. What am I supposed to think?'

'I wasn't pissed. I didn't drink more than a glass of wine. And—'

'It's not looking good, Ranald. Not looking good at all.' Marcus drummed his fingers on the table. Ranald saw his mobile phone lying there, just within reach. He thought about grabbing it, trying for a signal and phoning the police.

'What do you mean?' he asked. 'It was an accident. It must have been an accident. I was asleep. Liz was in the shower. I fell asleep…'

'Let me tell you what's happening, Ranald.' Marcus fixed him with a glare. 'Or what *never* happened. That woman was never here. She never drowned in that pool. You never met her. Never fucked her—'

'The police. We need to contact the cops. I'm innocent. I did nothing wrong. Surely the evidence will point to that?'

Marcus leaned forwards, his eyes full of loathing. He had clearly already convinced himself that Ranald was guilty. 'Twenty-five years in criminal law and I've tried any number of murder cases; you are looking at a life sentence here, cousin.'

'What are you on about? It was an accident. It must have been.'

'Ranald, here's what the prosecution will tell the jury. An empty bottle of wine. Your DNA all over her, and inside her. A telling bruise on the side of her head and lungs full of chlorinated water. All they will have trouble with is intent. Murder or manslaughter.' He wiped one hand off another. 'As open and shut as I've ever seen it. You killed that woman, Ranald.'

'No!' Ranald shouted. 'No…' He looked from Marcus to Mrs Hackett. Beseeching her, *back me up*. But she cast her eyes to the table top and said nothing.

'We simply can't allow another scandal in this family,' said Marcus with certainty in his voice. 'So this is what we are going to do. What we *are* doing. Danny is, as we speak, driving that poor woman and her car up to Loch…' He paused. 'Best we don't tell you which one. Suffice to say, her and her car will end up in deep water.'

'You're a lawyer. How the hell can you—?'

'Do you want to go to prison?' Marcus seemed to be fighting for some calm now.

'Of course not. But—'

'Mrs Hackett,' Marcus looked over at her, '… would you leave us for a moment, please?'

Without a word, she left the room.

In a blur, Marcus was in Ranald's face. He grabbed the collar of his t-shirt and pulled him closer. 'You murderous little cunt. If you weren't part of this family I would have you. You'd never see the light of day.' He pushed him away again as if trying to regain control. He took a deep breath and stepped back. Walked round to his side of the table and sat down.

Marcus stared at Ranald for a long moment.

'Having witnessed that little scene in the pool, I could begin to believe you really are a product of two sets of Fitzpatrick blood.' Then, as if he had reached a decision, his eyes gleamed. Ranald felt his gut twist. His mind was working at a hundred miles an hour, and, despite his protestations that the police should be called, he could not but feel relieved that they weren't going to be involved. Sure, he *was* innocent, wasn't he, but Marcus had a point, he had no idea how he would defend himself against this.

He looked into his cousin's eyes, read the disgust and tried to work out if he knew anything about the real story behind Helena and

Gordon's apparent double suicide. If Marcus did know his mother had murdered his father, now would be a perfect time to drive that nail into Ranald's conscience. Like mother like son.

He held onto the edge of the table. There was a keen expression on Marcus's face. 'You've obviously come off your drugs. You will go back on them.'

Ranald's head was flipping over and over. How did Marcus know about his mental-health situation?

As if reading his thoughts Marcus smiled – a mean grimace. 'I'm a lawyer, Ranald. Don't you think I had you investigated as soon as we found out about you? Now, as I was saying, you'll go back on your meds—'

'No, I can't do—'

'You've just murdered someone, Ranald,' Marcus said it in a matter-of-fact tone, as someone might discuss the weather. 'We've got to make sure you are not a risk to yourself or anyone else.'

'I didn't…' Did he? He thought about his mother, and crossed his arms against his fear that in this, he was his mother's son.

'Sit your arse down.'

Ranald did as he was told.

'If you don't go back on the drugs, I will have you committed.'

'What?' Ranald jumped to his feet so sharply, his chair clattered to the floor behind him.

Marcus crossed his arms. 'You were found sleeping in the lift. You were seen walking naked in the garden and through the house. You've been heard talking to yourself. And today, one of my friends in town phoned me to say they'd seen you step in front of a van. With your medical history and all of that, there's enough evidence to commit you to a mental institution.'

'You utter, utter bastard.'

'And you've been sectioned before.'

So he knew all of this?

'Sit down, Ranald. I know everything about you…'

'You complete—'

'Now.'

Ranald sat down again.

Marcus smiled as if he was preparing to deliver his coup de grâce. 'Here's what's going to happen. No prison. No loony bin. Instead, your mental state will be managed by the proper medication. We will find you other lodgings, large enough to house all those fucking books and you can lose yourself in them well past your dotage.'

'What a minute. What about the house?'

'The developers are waiting to begin work. They will be here by the end of the year. All we need to do is get things in motion. You will sign the necessary forms and authorise the trust—'

'I won't do it. I'll not do it.'

Marcus slammed the palm of his hand on the table. 'You. Will. Fucking. Do. It. You murdering little shit.' He lifted up his phone. Turned it around and showed the screen to Ranald. It showed Liz's body in the pool and Ranald, slack on the lounger in the far corner.

How the hell did the cold bastard have the presence of mind to take this photo after walking in on what appeared to be a dead body?

As if he read Ranald's mind, Marcus said. 'I've been at lots of murder scenes. Seen lots of dead bodies.' He paused a beat. 'And I'm always working an angle, cousin.' He put his phone back down on the table. 'I've not seen anything yet that fazes me.'

Ranald fought for a solution. Tried to force his mind to think, but all he could see was Liz … lifeless. He felt the emotion build. Bit down on his lip. Didn't want his prick of a cousin to see him any weaker.

'Think about it, Ranald.' Marcus tried to adopt a more conciliatory tone. 'You'll receive a fair share of the proceeds – enough to buy a house that can accommodate you and all of our mad great-uncle's books, and give you a small annual income on the side. The drugs will keep your murderous rage under control. And in this space' – he held out his arms – 'a beautiful development will be built.'

Ranald sagged in his chair. Alexander's library would be lost. Which, in the grand scheme of things, hurt him, but it paled against the knowledge that he may have inherited a sick woman's impulses.

Liz was dead.

Could he really be a murderer, like his mother?

Marcus tapped the back of his phone. 'We will have the papers drawn up straight away. And just in case you change your mind, the wine bottle and glasses have been preserved in a safe place. Lots of lovely DNA there. We have the photo here and we can release the exact location of the car and the body.' With a triumphant look he sat back in his chair.

Ranald felt a flare of rage. In that moment, he thought he might well be capable of another murder. He imagined himself reaching into the kitchen drawer, pulling out a bread knife and slashing it across Marcus's throat.

The image took his breath away.

'You will sign the papers, cousin, won't you?' Marcus asked, his tone level.

'Fuck off,' replied Ranald, but it was an empty gesture. Nothing but a last act of defiance. He had no other way out of this situation.

27

Mrs Hackett sat in the doctor's reception area with Ranald while they were waiting to see the GP. She'd been adamant that he leave his usual practice and join one that was more local to them. He was in too fragile a state to argue.

'You don't think I did it, do you?' he whispered to her, yet again, before his name was called. 'I couldn't … I wouldn't…' Who was he trying to convince?

'It doesn't matter what I think, son. I'm here to serve the family I've served all my days.'

'I didn't do it, Mrs H, I promise you.' As if to reinforce his argument, he placed his hand on top of hers. With a barely disguised shudder, she snatched it away.

'It will all be fine, Ranald,' she murmured. 'Once you're back on the medication, you'll be your old self once again.' The cheer in her voice was false.

A buzzer sounded and his name popped up on the announcement screen.

╫

The doctor was a young, Asian guy with designer stubble and a huge Adam's apple.

'What can I do for you, Mr McGhie?'

Ranald nodded. Thought about saying, *I think I might have killed someone*. Instead he said nothing and stared at the patterns in the wood of the doctor's desk.

'Mr McGhie?'

The doctor might be young but he already had that deep, sooth-ing voice to which patients would respond.

'I was on some stuff at my last doctor's and … I came off it without, you know, checking it was okay to do so.'

'Right.' The doctor sucked on his lower lip. He swivelled in his chair and faced his computer screen. 'Let's see…' Pause. 'Yup, your records have been transferred across.' He read quietly. 'You were on…' He read out a couple of scientific-sounding names that Ranald vaguely recognised. He'd always been in denial about his condition and invested as little time as possible in his own care.

'Why did you come off them?'

Ranald shrugged a 'dunno'. Wrists resting on his lap, he used the nail on his right index finger to dig dirt from behind his left thumb-nail. He quickly realised that this made him look like a recalcitrant schoolboy and sat on both hands. He looked squarely at the doctor. He was a grown-up, for crying out loud. Why was he reverting to this childhood state?

'New situation,' he answered. 'New house. Some security? I didn't think I needed them any longer.'

'What was the effect?'

'A mix of stuff. I saw things and I was incredibly, you know … horny.' His memory served up a memory of him making love to Liz, followed by her dead body; he nearly gagged. The thought came to him that he'd never be able to do that again. If he did, might he also kill? Was his lust and the killing linked? The sooner Marcus sold the house and he bought a little cottage in a forest somewhere, the better. Preferably a forest no one ever visited.

The doctor was saying something else. Ranald refocused. 'Sorry, what did you say?'

'A return of libido is quite normal for a young man of your age. When you say you saw things, what do you mean?'

The woman in the mirror.

Could he say the words out loud?

'Ghosts and stuff. It was quite scary.'

'Have you been sleeping okay?'

'On and off,' replied Ranald. 'Some nights like a baby. Some nights I sleepwalk, and some nights I can't sleep at all.'

The doctor made some reassuring noises. Then he read from the screen. 'According to your hospital notes you were diagnosed with bipolar and hospitalised after a manic episode that saw you on top of a roof…'

…Thinking he could fly, and Ranald felt a stab of resentment that the doctor would bring that up, but he knew the guy was reading all of this out to remind him that if he let things get away from him, the next journey up onto the roof might end very differently.

'…it also says you suffered from hypersomnia and insomnia. Agitation…' Ranald stopped listening. He didn't need to hear this. '… episodes of psychosis … displayed evidence of suggestibility.' The doctor paused, clearly noting that Ranald was distracted. 'If you take one thing from this meeting, it's that you should never go cold turkey with these drugs. You need to taper your way off them.' He swallowed and his Adam's apple bobbed. There were a couple of hairs growing out of it that he obviously missed each time he shaved. Ranald stared at it. It had to be better than the mess going on in his head. The doctor continued. 'There is a lot of evidence that stopping and starting your meds actually makes your condition worse. It can dramatically shorten the time between episodes.'

'So, anyway,' Ranald said, 'I need to go back on them.' He drummed his fingers on the desk. 'Soon as, please.'

'Any other symptoms of withdrawal?'

'I get very fucking annoyed, doctor.' He quickly reined his frustration in, forcing a laugh. 'Mood swings. Anxiety. You name it. I'm a basket case.'

'Not so, Mr McGhie. These drugs contain powerful compounds. Anyone would find themselves reacting like that if they came off them without proper management.' His tone was supportive.

Aye, but, would they murder someone?

Ranald didn't say it, even though, just for a moment, he wanted to. Perhaps then the doctor would phone the police and he would pay for what he'd done. He shouldn't get away with it. The family of that poor woman would be sick with worry. What would her husband be thinking?

All of this remained firmly locked behind his tongue, though, like ground glass in his throat. He deserved to pay, but he didn't have the moral courage to make sure it happened.

'I was saying…' the doctor raised his voice slightly '…two months' course for now. Get you back on an even keel.' He paused. 'No thoughts about self-harming?'

'No.' He realised as he said the word that he was nodding. 'I did step in front of a moving van. But that was just cos I forgot to look,' he lied.

'Happens to the best of us, Mr McGhie.'

The doctor typed. Clicked his mouse and a completed prescription came out of a small printer at the side of his computer. He signed it and handed it over to Ranald.

'And I'll refer you back to your mental health practitioner to get you back into some good habits, okay?'

Mrs Hackett was waiting for him at the front door of the surgery.

'These places make me nervous,' she said to Ranald when he walked up to her. 'God knows what germs there are.' Her expression softened. 'Ready to go home?'

Ranald nodded, trying to work out how she was feeling about him. One minute she seemed scared to even look at him. The next she was as solicitous as a new mother.

†⊦

At the chemist, while he was waiting for his pills to be handed over, he bought a bottle of water, so he could take the first dose immediately. The sooner the mess in his head was silenced, the better, he thought.

By the time he got home, the early sedative effect of his pills was taking hold. He walked in the door, his chin almost on his chest. He made for the stairs, wanted to say, he'd just go to his room, but the words were beyond him. When he got to the top, he remembered this was why he usually took these pills at bedtime.

He made his way to the side of the bed and allowed himself to fall forwards onto the mattress, from there managing to worm his way up to the pillows.

He closed his eyes and allowed the pills to work their magic. This was a world where nothing happened. Nothing could go wrong. Every thought was edged in cotton wool. Each word bandaged with care.

He opened and closed his mouth, and realised how dry it was already. He considered going to the bathroom for a glass of water. In a minute, he thought, turning on his side and pulling his knees up to his chest.

Here he was safe. Warm and dry. He could wait out the world. Pretend nothing had happened. No Liz. No dead body.

No *her*, he thought, with a pang of missing.

28

The next few weeks passed in a haze. Everything came at him as if from a distance. As if it was happening to someone else and he, the owner of his body, was sidelined. Food tasted either of cardboard or nothing at all, and he wouldn't have bothered eating if Mrs Hackett hadn't prepared each meal and then sat with him until he had eaten at least part of it.

Soup was a good choice, she said to him one day. And look, she added, you barely needed to chew.

Which was a bonus. Chewing took effort.

He passed his days lying on a Chesterfield sofa in the library. Picking a book – making that sort of decision – was beyond him. Instead, he lay among them and pretended they were whispering down at him. Laying a carpet of soothing words over the soft mush of his mind.

Work was beyond him, so he emailed his agent a short message. He wrote 'On holiday' in the subject line and hoped that would be enough. Clarity of thought and the ability to express ideas – they really were on holiday; but explaining that was outwith his ken.

Thoughts of his parents regularly popped into his head. They were the reason he first went on the pills. Such a lot of grief for such a young mind to handle, his doctor had said. He was an older man, close to retirement, lined and worn down by his service to the community. Ranald often thought of putty when he looked at him. Wanted to push his finger into the man's cheek to see how long the indentation stayed there.

He thought about the moment he found his parents. Now, under the influence of a chemical removal from emotion, he was willing to prod the memory.

His mother did *that*.

And she had a baby with her brother. Ranald knew Marcus was lying about the two of them being brothers ... but even that thought was simply another stone on the dark path he walked down.

Here he was keeping up the family's murderous tradition.

But the further he went, the more he realised that the sadness he felt was now only vague, as if his parents' sudden deaths were no more than a shame. A shitty thing to happen. Perhaps the truth was that he was still that emotionally inarticulate young man, frozen in that moment, unable to deal with what had happened. Unaware of his stuckness – as a self-help book Martie bought for him had termed it.

The good thing was, nothing much mattered anymore. The drugs saw to that.

Now and again his mind went to the body in the pool, and the thought also occurred to him that he was complicit in betraying his great-uncle's dying wishes. But these musings were no longer accompanied by any bone-crushing guilt.

⊩

Eventually the fog began to recede a little. His emotions were still on hold, but he could function to a degree – make decisions about when to go to bed, when to get up, when to eat, what to eat. How much work to do. He'd even got back into the pool and felt the pleasure and caress of cool water the full length of his body.

One particular morning he received a phone call from Quinn.

'Mr McGhie, I have something for you.'

'Right,' said Ranald. 'How am I going to get it?' he asked, thinking, *Can't you just stick it in the post?*

'I can't put it in the post,' Quinn said, as if reading Ranald's mind. 'The instructions are to put it directly into your hand. I have space in my diary for you this morning. A taxi will be at your door within the hour. I'll see you when you get here.'

For the first time in a long time, Ranald dressed with some care. A dark-blue suit, pale-blue shirt and a red patterned tie. Checking himself in the mirror, he almost didn't recognise himself. His haircut had almost grown out, the layers on the top of his head falling forwards into his eyes. And it was those eyes that struck him most. They looked haunted among the shadows of his face.

ⱵⱵ

Quinn started when he saw him walk into his office.

'The resemblance is…' He stopped, as if remembering his own personal diktat not to exchange personal comments with clients. 'Good to see you, Mr McGhie. Thank you for coming in.'

'Why do you need to see me, Mr Quinn?'

'Your great-uncle,' Quinn began in a not-beating-about-the-bush tone, 'left instructions, telling me that, were you enticed into adapting the trust to allow for the sale of Newton Hall, I was to give you this.' He opened the file on his desk and lifted out a small brown envelope. Ranald recognised the shape and colour of it. There was a pack holding similar envelopes in his desk back at the house.

His desk.

Ranald reached forwards to pick up the envelope. He looked at Quinn.

'I believe everything you need to know is within the envelope. Mr Fitzpatrick was a highly articulate man. I've no doubt you'll understand everything he wants you to.' Quinn stood up. 'I'm to leave you here to read it, so I can … assess your … temperature once you've digested the contents.' And with that, Quinn left the room.

There was a small, silver paper knife on the desk. Ranald picked it up and used it to slice open the envelope. The sharp, clean tearing noise seemed to echo around the large room.

He pulled out the paper and began to read.

My dear Ranald,

As I write, a clock is chiming the hour in my ear. Midnight. An illustration, just when I don't need it, of the relentless march of time. For assuredly my time approaches, leaving me with just enough to make right some of the mistakes of my life.

One of those mistakes was not to ignore the wishes of your grandmother and take more interest in you and your development. She was a vain, proud woman, and she felt the loss of your mother (into what she argued was a deserved life of penury) very deeply. On her deathbed, she made me swear that Helena's progeny (that was how she talked about you) would not receive any of the benefits his mother had denied him by walking out.

Deathbed promises are not something one breaches lightly, and it is only now, as my end approaches, that I feel able to follow the instincts that told me your grandmother was a bitter and lonely old woman who should have been ignored.

I did intervene when your parents died. I couldn't sit back and watch as you struggled to deal with this. And I had to protect the reputation of the family. There is no benefit in detailing here what steps I took, but I did have occasion to meet the wonderful young woman you eventually chose as your wife, and I approved of her thoroughly.

I was in the back of the hall when you graduated and I sneaked into the back of the church when you got married. Each time I wanted nothing more than to walk up and introduce myself, but my own shy nature and lack of courage would not allow me too. Instead, I watched on from a distance, with pride squeezing my heart. It's a wonder you didn't hear me sob.

But enough of my emotional outpourings and on to the matter at hand. You will by now know of my library and I hope and pray that you have enjoyed being in that space as much as I enjoyed creating it. I did so partly with you in mind, and I hope that you might enjoy for years to come the haven it provides.

If you are reading this letter, then, as I feared it might happen, that haven is under threat.

You might ask why I didn't make the conditions of the trust tighter – impossible to breach. My reason may well yet prove to be foolish, but I wanted you to have a choice. You have been such a slave of life's misfortunes, Ranald, I wanted you to eventually have an element of control, even if the choice this control delivered meant the breaking up of the one thing I hold dear.

Your cousins, Marcus and Rebecca, are the other beneficiaries of my will. They each benefit handsomely, although I fear their distinct lack of moral fibre will mean my bequests are wasted. My gift to them comes from duty. They are family and for the Fitzpatricks that connection is paramount (another reason your grandmother found it difficult to forgive your mother for walking away).

My gift to you, however, comes from a place of affection and I hope that reading this letter you come to see that affection as being very real indeed.

To the point, dear Ranald. As I write, I am aware of your cousins' financial difficulties and I am also aware of both their hope that they might inherit this house, and their plans for what they would do with it. (They have forgotten all about you, and I don't plan to remind them. I'll leave that to the reading of the will, which, if you forgive my indulgence, gives me a moment of pleasure in its consideration.)

I warn you that they will do what they can to persuade you to join in their project. And I pray that this warning is not diminished in any way as it moves from my mind on to the page. William's offspring are my family, but they inherited none of his charm and all of his venereal, wasteful ways.

William was a terrible, terrible man. An affront to the grand Fitzpatrick name. He even claimed to have had relations with another member of the family, but I paid that no credence whatsoever. The man would have said and done anything to get a reaction out of me.

I will draw a line there, Ranald. There is only so much I can commit to paper before my guilt at this betrayal – I acknowledge the contradiction with a faint smile – stops me from continuing. I must sign and seal this letter before I reconsider and tear it up.

The word 'apology' is a collection of letters, an arrangement of syllables. A word that I fear comes nowhere near to explaining the sense of responsibility and sorrow I feel when I think about how our family has failed you. The library and the house is my way of redressing that balance, giving you a home, a haven and the security that you have lacked for most of your adult life.

With love and affection (and some tears)

Alexander Fitzpatrick

29

Ranald read the letter again. And again. He imagined his uncle leaning over the desk, writing the letter, his face full of concentration as he carefully chose his words.

He followed the lines of the man's signature, wishing he knew enough of the science of handwriting to glean from it any of the signs of his uncle's character. Following that thought he reflected that the letter itself was full of clues.

Several words and sentences echoed in his mind. 'Venereal'. Sexually indulgent – was that what Alexander was suggesting? Was he referring to William and his mother? He all but discounted it in his letter, though. So did William have a series of scandalous encounters with women?

The door behind him opened, the base brushing over the thick carpet. Footsteps, a cough and Quinn took his seat on the other side of the desk.

'You've read the letter, Mr McGhie?'

Ranald nodded.

'Your thoughts?'

'I…' Ranald shook his head. 'I can…' He coughed as if trying to free the words, and as he did so he knew this was a betrayal of his uncle and his intentions. 'I can use the proceeds to buy another, smaller house, but one that still has enough space for all the books.'

'Would that be the same, Mr McGhie?'

'They'd be safe. And still be together as a collection.'

'Right,' said Quinn.

Ranald studied him, looking for some sort of absolution. Permission.

'I'm not here to offer an opinion, Mr McGhie. I'm simply here to pass on my client's instructions and to record the result. And to enable what comes next.'

'Yeah, but you're looking at me like I'm a piece of shit.'

He wasn't, but Ranald needed to strike out. He knew he was in the wrong, but was tired of constantly aiming his scorn against his own life inwards.

Quinn was too smart to be affected by Ranald's words, though. 'You have two days to consider the words of your great-uncle,' he said. 'A meeting has been called by the other signatories to the trust: Marcus, Rebecca and myself. That's when we will all vote for the motion to change and sign the necessary papers if that is required.'

'You're also a signatory, Mr Quinn?' Ranald asked.

A nod.

'You don't need me, then, do you?' This was great, this could happen without Ranald betraying Alexander. 'You just vote along with my cousins, and the developers can move in.'

'That's assuming I think that is the right thing to happen.'

This was a surprise. Ranald assumed Quinn and Marcus were as thick as thieves.

'You're going to vote against it?' asked Ranald.

'The trust states a majority vote is required. You, Marcus and Rebecca will be enough to carry the motion regardless of what I think should happen.'

Ranald stared at Quinn, trying to get a sense of which way the man might vote, but the lawyer's face was as blank as a mask.

Ranald pushed himself to his feet and as he did so, noticed the weakness in his thighs. Even his body was telling him this was wrong.

'One last question, Mr McGhie. As you know, Alexander did not trust Marcus and Rebecca. Can you confirm that whatever you decide to do is your own free will? Your cousins haven't offered you any enticements?'

Ranald stared at the top of the desk. He wanted to say there was no need for enticements – he had managed to mess everything up all on his own. For a blink of a moment he considered coming clean.

But then he imagined himself in a jail cell waiting to be tried for murder. He shuddered.

'No.'

Before Quinn could say anything else, he left the office.

╫

Walking in the front door of the house he immediately felt himself relax. He hadn't realised he was apprehensive about being away from these walls until he came back inside them and felt an easing.

This was home. At last.

Just a short time ago he was anxious about walking in that door. All this space had served only to highlight his aching sense of loneliness and the lack of people in his life. Now – was it the drugs, or was he growing into the place? Whatever it was, he should access this new feeling, for the good of his health. Grab a blanket and a book and go into the lift for a little reading session.

And the thought of what he was about to do came crashing down on him.

He made his way through to the library as if he was dragging a block of concrete behind him and sat behind the desk. He fired up his laptop to check his emails, trying to ignore his feeling of discomfort. What choice did he have? Sell the house or go to prison … it was no choice at all.

But he did kill someone. Didn't he? He had prodded at the memory but nothing came back to him. At the least he was complicit in someone's death. He should be punished for that.

The first email was from his agent: 'Still on holiday?'

He ignored it and hoped the fact that it had gone unanswered was all that was needed.

The next email was from an address he didn't recognise. There was an attachment, and despite his best intentions – it would have gone straight to his spam box if it was in anyway dodgy, right? – he clicked it open.

It was the image he'd last seen on Marcus's phone. Poor Liz in the foreground and him, clearly there, behind her. He jerked his seat back from his desk, as if to get away from the picture.

Fuck.

He did that. Whatever happened in that conservatory, a woman was dead, and he was a worthless piece of shit. He crossed his arms, held himself tight. He deserved nothing good. Should he just give himself up to the police?

Ranald saw himself in a prison cell. An aluminium toilet in one corner, a snarling cellmate in another with a shank in his hand, bars in the small head-height window and nothing but grey skies beyond.

He didn't have a choice, did he? He had to sign the papers.

Anxiety making his body tremble, he stood up. Unable to stay in one place, he wandered through to the kitchen and absentmindedly began to make coffee – for want of something to occupy his hands. As he waited for the kettle to boil he had a thought: this email from Marcus – who else could have sent it? – had arrived just when he got back home from talking to Quinn about saving the house and stopping the development.

Was Quinn in on it? How else would Marcus know to terrorise him on this particular morning?

And what about the developers – were they in on the act, too? He realised he didn't know the first thing about the company – what was its name ... McIntyre? He needed to know more about what was actually happening with the project. But how could he find out?

He slapped his forehead. Of course, Marcus had given him a folder with all the particulars. Refusing to look at it, Ranald could remember throwing it down on the flower table in the hall. How long ago was that? It seemed a different age.

Mrs Hackett chose that moment to walk past the doorway. He got up from his chair and chased after her.

She turned when she heard him, looking at him as if assessing his state of mind. 'I'm just about to finish for the day, Ranald. Is there anything I can do for you?'

'I'm looking for a folder,' Ranald said. 'Last I saw it, it was on the table in the hall.'

'Yes,' Mrs Hackett said, her mouth pursed in disapproval. Then she gathered herself. 'It's still there, Ranald. Now, I must go. Danny will be waiting for me.'

Ranald blinked at the mention of Danny, realising he hadn't seen him for … how long? Since the day he'd got rid of Liz's body. Was Danny avoiding him? How had he been affected by having such a job to do? He'd have to be a pretty callous bastard to dispose of a human being like that. When he looked at Danny, Ranald always got the feeling of a man who knew his place in life. He was a servant and took pride in doing a good job. Like his wife, he was loyal to the family. But that kind of action was beyond loyalty. What was Ranald missing? Was Danny more than the humble gardener? Or did Marcus have some kind of hold over the Hacketts?

As Ranald walked to the hall he thought about Mrs Hackett's reaction to his question. She wasn't happy with him. Or, to be fair, she was even less happy with him than she normally was. He needed to get to the bottom of that. Things were bad enough without losing her support.

Sure enough, the file was on the table. He wondered whether Mrs Hackett had read it. Why shouldn't she? She was bound to be curious. This was going to affect her as well.

Back in the library he sat down at the desk and opened the folder. It contained lots of paper. With lots of diagrams. Most of it was meaningless at first, but his mind slowly made the shapes on the pages correspond with the house as it stood.

His bedroom and the other rooms off that corridor made up one apartment, as did the rooms below. The pool was to be given an extension, turning that area into a two-bedroomed apartment.

He turned over the page and studied the one below it. This was of the gardens. There, at the side, it looked like the garage would be converted into a mews cottage and in the far corner a block of four apartments, two storeys high.

He positioned that in his mind, turned in his seat and looked out of the window.

But that apartment block was where the Hackett's cottage was. Where were they going to go? Had Marcus made them an offer they couldn't refuse?

Was that why Mrs Hackett was being more off-hand with him?

Ranald closed the file and pushed it away from him, shaking his head. He needed answers. There was too much going on here that he knew nothing about.

How to get those answers? It wasn't like he could phone Marcus and demand to know if he was planning on putting them all out of their homes.

Oh, come on, that was stuff and nonsense. It was as if he heard Great-Uncle Alexander in his head. That was something he might have said. And he would have had a point. *Admit it, Ran,* he thought, *all this crap about some grand plan of Marcus's was displacement.* He sighed; he knew his mind was seeking a target, someone to focus on, someone else who could be a villain; someone – anyone – who could replace the crushing thought that he was a killer.

Seeking a way to corral the crazy in his head, Ranald pulled Alexander's letter out of his pocket and placed it on the desk. Smoothing the paper out with his palm, he read it again. He imagined seeing an old man, hunched in the last pew of the church. He sent him a smile of thanks and saw his uncle's eyes twinkle in response.

He sat back in his chair, shaking his head at his whimsy.

Looked back down at the letter. How could he keep the house and satisfy his uncle's wishes, without going to jail?

Wasn't that what he deserved? For probably the thousandth time, he cast his mind back to that afternoon. The last he remembered of Liz was her heading over to the showers. Then he fell asleep. Next thing he knew Danny was shaking him awake.

What really happened in the interim?

He had been sleepwalking. Had he struck Liz in his sleep? That kind of thing happened, didn't it? Was he a murderer? He crossed his arms, as if protecting himself from the thought. He didn't have a violent bone in his body. Even when he was a kid, he walked away from every fight. He couldn't remember ever striking anyone. So, why would he do it now, in his sleep?

Her.

Had she affected him somehow? She was clearly jealous of any thoughts he might have of another woman. Had she – could she – influence his behaviour in that way?

Ranald planted his elbows on the desk and rested his forehead on the heels of his palms. He stayed like this for a long moment. The drugs were keeping the worst of his emotions at bay, but still, he needed answers.

How could he get them when he wasn't even sure what the questions were?

⊩

He had to do something. Sitting around the house under the combined weight of his guilt over Liz's murder and the subsequent part he had to play in Newton Hall being sold was too much for him to bear. He should either increase his prescription or go looking for answers. On top of what he now knew about his mother, what was his family history? Who exactly were these people? He thought about the old man at the barbers' – Ken Welsh. Ranald was in no doubt that he had some opinion about the Fitzpatricks. And was it a coincidence that wherever Ranald went, Ken seemed to be nearby? Surely it wouldn't take much to get him to talk. Before he knew it he was shrugging himself into a jacket and was on his way to Dan and Stan's.

Once there, he was pleased the place was all but empty. He was directed towards Dan's seat with a grin. He looked around himself, noticed a Halloween display in the window. It was nearly the end of October already?

'What can I do you for?' Dan asked.

'Same again, please.'

Dan reached for his water bottle and sprayed Ranald's hair. 'I suppose one hairstyle change every ten years is enough, eh?'

'The old guy who was in here the last time I was in…' Ran said, getting straight to the point.

Dan stopped spraying and looked at him in the mirror. 'Old guy?'

'Aye, he let me go before him. Said he was in no rush.'

Dan stared off into memory. Sifted. Sorted. 'Oh, aye. Mr Welsh? What about him?'

'Is he all right?'

Dan looked surprised by the question. 'As all right as any of the old duffers that come in here.'

Stan sent a look of warning across the room. 'That's our bread and butter you're talking about, mate.'

Dan waved a hand in the air, dismissing Stan's comment. 'They know I'm only joking.' He gave Ranald a look in the mirror that said, *I'm not joking.* 'Why do you ask?' he said to Ranald.

'Just something he said to me about my family.'

Dan nodded slowly. 'If anyone knows anything about folk in this area it's old Ken Welsh. He's like a walking community notice board.' He began to snip at Ranald's hair.

'Not much of a notice board if he wouldn't give me any details.'

'The thing with people like that' – Dan waggled his comb at Ranald – 'is to pretend you're not that bothered hearing about the gossip he has. It will drive him nuts. Then he feels he *has* to tell you everything.'

How on earth could he manage to do that? Ranald wondered.

'Talk to him about something he might be interested in and see if the conversation develops from there,' suggested Dan.

'First, I just need to engineer a meeting with him that will feel random.'

Dan pointed towards the window. 'I see him popping in across the road, into The Station. He's in there almost every day.' He turned to look at the clock on the wall. 'It's just gone two pm. He's usually in there about four. Must be for a wee pre-dinner snifter.'

╫

Once his hair was cut, Ranald made his way to The Station, which looked just as its name suggested – a former railway building: long, low, grey brick, with regularly spaced windows, and plenty of hanging flower baskets to add colour.

Inside, he was surprised by the modern feel to the bar. Lots of light. Light tan floorboards, a marble bar fronted with blue tiling. He would have suspected Mr Welsh to be an old-school drinker. Lots of dark wood, brewery sign mirrors, Formica table tops and any drink you wanted as long as it was beer, lager or whisky. The only nod to modernisation in such a place would be a fruit machine and a flat-screen TV.

He ordered a pint of lager at the bar, nabbed a newspaper from a rack and took one of the seats by the window. He settled down to read, thinking, this was what it was like to be a normal person. He sent a silent thank-you to whoever had developed and manufactured the drug he was on. But despite the mind balm of the chemicals he couldn't help but feel a surge of guilt that he was only on them because someone had died.

Liz.

And she was there in the pool. Sodden cloth sticking to her skin. Sightless eyes staring up at the roof.

Another shot of guilt. Liz didn't deserve his chemically induced withdrawal from the truth.

A voice in his ear disrupted his chain of thought.

'If it isn't the young Fitzpatrick.'

He looked up from his paper. It was Ken Welsh, just as predicted.

'The name's McGhie, actually. Ranald.'

'Aye, son, aye,' replied the old man, as if locking that piece of information away. 'I forgot your mother ran away to get married.'

You forget nothing, Mr Welsh, thought Ranald.

'This is nice,' said Ranald. Then, remembering Dan's advice said,

'I felt like getting out of the house for a while, you know. Big houses get a bit lonely.'

'Aye, son.' Ken's eyes shone a little brighter. 'What's happening with the house? Are the developers moving in soon?'

'Has this place been open long?' Ranald asked, looking around. 'I assume it used to be a train station or something?'

'Wonder what gave that away?' said Ken with a hint of a smile. 'The railway line running along the back there?'

Ranald made a face, as if admitting he'd said something stupid. He made a pretence of going back to his newspaper.

'Aye,' Ken said again. He was quiet for a moment, then said, 'I should be getting the new boy a wee drink to welcome him back to the area, eh?'

Ranald looked back up at him and pretended he hadn't heard. 'Sorry?'

'Get you a wee drink, Ranald? Welcome you back.'

'That's very kind of you, Ken. A pint of lager, please.'

Looking pleased with himself, Ken walked across to the bar and returned a few moments later armed with two full pint glasses.

'Cheers, son,' he said as he placed them on the table and sat down, groaning as he did so. 'S'good to take the weight off.' He took a sip. 'So, what's happening up at the house then?'

'You'll probably know as much as me.'

'Really?' Ken sat back in his seat. 'Last I heard, you inherited the house, but if you sold it you'd have to share the proceeds with your cousins.' He took another sip. 'Which, if you ask me, is a strange way to organise an inheritance.'

'Sure is,' said Ranald, thinking Ken had strong sources. 'I think my old uncle was trying to test me.'

'Hmm. I don't understand it myself. Either he wanted you to have the house or he didn't.' He sucked on his top lip. 'As much of a prick in death as he was in life.' He paused. 'Ach, that's no' being quite fair on him, even though I can't stand him. *That* was the young man. The older man? He did seem different.' Ken's eyes grew distant. 'I moved away for a few years, came back twenty years ago. First day back I saw Alexander Fitzpatrick up at the Cross, I almost walked past him – barely recognised him. He was a shadow of what he was. Not cowed, exactly. Just … less. As if he'd been rubbed away by something. A guilty conscience, I like to think.' He flavoured his smile with a sense of self-mockery. 'Hark at me, sounding all intelligent.' Ken looked at Ranald over the top of his pint. 'So what are you going to do?'

'I'm going to give it serious consideration.' He felt satisfied with that answer; it gave nothing away.

Ken studied him for a minute. 'You know exactly what you're going to do, son,' he said. 'You just don't want to admit it yet.'

Ranald shrugged. Then thought about something Ken said earlier.

'That's a couple of times you've called Alexander a prick. What's he to you?'

Ken's eyes narrowed. 'I hate it when rich folk think they own the rest of us.'

Ranald said nothing, hoping Ken would expand on his comment. But the old man returned to his pint. Ranald was the first to crack.

'There's any number of rich folk in this place. Are the Fitzpatricks the only ones who piss you off, or do they all get your goat?'

Ken smiled. 'Oh, your family manage to take it to another level.' He placed his glass back on the table and rested his hands on the table edge. There was a faint tremor in his right hand. The skin on the back of it a map of fat veins, deep wrinkles and liver spots. 'To be fair, as I said, Alexander seemed to be a different guy than the one who went to war.' He exhaled. 'War tends to do that, you know.' He shook his head. 'You seem a nice young fella. Maybe being kept away from them has done you some good.'

To hell with it, thought Ranald. He should just ask.

'I need to know what those people were like, Ken. It might help me make a decision about the house, you know?' He adopted his best hangdog expression and looked into the older man's eyes. 'Last time we met you hinted that you knew … stuff. That there might even have been a scandal?'

'Just the one?' Ken snorted, and then shook his head, the disdain he felt for the family evident in that small movement.

'We're talking about Alexander,' Ranald replied. *Just tell me*.

Ken studied him. Narrowed his eyes as if making a decision. 'There was a young lassie on the staff. A bonnie wee thing apparently. Your uncle got her pregnant.' Pause. 'Good as raped her if you ask me…'

'Aww, c'mon,' said Ranald. 'That's a bit harsh.'

'What would you call it?' Ken leaned towards him. 'He's got all the power. She's worried about keeping her job. He forces himself on the wee lassie.'

Ranald studied Ken and for the first time saw how old he really was. The pale, fragile skin under his eyes, puffy and threaded with small, red veins. The sparse, but overly long eyebrows. There was more to this antagonism than a neighbour looking in envy at another.

'She was your big sister, wasn't she?' Ranald said. The realisation came at him and he'd voiced it before he could give it more consideration. 'What happened to her?'

Ken widened his eyes, clearly surprised at Ranald's reading of him. Then he slumped a little in his seat and took a long pull at his pint before speaking. 'I was just a kiddie when our Jennie got that job, but I remember her leaving our house for her first day at work. Wearing her best hat and gloves. You should've seen the smile of excitement on her face when she turned at the end of the path to wave cheerio to me and my mother. She would have been eighteen, just fresh out of secondary school.'

He shook his head slowly, and Ranald could see that for Ken, his sister would be forever eighteen.

'Most kids in those days left school at fifteen, you see. But Mum and Dad were keen for her to get an office job or something, maybe even go to university. But Dad took a turn for the worse. Some old war wound or something, and Jennie had to give up her dreams and go into service. I don't remember much about her after that. The big house was only a few miles away, but in those days, that might as well have been a million. And folk rarely got any time off. Sometimes at

New Year and the like.' He sniffed and rubbed at his nose. 'He tried to buy my mum and dad off, you know,' he said. 'After the war. Big as you like, in his best clothes. Said that he loved her. Said he wanted to pay for a proper tombstone.'

'She died?' Ranald asked, rather unnecessarily.

'Fucking brain of Britain, you, eh?'

Ranald acquiesced to that with a shrug. It was a stupid question. 'What happened to her?'

Ken was silent for a long moment. He stared at the top of his drink as if it was displaying all of his memories.

'My big sister was my hero,' he said eventually. 'It seemed like she'd found a good life for herself. Lots of kids wanted to work in service in the big houses in those days. And the Fitzpatricks had plenty of cash. She wrote me a letter once, telling me all about life in Newton Hall. About the grand feasts and the posh people with their fancy clothes.'

In Ranald's mind, a bat-squeak of recognition sounded through the fog.

'Don't know what happened to that letter.' Ken looked about himself as if it would appear magically in front of him. 'I read it over and over again. Tried to keep it safe, but you know what you're like as a kid. Careless doesn't cover it, eh?' He wiped at the side of his right eye. 'Sorry, son. Old age makes you get sentimental.'

Ranald motioned that there was no need for an apology. He felt absurdly responsible for the older man's age-old grief.

'The head bummer up there hated her. Old Mrs Winters was in charge of the staff.' He paused. 'That one was well suited to her name. Constant winter around Mrs Frosty Knickers.'

Ranald wanted to urge Ken to get to the point, but knew he'd best let him ramble.

'It was her fault really, you know. All of it.'

'All of what?'

'It was her that found Jennie. Said she had gone mad and had her committed.'

'Ken, I don't understand. What are you saying?'

The old man sighed like there was decades of pain in his breath. 'It was weeks after Alexander had gone off to war. Jennie had managed to hide her pregnancy from everyone. Even Alexander said he didn't know.' He wiped at another tear. 'I'm amazed this has still got the power to hurt, son. It was such a long time ago.' He looked into Ranald's eyes. 'You look so much like him, I'd give you a good kicking if I thought it would help.'

Ranald faked a smile in response. He was irritated, keen for answers, but knew the old man was taking his time because it was painful.

'So, anyway. The old bitch, Winters, found her. Accused her of giving herself an abortion. Said she was some kind of witch and was trying to eat the foetus as part of some kind of spell...'

'What?' A terrible image formed in his mind. *Her* with the dead thing in her arms.

'Aye. Anyway. Different times.' And then he added, as if it explained everything: 'And let me tell you son, mud sticks. Of course, no one knew about the pregnancy and Alexander wasn't there to defend her. Unmarried girls who found themselves in the family way were treated appallingly in those days.' A film of water covered the lower part of his eyes. 'She was carted off to the asylum. Died a few weeks later.'

'Dear God,' said Ranald, feeling an ineffable sadness. What a waste of a life. Then his mind brought him back to what Ken had said moments earlier, about a letter.

'Your sister wrote to you?' he asked.

'Well, to my mum and dad.' Ken nodded. 'Just that one time. That was a disappointment to my mother, that she didn't keep in touch. Thing is, as my parents told it she was always a girl of her word. After she died, they would point to that letter and the words at the bottom. She had even underlined it, saying she would write again soon. But,' he shrugged, 'we didn't get any more letters from her.'

The letters in his grandmother's desk.

Ranald jumped to his feet. 'I've got to go check something,' he said, abandoned a mystified Ken at the table, and ran nearly all the way back to Newton Hall.

ๅⵏ

He was panting when he dropped onto the seat in front of his grandmother's desk. Sweat dripped from his face as he pulled the drawer open and laid the folder on top of the desk. He opened it and scanned down to the signature. When he'd first read it, he was unable to decipher the signature, but with Ken Welsh's voice ringing in his ears, the small name became instantly clear.

Jennie.

30

Ranald was curled up on a sofa in the library. He needed food, but he was now too afraid of going near the lift to walk along to the kitchen. All he could think about was what Ken Welsh had told him. And the letters in his grandmother's desk.

Jennie – was she his 'ghost'?

There were no bloody ghosts, he thought. It was just the effects of coming off his meds for all those weeks. He'd experienced similar kinds of things in the past.

Then he thought about the times he'd spent with her. Slept beside her image in the mirror. Dreamed of her mouth on his. Her hand in his. That had all been, well, pleasant. He revised this thought. Better than that. It had felt like love.

He laughed at the notion.

Love.

With a ghost.

An imaginary ghost, even. How messed up was that? And in those letters she was not much more than a girl. He considered them, what they said, and kept going back to the word that had jumped out at him when he read them – 'safe'. The poor girl was trying to ask for help and there was no one there for her.

And how could they be, if his grandmother had kept the letters, if they'd never been sent? Then it occurred to him that his grandmother herself would have been young. How did she come to have them, then?

He lay back, head against the arm cushion and sighed. That was the ghost he was in love with?

A memory: he was in his room at the hospital, scratching at his right arm, convinced something had burrowed under the skin there.

He was speaking to Martie at a hundred miles an hour. He had no recollection of what he was saying, but the horror he could remember seeing on her face told him it was far from healthy. It was her reaction more than anything that bothered him. He saw real fear there.

He could deal with remembering the mania. That wasn't really him. But what shamed him, what burned into his brain, was the fact that he had made life so difficult for Martie. She was so young, how had she found the strength to deal with the change in him, while helping with all of the funeral preparations for his parents. While dealing, alone, with the truth of what happened…

No, this *thing*, whatever it was – this obsession with a ghost, with the spirit of a wronged girl – it wasn't love. It was a shift in brain chemistry. His condition. God knows how that would have affected the workings of his brain. He was imagining things. He was prone to psychosis, wasn't he? And what the successive discoveries he'd made since coming to Newton Hall – blow upon blow upon blow…

And he'd been so bone-crushingly lonely with all this space around him. Still was, despite going back on the meds. It would drive anyone to imagine a companion, someone to turn to for solace.

He looked at his laptop. Stood up from the sofa, went and sat at the desk and opened the lid. Wouldn't it be better to go online like the rest of the world? Get lost in social networking, dating apps or whatever echo chamber of banality he could find? It might even make him feel sane.

He closed the lid.

No, he wasn't going there.

He pushed his laptop away, knocking his great-uncle's letter further along the desk as he did so. He thought about giving it another read and stood up to reach it. As he did so he pressed his thigh against the underside of the desk.

Bending forwards to rub the sore spot on his thigh, he saw that one of the desk's drawers was pulled out slightly. Had he left it open? He reached down to push it shut and then remembered that this was where he'd stored Alexander's laptop. He opened the drawer and pulled the machine out. The power cables were attached.

He pushed open the lid and pressed the on button. The battery was low, so he plugged it in.

As when he'd first opened the machine, all those weeks ago, it had demanded a password. His right index finger hovered over the mouse. This time a hint came up on screen: 'Ranald' it said.

What?

No, he thought, it couldn't be that easy. Could it?

With a shrug he typed his full name in the password box, and was allowed entry.

The home screen was a generic Windows image and right in the centre of the screen was one icon: a Word document thumbnail. He clicked on it and began reading.

31

Dear Ranald,

As my hour comes, I regret more and more that I didn't defy my sister's wishes and get in touch with you. And somehow the thought that you may read my words here does warm me.

I do have a number of notebooks spread around the house that you may have read, but they were simply for my pleasure. This is going directly to you.

My lawyer, Mr Quinn, has another letter for you. As I write this I have no way of knowing which of these missives will find their way to you first. But I can tell you that the letter I sent to you via the lawyer tells you only part of the picture. This will fill in the rest. Why didn't I just include this with the other letter? Because it contains information that if read by anyone outside of the family would be incendiary. I trust Mr Quinn almost completely, but he is a mere human and, as Seneca once said, *errare humanum est*.

What age are you now, Ranald? Late twenties? Do you look back at your younger self and wonder at the change time has wrought? Do you look back at him as if he is another person and wonder how he could have done the things he did?

I do. Every single day of my life; it has coloured my every waking second and chained me to a moment I wish was confined to another's memory.

I was young, immature and born in to a life of privilege. And that wealth and the licence it offered did not have a positive impact on my burgeoning ego. I thought I was untouchable. I thought that everything and everyone was there for my use.

As I sit here and write this I'm shaking my head, judging my early character and finding it seriously lacking. Forgive me, but I am an old man and my mind is wandering. I will get to the point.

Have you met her yet? My Jennie?

She was employed to look after my mother and my younger sister, your grandmother. I first saw her on the first day of her employment here. What beauty. I can still remember her wide-eyed, flushed innocence as she stood in the main hall, holding her hat in her hands in front of her as she looked around the space in wonder.

She had just turned eighteen. I was twenty-three and I had to have her. I was the young master of the house. She was a lowly servant and no one could gainsay me. But she did, at first.

Good lord, but was she a clever one. She recognised my attentions for what they were and for the most part she managed to avoid being in the same space as me on her own. If ever it did happen she would gracefully slide out of my reach.

I couldn't get her out of my mind. I saw her everywhere. Even heard her laughter in birdsong. No one else could compare. Not one of the daughters of the other Glasgow families held a candle to Jennie. They all faded when compared to her light. I would not be satisfied until I had her. I somehow convinced myself that once I did get her out of my system, as it were, I would go to my parents and tell them I was ready to pick a wife from one of the more desirable families in the city.

That was until the night when everything changed.

It was Hogmanay. The house was full to bursting – not an easily achieved endeavour with all this space – and my whisky-fuelled lust would not be refused. I tracked her down to her quarters, having checked first that the rest of the staff were lost in their own revels.

She cowered in the corner, her face pale with fear. But I could see nothing but my desire to conquer her. I ordered her to strip and lie on the bed or I would have her sacked. (Still, now, at those words my heart quails.)

What skin. What a form she took. Like a classic statue given flesh.

I was poised above her. My knees forced her thighs apart and I could feel her muscles trembling. She had turned her head to the side and her eyes were screwed shut. Then she gathered the last scraps of her courage and turned her head so she could look into my eyes.

'You are better than this, master.'

She spoke so quietly I couldn't make out the words. She repeated them and I was so taken aback that I met her eyes; and in that second something passed between us, and I was instantly shamed. Jennie was at my mercy but she showed such courage and dignity, despite what was happening, that I couldn't fail but be moved. With that simple look she managed to reach the human in me and tell him she was also human, not a thing to be used with such lack of care, and cast aside.

I fear this description does little to illustrate the profundity of that moment; but I beg you to accept it as fact and know that it changed my life.

Burning with shame, I removed myself from her, made myself decent, and I bade her dress. I muttered some pathetic apology and left the room to find more whisky and prayed that if the golden liquid judged me that it would not also find me so wanting.

For a few weeks thereafter I avoided her, which was surprisingly difficult in such a large house, particularly when my sister was constantly chasing me to play with her. Jennie was her maid, so she was never far behind.

I acknowledge that this must have been terribly difficult for Jennie – to come face to face on an almost daily basis with her would-be attacker. But – I'm searching for a silver lining here – perhaps what it did do was let her see that there was more to me than the monster who appeared in her quarters that fateful evening.

My sister was a determined girl even then, and she would persist until I read to her or played checkers or snakes and ladders, or, on summer days, she would pester me until I played games with her on the lawn.

I found myself in those moments – when I finally acquiesced to my sister's demands – playing to Jennie, trying to win a smile from her. I was ostensibly pleasing my sister, but simultaneously trying to win the good favour of her maid. If any of my university friends could have seen me, how they would have laughed.

At first, Jennie resisted my attempts to persuade her of my more lofty intentions. I was a good man, not the monster she'd had brief glimpse of, and I would prove it to her. Then, one day in the garden with my sister, I sensed a swing in Jennie's poor opinion of me. It may have been the sunshine, or the warm breeze, or the perfume from the flowered borders, but something changed. We were playing at quoits and the girl who became your grandmother was being particularly petulant. I gave into her mood and allowed her to win, deliberately missing the target when it was easily mine.

Jennie was in attendance as usual, and she noticed my ploy. She didn't meet my eye, but her mouth twitched in a suppressed smile. How can I convey what that moment meant to me? Was this forgiveness? Acceptance? An acknowledgement that we two older people were at the behest of this small girl? Or was it more? I could only dream that it was and I sought out that reaction more and more until she was all I could think about.

I managed to meet her regularly in the house as she carried out her other duties and if ever I won a smile, I would chalk that up on my board of success.

Trying to get her on her own was hellishly difficult. We were from different classes, and our social positions defined us utterly. Change was happening in other strata of society, but at a glacial pace, and it was happening even slower with the rich. For what were traditions but a way to protect our privilege?

I was determined to win her, not as a thing to possess in a moment of lust, but as my wife. One afternoon, we managed to persuade my sister that the heat meant she had to have a nap, and I cornered Jennie at the far end of the garden. I say cornered, but I kept my distance, frightened that I may scare her.

But she could see my intentions had transformed and she listened to me. She agreed that our situation could not be much worse, but she would welcome my attention provided the outcome would be honourable and that she would not be thrown on the scrapheap.

I was energised by this. I said I would go to mother and father and tell them I was in love and demand that they accept my choice of wife. This was almost the 1940s, I heard myself say.

Jennie counselled caution. She could now see that I was a good man and that I had been driven to force myself on her by a combination of youthful lust and whisky. She would consent to me wooing her in secret and we would take it from there.

Soon she admitted she was also in love with me – how wonderful that news was to my ears – and consented to long, languorous kisses under the shade of the willow tree where we would be out of sight of the rest of the household. Which was not easy, let me tell you. Mrs Winters, the housekeeper, seemed to dislike Jennie and watched her like a hawk. She always gave her the worst possible jobs to do and went out of her way to make life difficult for her.

A little power can make a large change in some people and I noticed this in Mrs Winters. Since she was promoted to her post, the power it afforded her went to her head and she lorded it over all the other servants. If she knew that Jennie owned my heart, her position would have been threatened; I'm sure she would have done anything to stop that from happening.

We made plans. We would get married and have a brood of children. There was talk of war at this point, but in our naivety we were certain we would be unaffected. My parents could be persuaded – they **would** be persuaded, I insisted – to accept her as my choice. And if they didn't then I would leave and earn my way in life some way.

Jennie tried to convince me this was folly. I should not give up my position in life for her, she said. She wasn't worth it. Even now her self-deprecation humbles me. Back then I determined I would prove to her that she was worth it and at the right time make whatever sacrifices it took to ensure she became my wife.

Then war was forced upon us. An Act of Parliament meant I was served a notice of conscription in October of that year. My choice was the army, navy or air force. I chose the air force, as many of my class did, and with a heavy and fearful heart I was sent off to war.

I promised Jennie I would come back to her and that the country would be a changed one after we had beaten Hitler into submission, as we were certain we would. Then surely a modern climate would allow for us to be together?

On my last night before I left for military training, Jennie came to my room in the dead of night. We made love. No three words can adequately describe what happened apart from those three: We made love. It was wondrous and sustained me through many truly difficult times during the war years. I tried to withdraw before I spilled my seed, but my Jennie held me close, whispering in my ear that, if the war took me, at least she might have my child.

The morning I left for war my parents called me into the reception room and announced that they were well aware of my – they called it a 'dalliance' – with one of the maids. Mrs Winters had discovered her leaving my room early that morning. My parents said they had put it down to youthful folly and the fear of never returning from the fighting. The girl would be sacked, of course, in case it gave her ideas above her station, and it would never be referred to again. I prevailed upon them to keep her in work, for where else could she go? The world was tightening its belt. There were no jobs. Besides, I convinced my parents that Jennie meant nothing to me. It was, as they said, folly. I knew it was less than Christian, I said, but I had used her before I went off to fight the Germans.

My heart quailed as I spoke these words and as I shrunk from the lies I was telling. I managed to add that, as my sister was fond of Jennie, wouldn't it be an added pain for her to lose her loving big brother and her maid, all at the one time? My parents were convinced by my argument and agreed that Jennie would not be released.

It was months before I was able to return home. I was sent to

London and engaged quickly in activities that were crucial to the war effort. While I was away I missed my Jennie terribly. I couldn't write to her, for that would have given away our secret. I did consider disguising my handwriting and writing anyway, under an assumed name, but I was certain that Mrs Winters would read the letters so anything I wanted to say to Jennie would be read by that woman first. That, I couldn't bear, so I resisted.

I prayed that Jennie might write to me, but she had no way of tracking me down. Everything was done in such secrecy in those days, particularly amongst the people with whom I was working.

Eventually I was given leave before an important mission – at last I was being sent to the front – and I was able to come home. And what a return. My world had collapsed. No one knew the real extent of our relationship – that Jennie and I were nominally engaged – so no one had considered that I should want to learn what became of her.

Can you imagine my state when I came home to find she was dead? The horror of it? The earth had caved in during my absence and I knew nothing about it. In my ignorance of Jennie's situation, I had been unable to do anything to help her.

It was Mrs Winters who found her and the picture she drew for anyone who would listen was one of unimaginable horror. Jennie was a witch, Winters said; she had found her eating a child while casting a spell. Can you believe that was given any credence? My parents were not stupid people, yet they were all taken in by the force of Mrs Winters' persuasion.

I was able to deduce that the child was mine and must have come into the world early. How she managed to disguise her state is anyone's guess, but she was unable to hide it any longer when the baby arrived. It was to all our shames that Winters was the one who found her and therefore was able to shape the narrative into one that best suited her purposes.

To give the woman the benefit of the doubt, I don't think that even she realised the experience would kill Jennie, for what woman would wantonly wish that upon another? But kill her it surely did. I managed to pull some strings and obtain her death certificate. Loss of blood was the reason given for Jennie's death. When I read that on the official document, my own loss was indescribable.

I could describe at some length here how I felt in the days after my discovery, but I will spare you that. It would run for pages and it would not make pleasant reading. Suffice to say, I cut my leave short and went back to my military life with an avowed determination to make someone pay for what had happened. I made sure I was sent to the front; if I managed to get myself killed in the process that was just fine by me.

Of course, suicide by Kraut didn't happen and I lived through what was undoubtedly the darkest period of my life – experiences that would scar anyone.

Until that is, I received a cure for my wounds from the most unlikely source: my Jennie.

Crazy as it seems, she came back to me.

I catch myself writing this and consider that you will no longer consider it crazy, for I'm sure Jennie will have made herself known to you. She is one of heaven's lost souls, I'm certain, trapped in this state by the force of the violence and betrayal perpetrated against her.

I used to lie in her bed at all hours and read to her. That was her favourite time, my reading to her. She didn't care what it was, just that my voice issued the words of great writers. It was how she made herself known to me the first time.

The war had been over for five years. Loneliness was a weight in my chest and the only way I could alleviate it was to go to her room and read out loud. The first time I felt her presence she came to me like a benediction. It was as if a feather was brushed against my cheek, then the weight of her was beside me on the bed.

I've spent the following years trying to ease her torment. I know she blames herself for the loss of our baby, and I know she will never forgive herself for this. I only hope my voice and presence gave her some sort of peace.

As for Mrs Winters' assertion of witchcraft? Utter claptrap. That was not Jennie, but the old bitch refused to counter her claims for the remainder of her life. I'm only pleased that her daughter, who also entered service in the family, turned out to be such a source of support to me in my declining years.

This has turned out to be quite the missive, my young Ranald. I only hope that I've held your interest. And I pray that its message is received by a welcoming mind. My Jennie, the library and the house is in your care. This is where she is at rest for evermore and the responsibility has fallen to you to look after her. It is almost more than I can bear to think that Jennie might be betrayed by this family once again. And I pray that everything I have provided for you and your security is enough of an enticement to see you carry out my wishes.

Your Uncle,

Alexander

32

Ranald was feeling far less woozy on his medication. His previous experience told him that the first few weeks might be difficult, and he was relieved that he was at last approaching something close to normality.

Sure, his emotions were being held at a distance by the drugs, and his libido had returned to a somnolent state, but at least he could process thought. Which helped when considering everything he'd learned and experienced recently, and the new details that Alexander's letters had just dumped on him.

Foremost in his mind was that *she* was real and her name was Jennie. He wasn't crazy. It wasn't a cocktail of drugs that was causing vivid dreams and experiences. Jennie was there and she was a ghost.

The house was haunted. It was a thrilling and terrifying thought.

But ultimately he'd found her presence a positive one. He enjoyed the dreams, the sex felt real, and reading to her in the lift was completely absorbing.

Another question occurred to him: was he sure he hadn't simply been experiencing a delusion – another symptom of his illness on top of everything else? How could he possibly rationalise the irrational otherwise?

It was like having two minds in one head. He stood up. Do something. Go somewhere. Talk to a real human being.

Only then did it occur to him – with a crush of guilt – that besides Jennie, he and Alexander held something else in common: both of their actions had resulted in the death of an innocent woman.

The Hacketts' cottage was at the far end of the property. It was built of red sandstone, had a red door and was set over two floors. As Ranald approached he thought what a shame it was that, under Marcus's plans, it would be destroyed. It was picture-box pretty, with a planter by the door filled with red and yellow blooms and window boxes on the lower-ground windows holding the same.

The door held a shiny, brass knocker in the shape of a lion's head. Worried that he was about to spoil it with his dirty fingers, he wiped his hand on his jeans before lifting it.

The door was answered almost instantly.

'Danny,' Ranald said in greeting, and took in the dark-brown cords and red-and-blue checked shirt. This was the first time Ranald had seen Danny wearing anything other than his working dungarees.

'Mr McGhie,' Danny replied, his eyes barely lighting on Ranald's face.

'Mind if I come in?'

Without a word, Danny stood back and allowed Ranald entry. The hall was a small, bright space, with a staircase and four doors leading off it. The walls were half covered in wood panelling, which should have made the space feel smaller, but it was painted in a light tan. One door was open; Danny pointed towards it.

'If you…' he said. 'I'll have to…'

'I need to speak to you, Danny,' Ranald said, aware from Danny's stance that he was about to leave. Ranald took a step closer and lowered his voice. 'I need to talk to you about that…'

Ranald heard footsteps behind him.

'Ranald,' said Mrs Hackett. 'Can we offer you a wee cuppa?' She was also almost unrecognisable in her ordinary clothes. She was wearing a light-blue twin-set and a matching knee-length skirt. For the first time Ranald really thought of her as an individual, not just a woman who worked for him. He shook his head at how easily his mind had become closed.

'Tea would be lovely,' he answered.

Mrs Hackett ushered him into a small kitchen, with dark wood cupboards and a small pine table with three seats in the far corner.

'Have a seat. The kettle is just off the boil.' She smiled and set about making the tea. Before long he was taking a careful sip.

'It's not like you to come up here,' Mrs Hackett said, as she sat down beside him.

'Where's Danny gone?' Ranald asked, looking through the kitchen door into the hall.

'He was just off on some errands,' she explained and made a face. 'At least that's what he tells me. You men need your time off on your own, don't you?'

Now that Danny had left, Ranald didn't know what to say. On the way over from the big house he'd thought about Alexander's letters: the story about his love affair with Jennie; going off to war and coming back to find out his love was dead. How he'd then devoted his life to protecting her spirit and keeping her company.

And how he wanted Ranald to do the same.

Ranald couldn't deny that he relished the job. Jennie fended off his loneliness. But surely she was stopping him from forming a relationship with a real, flesh-and-blood woman. Was Jennie worth that sacrifice?

He took a sip of his tea, fighting for time. Now that he was here, could he ask Mrs Hackett about Jennie? Could he broach that subject and expect a sensible response?

'This is lovely,' he said, finding safe ground in the banal. He was struck by how this place felt like a home – such a contrast to all of that space and grandeur just beyond the trees.

'My family has lived here for a long time, Ranald.'

The way she said it made Ranald start. He looked into her eyes. Was that a challenge of some sort? Something shifted in her expression and the congenial servant was back.

'Yes,' said Ranald, thinking he would park that and come back to it later. 'Mrs Winters was your mother, I believe?'

Mrs Hackett sat back in her chair, taken by surprise. 'You know about my mother?'

'My uncle left some diaries and notebooks around the house. I found her name in them.' He paused. 'He mentioned you, too. He said you were great comfort to him in his later years.'

'Why, thank you, Ranald,' she said, placing her hand over her heart. 'You don't know how lovely it is to hear that.'

'I'd really like to talk to Danny,' Ranald said. 'When will he be back?' And he silently added, *Is he avoiding me*?

'No idea, Ranald. He goes off on his wee trips and I see him whenever I see him.' She raised her eyebrows. 'My husband is his own man. He likes his own space now and again. I've learned not to ask where he goes.'

Ranald couldn't disguise a look of surprise.

'Oh, he's not doing anything dodgy,' she went on. 'I know that. And he always comes back in time for his tea, so where's the harm?'

Where's the harm? He could be off hiding more dead bodies for all she knew, Ranald thought.

'That afternoon,' he began. 'What happened? How come Marcus and Danny were there?'

'Now, now, son,' Mrs Hackett said, reaching across the table. She placed her hand over his. 'Now, let's not upset ourselves. What's done is done.' She pursed her lips. 'And everything is sorted.'

Something wasn't quite right here.

'How can you be like that? Someone – a woman – died in my pool and you're saying, what's done is done?' He stood up. 'Why aren't you terrified of me? It could well have been me. I could have killed that poor woman.'

She looked up at him as if he was nothing more than a recalcitrant child.

'Ranald, if there's one thing I know it's people. And you are not a killer.' She looked at his chair pointedly; it was a look that said, *Please, sit back down*. He did.

'Besides. It's all taken care of. Marcus Fitzpatrick is one of the finest lawyers in the country; if this is an outcome he is happy with, then I'm happy with it, too.'

'Your loyalty to the family goes that deeply?' Ranald asked, wondering as he said it what she knew about William's relationship with his mother. If she suspected even a little about that, surely it would stretch her loyalty very thin?

'Why, yes,' she answered, as if he was insane to think anything else.

'I don't understand how you can be like that. Don't you know they take your existence for granted? Don't you know they plan to demolish your house?'

'Yes, well.' She crossed her arms, her look accusatory. '*That* part of the plan has been shelved. Marcus has come up with something else. Something more suitable for all parties concerned.'

Ranald thought of the plans back on his desk. They'd been changed? Why hadn't Marcus informed him? This was all very strange. He felt that he was missing something vital and for the life of him he couldn't think what it might be.

'Marcus said something that troubled me…' He scratched at this side of his head as he considered the best way to get the information out of her. 'About my mother and his father, William.'

'Really? What?' Mrs Hackett looked mystified.

Ranald studied her. He would have been surprised if anything got past her nowadays, but she had only been a young woman back then. Had she missed what was going purely through naivety?

'Something…' He could barely bring himself to say it. 'Something untoward.'

She snorted and crossed her arms. 'Why on earth would Marcus say something like that? Surely you misheard him.'

'I heard him very clearly, Mrs Hackett.'

She looked at him as if assessing his state of mind, and he knew she was wondering if he'd only imagined Marcus saying that while he was ill. 'Your mother and William argued a lot, like siblings often do, but I remember nothing *untoward*.' She reared back in her chair as if to get away from such a strange topic and took a quick sip of her tea.

'What else has the old fella been saying in his notebooks?' Mrs Hackett asked, as if it was her turn to move the subject onto less contentious issues.

'He told me about Jennie.'

'Ah,' she said after a long pause.

'You don't seem surprised.'

'She was a big part of his life, Ranald. Even though she was only in it for a short time.' Her face pinked a little as a thought moved across the screen of her eyes.

'Have you met her, too?' he asked.

'Met her?' she asked. Then, as if realising he was speaking in the present tense. '*Met* her? Good Lord, no. Your uncle was a sick man, Ranald. He imagined all sorts. If you read any more of those notebooks, please ignore them. Alexander punished himself for many, many years. Retreated from life for an absurd ideal.' She paused. 'I'm sorry. It's not my place to talk about these things, but I would hate to see you influenced by your uncle's words.'

'What do you know about her?' Ranald asked.

'Please don't ask me this, Ranald.'

'Did Uncle Alex fall asleep in the lift as well?'

She said nothing, placing her hand over her mouth as if to keep it shut. But almost involuntarily, she gave a tiny nod. Her eyes widened, as if that small action was a huge betrayal of a confidence.

'Isn't it strange that I'm doing the same things as him? I look like him. I dress like him. Doesn't this all strike you as very, very odd?'

'Ranald, please.'

'These letters.' He looked up from studying the back of his hands and stared into her eyes. 'He told me everything about Jennie. About how he wanted to marry her. How his parents refused. And how your mother accused her of eating her own baby. How messed up is that, for God's sake?'

Mrs Hackett studied the surface of the table.

'What the hell is going on?' he asked.

She opened her mouth. Closed it again as if she was afraid of the words that might spill out.

Finally, she raised her eyes and studied his. It looked as if she couldn't make up her mind whether she wanted to hug him or harm him.

She stood up. 'Time you were away home, Mr McGhie. While you still have the place, eh?'

'What about the mirror?' he asked.

She paled. Her eyes large.

'Tell me about the mirror.'

She shook her head turning away.

'Please, Mrs H, I need to know.'

'I told him to get rid of it, all right?' Her voice was suddenly raised. 'I told him. But he refused. Told me I was imagining things.' She tutted. 'Me, imagining things? Every now and then I'd go in the lift and give everything a dust, you know?' She shivered. 'Gave me the creeps. I used to hear whispers coming from it. From the mirror. Thought I was going nuts.' She took a curious double breath as if one had got stuck in her throat. 'One weekend, when Mr Fitzpatrick was away on business I moved it, as a kind of trial. Carried it out to the garage.' Her eyes grew large. 'I couldn't believe it. I was sure Danny was playing pranks on me, but when I asked him, he looked at me like I was a crazy woman.' She paused, her hand held over her heart as if to slow its rapid beat.

'Next morning the mirror was back in the lift.'

33

It was the night before Ranald was due in at the lawyer's to sign the necessary papers. He half expected another emailed image of the newly deceased Liz to appear in his inbox. Not that he needed the reminder. It was a sight that would be forever locked into memory and one he dwelt over at least once a day.

He was lying in his bed, the curtains drawn, thinking again that he should go to the police and put himself at their mercy. Let them know how Marcus had manipulated the tragedy. But, he discounted this; his cousin would find a way to make such an accusation spring back on him. He was dealing with a clever, cunning man; even if his brain had been clear enough to think and plot, he was certain Marcus would get the better of him.

What should he do?

He dismissed the question. Prison or a nice big flat in a desirable part of the city – it wasn't much of a dilemma, he thought.

Except it *was*. It wasn't so much about the books; he'd simply buy a place with enough room for all of them. No, the real dilemma centred around Jennie.

Alexander was clearly upset about the idea of her spirit somehow being uprooted. What affect would the renovations have on her? He cast his mind back to the plans. He couldn't remember the lift being noted anywhere. In which case, it would simply be rooted out, filled in, and the space would become part of something else.

The mirror, then. Why was she focused in the mirror? Perhaps if he took that with him, he would take her along, too? Then he remembered what Mrs H said about the time she moved it. Would it then reappear in some poor buyer's new home, just where the lift used to be?

He crossed his feet at the ankles, crossed his arms over his chest and thought about life away from this house. He felt himself grow sad. Sure, it was huge and sometimes accentuated his loneliness, but there were compensations. He would miss the place. And he realised that he would miss her.

Her presence hung in his mind and it was so real he sat up, shuffled to the end of the bed and peered out from behind the drapes. He almost expected to see her standing there, so strong was his feeling of anticipation.

Without another thought, he walked down the stairs and along to the lift. There was a book on the chair from the last time he'd sat there: *The Cone Gatherers* by Robin Jenkins – it was set during the Second World War in a country estate in Scotland, and he had thought the time and setting might appeal to Jennie.

He picked the book up and sat down, his naked skin retreating from the cool of the material. He considered going back upstairs for a blanket of some sort but decided against it. The day had been a warm one for this time of year

He relaxed into the seat. Felt the house grow calm around him, as if now that he was still it could settle, too. Looking into the mirror, he sent her a silent message. Then, stretching his legs out in front of him, he located the place he'd last read from, rested the book on his chest and began to read.

†⊦

He snored himself awake. The book was resting on his chest, pressed there with his left hand.

He couldn't remember falling asleep.

He'd dreamt; he could remember that. He was standing in a place he knew she loved. He couldn't see around him as everything was clouded in a thick, comforting mist, but he knew – just knew – this was a place of quiet joy.

She was walking through the haze, waving her hand, as if clearing condensation from a window. Then she stopped and with a delicate finger drew a heart shape. Next they were sitting side by side on a park bench, hands as close as they could be without actually touching. The space between them sparked. Electric. He reached out a finger and touched hers. Her answering chuckle delighted him.

They were surrounded by children. Their children. And they all, as if given a silent cue, lay down, folded and became books.

They were on a beach and she was saying that the young master once brought her here. She loved the expanse of sand, the white-crested waves and there … footprints. He turned and looked behind him. Nothing. Ahead, his and hers, side by side stretching off into the horizon. She gave his hand a squeeze as his mind sent her his understanding.

She was telling him that death has a wondrous shadow.

She was telling him that they would have their time.

And that time was nigh.

34

Ranald was in the chrome-encased lift in Quinn's building, tucked into the corner, arms and legs crossed, heading up to the lawyer's office. He had dressed with care that morning. Grey herringbone suit, white shirt and red tie. He wanted to make a point; show them how much he had changed.

And he didn't need the drugs. He'd barely been taking them over the last week or so. He hated the way they made him feel, so the previous morning, in an act of defiance and with a sense of satisfaction, he had tipped all of the pills he could find into the toilet and flushed them away.

Whatever had happened that day to Liz, he wasn't a murderer. It was only his delusions that helped him to take that on. There was a complete absence in his mind, when he sought answers for what happened that night. Nothing had flicked forward from deep memory. However Liz died, there was no way he was a killer. Over the years his illness had made him do, say and see strange things, but he'd never harmed another soul. Unlike his mother. He'd go along with this whole thing because, as he saw it, he had no choice; but no drugs would be his stipulation.

Just before the lift began its ascent, the door pinged open again; but his mind was so caught up in his thought he didn't raise his eyes from his shoes to look at the couple who had entered. He could just see that they stood side by side in front of the doors.

The woman was humming a song. He heard her whisper to her friend. 'Heard that in the car as I came here. One of my favourites.' She began to hum again.

The man dismissed her with a loud, 'For God's sake.'

Ranald recognised his voice. He finally looked up. It was Marcus.

Marcus must have caught the movement in his peripheral vision because he turned and raised his eyebrows in acknowledgement. Perhaps it was too much effort for him to actually speak, thought Ranald. You'd think, now that he was about to get everything he wanted, he would be a little more energised.

Ranald looked at the woman by Marcus's side. Rebecca. She was wearing a bright red leather jacket, a pair of black jeans and high-heeled sandals with bare feet. He opened his mouth to address her but the lift slowed to a stop and the doors opened.

Marcus gave him a small smile as if fighting to acknowledge his moment of triumph and walked out of the lift with his sister. If she was aware that Ranald was even present, she gave no sense of it; she simply adjusted the straps of her large handbag onto the crook of her left arm and walked with Marcus along the corridor to the lawyer's room.

Marcus pushed the door open for his sister and followed her inside, Ranald behind them.

'Ah,' Quinn looked up from his desk. 'Good. You are all here. Have a seat everyone.' He gestured to the three chairs arranged in front of him.

Rebecca sat at one end and Marcus sat in the middle, leaving the seat at the other end for him.

'Right,' said Quinn placing his hands on the desk in front of him, either side of a manila folder. 'We all know why we are here, so let's get on with proceedings.' Was Ranald imagining things or did Quinn give a slight sniff of disappointment after he said that?

'Yes, let's get on with it, Quinn,' said Marcus, his voice high with excitement. 'I have a building site to get organised.' He rubbed his hands together.

Ranald felt another twist. He wanted to run out of the office, but his legs were leaden. The role had been chosen for him, he'd played his part to perfection and now he was reaping the dubious rewards.

Quinn was speaking, but all Ranald could see was Jennie's face, white and silent among the shadows, the plump pale of her lower lip quivering as if emotion was contained just under the surface of her skin.

I'm sorry, my love, he sent her.

'What did you say, Mr McGhie,' asked Quinn.

'Nothing,' he mumbled. Then cleared his throat and repeated: 'Nothing.'

'God, he's even talking to himself,' said the woman at the end. Then she laughed – a loud mocking noise. Ranald's head shot round. He recognised that sound. He'd heard that laugh before. But where?

As if aware of his scrutiny Rebecca looked across at him. Her eyes sparked from behind heavy eye make-up and a long black fringe. Her lips formed a small moue of disapproval, and her eyes flicked from him to Quinn. 'The papers, please?'

Marcus appeared to grow nervous at his question, but when Ranald shifted his position to look away from Rebecca, he could sense his cousin relax a little. What was up with him? wondered Ranald. From the corner of his eye, he looked at his cousin and tried to assess what was going on in his mind.

'Yes, the papers,' said Marcus. 'Where do we sign?'

Quinn opened the folder and pulled a black pen from the inside of his jacket. He turned the folder round so that the print was facing the three of them.

'I've marked the places where we should each sign. Rebecca,' Quinn pointed, 'you should sign here.' He handed her the pen.

She crossed her legs and leaned forwards. Her foot moving up and down and the sandal making a faint slapping sound each time it hit her heel. She reached for the pen, signed with a flourish and sang a couple of notes from whatever song had been entertaining her in the lift.

What was that tune? wondered Ranald.

'My turn,' said Marcus, and he reached over and pulled the file so it was in front of him. He signed. Rebecca's heel slapped against her sandal. Marcus pushed the file along to Ranald.

With a look at Quinn, Ranald took the pen from his cousin. The heavy metal barrel of the pen was warm from his cousins' hands. Ranald cleared his throat. Leaned towards the file and saw the spot where he should sign. He pushed down the end of the pen with this thumb, closing up the nib. He pushed down again so that the nib once again shot out of the hole at the bottom. Ready to spill ink.

Could he do this? He was about to betray his uncle and Jennie.

His stomach twisted again. His tongue soured in his mouth.

What choice did he have?

Rebecca's heel continued to slap quietly against her sandal. The noise was suddenly becoming very annoying. He looked down at her foot as if sending it a message to stop.

And there, just under her ankle bone, a tattoo.

A very familiar tattoo: a blue butterfly.

He looked from there to her face. Aware of his scrutiny, she turned to face him.

'You need to sign it,' she said, as if talking to a child.

'That tattoo,' he said as information slowly uncurled in his brain. Then, without thinking about what he was saying, he allowed the words to fall from his mouth. 'I've seen that tattoo before. You've got another one at the top of your right thigh. A pink heart.'

Oh my God, he thought.

He stood up. Looked from Rebecca to Marcus.

'What have you people done?' he shouted.

They were all standing now.

'What are you talking about?' Rebecca and Marcus demanded at the same time. Quinn was also saying something, but Ranald couldn't hear him. He was seeing a woman in his bedroom. In the toilet at the café. Cheerful, naughty, fun. Dead in his pool. And now, she was here, in front of him.

She was different somehow. Not just in the clothes she was wearing, and her hair, but in her cold, assessing eyes, her voice, the set of her shoulders.

But it was her, he was certain.

Alive.

'How could you? How could you?' Ranald asked, taking a step closer to Rebecca. 'Oh my God. You people…' He looked from Rebecca to Marcus.

Marcus moved his body between them, leaned towards Ranald, his face close. 'What rubbish are you talking about, Ranald? Are you back off your pills?' His face was bright red, saliva sparking from his mouth. 'Sit your arse down and sign that fucking document.'

Ranald took a step back, almost tripped over his chair. 'What did you do?' he shouted. 'What did you do?'

Louder than anyone else, Quinn shouted. 'Will everyone sit down, shut up, and tell me what the hell is going on?'

'Ask my cousins,' Ranald answered. He looked around the room as if the solid wood furnishings would offer some understandable shape to the memories, thoughts and emotions that were crowding his mind. The evidence was there in front of him, but still he struggled to piece it all together.

'Ranald, what the hell is going on?' demanded Quinn.

Ranald looked from the lawyer to his cousins. Read the defiance in their faces. They would deny everything he threw at them. Try to say that he was crazy. That he should be put on stronger drugs.

'Oh my God,' he said again. He stared into Rebecca's eyes and tried to locate the woman he'd laughed with. The woman he'd made love to. But he saw nothing of her, just this dark-eyed woman who was looking at him as if he was certifiable.

So strong was her certainty, so different from Liz's, for a moment he questioned himself. He thought about her voice, her tattoos, her singing. This was her. There *was* no doubt.

'You…' He stared at her. 'How could you do…?'

'Ranald, you are going to have to explain yourself,' said Quinn.

With a supreme effort, Ranald contained the riot of emotion surging through his mind. He tried to think of what his uncle would do in this moment. How he might be and act.

He drew himself to his full height, and looked at Rebecca and Marcus with a certainty chilled by the realisation of just what kind of people his cousins were. For, without doubt, they had orchestrated the whole thing together.

'Mr Quinn, this meeting is over.' He looked at Rebecca and shook his head. 'I will not be signing the papers. The house will remain in my sole ownership as per the original reading of the will.'

It may have been his imagination, but Quinn almost smiled.

Marcus and Rebecca weren't smiling though. They began shouting – at each other, and at him. Marcus pulled his phone out of his pocket. Held it up for Ranald to see the image displayed there.

'I just need to press send, cousin, and your fucking life is over.'

Ranald stepped forwards. 'Go ahead. Press send, you detestable prick.'

'People. People,' Quinn rushed round from his desk, trying to play peacemaker. 'Will somebody please tell me what the hell is going on?'

'Ask them,' answered Ranald.' Ask Rebecca here.' He stared into her eyes. 'Or do you prefer "Liz"?'

35

Ranald hailed a taxi as soon as he was out of the building and asked the driver to take him home.

As he sat back in the seat he wondered about everything he had just discovered.

How could anyone do something like that? For his home? For money?

Shame scoured him. He was such a fool. How could he be such a dupe? They'd sized him up so easily and manipulated him like he had all the brain power of a newborn.

She'd slept with him.

Several times.

They were family. And he'd enjoyed it, really enjoyed it. What did that make him? He was sure Marcus's taunt that they were more than cousins was a malicious invention, but still. He shuddered. It felt like something else he could enter in the column of his life marked 'Just like Mother'.

He thought of that afternoon. Waking up to find Danny bending over him. Liz in the pool. Marcus, fully clothed, carrying her out. How stupid had he been?

And then he considered the Hacketts. What was in it for them? In the first plans he'd seen they were going to lose their house. But Marcus had clearly changed the design; was that in order to persuade the couple to go along with his scheme? Was that the hold he had over them?

When the taxi dropped him off, he made straight for the Hacketts' house, grabbed the brass lion knocker and rapped loudly on the door.

The door opened almost instantly. It was Danny, and one look at his face told Ranald that they'd been warned by Marcus about what had happened.

Without a word, Danny stood to the side and let him in. Questions, thoughts and ideas all jumbled within Ranald's mind; he didn't know where to start first.

Mrs Hackett appeared in the hallway.

'In here.' She turned and led him into a small living room. The room was fronted by a large bay window, looking out into a small part of the garden Ranald had never been in. Mrs Hackett sat in a chintz armchair, every inch the power in the room. She was sitting slightly forward, her feet crossed at the ankles, her hands clasped in front of her and her face a quiet simmer. She appeared ready for anything Ranald might throw at her.

Danny stood behind her chair, his hand on her shoulder.

Ranald opened his mouth to speak.

'Sit, please, Ranald,' Mrs Hackett said. 'Let's at least be civil about this.'

At this polite request, he felt the fury within him fizzle out, and he slumped into a seat.

He simply asked. 'Why?'

'We…' began Danny.

'We helped hide the body…' Mrs Hackett completed his sentence, her tone wrapped in denial.

'You're still going with the dead body thing then?' asked Ranald, his anger returning.

'We helped hide…'

'Oh, for crying out loud,' Ranald said. 'I know.' He repeated. 'I *know*.'

But Mrs Hackett persisted until Danny interrupted.

'It's over, dear,' he said. 'The man knows it was all a ruse.' Mrs Hackett looked up at her husband, mouth open. 'We're sorry, son. It was just—'

'Shut up, Danny. Shut up. He'll put us out of our house,' she hissed.

'It's no more than we deserve,' he replied, his voice a hushed admonition.

'Wait.' Ranald sat forwards in his seat. 'What the hell are you talking about – put you out of your house?'

'Marcus told us everything,' said Danny, looking into Ranald's eyes for the first time.

'I saw the plans in that folder on the hall table, in which you…' Mrs Hackett began. Ranald could see large red blotches had flowered up and down her neck. 'You were planning to pull this house down and put up a small block of flats.'

'What? I had nothing to do with those plans. And what's more I have no plans to sell this house.'

'What?' asked Mrs Hackett, her tone one of disbelief.

'I have no intention of selling. Never have had. I want everything to stay as it was.'

'You have no plans to…' Danny repeated, his face going pale. He sat on the arm of his wife's chair. Rubbed at his head. 'Good lord. What have we done?'

'Your name was on those plans. Your signature was at the back. I saw it all, Mr McGhie.'

'You may have seen those plans, but you saw them just after I saw them for the very first time – after Marcus dropped them there. I can assure you they were as much a surprise to me as they were to you.'

'Well, what…'

'Mrs Hackett, why don't you start at the beginning and explain what my cousin told you.'

She took a deep breath and looked at Danny. He gave her a small nod.

'I saw those plans and your name on them and I contacted Marcus and asked him what we could do to stop you from tearing down our house…'

'So, you thought that pretending I had killed someone and Danny burying the body was what – some kind of thing that reasonable human beings would do? It's fucking nuts.'

'Please don't swear in my house, Ranald,' said Mrs Hackett.

'Right, cos using the f-word within these four walls is beyond the pale, while tricking someone into thinking they had actually committed murder is acceptable. That's a screwed-up value system right there, Mrs Hackett.'

'Marcus was very convincing, Ranald,' said Danny. He was twisting his fingers in his lap. He looked like he wanted to combust with embarrassment.

'That man has spent a lifetime arguing in our top courts. We were putty in his hands, Ranald,' added Mrs Hackett.

Ranald could see where they were coming from, although, from his point of view, it was Liz's – or Rebecca's – performance that was the more convincing.

'Right. The plan?' he asked.

'Marcus said that you had the final say on any plans. That your intentions would be carried out, and the only way to overturn them would be to completely discredit you. Bribe you in some way. He said that he and Rebecca had already started on their plan and that I had come to them just at the right time.'

Ranald sat back in his chair, his anger fading again. 'He manipulated you as easily as he did me.' He paused for a moment, considering the lengths of Marcus and Rebecca's plans; he couldn't help but admire their cleverness.

'Here's the truth, Mrs H, Danny: the will states that the house and grounds are mine. And that you guys have to stay on as staff for as long as you live. If I sell up I have to share the proceeds with Marcus and Rebecca.' He looked at Mrs Hackett to check if she was following him. She was. 'The plans were dropped there for you to see, Mrs H. He knew you would come to him for help and then you would be drawn in to assist him.'

'We truly thought we were going to lose our home, Ranald,' said Danny.

'Again, and that's enough to make someone think they were a murderer?'

'I would do anything … anything, to keep my home, Mr McGhie,' answered Mrs Hackett, her eyes brimming with tears and her jaw set with indignation. 'My family has done everything to help your family over the years, and I would not – could not – allow another one of you to…'

'Dear,' Danny put a hand on her shoulder, 'you've said enough.'

Mrs Hackett closed her eyes, visibly pulling herself together. She opened them and glared at Ranald. 'I was keeping my home whatever it took.' And Ranald could see what a formidable adversary Mrs Hackett might be if she put her mind to something.

'Marcus came up with another set of plans,' Danny took over. 'Where this house was untouched. Said he couldn't stop the sale of the big house, but he could make sure we were safe if we helped him.' He looked at Ranald. 'After you giving me that car…' His voice faded. He stood up as if he had come to a decision. 'Give us till the end of the week, Ranald, and we'll be out of here.'

'What?' said Mrs Hackett.

'No one's going anywhere,' said Ranald.

Danny was all but at attention; a soldier at his court martial. 'Our position here is untenable. We simply can't stay on.'

'Yes, you can,' said Ranald. 'My uncle's wishes were that you are retained in service till you retire and then stay on in the cottage for life.' He shook his head. They were good people who had been fooled just as he had. And, anyway, he needed some kind of constant in his life. 'No one's leaving,' he said, 'and I'm not taking no for an answer.'

Mrs Hackett looked over at him, sending a silent 'thanks'.

'You've known these people all your life, Mrs H. What on earth would make them behave like that?'

She exhaled. 'When you've been a servant for as long as I have, Ranald, you learn to look away. If you didn't, you couldn't live with yourself. But what I will say is this: those two children were spoiled rotten. Everything they ever wanted they got. And Marcus was always about *stuff*. He wanted the biggest car, the biggest house, the prettiest wife, and he would do anything to get them.'

'And Rebecca?' Ranald asked.

Mrs Hackett sat for a moment as she considered her response. 'She has always been a strange one, that girl. Less interested in the material things in life.' She paused as she considered this. 'Don't get me wrong, she always liked having nice clothes, but it was like something else motivated her. And she had a gleeful disregard for what other people thought of her. She simply didn't care.'

'First day I worked here she turned up,' Danny joined in. 'Said she would give me a blowjob for a tenner.'

'What?' Mrs Hackett demanded. 'You never mentioned that before.'

'She didn't mean it,' said Danny. 'Not really.'

'What do you mean, not really?'

Danny thought about his answer for a moment. 'It didn't matter to her either way. If I went for it she would have complied. When I said no thanks, she just laughed, showed me her boobs and ran off. It was more about her trying to shock me as much as she could.'

'Good grief,' said Mrs Hackett and pressed the back of her right hand against her forehead as if blotting the sweat there. 'The more I learn about this family the less I understand.'

'You and me both, Mrs H,' said Ranald. 'You and me both.'

Mrs Hackett grew quiet, her blush reasserting itself.

'All that trickery, Ranald,' she said at last. 'I'm really sorry.'

'Trickery?'

'The drugs … and the mentions of the mirror. I said too much to Marcus. He knew your medical condition could cause all sorts of strange things. He encouraged me to have you think all the strange stuff about the lift was real.' She focused on her hands where they lay in her lap, watching as she twisted her own fingers. 'That stuff I said about the mirror was all nonsense. It was manipulative when you were in a bad place.' She swallowed as if gathering the strength to look up at him. Eventually she managed. Her eyes heavy with apology. 'The mirror in the lift, Ranald. It really is just a mirror.'

36

Back at the house, in the library, Ranald's mind was part fog, part crystalline clarity.

The phone on the desk rang. It was Quinn.

'What just happened, Mr McGhie?' He sounded completely flustered.

'Why don't you tell me?' demanded Ranald.

'I can assure you I couldn't be more at sea.'

Ranald talked, and over the next few minutes, as if putting all the pieces into place, he explained his cousins' plot.

Silence. Then.

'Good lord.' Quinn paused. 'I don't know what to say, Mr McGhie. Do you have any proof of this? Do you want to press charges? We could take out a civil suit on your behalf and sue them for emotional distress.'

'Stand in front of a court and say my cousin had sex with me; told me she was hearing things in the walls – crying babies and ghostly women – all to get me to sell the house? And that she and her brother then faked her death? How well do you think that would work, Mr Quinn?'

'Marcus *is* a formidable lawyer,' he replied, doubt in his voice.

'He will have covered his tracks. I doubt Mr and Mrs Hackett will have the stomach for it and, besides, who would believe that they would go to such lengths?'

'And the burden of proof is yours, Mr McGhie.'

'Quite,' said Ranald. 'I'll settle for knowing what I'm dealing with and plan never to meet either of them ever again.'

That night he didn't even bother with the pretence of going to bed. Instead, he grabbed his quilt, pillows and a book and settled in the lift for a read. Mrs Hackett might have tried her best to push him away from *her*, but he needed to believe.

As he lay there, he listened as the house settled around itself. Floorboards shifting, pipes creaking, slates clicking. The sounds of a living, breathing home.

He felt a breeze and she was there leaning into his side.

He turned to hear, feeling his heart swell. She still cared for him. He wished he could demonstrate in a very real way how he felt about her. How her presence was making everything that happened more bearable.

I know, Jennie, he sent her as he thought about his Uncle Alexander's letter. *I know everything.*

He felt a slight pressure on his cheek as if a pair of lips had been pressed there. Then heard, 'You know nothing, my love. Nothing.'

And her scream was a sharp, endless note that lasted through the night.

╫

The following morning, he was woken by a nudge on his shoulder.

'Ranald.' Pause. 'Ranald, you really must learn to sleep in your bedroom.' It was Mrs Hackett. 'I thought I was finished waking up you Fitzpatrick men in this lift.' She shuddered. 'I told you that stuff about the mirror was rubbish.'

He sat up and pressed his thumbs into his eyes as if that might push away his early-morning fatigue. 'What's the time?' he asked, the words poorly formed in his mouth, as if his tongue was fighting against cotton wool.

'Almost noon,' she replied. 'I saw you here when I arrived, but you looked so … cosy, I thought I'd let you sleep.'

He stood up willing the fog of his tiredness to lift.

'Get dressed, Ranald, and come meet me in the kitchen, will you? We need to talk.'

†⊢

Minutes later, wearing a blue t-shirt and jeans, Ranald was sitting at his kitchen table, both hands wrapped round a mug of freshly poured coffee and poised over it like the aroma was the only thing keeping his eyes open.

'A long night?' asked Mrs Hackett.

'You don't want to know,' Ranald replied.

Mrs Hackett took a sip of her drink and sat back in her chair, as if using the wooden back to strengthen her spine.

'If I am going to carry on here as your staff, Ranald, I need … *we* need to talk about what happened yesterday.'

'We do?' Ranald leaned on the table, resting his forehead on the heel of his right hand. 'As far as I'm concerned, what's done is done. I've moved on.'

'You may have. I haven't.' She paused a beat. 'We haven't.' She looked into his eyes, her own sending messages of humility, sorrow and not a little injured pride. 'We made a terrible error of judgement and we want you to know that you have our complete loyalty from now on; and if we *ever* betray that…'

Ranald was about to answer with flippancy, but stopped himself when he realised that it would be ill judged. Mrs Hackett was being deadly serious and she needed something similar in return in order that she could, indeed, move on herself.

'Thank you, Mrs Hackett,' he said and dipped his head. 'I appreciate the sentiment and the courage it would have taken you to say all of that.'

She gave a little smile in response and her shoulders sagged a little as if she had been holding herself tight.

'Now, if we are back to normal I'm going for a swim.' He stood up.

'Mind if I detain you a little while longer?'

'Aye?' He sat down, a little confused.

'In some ways, I think it would have been better for you if you *had* sold the house.' Her mouth shaped a smile of apology.

'What do you mean?' he asked as he considered Donna's warning to sell up before he became the latest victim of whatever was going on in this house.

Her arm moved up and away from her body as if it was pointing at the lift.

'You need to meet someone. This thing you have about Alexander and Jennie … You need to get out and about. Meet real people, not some woman in a mirror.'

'You know that there is something going on in this house.'

'And that is why you need to go.'

'But my great-uncle provided all of this for me. He spent decades trying to make up for his early mistakes. He spent all this money trying to set up a home for me. He built that library for me. He sought me out, Mrs Hackett, and, a bit late, I admit, he tried to look after me. I can't let him down.'

'Yes, he did all that. I remember him coming back from your graduation ceremony. The smile on his face. He was so very proud of you, Ranald. But if you are going to take on this house – and I mean really take it on – you have to know everything.'

'Go on…' Ran folded his arms tight around himself.

'She – Jennie – worked under my mother. And mum told me everything. She was haunted by it.'

Ranald thought about the details he'd read in the letter. 'I should think so.'

Mrs Hackett raised herself in her seat slightly as if she was going to rush to the defence of her mother, but then seemed to rein herself in.

'You said my mother *should* be haunted by what happened. What did he tell you in that letter?' she asked.

'That Mrs Winters, your mother, had it in for Jennie from the moment she met her…' Mrs Hackett took a sharp breath and held a hand to her mouth. 'That she told everyone Jennie was a witch and was trying to … eat a child while casting a spell…'

'The old…' She interrupted Ranald, then stopped herself as if she was about to say something she considered too foul to be uttered. Her mouth was a scolding thin line as she worked through her anger at what Ranald said. 'The guilt might have tortured him, but he clearly didn't want you to think badly of him.' She gathered her thoughts. 'My mother did watch out for Alexander and Jennie, that bit is true. But not in the way he said.'

'In what way then?'

'Right enough, she didn't believe the wee lamb at first. But then she did what she could to help her. The poor girl was terrified of him.'

37

'Do you really want to hear this, Ranald?'

He shook his head. He didn't know what to believe. *Who* to believe. He felt like he was swimming through smog. That everything solid he touched would fade into vapour. First Marcus and Liz ... or Rebecca or whatever the hell her name was. Was he really so suggestible that all she'd needed to do was a bit of theatrics and he'd ended up imagining a whole *person* – for week upon week? But Jennie seemed so real. The girl in those letters certainly was.

Then he thought about his mother. Incest and murder. He searched his memory of her for clues that might suggest what she was capable of, but his brain came up short. In any case, how could he possibly remember someone in a 'normal' activity and then conflate that with something so heinous?

If all of that wasn't enough to deal with, then there was the betrayal by Danny and Mrs Hackett – they'd seemed so down-to-earth and honest.

And now even in his letters written before he died, the old man had been hiding some of the truth.

He planted his feet on the floor, squared his shoulders and looked into Mrs Hackett's eyes. What he saw there offered some reassurance. She wanted to tell him; needed to tell him. And the information she was about to impart, she believed to be the absolute truth. He could see that.

'Go on then,' he said.

'It wasn't that long ago, but you have to remember that this was a different age. There were very clear lines between the classes. Very strict codes of behaviour. As part of the ruling classes, the wealthy, your uncle had a lot of power over the people who worked for his family.

'For a young woman from a working-class family, in her first job in the big house, it would have been terrifying. You also have to remember that there was little in the way of social security back then. Children in her situation – and she was little more than eighteen at the time – had to go to work to send money back to their families. Lose a job and it could be disastrous.' She paused and rubbed at her mouth while trying to work out how to go on.

'She went to my mother, not sure how to handle your uncle. She said that every time she turned round he was there, staring at her or saying how pretty she was. Trying to touch her hair, her face. Nothing sexual at first, she said. It was more like he was infatuated and was reaching out to touch her as if to prove to himself that she was real, you know?' Mrs Hackett shook her head. 'It was, as I said, a different time; children didn't have the rights they have now. It was the age of being seen and not heard, and if something bad happened, people would shrug and dismiss it as just one of those things. Anyway,' she exhaled, her facial muscles formed into a shape of inherited regret, 'my mother said she told Jennie not to worry. It was just a phase and it would pass. To keep on with her work. Keep busy, she told her, and Mr Alexander would get bored and leave her alone. Except he didn't, it got worse.'

Ranald slumped in his chair, feeling a chill; he crossed his arms as if that might help to warm him.

'Alexander suggested to his mother that Jennie be promoted and become her and his sister's chambermaid. This meant she was given a small room of her own in his mother's wing and that he could visit her there.'

'No…'

'Sadly, yes. He began to go to her after everyone was in bed.' She swallowed. 'Your uncle effectively raped this young girl, night after night, for months, and there was no one – *no one* – she could turn to.'

'Oh my God,' said Ranald. 'But his letter…' He completed the sentence in his head: *…told a vastly different version.* He was moving on from his earlier position of doubt. Everything he was hearing had a ring of truth. 'Couldn't she go to your mother?'

Mrs Hackett shook her head. 'She did. But – and the guilt of this haunted Mum to her last breath – my mother didn't believe her. She told her off for telling lies and threatened to have her sacked if she repeated them again.' She pursed her lips and exhaled slowly, as if releasing some of her own pain. 'She said Alexander was a fine young man. The future of a great family, and a likely pillar of the community. There was no way he would be involved in anything so awful. She sent the poor girl away with a flea in her ear.

'Next thing, Alexander was sent off to war and Mum noticed a change in Jennie. At first she seemed more like the young girl who first arrived at Newton Hall – lively and curious. Sometimes it's only when something returns that you notice it was missing, you know? That was the first time Mum thought that Jennie might indeed have been telling the truth. But then she seemed to revert to being overly shy and sensitive. She started taking her food up to her room and avoided being with any of the other members of staff.'

Mrs Hackett held her hands on the table in front of her. She slowly rubbed the back of her left hand with her right thumb.

'God knows how she managed to keep her pregnancy a secret.' She shook her head slowly. 'Then it all came to a head. Mum was helping Alexander's mother with something when they heard an awful scream. It came from the lift. They ran there and found Jennie covered in blood from the waist down. She had just given birth – Mum guessed that Jennie hid there when she realised she was going into labour – to keep away from everyone.

'Mum said the sight would haunt her to her dying day. Jenny was trying to cradle the baby while chewing through the cord. The poor girl was terrified, exhausted and in a panic. The baby was stillborn, poor thing. Mrs Fitzpatrick ordered that everything be cleaned up and that the girl be sent from the house in disgrace. Jennie spoke up for the first time and told her that the baby was Alexander's, that he had forced himself upon her and that she was frightened that when he came back from leave the rapes would start up again.'

'Dear God,' said Ranald, and heard his voice echo in the space. Rough and masculine, so out of place in this story of abuse. He shuddered at the thought of what poor Jennie had gone through.

Mrs Hackett stood up. 'I need something to drink. Just a shame it's not later in the day. This is a story that should be served with a large whisky.' She replenished her tea and sat back down to continue.

'Of course, Mrs Fitzpatrick was having none of it. This girl had thrown herself at her son, she thought, trying to worm her way into a position of wealth and privilege. And she had Jennie carted off to the asylum, telling everyone that she'd been found eating her own baby and that she must be insane or a witch or something equally vile.' She paused a beat. 'The poor girl didn't stand a chance. Who was going to believe her against the Fitzpatricks? Sadly, she died shortly after. Loss of blood apparently.' Mrs Hackett blessed herself. Her right hand finding the places to touch on her body, quickly and by long habit. Forehead. Heart. Left shoulder. Right shoulder.

'What happened to the baby?' asked Ranald.

Mrs Hackett looked at him. 'That was something my mother remembered as being odd. Mrs Fitzpatrick was determined that the girl was lying, that her son hadn't laid a hand on her, but she had the baby buried in the garden and a wee statue erected. Made a wee memorial spot, if you like.'

'Really?'

Mrs Hackett nodded. 'I think she was hedging her bets. I don't know what they would normally do in that situation, back then. An unmarked grave in the council cemetery, maybe? But she had a little spot in the garden dedicated to him.'

'It was a boy?'

Nod.

'Whereabouts in the garden? Is it still there?'

'Yes,' she replied. 'Beyond the big rhododendrons. There's a small sort of clearing.'

He made a mental note and decided he would look for it later.

'That would have been a source of comfort to Jennie. If she knew,' Ranald said.

'Poor Jennie. What that girl lived through.' Mrs Hackett's face was long, mournful. 'Any woman who got pregnant out of wedlock in those days was treated abysmally. It was shameful. And it's something we rarely talk about these days, like it's a convenient community memory loss.' She cleared her throat. 'And then Mr Alexander came home on leave. He was furious that no one had told him about Jennie.' She looked into Ranald's eyes and held his gaze, as if it was essential that he understand the importance of her next few words. 'He was a changed man. The war changed him, whatever went on over there. He had convinced himself that he was in love with her, and he confided in me in his later years that he was certain that in her own time, had she lived, Jennie would have realised he loved her and would have forgiven him for his youthful impatience.'

'Youthful impatience?' Ranald repeated. 'That's how he excused his rape of this girl? For fuck's sake.'

'Language, please, Ranald. I can't abide that word.'

'I'm not going to apologise, Mrs H. It's the only word that works in the situation. It appears that everything he said in his letters was true. Apart from the events surrounding Jennie's death, and that poor stillborn baby.' He saw her in that lift, mouth open in a soundless howl, blood-stained teeth, and that little bundle in her arms. 'He never admitted to any of that. And that's where true repentance lies.'

She gave him a look that conceded agreement and continued. 'In any event, as my mother would tell it, he went back to war and at the end, came home, utterly different from the man who first put on that uniform. Mum said she would come in early to do her work, avoiding his rooms because he always slept late, but she would hear his screams throughout the house. Blood-curdling they were. She said he must have had terrible nightmares.' She shook her head. 'He devoted his life to the family business, told his mother that Jennie was the only one for him and to get used to the fact that he wasn't ever going to get married and have children.' She considered that for a moment. 'I think, unable to deal with his guilt, he twisted his own thinking, blamed his mother for Jennie's death and this was his way of punishing her.'

'So, he never met anyone else? Didn't have so much as a single girlfriend?'

'Not that we know of.'

'Unbelievable,' said Ranald. He held a hand over his stomach and pressed there as if trying to contain the conflicted emotions he was feeling. 'You *knew* all of this, Mrs H. How could you spend so much time with him? What he did? It was vile.'

Mrs Hackett listened to his questions and leaned forwards on the table, her hands clasped in front of her as if in prayer.

'I've been a regular churchgoer all my life, Ranald, and the Bible tells us that the person is not the sin. Or at least that's what I believe. And it tells us that God is the judge. There's far too many people willing to take on that role. I don't presume to think I'm in a position to sit on judgement on anyone.' She stopped speaking and looked down at her hands. She stretched her fingers out and closed them as if returning to prayer. 'Besides, I firmly believe he repented. He took the knowledge of that sin and wore it like an emotional sackcloth for the rest of his life.' She gave him a small smile. 'What form of judgement or penance could I suggest that would match that?'

'I think we should just have a proper drink, Mrs H regardless of the time of day.'

'The tragedy is, Ranald, it's not just a story.'

'True,' he said as he got to his feet. 'True.' And he thought about Ken Welsh. The old man still grieving for his big sister – carrying the weight of that all these years later.

Mrs Hackett stood and stepped forward. She took his hands in hers and, with eyes full of an empathy Ranald wasn't sure he deserved, she said, 'Thing is, it has to end here, Ranald.'

'What do you mean?'

'That girl you think you saw in the mirror? That's a figment of your illness.'

'But how did I know about her to see her?' He paused and checked what he just said for sense. 'If you know what I mean.'

'You must have read one of your uncle's notebooks and the suggestion of her was taken up by your subconscious?'

'That feels a bit far-fetched.'

'As far-fetched as a woman only you can see in a mirror?'

'Well...' His voice faded. The justifications that rallied in his mind weren't strong enough to beat her use of logic. Then he remembered the album. 'But I saw her photograph. I found an album in the other wing, and she was with Alexander. And she was just like the woman in the mirror. Explain that.'

'You must have seen the photograph before,' she said. 'That could be enough to plant the suggestion.'

'But I hadn't. That was the first time I went into that room.'

She looked at me confused. 'When was this?'

'I can't remember. Not that long ago.'

'But, son,' she stretched a hand out to touch his. Her face long with sadness, as if she was somehow complicit in this. 'Your first weekend here, I found you up there. Don't you remember?'

'My first weekend here? You don't work weekends.'

'I did then. Just to be sure I could help if you needed something.'

Ranald scoured his memory and came up with nothing.

'You say you found me?'

A nod. 'You said you had no idea how you got into your grandmother's sitting room. Thought you might have been sleepwalking.'

'I did?'

'You see, Ran. You have to forget all of this. You've read his memories and ... and somehow taken them on. Some sort of weird gratitude? Jennie was a real person. Your great-uncle treated her appallingly, went to war and came back a changed person. He persuaded himself he had loved her and the tragedy of that twisted his mind over the years.' She looked at him with kindness. 'Maybe he had an undiagnosed condition. Maybe that's what you inherited from him. I'm really not sure of any of this. But what I am sure of is that you need to leave that tragedy to die with him.'

He was aware that his physical self was wearing a mask of acceptance. He felt he had to let her think she was convincing him, but all the while his mind was rearing back from this version of events. Surely Jennie was as real as the clock on the wall, the books on the shelves, the clothes covering his flesh.

But what if Mrs Hackett was right? If Jennie was real, wouldn't she run from him – a Fitzpatrick – not take him into her arms?

'Right.' Without making it seem to obvious, Ranald slowly pulled his hands away from hers. He felt heat building up in his neck and tried to understand where his new feeling of awkwardness was coming from. He broke eye contact with her and looked out of the window; read the gathering clouds in the distance and the sway of the leaves at the top of the trees.

He had heard her, but he could not allow himself to accept what she was saying. He was silent for a moment. 'I found her letters, you know.'

'What?'

'Letters,' Ranald repeated. 'Jennie wrote to her family regularly, except the letters were never delivered. I found them in my grandmother's desk.'

Mrs Hackett looked utterly mystified at this disclosure. 'How on earth would they get there?'

'You have no idea?'

Mrs Hackett shifted in her seat, and twisted again, as if that might dislodge some memory. 'I remember Mum saying that as a young girl your grandmother was a spoiled little madam.' She stopped speaking as if examining her thoughts. 'Mum said she was hugely attached to Jennie and was devastated when she died.' She took a deep, shocked breath as realisation hit. 'Her bedroom was right next door to Jennie's. Might she have heard her brother on his visits?' She clasped at her throat. 'Perhaps this was your grandmother's way of punishing

Jennie? Withholding the letters from her family? It would be easy enough for her to do. All the mail was piled on a table in the main hall for the doorman to see to. It might make sense to a girl that young: Jennie was hers, and her big brother took her away from her...' Mrs Hackett's eyes were full. She shook her head, back and forth, back and forth.

'In what other family would any of that make sense,' Ranald said, his voice heavy with certainty in the truth of what he just said.

Ranald made his way to the door, turned before he left and saw that Mrs Hackett had her mouth open as if to say something.

'What?' he asked.

'You'll think I'm a silly old woman.'

Ranald made a dismissive sound that he hoped encapsulated their previous conversations about women in mirrors and men reading to ghosts in lifts. 'I'm sure nothing you could say would surprise me, Mrs Hackett.'

'Alexander Fitzpatrick may have been changed by what happened to Jennie, but so was my mum.' Her expression showed she was keen that Randal no longer thought badly about her mother.

'I believe you, Mrs Hackett.'

'The thing that haunted her most?' She paled and held a hand to her throat once again. 'Mum was feeling so bad about misjudging her that she went to visit Jennie in the asylum just before she died. She said there was no trace of that sweet little girl who first came to work for her. There, restrained on the hospital bed, hair plastered to her head, she screamed at Mum, said she would find a way to come back from the grave and make every Fitzgerald's life a misery. She swore she would use her very last breath to curse the house and everyone in it.'

38

Ranald slept little that night, his mind a melee of images and emotions, and early the next morning he gave into his restless mood and made his way down to the library, hoping that the ranks of books would offer a soothing. It didn't work. All he could think about was Mrs Hackett's words and the curse of a desperate, maltreated young woman.

He walked along the rows, running his fingertips over the books, before picking one at random, taking it over to one of the sofas where he lay down and began to read.

Few of the words made any sense to him. They were just a jumble of black marks on the page, and eventually he gave up, dropped the book onto the floor, turned on his side and stared blankly at the back of the red leather sofa inches from his face.

Unable to lie still, he turned on his back and shifted across the sofa so that his head was hanging off. From this vantage point he looked over at the stacks of books. For some reason, today, they had failed to work their magic on him. He looked up the rows and noticed that from this angle the amount of each row of books he could see got smaller and smaller as they stretched up to the top, and there all he could see was about an inch of book. He turned his head slightly to see a top row that was bound in a light-tan leather, and it occurred to him that each book top was like the knuckle of a vertebrae. He sat up, head reeling. He could see bones everywhere. He was living in a house of spines.

⊣⊢

Sometime later, when daylight was stronger and he judged that other people might be up and about, he sat behind the desk, picked up the phone and called Martie.

No answer.

He called Donna and let it ring beyond what was sensible. No answer either. Next he called Quinn to be told he was out of the office. He thought of calling *War and Peace* girl, Suzy. But he couldn't remember if he'd ever taken down her phone number.

Why was he calling all these people?

No one was going to help him with this situation. What happened next was up to him and him alone.

But, if only he could just speak to someone. They didn't even need to talk about the house or anything else, but the sound of their voice, the energy they might transmit down the line would be enough to take him out of himself, just for a moment.

That was all he needed to achieve some clarity.

Should he go back to the doctor? Renew his prescription? Chase that emergency appointment with his mental-health team? He knew he should, but he also worried that, if he did so, Jennie might never speak to him again. He swung in his seat and looked out of the window. The leaves on the trees around the house had all but given up the fight. Just one or two stragglers persisted on the branch as if afraid of that final fall down to earth.

He could go to the café.

But he discounted that. They all just stared at him. They knew who he was, where he was from. What his family had done. And he could do without that silent, communal judgement.

Something was building in him, he could feel it. His fingers were drumming at the desk as if charged, as if the force of his fingertips could drive through wood. This was the moment he should take a step back. Find the app on his laptop and chart his mood.

Fuck it, he thought.

He reviewed everything he'd learned about his uncle and considered how, even from the grave, the man had tried to manipulate him into thinking he was entirely innocent of any wrong doing when it came to Jennie.

Since moving here, everyone had tried to handle him in some way.

He went through to the fitness suite, stripped off and dived in, hoping the meditative action of working his way up and down the pool would help him. After sixty lengths, his shoulders were aching and his breathing was losing its rhythm, but clarity still eluded him.

Reaching the end of the pool by the wide, glass doors, he rested on the pool edge, arms and chin resting on the side, his legs kicking in the water. He looked out into the garden and saw Danny trimming the grassy edge of a border with a pair of long-handled shears. Every now and then he would stop and look up at the sky to assess when the rain might start. It was as if this job had to be done that day and he resented the rest that a spell of rain would enforce on him.

Ranald was yet to learn the names of the wide variety of trees, bushes and flowers that Danny and the previous gardeners had planted over the years.

He'd miss all this if he had to go.

Both Donna and Mrs Hackett had said it would be better for him if he left. Mrs Hackett stopped short of saying his uncle was crazy and he would end up the same way if he stayed. But that was what she was saying, wasn't it?

He could always sell up to a development company with whom Marcus and Rebecca had no dealings. This would mean they would still get something from the sale, but not quite so much as they wanted.

No. That's not happening, he thought as he rested his hands on his chin. No way are they getting anything. They took advantage of his mental state and tried to convince him he'd had a hand in killing someone. They deserved nothing.

Nothing.

Rain pattered against the glass, like an introduction. Then daylight all but failed and the rain fell with surprising speed and force. He could see a bush at the side of the patio being whipped back and forwards.

He watched the storm for several long minutes, caught up in its simple beauty. I am here, it was saying, and there's nothing you can do to gainsay me. I will stop in my own good time.

Being too still in the water for too long made him cold. He pulled himself out and walked up to the glass. Pressed himself against it with his whole body, arms up and wide, legs shoulder-width apart. But that was symbolic. If the storm was to take him he had to be outside at its mercy.

He pulled open the door and ran out into the middle of the lawn. There, he adopted the same stance and threw his head back and opened his mouth.

The wind and rain buffeted his forehead, his shoulders, buttocks and thighs: every inch of his naked flesh. The squall howled round him, circling him like a pack of baying hounds, deep-chested and hollow-bellied. The water filled his eyes and lashed into his mouth.

He let out a scream, an ululation.

'Take me,' he ordered. 'Or tell me what to do.'

With the suddenness of a falling axe, the storm stopped. He opened his eyes and looked around him. He saw a spot of blue in the approaching sky. A bird started to sing, as if checking to see that its song had not been drowned.

Ranald dug his toes into the thick, wet grass and felt his connection with the earth. He looked to the side and saw the flat plate of a large leaf shine with rain and watched as drops slid from it to the earth with a slow reluctance.

What was that? he asked himself. A cleansing?

Or acceptance.

Now shivering against the cold, he remembered what Mrs Hackett said about the boy's memorial. He went back into the pool area, roughly dried himself off and put on his clothes. Decent again, he stepped outside and walked to the far reaches of the garden searching for the spot Mrs Hackett had described.

This area of the garden was darker, less well tended. The path was slick with moss. The rhododendrons had long lost their bloom and, as he passed, he could see the small, dark stems from where the flowers would have sprouted in the spring, sticking up like withered fingers.

The path led to a small clearing with a low stone bench to one side, and there, on a waist-high granite plinth was the boy. He was naked, balanced on one foot, the other leg raised and bent at the knee. His arms were plump, positioned wide, palms down as if that pose might help him better maintain his balance. The sculptor had bent his neck so the boy was looking down and to the side at a slight angle. The aim might have been to give him a playful look, but time and weather had worked at his features, blurring them slightly, giving his smile a melancholy cast and his eyes an aspect tinged with regret.

Ranald sat on the stone bench and placed his hands either side of him. The garden was quieter here. The tall, wide trees and bushes muffled the sound around them. Even the birds in this area seemed quieter, more reserved.

He stretched his hands out to the side, running his fingertips over the rough, cool sandstone. Doing so, he noticed the seat there was worn. He tilted his head to the side, judged the shadow and saw there was a slight grove there, as if a small, narrow-hipped person had sat there through countless lonely evenings.

Who might that have been, he wondered? Alexander's mother? Mrs Winters? It could have been anyone, really. The bench looked long-weathered and very old. It could have been well worn even before the bench was sited there.

The garden grew still around him, a cool breeze fingered through the hair on the top of his head, blowing his fringe in front of his eyes. He brushed it away and realised that the day had darkened again. In front of him the undergrowth formed an edge of dark leaf, and it was harder to distinguish one species of bush or tree from another.

The air cooled even further, the shadows thickened around him and he felt her hand take his. Warm and light, her bones as fragile as the breast cage of a wren, and he was certain, in that moment, what his future should look like. And he accepted it without a single note of regret.

I'm here, he sent her. *And I'm yours.*

'You are,' she answered, her words no more than a breath on the fine hairs on his earlobe. 'Come,' she said and he was aware of movement as she stood. The light flickered. Her long skirt fluttered in the wind.

He got to his feet, feeling as light as a seed borne on a breeze – truly calm for the first time in his life. An image of the library flowered in his mind. Shelves upon shelves of unread books. Bound papers and the scent of vanilla and burnt almond. Realms beyond count that he had yet to witness. The real world held at a distance by imaginings that were untarnished by fact.

'What have people ever done for you?' she asked.

He saw the pale silk of the inside of her forearm and the long, thin thread of a blue vein as she stretched out towards him. 'Come. We are young yet and we have dreams and a long sleep to share.'

He walked back into the house, into the kitchen where he found a blister pack of drugs that had survived his last purge of them, and swallowed a mouthful. Guessing that he might need more, he swallowed another handful, took a drink of water and then walked to the conservatory, pushed open the door and stepped inside.

For once he used the ladders and climbed down into the water. For once he kept his clothes on. It seemed too much of an effort to take them off, and, besides, when someone found him he didn't want the task to be too unpalatable.

That was him all over, he thought, as he stretched out across the surface of the water face down; considerate to the last breath.

He opened his eyes, ignoring the nip of chlorine and looked down into the depths. There, from the bottom *she* looked up at him, her long dark hair waving in the water around her head like kelp. As the drugs began to take effect, weighted his mind and his muscles with fatigue; making it difficult for him to understand why he couldn't breathe, and how he could restore motor function, enough to find some air, he read the look on her face.

Triumph.

39

Breathing.

That was the first thing he heard. Slow and deep and evenly spaced.

Where was it coming from? Who was it coming from?

He tried to take stock. His head and neck were cushioned and his legs pinned down by something. Cloth. He stretched his arms out, and they reached the sides of the bed with ease. Where would he find such a narrow bed? Where was he?

The breathing continued. It wasn't him. It sounded like it was coming from the left of where he lay.

He sent a command to open his eyes. Nothing happened. He tried to wiggle a toe and felt the movement, heard the whisper of skin brushing cotton.

The last thing he remembered was a storm. Standing under a dark, bruised sky, naked as the day he entered the world, screaming into the wind. So, how did he get here, wherever *here* was?

Without casting a thought or command, his eyes opened onto … a white ceiling so bright it looked like it must have just been painted. Then he took in the rest of the space. A curtain rail. Walls painted an institutional cream.

Hospital.

He opened his mouth; it felt dry, which was odd given … did he end up in the pool? He had been clothed, he now remembered, which was not like him. Wet cotton like a heavy, cold second skin had encased him, weighed on his limbs. Making movement more of an effort.

And then another slice of recall slid in, like his brain was choosing random shots. She was there; her pale arm reaching for him; a blue thread of vein. She was beckoning. Telling him to come with her. Join her on the other side. And he had followed her, despite everything. Despite all sense and logic. Despite his mind telling him that she was simply a product of his fevered, drugged imagination, his heart had insisted she was real, and had instructed him to obey.

He had entered the water.

Then.

War and Peace girl there in the pool. Suzy. Holding his head. Saying something. Her mouth moving, but the noise coming at him as if through wool. Movies. She was saying she came round to see a movie. Or borrow a book. A fake laugh, tinged with desperation. *What a shock you gave me.*

Breathe, she commanded. Begged. *Please breathe.*

A breath.

He turned his head and she was there at his side. Curled up on the hospital armchair.

Suzy opened her eyes as if she heard his thoughts. 'Great, you're awake.' She rubbed at her eyes and yawned. Then she leaned forwards and reached for his hand. 'How are you feeling?'

'Like…' Ranald croaked. Sat up. Cleared his throat and tried again. 'Like I swam a marathon.'

Then, as if his brain noted that he was now able to cope, it released all of his memory at once. Slapped it into the forefront of his mind. He groaned. Pushed it away. Not now. Perhaps not ever.

'Welcome to The Death Star,' said Suzy, and Ranald could hear note of humour in her tone, as if she was seeking the same in him. 'The Death Star': that was the name the citizens of Glasgow had given the colossal new hospital.

'Something to drink?' Suzy turned from him to the tall bedside cabinet and poured some water into a glass. She handed it to him.

Relieved that he had something to do – something that did not involve sifting through the events of that day – he accepted the glass from her, set it to his lips and drank. He savoured the cool and wet of it as it coated the inside of his mouth and slid down his throat.

But he'd have to go there, wouldn't he? Or he'd end up back in that pool. Face down again. He took another sip.

'It's the simple things in life, eh? A glass of water. This is nectar.'

'Refill?' Suzy asked.

'Sure. Thanks.' He held the glass out to her, grateful for the time this afforded him. No awkward questions. No recriminations. If Martie was here…

'I met your ex-wife,' said Suzy, as if, again, she'd read his mind. 'And your neighbour, Donna. They've just popped downstairs for a coffee. I said I would sit with you in case…' she brightened '…this.' She held a hand out like a magician who'd just performed a trick.

'You saved me,' Ranald said and slumped back onto his pillow. He sent his thoughts inward. Probed for *her*. Found nothing. There was nothing in there but numbness. *Only him*. He opened his mouth as if to explain. This was a silence that needed to be filled.

Suzy put a hand out. Held his.

'If you're not ready, now might not be the time.'

He met her gaze and found a wealth of understanding there. Understanding without judgement. She *knew* and she didn't find him wanting. The relief of this cheered and choked him. He felt his throat tighten with emotion. Tears flooded his eyes. He resisted the impulse to turn away and hide them. But she saved his life, if anyone deserved to see him truly naked, it was her.

He cried.

He cried for the nine-year-old so desperate to be loved by his mother that he joined her naked and danced under an uncaring moon. He cried for the eighteen-year-old unable to articulate his horror at finding his parents dead, realising that this was the first time he'd cried in all these years since he'd stood at their grave.

He cried for the father he accused of abandoning him, murdered by his own wife.

He cried for the woman whose genes he shared, and her unceasing pain. He wept for the young man stuck for years in an emotional limbo, desperate to articulate his feelings, but not knowing how to work them into language: how to force them from the dark of his mind and out between teeth and tongue.

Once the tears eventually stopped, he offered her a smile. A smile that said a simple thank you, for what else was there?

Then he asked.

'So, you read any good books lately?'

40

Ranald willingly gave himself up to the advice of his doctors. If they said he needed three months in hospital to get himself back on an even keel, then that was what he would do.

Being there over Christmas and into the New Year was difficult, but the medical staff did their best to make the place feel homely, and Martie, Donna and Suzy all visited regularly. Reminding him that outside those walls the real world still went about its business.

Quinn also visited, and each time he did he apologised again for not realising the depths that Marcus and Rebecca had reached. Danny and Mrs Hackett, he assured him, were making sure everything was being looked after at Newton Hall until the doctors said he could return.

Newton Hall.

Could he go back there?

Of course he could. It was just a house, right? There were no ghosts. There was no Jennie. He could see now that it was all a product of his fragile mental health, and his willingness to adopt the burdens and delusions of his great-uncle; a combination that had made the illusory so, so real.

Eventually, the specialists all agreed that he had recovered and that he was no longer a risk to himself. He was reminded of the effectiveness of charting his moods, how to read them and what to do if they suggested he was at risk of another episode, and how the correct medicines, exercise and a healthy diet would help make sure that another collapse was reduced to a remote possibility.

The day came for him to return to Newton Hall and he was cheered that when he went downstairs to the main hospital entrance his taxi driver was the same man who took him home all those months ago. *All those months.* It felt like years. Almost as if it had happened to someone else.

Other than the chatty driver, the journey to Newton Hall was very different this time around. The skies were a stark winter blue, the air looked sharper and the trees were bare.

What had also changed was Ranald himself. Older and shrewder. Calm and centred. He was a man of property. A man who knew his place. He was a Fitzgerald and proud of it.

He asked the driver to take him on a little detour before he went home. There was a small pile of letters he wanted to deliver, decades late, to their proper recipient. He'd had Martie collect them from Newton Hall and bring them to him on her last visit, along with the address of the man who should now be their owner.

With a churn in his gut at the thought of how huge this was going to be for Ken Welsh, he knocked on the old man's door. It opened quickly.

'Ranald,' he said with some surprise. 'You're looking well. Have you been away?'

'You could say that, Ken.'

The old man looked down at Ranald's hand, at the folder he was holding. 'Is that for me?' he asked with an inquisitive smile. Then he stepped back, a wariness in his posture, as if he was afraid to come across as too friendly. 'Want to come in for a cuppa?' he said, almost grudgingly.

'No, thanks,' Ranald said, and turned his head to the side to indicate his waiting taxi. He coughed. 'Remember that last time we spoke, you mentioned something about a letter from your sister, and I ran off like the hounds of hell were after me?'

Ken pulled his head in. 'Aye. You weren't quite yourself that day, son.'

'Well, I found these up at the house…' he held the folder out '… and thought you should have them.'

'What's that, son?' Ken accepted the folder from Ranald. 'What is it?' he asked again as he opened it.

But one look at the handwriting and his question was instantly answered.

'Oh my,' he said. His bottom lip trembled and his eyes filled with tears. His right hand was over his mouth and it was shaking hard. He looked from the letters up to Ranald. 'It's our Jennie,' he said as if he could scarcely believe his own eyes.

'She wrote more than that one letter, Ken,' said Ranald gently. 'It's to my shame that they were never delivered.'

'Oh my,' Ken said again, in a whisper. 'Jennie.' He stepped forwards and pulled Ranald into a hug, and Ranald could feel the force of the little man's emotions, his body quivering within his arms.

'I don't know what to say,' Ken managed a whisper to the side of Ranald's face.

'I do,' said Ranald. 'Sorry.'

With that, he gently disengaged from the old man and turned and walked away up his garden path and climbed into the taxi.

ᛏᛏ

Minutes later, the car stopped again, in that familiar wide drive, and after paying the driver Ranald climbed out. The front door opened and Danny and Mrs Hackett stepped outside to welcome him. The house looked like it had been sleeping, waiting for him to return before resuming its position in the world.

With a huge sigh Ranald realised just how much he was looking forward to being at home. The first thing he was going to do was jump in the pool. Then spend a few hours in the library before going up to his bed. Just then he looked up at the first floor windows. He wasn't sure what grabbed his attention. Some movement behind the window? A flicker of sunlight? But there, behind the glass, just beyond the thick, dark drapes he saw her slight frame, her ageless, pale face, and a slender hand raised in greeting.

Acknowledgements

To my first readers of this book – Douglas Skelton and Mike Craven. Thank you, you saved me from some silly mistakes.

When I turned this book into the editing team of Karen Sullivan and West Camel, I thought it was a good read. Their diligence, patience and hard work has made it SO MUCH better. Thanks for pushing me.

To everyone on Team Orenda – you guys rock!

I thank my lucky stars for the day I met my publisher, Karen Sullivan. Is there anyone in publishing today who works harder? Anyone who invests so much of her time into author care? I seriously doubt it. Thanks, Karen it is very much appreciated!

And finally, to all the bloggers, reviewers, booksellers and readers – all of those dedicated people who make the world of books such an amazing place to work, a HUGE thank you.